OXFORD WORLD'S CLASSICS

# THE WATER-BABIES

CHARLES KINGSLEY (1819–75), novelist, poet, historian, clergyman and amateur scientist, was born at Holne, Devonshire. He studied at King's College, London, and at Cambridge, and took orders in the Church of England, becoming rector of Eversley, Hampshire, in 1844, a living he retained until his death. He later became canon of Chester and finally of Westminster, and returned to Cambridge as Regius Professor of Modern History in 1860. As a writer, Kingsley gained early notoriety with two novels that sprang from his involvement with the Chartist movement: *Yeast* (1848) and *Alton Locke* (1850). Energetic and volatile, he also produced panoramic historical novels such as *Westward Ho!* (1855), an adventure story that established him as a writer of appeal to both adults and children. *The Water-Babies* (first serialized in *Macmillan's Magazine* 1862–3) remains one of the most enigmatic of all children's classics, at once a fantasy of redemption, an argument about evolution, and an anthology of different literary styles.

BRIAN ALDERSON has been involved in work on children's literature for many years, as editor, translator, lecturer, and writer. He has been the children's books editor for *The Times* since 1968, and he has a special interest in the history of English and American publishing for children. He has long been intrigued by *The Water-Babies*, not just for itself but for the many sidelights that it casts on Kingsley's ideas about children and about the children's books of his time.

ROBERT DOUGLAS-FAIRHURST is Fellow and Tutor in English at Magdalen College, Oxford. He is the author of *Victorian Afterlives: The Shaping of Influence in Nineteenth-Century Literature* (2002) and *Becoming Dickens: The Invention of a Novelist* (2011), and has edited Charles Dickens's *A Christmas Carol and Other Christmas Books* and Henry Mayhew's *London Labour and the London Poor: A Selected Edition* for Oxford World's Classics.

# OXFORD WORLD'S CLASSICS

*For over 100 years Oxford World's Classics have brought
readers closer to the world's great literature. Now with over 700
titles—from the 4,000-year-old myths of Mesopotamia to the
twentieth century's greatest novels—the series makes available
lesser-known as well as celebrated writing.*

*The pocket-sized hardbacks of the early years contained
introductions by Virginia Woolf, T. S. Eliot, Graham Greene,
and other literary figures which enriched the experience of reading.
Today the series is recognized for its fine scholarship and
reliability in texts that span world literature, drama and poetry,
religion, philosophy, and politics. Each edition includes perceptive
commentary and essential background information to meet the
changing needs of readers.*

OXFORD WORLD'S CLASSICS

CHARLES KINGSLEY

# The Water-Babies
## A Fairy Tale for a Land-Baby

*Edited by*
BRIAN ALDERSON

*With an Introduction by*
ROBERT DOUGLAS-FAIRHURST

OXFORD
UNIVERSITY PRESS

# OXFORD

## UNIVERSITY PRESS

Great Clarendon Street, Oxford OX2 6DP
United Kingdom

Oxford University Press is a department of the University of Oxford.
It furthers the University's objective of excellence in research, scholarship,
and education by publishing worldwide. Oxford is a registered trade mark of
Oxford University Press in the UK and in certain other countries

Note on the Text, Appendix I, Explanatory Notes © Brian Alderson 1995, 2013
Introduction, Select Bibliography, Chronology © Robert Douglas-Fairhurst 2013

The moral rights of the authors have been asserted

First published 2013
First published as an Oxford World's Classics paperback 2014

Impression: 8

Published in the United States of America by Oxford University press
198 Madison Avenue, New York, NY 10016, United States of America

British Library Cataloguing in Publication Data

Data available

Library of Congress Control Number: 2014933809

ISBN 978-0-19-968545-5

Printed in Great Britain by
Clays Ltd, Elcograf S.p.A.

# CONTENTS

# CONTENTS

# INTRODUCTION

### *'the unseen wonders of the water-world'*

IT comes as something of a surprise to learn that the favourite pastime of Charles Kingsley, the volatile Victorian clergyman who inspired the term 'muscular Christianity', was fishing. In a fisherman's hands, he once wrote, 'the twelve-foot rod is transfigured into an enchanter's wand, potent over the unseen wonders of the water-world, to "call up spirits from the vasty deep" '.[1] But Kingsley was also capable of taking a more robust approach to his hobby. In 1854, while on holiday in the seaside resort of Torquay, he paid a 'strong-backed quarryman' to lever up rocks with a crowbar so that he could investigate what had been left behind by the tide. In 'The Wonders of the Shore', an essay published in the *North British Review* (November 1854), he described what he found. The rock pools were teeming with life—so much life, in fact, that Kingsley soon found himself happily scrabbling around in questions:

What are they all? What are the long white razors? What are the delicate grey-green scimitars? What are the tapering brown spires? What the tufts of delicate yellow plants, like squirrels' tails and lobsters' horns, and tamerisks and fir-trees, and all other finely cut animal and vegetable forms? What are the groups of grey bladders, with something like a little bud at the tip? What are the hundreds of little pink-striped pears? What those tiny babies' heads, covered with grey prickles instead of hair?[2]

Confronted by this array of creatures, Kingsley's descriptions make them sound both surprising and as natural as the hair on a baby's head. 'Look, again, at those sea-slugs' (*NBR*, p. 35), he urges, and that is what his essay does throughout: it discovers 'grandeur in the

---

[1] *Yeast: A Problem* (London: J. W. Parker, 1851), ch. 1; Kingsley is quoting from *Henry IV Part 1*, in which Glendower boasts that 'I can call spirits from the vasty deep', and a sceptical Hotspur responds 'Why, so can I, or so can any man; | But will they come when you do call for them?' (III. i. 52–4).

[2] *North British Review*, 22/43 (Nov. 1854), 17, hereafter abbreviated to *NBR*. The opening pages of this article are reprinted as Appendix II, below.

minutest objects, beauty in the most ungainly' (*NBR*, p. 10); it encourages us to look again at a world our ignorance hid from us even when it was in plain sight. Above all, Kingsley makes us realize that a world which might at first appear static is in fact pulsing with energy. His writing responds with busy verbs and thrusting syntax, from the red capsicums that are 'poking, snapping, starting, crawling, tumbling, wildly over each other' (*NBR*, pp. 17–18), to a slimy piece of black tape that 'hangs helpless and motionless' in the water until an unwary fish approaches, at which point it turns out to be a cunning combination of fishing line and fisherman, seizing the fish and slowly ingesting it until 'macerated to a pulp' (*NBR*, p. 38).

For Kingsley, the moral of this relentless activity is clear: if we find ourselves on the coast, we should avoid falling into lazy habits—his list of the leisure pursuits enjoyed by other holidaymakers includes sauntering along the pier, staring out of the window, and 'interminable reading of the silliest of novels' (*NBR*, p. 15)—and should instead follow nature's lead, by grabbing a collecting bucket, finding a rock pool, and having a good rummage around. The results will not only make us fitter in mind and body; they will also make us appreciate the fitness of every other creature for its environment. Taking our treasures home for more leisured study (Kingsley's essay explains how to construct and stock a domestic aquarium) will even provide us with a 'miniature sea-world' (*NBR*, p. 53) that has been put under man's benevolent control. In the meantime the essay itself is something like a virtual aquarium constructed from paper and ink. If the sea's variety astonishes and bewilders—'From the bare rocks above high-water mark, down to abysses deeper than ever plummet sounded, is life, everywhere life' (*NBR*, p. 40)—Kingsley's writing rearranges it into a settled order. He makes us feel at home in a strange world.

Kingsley's company on the beach in 1854 would not have been restricted to lobsters and sea slugs. The seaside was an increasingly crowded place. In the same year that Kingsley was busy with his bucket and crowbar, William Powell Frith exhibited his giant painting *Ramsgate Sands (Life at the Seaside)* (1852–4), which depicted dozens of holidaymakers squashed together on a small patch of sand, enjoying themselves by paddling in the sea, reading newspapers,

picnicking, playing games, snoozing in the sun, or sheltering beneath
dainty coloured parasols. The more genteel resort of Torquay was
becoming equally lively. Although in 1854 *The Handbook for Torquay
and Its Neighbourhood* pointed out that the location's 'real benefits,
alike conducive to mental refreshment and to bodily health' were its
climate and the 'diversified scenery' of its surroundings, and complained that the only public baths were 'quite unworthy of the town',[3]
within a few years a later edition (published in the same year as
*The Water-Babies*) was boasting that a new set of baths was 'of first-
rate excellence', built to serve a growing number of tourists and a
resident population that had increased from 11,000 to 17,000.[4] And
the development of both resorts was part of a much larger Victorian
movement—at once a social drive and an imaginative drift—
towards the sea.

The first verse of the Edwardian music-hall song 'I do like to be
beside the seaside' opens a window onto a period that transformed
whole stretches of sleepy coastline into the nation's playground.
'Everyone delights to spend their summer's holiday | Down beside
the side of the silvery sea', it explains, but if you're an ordinary Smith
or Brown 'At bus'ness up in town', a trip to the seaside is a special
annual treat: 'You save up all the money you can till summer comes
around | Then away you go | To a spot you know | Where the
cockle shells are found.' The rapid spread of the railways, and the
introduction of paid holidays, meant that coastal resorts were increasingly being filled by clerks and factory workers dipping their toes into
a previously exclusive world of leisure. Many of the features that now
seem central to these resorts were a response to their tastes, from fish
and chips (previously an urban speciality) to the iron piers which
stretched out into the sea in ever larger and more elaborate forms, as
if each town was poking its tongue out at its neighbours. Before then
the coast had mostly been a place to be avoided; the home of smug-
glers and the untamed roar of the ocean, it was where civilization
fell away into savagery. Two eighteenth-century fads changed all

[3] *The Handbook for Torquay and Its Neighbourhood, with the Natural History of the
District* (Torquay: E. Croydon, 1854), 5–6, 290.
[4] Ibid. (1863 edn.), 285.

that: the consensus among doctors that bathing in seawater was a cure for everything from leprosy to gout, and theories of the sublime that made the sea newly alluring as a place where one could literally immerse oneself in nature. Soon Brighton had been adopted by the more sickly members of the royal family as their unofficial holiday residence, taking the waters being a much more straightforward remedy than that prescribed to the Duke of Gloucester in 1771, who was advised to suckle at 'the breasts of some healthy country women that were sent for from the mountains'.[5] By 1797, the word 'seaside' had come to mean a destination for health or fun,[6] and where holiday-makers led, entrepreneurs followed: by 1904, the Palace in Rhyl boasted a huge ballroom with 2,500 springs under the parquet floor, a waxworks show, ping-pong rooms, and an imitation Venice featuring 'real Gondolas propelled by real Italians'.[7]

Alongside these impressive leisure facilities there was also a craze for 'improving' or 'rational' amusements, of which by far the most popular was beach-combing. As early as 1763, a local guidebook to Margate noted that 'When the tide is ebbed, many persons go on the sands, to collect pebbles, sea-weed, shells, &c.',[8] and by 1856 G. H. Lewes could think of no better way to spend his holiday in Ilfracombe than studying rock formations and anemones, carefully recording each day's discoveries in his journal.[9] The 1854 *Handbook for Torquay* had included separate chapters on 'Geology', 'Botany', and 'Conchology', promising that the neighbourhood was 'peculiarly calculated to interest men of science' (p. 248). Other publications were even more detailed. Kingsley's essay 'The Wonders of the Shore' was originally published as a review of half a dozen recent books in the field, including *The Sea-side Book* (1849) and *Things of the Sea Coast* (1850), which accurately indicates how popular such studies were. Indeed, when *Punch* included a poem on what happens

[5] Travis Elborough, *Wish You Were Here: England on Sea* (London: Sceptre, 2010), 43.

[6] *OED*, 'seaside'.

[7] John K. Walton, *The English Seaside Resort: A Social History 1750–1914* (Leicester: Leicester University Press, 1983), 180, 176.

[8] Ibid. 16.

[9] See John Hassan, *The Seaside, Health and the Environment in England and Wales since 1800* (Aldershot: Ashgate, 2003), 32.

when a young man falls into a rock pool—'And hauling, sprawling, crawling crabs | Have got into my socks with starfish and dabs; | And my pockets are swarming with polypes and prawns, | And noisome beasts with shells and horns'—the joke is that he has managed to collect more by accident than many other people did on purpose.[10] Tourists peered into rock pools with all the eagerness they had previously given to peering into microscopes, and treated them in much the same way: they were lenses that refocused the world.

Of the many amateur naturalists encouraging this fashion for marine biology, by far the most influential was Philip Gosse, whose meticulously detailed studies *A Naturalist's Rambles on the Devonshire Coast* (1853) and *The Aquarium* (1854) were among those reviewed by Kingsley in 'The Wonders of the Shore'. Many of Gosse's ideas chimed with Kingsley, particularly the conviction that no part of God's creation—from a straggling line of seaweed to a knobbly cluster of barnacles—was beneath notice. That is why, when Kingsley once saw a dead mole, his first thought was to show it to his fiancée 'and preach her a whole sermon about moles and their use and try to find some mystic meaning in them'.[11] Every earthly creature offered a little glimpse of eternity. The same was true of creatures that lived under the sea. After years of tortured self-questioning, Kingsley's vocation as a clergyman had finally been confirmed on the night of his twenty-second birthday, when he spent an hour on the seashore and 'Before the sleeping earth and the sleepless sea and stars I devoted myself to God',[12] and for him the seashore remained a place of divine revelation. Its busy natural order offered an alternative to 'the ever restless sea of doubt and disbelief' that crippled many of his contemporaries (*NBR*, p. 12), not least because it offered straightforward lessons that observers could apply to their own lives. Just as Gosse hymned the humble prawn as evidence that nature cleaned up after itself ('See the Prawn . . . washing himself after dinner, or at any other

[10] 'The Lay of the Last Lodger', repr. in *Mr Punch at the Seaside* (London: Educational Book Co., 1910), 74.

[11] Unpublished letter (1843), cited in Susan Chitty, *The Beast and the Monk: A Life of Charles Kingsley* (London: Hodder and Stoughton, 1974), 43.

[12] Ibid. 60.

spare moment, for he is careful to maintain his polished coat of mail most scrupulously clean'), so Kingsley developed the analogy with man's 'constant unremitting war with DIRT' in lovingly extended explanations of how seawater was kept clean by oxygen-producing plants and spider crabs.[13]

Kingsley was in no doubt that seaside science was worthwhile; indeed, by the time he came to write his novel *Two Years Ago* (1857), all he needed to confirm the moral credentials of his hero Tom Thurnall was an account of him at low tide, with 'an old smock over his coat and a large basket on his arm', as he 'comes hopping towards you, dropping every now and again on hands and knees, and turning over on his back, to squeeze his head into some muddy crack, and then withdraw it with the salt water dripping from his nose'.[14] During 1854 Kingsley even attempted to play a part in the development of marine biology as a scientific discipline. Alongside specimens for his own use ('After each low tide,' his wife recorded, 'some fresh treasure was discovered, and drawings and a minute description made'), he assembled 'hampers of sea beasts, live shells, and growing sea-weed' that were 'sent off to Mr Gosse, in London'.[15] Unfortunately, the history of their friendship revealed that human relations were far less predictable than the settled order of the ocean. As Edmund Gosse explained in his memoir *Father and Son*, his father could never reconcile his religious faith with growing geological evidence of the Earth's true antiquity, and his hopeful attempt at a compromise—satirized by the press as an argument that 'God hid fossils in the rocks in order to tempt geologists into infidelity'—was roundly derided. His friendship with Kingsley failed to survive the storm, with his former acolyte writing that Gosse could not 'give up the painful and slow conclusion of five and twenty years' study of geology, and believe that God has written on the rocks one enormous and superfluous lie'.[16]

---

[13] *The Aquarium: An Unveiling of the Wonders of the Deep Sea*, 2nd edn. (London: John Van Voorst, 1856), 170; 'The Wonders of the Shore', *NBR*, 49–52.

[14] The example is discussed in Chitty, *The Beast and the Monk*, 182.

[15] *Charles Kingsley: His Letters and Memories of His Life*, 2 vols. (1877; London: Macmillan, 1910), i. 317.

[16] Edmund Gosse, *Father and Son* (1907), ed. Peter Abbs (London: Penguin, 1986), 104–5.

Kingsley, by contrast, saw no conflict between science and religion: the 'wonders' of nature were an invitation to speculation as well as worship. Unlike most churchmen, he was prepared to accept that the Earth was hundreds of millions, rather than mere thousands, of years old, and that man had descended from apes rather than their biblical forefathers. He even corresponded with Darwin about the evolution of flatfish, and was quoted in the third edition of *On the Origin of Species* (1861) as a 'celebrated author and divine' who had come round to the view that God 'created a few original forms capable of self-development into other needful forms'.[17] In fact Kingsley did more than grudgingly accept the scientific principles of evolution. They fired his imagination. What some of his contemporaries saw as nature's terrifying prodigality, 'from the growths of the tropical forest to the capacity of man to multiply, the torrent of babies',[18] for Kingsley was proof of God's endless creativity and generosity. His writing took up the challenge. In 1855 he expanded 'The Wonders of the Shore' into *Glaucus*, an illustrated book-length study that added even more examples as it abandoned the beach and plunged further into the ocean. Here too he saw evidence of a 'LIVING GOD' wherever he looked, and his writing had to work even harder to keep things in proportion.[19] One of the ways he did this was through metaphor, describing the 'tiny rabbit mouths' of one species of fish, and the 'parrots' beaks' and 'bright lizard-eyes' of another (*Glaucus*, 163), as if God created different life forms through a peculiar combination of fecundity and thrift, forever reusing old ideas in new combinations. Another way was by reducing the scale of his comparisons: the capsicums that are 'as big as a man's two fists' in 'The Wonders of the Shore' (*NBR*, p. 18) are no larger than 'a child's two fists' in *Glaucus* (p. 64). However, by far Kingsley's largest change was to introduce an element of narrative, so that 'wondering' took on a new momentum and direction. The title of his book summoned up the mythological figure of Glaucus, a fisherman who, according to the

[17] See Gillian Beer, *Darwin's Plots: Evolutionary Narrative in Darwin, George Eliot, and Nineteenth-Century Fiction* (London: Routledge & Kegan Paul, 1983), 138.

[18] Tennyson, cited ibid. 124.

[19] *Glaucus; or, The Wonders of the Shore* (London: Macmillan, 1855; repr. 1890), 102.

legend told by Ovid in *Metamorphoses*, grew fins and a fish's tail after
eating a herb that made him immortal, and was forced to live for ever
in the sea. Even this allusion involved a strange compound of myth
and science: when Kingsley recalled how, 'standing on the shore at
low tide', he had 'longed to walk on and in under the waves . . . and
to see it all but for a moment' (*Glaucus*, 146), he was mixing together
the story of Glaucus and news reports of early diving suits, like that
shown by Joseph-Martin Cabirol at the 1855 Exposition Universelle
in Paris, which included a helmet fitted with four portholes, an air
hose, and weighted boots that allowed the wearer to clump along the
seabed at depths of up to 40 metres. The same is true of Kingsley's
comparison of the naturalist to a 'knight-errant of the Middle Ages'
('strong in body', 'gentle and courteous', 'brave and enterprising',
and 'of a reverent turn of mind', *Glaucus*, 44), which turned rock-
pool exploration into a modern quest narrative, or perhaps a rehearsal
for larger conquests overseas.

Eight years later all these elements came together in *The Water-
Babies*. In an early scene we are introduced to a young girl walking along the seashore with a fussy old scientist called Professor
Ptthmllnsprts. As his name indicates, his only desire is to trap
as many of the 'beautiful and curious things which are to be seen
there' (pp. 80–1) as possible, and then pickle them in alcohol. The
girl is unimpressed. 'She liked much better to play with live children,' we are told, 'and at last she said honestly, "I don't care about
all these things, because they can't play with me, or talk to me. If
there were little children now in the water . . . and I could see them,
I should like that"' (p. 81). A few minutes later the Professor gropes
under some weeds with his net and fishes out Tom, a boy chimney-
sweep who has been turned into a water-baby. ' "Why, it must be a
Cephalopod!"', he cries, and receives the uncompromising reply
from Tom '"No, I ain't!"' (p. 83). Clearly the rock pools contain
wonders that are not to be found in biological textbooks, and as
Kingsley's story continues, this is the middle ground it gleefully
occupies, between the unknown marvels of the natural world and the
unfathomable depths of the human imagination. The fecundity of
nature produces a fictional version of evolution's 'torrents of babies',

as Mrs Doasyouwouldbedoneby picks up two huge armfuls of the children who were surplus to requirements on earth, 'nine hundred under one arm, and thirteen hundred under the other—and threw them away, right and left, into the water' (p. 111). The connection between scientific exploration and empire-building is confirmed by Kingsley's bossy narrator, who is never prouder of Tom than when he is proving himself to be 'a brave, determined little English bull-dog' (p. 72) by voyaging through the world's oceans. Above all, the desire to unite a naturalist's accuracy with a novelist's plot is reflected in writing which is repeatedly stalled by descriptions of remarkable sea creatures, but which incorporates them into a story where the overwhelming need of everyone and everything is to keep moving. Any other writer might have baulked at the work required to reconcile so much into a single novel, but not Kingsley, who in *Glaucus* had written about 'the labours of the happy, busy day' (p. 150), and who often seems to have thought of 'happy' and 'busy' as more or less synonymous terms. In 1862 he picked up his pen and dived in.

## 'plunging in and out of the water'

The book Kingsley produced occupies an ambiguous place in the public imagination. *The Water-Babies* is simultaneously one of the most loved and one of the most neglected stories in the history of English literature. Received with some puzzlement when it was originally published, it remains one of a handful of Victorian works—others include Dickens's *Oliver Twist* and 'A Christmas Carol'—that far more people know about than have actually read. For many years a popular gift book, it is still routinely bought by well-meaning adults for children, most of whom receive it with expressions of delight before carefully placing it unopened on the shelf. Yet anyone who ventures past the book's cover is likely to discover something far stranger than they were expecting: a jerkily episodic narrative, crammed with topical satire and linguistic oddities, in which fact repeatedly rubs up against myth, and science and religion keep swapping places. The plot is straightforward enough. Tom, the boy apprentice of a bullying chimney-sweep named Grimes, takes a

xvi                                   *Introduction*

wrong turning one day in the chimney of a grand house, and finds
himself in the bedroom of a beautiful young girl. Her screams force
Tom to run away, hotly pursued by the Victorian equivalent of the
Keystone Kops, and he escapes by diving into a stream, where he is
transformed into a water-baby. The rest of the story describes his
underwater adventures, as he narrowly escapes being eaten, encounters a wide range of real and imaginary creatures, and is finally
reunited with Grimes at the 'Other-end-of-Nowhere'. It sounds simple, and writing in her memoir of Kingsley, his wife Fanny offered an
equally straightforward explanation of how it came to be written:

one spring morning, while sitting at breakfast, his wife reminded him of an
old promise, 'Rose, Maurice, and Mary have got their book [*The Heroes*,
1856] and baby [Grenville Arthur] must have his.' He made no answer, but
got up at once and went into his study, locking the door. In half an hour he
returned with the story of little Tom.[20]

That makes Kingsley's methods of composition sound less like a form
of literary genesis than a homage to the Book of Genesis: little Tom
emerges from the study like Adam from the clay; creation occurs as
quickly as thought. Perhaps Fanny's memory was filtering the scene
through her later knowledge of the story itself, where several creatures enjoy equally sudden births, such as caddis flies that retreat into
silk cocoons until they are ready for their grand entrance into society,
or dragonflies that shed their dull casing before whirring away like
iridescent fairies. Yet rather than being the result of a single burst
of inspiration, in many ways *The Water-Babies* was a distillation of
Kingsley's eccentric life so far. Being a churchman who believed
equally in God and Darwin was only one of the contradictions
that animated a writer who had a good claim to being the strangest
figure of his age. Unlike most eccentrics he ended up at the heart of
the establishment, being appointed at various times Regius professor
of modern history at Cambridge, royal chaplain, and canon of
Westminster Abbey, but none of this professional success could disguise the fact that he was an essentially contrary figure, who would
argue with himself when nobody else was around. Indeed, there were

[20] *Letters and Memories*, ii. 126–7.

times when he gave the impression of being a bundle of different people who merely happened to inhabit the same skin.

He was a shy extrovert; a no-nonsense sentimentalist; a mesmeric preacher who suffered from a debilitating stammer; an apostle of healthy living who hid pipes in the bushes around his rectory in Eversley in case a sudden urge to smoke came upon him while taking a walk. In public he fought for the rights of the working man; in private he referred to the Irish as 'white chimpanzees' and blacks as 'ant-eating apes'. An enthusiastic hunter, he once befriended a wasp he had saved from drowning. On a lecture tour to America he complained about the central heating in hotel bedrooms, and insisted on sleeping with the windows open, before returning home to die of pneumonia at the age of 56.[21] A man of fads and crazes, he directed his energies towards one object after another, without ever settling on anything for long enough to make a lasting impact. Thomas Hughes, his friend and fellow author, said that Kingsley reminded him of a boisterous Newfoundland dog being taken for a walk, 'plunging in and out of the water' before rubbing himself up against neatly dressed bystanders, 'and all with a rollicking good humour which disarmed anger, and carried away the most precise persons into momentary enjoyment of the tumbling'.[22] But there was also a quieter and sadder side to Kingsley. By the late 1850s, despite a growing literary reputation, he had suffered a series of personal setbacks that left him in a mood little short of despair. His life had settled into an unhappy rhythm of overwork and breakdown, interspersed with short periods of recovery on the Devon coast. Fanny had become increasingly demanding over money, and was keen to live in the style of an aristocrat on the income of a parson. Even his pen seemed to be failing him: although the publishers Macmillan were prepared to pay him the large sum of £2,000 for his next novel, several stories were started and then abandoned, with Kingsley sadly describing his last attempt in 1859 as 'twaddle and a failure'. More positively, he continued,

[21] This summary of Kingsley's contradictions is taken from Chitty, *The Beast and the Monk*, 16–17.

[22] Quoted in R. B. Martin, *The Dust of Combat: A Life of Charles Kingsley* (London: Faber & Faber, 1959), 120.

'I am only like a spider who has spun all his silk, and must sit still and secrete more'.[23] The natural metaphor was a clue to the kind of story he was contemplating: one in which the animal world would start off as the background to human activity, like the spiders which shake their webs 'so fast that they became invisible' when they see Tom coming (p. 22), but would end up swimming and swarming its way to the centre of things.

The speed with which Kingsley wrote *The Water-Babies*—according to Fanny it was 'perhaps the last book he wrote with any real ease'—reflected more than just another sudden enthusiasm overtaking him.[24] It also allowed him to gather together all the private obsessions that underpinned his changing moods. In *Glaucus* he had glimpsed a form of natural order existing beneath an ever-shifting surface, and in *The Water-Babies* he gratefully seized on the parallel. Almost every major incident in this new story was a distorted version of something he had written before. When Tom tumbles into the river, he is following in the footsteps of many of Kingsley's other fictional characters who must undergo a figurative death before being reborn: the hero's fever in *Alton Locke* (1850); Lancelot's hunting accident in *Yeast* (1851); the lightning bolt that strikes Sir Amyas Leigh in *Westward Ho!* (1855). Kingsley's new story pushes the idea even further, because Tom's regeneration as a water-baby comes about only after his death as a human being, like a strange combination of baptism and resurrection, although this too carries echoes from earlier in Kingsley's career. The church bells that ring in Tom's head, encouraging him to enter the water and be clean, are not far removed from the glittering pistols that tempt *Yeast*'s Lancelot to commit suicide, calling out to him 'Come to us! and with one touch of your finger send that bursting spirit which throbs against your brow to flit forth free, and never more defile her purity by your presence!' (ch. 10). The only difference, reflected in the greater urgency and conviction of the later scene, is that for Kingsley a bullet through the head never held quite the same imaginative attraction as drowning. There may have been private historical reasons for this. One of

---

[23] Martin, *The Dust of Combat: A Life of Charles Kingsley*, 217.
[24] Cited in A. N. Wilson, *The Victorians* (London: Arrow, 2003), 295.

his best childhood friends was the son of a fisherman, 'a little, delicate, precocious, large-brained child, who might have written books
some day if he had been a gentleman's son', but who died at sea and
was later discovered lashed to the rigging of his father's boat 'cold
and stiff, the little soul beaten out of him by the cruel waves'.[25] There
were also rumours that Kingsley's brother Herbert, who officially
died of rheumatic fever, may in fact have drowned himself after running away from school following the theft of a silver spoon, rather as
Tom flees Harthover House with shouts of 'Stop thief' ringing in his
ears.[26] Kingsley's poems had already explored the theme in some
detail: in 1849 he had written in 'The Sands of Dee' about a young
woman caught out by the inrushing tide, comparing her golden
hair to seaweed and a salmon's glittering scales, while in 1851 'The
Three Fishers' had described how the drowned crew of a fishing boat
are cast up 'on the shining sands | In the morning gleam as the tide
went down'.[27]

An even more powerful force driving Tom's desire to wash himself in the river was the private mythology that led Kingsley to associ-
ate physical cleanliness with moral goodness. This had already been
rehearsed in *Glaucus*, where it is suggested that a man who studies
seaside flora and fauna can 'wash his soul clean for a while' from the
pollution of the city (*Glaucus*, 222), and it had also made several
appearances in some of his earlier stories, bobbing to the surface of
his writing in increasingly strange forms, like his lingering description in *Andromeda* of the heroine being tied naked to a rock and lashed
all night by the sea's spray. The same association had taken on even
stranger forms in Kingsley's life. The assumption that a clean body
was the only suitable refuge for a clean mind was a common one in
the nineteenth century, as was its dark double, the fear that dirty living conditions would encourage filthy habits and impure thoughts,
but few Victorians devoted themselves to this idea with Kingsley's
particular combination of stubborn literal-mindedness and imaginative zeal. 'The poor man's child has no means of washing himself

[25] *Prose Idylls* (London: Macmillan & Co., 1890), 279.
[26] Chitty, *The Beast and the Monk*, 39, 45.
[27] *Poems* (London: Macmillan & Co., 1902), 246, 255.

properly', he explained in a lecture to the Mechanics' Institute in Bristol, 'but he has enough of the innate sense of beauty and fitness to feel that he ought not to be dirty.' For adults, he continued, liberal use of cold water also prevented them from turning to less healthy liquids such as beer or gin: 'With a clean skin and nerves and muscles braced by a sudden shock,' he urged, 'men do not crave artificial stimulants.' While the idea that 'If you will only wash your bodies your souls will be all right' may have been theologically suspect, and generations of public schoolboys would later curse Kingsley for encouraging the idea of a daily cold bath, nobody could accuse him of failing to live up to his own ideals.[28] When staying in country houses, he 'always sent home meticulous descriptions of the arrangements made for his own ablutions',[29] and could not bear to wear clothes that were dirty: 'If I have a spot on my clothes,' he explained in an early letter, 'I am conscious of nothing else the whole day long.' Water made everything clean—even sex, which had troubled Kingsley a good deal until he discovered in Fanny a woman who was not only prepared to go along with his obsessions but actively encouraged them. His first thought after their wedding night was that he would soon 'wash off the scent of her delicious limbs'; later in their marriage he planned to build her a rustic bathing pool in the garden, while his love letters to her repeatedly urged her to kiss herself all over in the bath.[30] One picture he drew of them showed their naked bodies lashed together on a cross that was riding the crest of a billowing wave, and for all the apparent oddness of this iconography it probably came closer than any of his published writings to capturing Kingsley's most intimate concerns. Sex purified the body just as prayer purified the soul, cleansing it as thoroughly as the salty tang of the sea.

Given Kingsley's dreamy equation of cleanliness and godliness it comes as little surprise to discover that he was terrified by the alternatives. In *Yeast*, a character with the punning surname of Lavington lies on her deathbed burbling about the need to introduce clean water

[28] Chitty, *The Beast and the Monk*, 192–3.
[29] Ibid. 210.
[30] Ibid. 220–1.

into the foul slum that has given her typhus: 'Make a great fountain in it—beautiful marble—to bubble and gurgle, and trickle and foam, for ever and ever, and wash away the sins of the Lavingtons, that the little rosy children may play round it, and the poor toil-bent woman may wash—and wash—and drink' (ch. 16). A scene in *Alton Locke* is even cruder in its symbolism, as Jem Downes discovers his wife and children dead and partly eaten by rats in the London slum of Jacob's Island, and responds by flinging himself into Folly Ditch:

The light of the policeman's lantern glared over the ghastly scene—along the double row of miserable house-backs, which lined the sides of the open tidal ditch—over strange rambling jetties, and balconies, and sleeping-sheds, which hung on rotting piles over the black waters, with phosphorescent scraps of rotten fish gleaming and twinkling out of the dark hollows, like devilish grave-lights—over bubbles of poisonous gas, and bloated carcases of dogs, and lumps of offal, floating on the stagnant olive-green hell-broth—over the slow sullen rows of oily ripple which were dying away into the darkness far beyond, sending up, as they stirred, hot breaths of miasma—the only sign that a spark of humanity, after years of foul life, had quenched itself at last in that foul death. (ch. 35)

Tom's leap into the river at the start of *The Water-Babies* provides a happier alternative, as he leaves behind his body like a black husk and enters a world where, whenever nature produces a mess, the water-babies are quickly on hand to clean it up. While Kingsley remained troubled by how easily this idyllic pastoral world could be polluted by 'horrid dirty men, with foul clothes on their backs, and foul words on their lips' (p. 70), reflected in the fact that the language of dirt and disgust continues to spread out through *The Water-Babies* like a stain, Tom slips through the water like someone enjoying an endless cold bath. The result is a narrative of moral evolution in which Tom's physical passage plots out the development of his soul. As he navigates this underwater world, he learns the values of loyalty, truthfulness, and self-sacrifice; he grows out of his earlier bad habits; eventually he changes enough to be able to rejoin the surface world as a responsible adult. Indeed, by the end of the story Tom is even capable of making his bullying former master Grimes produce his own dribbles of salt water in the form of tears, suggesting that we all contain

hidden pools of cleansing fluid that are simply waiting for the opportunity to rise to the surface.

In becoming a baby who looks like an eft, part of the life cycle of a
newt, Tom is regressing to an earlier stage of life as both an individual
and a species, and for the most part Kingsley's approach to the idea
of evolution is a light-hearted thought experiment, rather than a serious contribution to the debates that surrounded the publication in
1859 of Darwin's *On the Origin of Species*. If man originally came
out of the oceans, Kingsley's story suggests, perhaps that would be
the best place to learn how to develop in a more satisfactory way.
Like Thomas Huxley, whose popular lectures on evolution were
published as *Man's Place in Nature* in the same year as *The Water-
Babies*, Kingsley was keen to see evolution in ethical as well as physical terms, as he questioned 'whence our race has come; what are the
limits of our power over nature, and of nature's power over us; to
what goal we are tending'.[31] However, also like Huxley, he remained
worried by thoughts of degeneration. Just as Huxley's book made
explicit an evolutionary link between men and gorillas that Darwin
had only discreetly hinted at, and associated early stages of evolutionary development with the so-called 'lower races of mankind', so *The
Water-Babies* contains numerous warnings about Tom's possible
reversion to an earlier state of savagery. (Kingsley's attitudes towards
race were at best ambivalent: while he loathed slavery, and once
entertained the Queen of the Sandwich Islands in his rectory, he also
wrote of an inevitable 'divergence . . . between the English man &
the savage or foreigner', and seems to have viewed 'savage' and
'foreigner' as more or less equivalent terms.[32]) Above ground, the
soot-blackened Tom has already been compared to a little gorilla, and
the threat does not disappear when he leaves the riverbank. The story
of the Doasyoulikes, who swiftly degenerate from lazy humans to
hairy beasts that climb trees and eat roots, provides an accelerated
version of the fate that awaits him if he fails to take advantage of
the opportunities for self-development offered to him by the story.

[31] *Man's Place in Nature and other Anthropological Essays* (London: Macmillan & Co.,
1894), 71.
[32] Cited in Martin, *The Dust of Combat*, 215.

The fact that the last of the Doasyoulikes is shot by the celebrated explorer Paul Du Chaillu contains an especially pointed warning, because in 1861 Du Chaillu had published an account of his travels in equatorial Africa that, in addition to boasting of the number of animals he had shot and stuffed, described his attempt to adopt the infant of a female gorilla he had killed. If his first surprise was that the infant had a face that was 'as white as a white child's', his second was that it quickly started to mimic human behaviour. 'I called him Tommy, to which name he soon began to answer', Du Chaillu reports, but although Tommy was 'extremely fond of being patted and fondled', there were times when he stamped his foot and howled 'like a badly-spoiled child'. Worse was to come:

He soon began to be a very great thief. When the people left their huts he would steal in and make off with their plantains and fish. He watched very carefully till all had left a house, and it was difficult to catch him in the act. I flogged him several times, and, indeed, brought him to the conviction that it was wrong to steal; but he could never resist the temptation.[33]

Substitute sea-bull's-eyes and sea-lollipops for plantains and fish, and the situation sounds strangely like Tom stealing sweets from Mrs Doasyouwouldbedoneby's hidden store. The difference is that she does not beat him, but instead sadly watches as he develops a prickly skin as an external sign of his guilt. The end of each story confirms that the gap between human and primate behaviour is a natural one, but must be carefully monitored if it is not to narrow too far. Tommy cannot learn from experience, and eventually sickens and dies. ('Alas! poor Tommy!', Du Chaillu sighs,[34] with an allusion to *Hamlet*—'Alas! poor Yorick!'—that confirms Tommy's role as the camp's resident clown.) By contrast, Kingsley's Tom discovers that he has a conscience monitoring his behaviour, and the revelation is also a reminder to the reader that biological evolution is only one of the ways in which human beings develop. Biology does not cancel out morality; when Tom is 'determined to be a very good boy' (p. 110) it is a matter of choice rather than compulsion.

[33] Paul B. Du Chaillu, *Explorations and Adventures in Equatorial Africa* (London: John Murray, 1861), 283–5.
[34] Ibid. 287.

## 'the Water of Life'

Kingsley's decision to serialize *The Water-Babies* in *Macmillan's Magazine* (August 1862–March 1863) indicates that such debates were at the heart of his story rather than merely decorative flourishes on its surface. A serious-minded journal, *Macmillan's* attracted equally serious-minded contributors; the topics of some of the other articles that surrounded *The Water-Babies* included new translations of the *Iliad*, the American Civil War, the 'natural and economic history' of oysters, cotton-weaving in Lancashire, the origin of language, the history of almanacs, 'national systems of bodily exercise', and whist. Viewed in this context, a story about a small boy whizzing through the oceans might have come as light relief, but Kingsley's topical allusions ensured that no matter how far Tom travelled his story never entirely detached itself from its textual surroundings. Indeed, there are times when his prose gives the impression of being the result of someone putting the rest of *Macmillan's* contents into a bottle and vigorously shaking them together. Barely a page passes without a satirical swipe at American foreign policy, or the British education system, or whichever contemporary issue happened to catch Kingsley's eye. Occasionally these swipes hit home. One of Tom's literary ancestors was 'The Chimney-Sweeper' in Blake's *Songs of Innocence and Experience* (1789), which features a young sweep named Tom dreaming about all the climbing-boys being set free by an angel: 'Then down a green plain leaping, laughing, they run, | And wash in a river, and shine in the sun.' In the poem this happy dream is contrasted with the miserable reality of another day being forced up chimneys ('Tom awoke; and we rose in the dark, | And got with our bags and our brushes to work'), but Kingsley has a good claim to being the man who really did set the climbing-boys free. Although the Second Royal Commission on the Employment of Children had been hearing evidence in 1862, it was *The Water-Babies* that provoked a flurry of public interest in the issue, leading to the passage of the Chimney-Sweepers' Act of 1864, which finally outlawed a practice that had led to dozens of small boys suffocating to death and countless more contracting diseases such as cancer of the scrotum.

Once we know this, it can be surprising to turn to the story's opening chapter and realize how little information it provides about the reality of Tom's work. What took the Royal Commission hundreds of pages to describe is briskly compressed into a single sentence: 'He cried when he had to climb the dark flues, rubbing his poor knees and elbows raw; and when the soot got into his eyes, which it did every day in the week; and when his master beat him, which he did every day in the week; and when he had not enough to eat, which happened every day in the week likewise' (p. 5). The repetitions give a suggestive sketch of each day's routine, but Kingsley is comparatively uninterested in the physical details of Tom's life; even the soot that marks him as its own quickly drifts from being a material fact to something more metaphorical, as Tom stands in Ellie's snow-white bedroom feeling dirty, 'and tried to rub the soot off, and wondered whether it ever would come off' (p. 17). The fear is not just that he is dirty, but that he might actually be made of dirt. It is an unusual idea, but Kingsley had long been worried about what he would later refer to as the nation's 'human soot'—the people who were at risk of being discarded as superfluous, like the waste products of an industrial process—and in viewing Tom as a piece of dirt he was developing the same line of thought.[35] Just as environmental waste could be put to better use (in *The Water-Babies* Kingsley criticizes people who 'are wasteful and dirty, and let sewers run into the sea instead of putting the stuff upon the fields like thrifty, reasonable souls', p. 100), so even the filthiest and most ignorant child could be redeemed.

Kingsley's treatment of chimney-sweeps establishes a pattern for his way of dealing with other pressing social issues. Rather than deploying them as a set of facts to ballast the realism of his writing, repeatedly he refracts them through the strange lens of his imagination. For example, the suggestion that Lady Harthover might have avoided taking her children to 'some nasty smelly undrained lodging' where they risked catching diphtheria (p. 79) reflects a far larger period concern with sanitation reform. This reached a crisis point in the summer of 1858, when London was hit by the 'Great Stink', as

---

[35] *Letters and Memories*, iv. 62; the idea is discussed in Valentine Cunningham, 'Soiled Fairy: *The Water-Babies* in Its Time', *Essays in Criticism*, 35/2 (1985), 131–48.

the stench of the polluted Thames became unbearable, and MPs were forced to drape curtains soaked in chlorine across the windows of Parliament. A year later *Punch* was still publishing satirical cartoons such as 'The London Bathing Season' (18 June 1859), which depicted a filthy boy sweep holding his nose as Father Thames invites him to 'have a nice bath';[36] as late as 1890 the crisis was still sufficiently alive in the public memory for William Morris to allude to it in his utopian fantasy *News from Nowhere*, which opens with a character swimming in a sparkling Thames of the future, where the blame for earlier mistakes is indicated by the fact that the old Parliament building has been converted into a manure warehouse. The Great Stink focused minds as well as noses, accelerating plans for a new sewerage system that would eventually thread its way under the city's streets, cleaning up the river and drastically reducing outbreaks of disease, but few Victorians were as passionately committed to the cause as Kingsley. In 1849 he wrote to Fanny from the cholera districts of Bermondsey, 'and, oh, God! what I saw! people having no water to drink—hundreds of them—but the water of the common sewer';[37] in 1873 he was still preaching in Westminster Abbey about London's 'murky alleys and foul courts', and praising 'every pious soul who now erects a drinking-fountain' for 'offering to the bodies as well as the souls of men the Water of Life'.[38] But although Kingsley's ideas were routine enough, his fictional treatment of them was far quirkier. Many of his contemporaries wrote about the need to avoid drinking contaminated water, but only Kingsley could have transformed it into a fantasy in which fairies protect Tom by 'turning him aside from millraces, and sewer-mouths, and all foul and dangerous things' (p. 71). Similarly, the fluidity of species revealed by Darwin encouraged many fantasies of hybrid or intermediate forms of life: 'With such a range and plasticity,' one newspaper joked in 1859, 'we know not where to stop—centaurs, dryads, and hamadryads . . . perhaps mermaids once filled our seas.'[39] Mermaids certainly filled the

---

[36] The cartoon is reproduced and discussed in Jonathan P. Ribner, 'The Thames and Sin in the Age of the Great Stink', *British Art Journal*, 1/2 (1999), 38–46 (at 43).

[37] *Letters and Memories*, i. 191.

[38] *The Water of Life, and other Sermons* (London: Macmillan & Co, 1897), 2–3.

[39] Cited in Beer, *Darwin's Plots*, 105.

Victorian imagination, appearing in poems like Tennyson's 'The Mermaid' and Arnold's 'The Forsaken Merman', fairy tales like Andersen's 'The Little Mermaid', paintings like Burne-Jones's *The Depths of the Sea*, and carnival attractions like P. T. Barnum's 'Feejee Mermaid', which had allegedly been caught in 1842 but was actually made from the stuffed top half of a monkey that had been sewn onto the bottom half of a fish. The popular enthusiasm for mermaid stories was such that in the 1820s a vicar had achieved some notoriety by making himself a seaweed wig and sitting on a rock out at sea, 'flashing the moon-beams about from a hand-mirror' and screaming until he attracted the attention of the superstitious locals.[40] Kingsley's hero is another hybrid creature, just as Kingsley himself once confessed that he felt himself to be 'made up principally of fish bones',[41] and at one point in the story Tom even starts to behave like a little mermaid, as he 'sit[s] upon a point of rock, among the shining sea-weeds' and cries out for the other water-babies (p. 77).

The difference, however, is that Kingsley does not merely describe a hybrid state. His writing embodies it. Science is grafted onto romance; the ordinary and the extraordinary are brought together until they become indistinguishable. Even an activity as simple as swimming takes on a new imaginative momentum in Kingsley's hands. The contradiction between his descriptions of the water-babies wearing 'the neatest little white bathing dresses', and the original illustrations that depicted them slipping naked through the water, reflected a larger debate in the period: by the 1860s, around half the men in Britain's seaside resorts had started to wear red-and-white striped bathing shorts, while 'the rest stuck to swimming naked'.[42] Such exercise was strongly recommended by medical authorities: one contemporary guide argued that exposure to seawater was especially good for children, capable of transforming 'weak, puny, decaying

---

[40] S. Baring-Gould, *The Vicar of Morwenstow: Being a Life of Robert Stephen Hawker* (London: King, 1876), 21. I am grateful to Matthew Kerr for some of these examples.

[41] See Charles Sprawson, *Haunts of the Black Masseur: The Swimmer as Hero* (London: Cape, 1992), 183.

[42] Judith Flanders, *Consuming Passions: Leisure and Pleasure in Victorian Britain* (London: Harper Press, 2006), 245.

beings' into robust and rosy-cheeked youngsters.[43] Some never grew
out of their love of the water. Apparently one of Swinburne's greatest
joys was being 'violently beaten to and fro between the breakers',
while in George Borrow's autobiographical novel *Lavengro* (1851) an
adult watches the fish darting about in a stream while longing 'to
bathe and cleanse myself from the squalor produced by my late hard
life'.[44] Matthew Arnold went further still: as a boy he had discon-
certed his father by 'spending an entire summer holiday imagining
himself as a corpse at the bottom of Lake Windermere', and some
years later when he dived into the sea a mile off the Italian coast he
found it so enticing that it was 'difficult ever to bring one's head up
out of it'.[45] Yet however closely Kingsley's contemporaries approached
his fascination with water, they could never duplicate the unembar-
rassed freedom with which he described his water-babies plunging
and frolicking in the sea; the hyphen he introduced between 'water'
and 'babies' was like an umbilical cord connecting them to their natural element.

## 'romantic, marvellous, heroic'

If Tom numbers newts and gorillas among his physical ancestors, his
literary ancestors are no less varied. In addition to Blake's *Songs of
Innocence and Experience*, they include Spenser's descriptions of
mutability in *The Faerie Queene*, Wordsworth's 'Ode: Intimations of
Immortality from Recollections of Early Childhood' (Kingsley was
especially haunted by the poem's lines about the 'immortal sea |
Which brought us hither', and their promise that our souls 'Can in a
moment travel thither, | And see the children sport upon the short, |
And hear the mighty waters rolling evermore'), and the robust phys-
icality of Rabelais's *Gargantua and Pantagruel*. This unusual patchwork of influences is further embroidered by an eclectic range of
allusions to the Bible and earlier fiction, including the sort of knowing winks to stories written for adults that were likely to go over almost

[43] T. D. Harries, *Guide to Sea-Bathing* (Aberystwyth: J. Morgan, 1874), 39.
[44] Sprawson, *Haunts of the Black Masseur*, 97, 149.
[45] Ibid. 82.

every child's head. It is hard to imagine many children enjoying the joke of a lobster caught in a trap and saying 'I can't get out' (p. 95), which replays the situation of the caged starling in Laurence Sterne's *A Sentimental Journey* who sings 'I can't get out—I can't get out'. In fact it is hard to imagine children enjoying many of Kingsley's jokes. Although it has long been viewed as a classic of children's literature, every aspect of *The Water-Babies*, from Kingsley's narrative style to his decision to publish it in *Macmillan's*, suggests that it was originally intended as a story *about* children rather than one aimed directly *at* them. (Kingsley's subtitle, 'A Fairy Tale for a Land-Baby', could mean that he was offering the story to his son as a gift, or merely that it was written in his honour.) Even if Kingsley did hope that *The Water-Babies* would have an uplifting moral effect on children, the complexity of his writing seems to assume an adult reader willing to act as an interpretive filter for the version that would eventually reach a child's ears. Indeed, a significant portion of the critical confusion that surrounds *The Water-Babies* can probably be put down to the fact that it is two stories in one. Like modern pantomime, which brings together a straightforward fairy-tale structure with knowing contemporary references, Kingsley's story often uses its tone of mock-innocence as a shield he could hide behind while lobbing his satirical hand grenades. Not all early reviewers were convinced by his tactics: in 1863 the *Saturday Review* grumbled that Kingsley was just another example of an author attempting 'to write a child's story really for grown-up people, but nominally for children . . . the sort of performance which is dearest to those who are made sentimental by a fantastic liking for an artificial childhood'.[46] Viewed in this light, *The Water-Babies* was not very different to a novel like Thomas Hughes's *Tom Brown's Schooldays* (1857), another story in which a boy called Tom is subject to a distant authority figure who punishes him with sadness rather than anger, and develops morally by learning to take care of someone else. Both encouraged adult readers to recover their dormant powers of imagination; both reflected a nostalgia for the sort of childhood that has only ever existed in the pages of fiction.

[46] *Saturday Review* (23 May 1863), 665–6.

Kingsley knew that the problem of unimaginative adults began early; in 1849 he complained that both the previous generation and his own had taken 'little or no proper care' of the love for everything 'romantic, marvellous, heroic, which exists in every ingenuous child'.[47] On the other hand, in a questionnaire he completed in the 1860s, he answered the question '*Favourite kind of literature?*' with 'Physical science',[48] and in 'The Wonders of the Shore' he had already praised scientists for retaining 'child-like hearts' (*NBR*, p. 11) in their readiness to be surprised by what everyone else took for granted. His essay 'The True Fairy Tale' made the distinction even plainer, arguing that the 'fairy land' of pantomime was nowhere near as astonishing as the real world: 'The theatre last night was the fairy land of man; but this is the fairy land of God.'[49] In *The Water-Babies* he attempted a compromise. Here scientific exactitude sits alongside descriptions of the world as it would appear if the imagination was in charge: a place where if there is 'sea-rock' then there is no reason why there shouldn't also be 'sea-toffee', and where Nice is so named 'because there are so many nice things in the sea here' (p. 105). By the end of the story, the sight of policemen's truncheons 'running along without legs or arms' is no more surprising than the *naviculae* (cells of algae) Tom has seen moving in the water 'without arms, or legs, or anything to stand in their stead' (p. 169). Even the biological terms that pepper Kingsley's prose, such as 'subanhypaposupernal anastomes of peritomic diacellurite' (p. 87), start to sound as magical as words like 'abracadabra' in their ability to unlock the world's secrets.

The scene in which Tom stares at Ellie in her bedroom, like a Prince about to release Sleeping Beauty from her spell, but is chased away before he can wake her with a kiss, prepares us for a story in which Kingsley playfully refuses to settle on any one narrative mode. From fairy tale to social realism, and topical satire to myth, he repeatedly switches between genres with all the energy of the fly that

---

[47] *Fraser's Magazine* (1849), cited in Jonathan Padley, 'Marginal(ized) Demarcator: (Mis)Reading *The Water-Babies*', *Children's Literature Association Quarterly*, 34/1 (Spring 2009), 51–64 (at 63).

[48] Chitty, *The Beast and the Monk*, 272.

[49] *Madam How and Lady Why* (London: Macmillan & Co., 1889), 114.

surprises Tom by jumping out of its skin (p. 55). The outcome is a story that appears to be based on accretion rather than design. Indeed, there are times when it threatens to turn into an anthology of popular Victorian writing, by turns a naturalist's handbook, an aquatic *Pilgrim's Progress*, a miniature *Palgrave's Golden Treasury*, an educative tract, a *Bildungsroman*, a tall tale to rival those of Baron Munchausen, and a religious alternative to the secular gospel of self-help. From page to page, and even from sentence to sentence, slap-stick violence makes way for pulpit oratory; biological processes blur into scenes of pantomimic transformation. In fact, when Kingsley's writing disintegrates into cluttered Rabelaisian lists, it is tempting to wonder whether he was deliberately experimenting with the printed page as a textual equivalent of Darwin's tangled bank: a world so crammed with squalling life that only the fittest ideas would survive. Repeatedly, 'and' takes over as the sole principle of connection (the sentence that describes Tom's life as a chimney-sweep sets the tone with sixteen uses of 'and', p. 5), and logical links are replaced by purely verbal ones ('a body's heart'll guide them right, if they will but hearken to it' (p. 37); 'he fell in with a deep, dark, deadly, and destructive war, waged by the princes and potentates of those parts' (p. 159)), as the narrative surges in different directions and spawns new ideas with the same irresistible energy as the world it describes.

   This was not a wholly new departure for Kingsley. As early as 'The Sands of Dee', he had written about the sea in a way that perfectly captured its own restless surface:

> They rowed her in across the rolling foam,
> The cruel crawling foam,
> The cruel hungry foam,
> To her grave beside the sea . . .[50]

Seen from one angle, these lines are like a set of cancelled variants that have somehow survived into the final version of the poem, as if Kingsley couldn't make up his mind how to describe a scene that exhausted synonyms. Seen from another angle, they perfectly capture a force that was always changing yet always the same. Kingsley's critics

---

[50] *Poems*, 246.

were not always so generous. Long before Louis MacNeice charac-
terized *The Water-Babies* as 'one of the most uneven and ragbaggy
books in the language',[51] a reviewer in 1860 had noted 'the inconsider-
ate confusion' which led events in Kingsley's stories to 'jostle and
stumble over one another', and 'the indistinctness with which many
of them are told'.[52] Three years earlier *Westward Ho!* had been similarly dismissed as 'straggling, tumultuous, incoherent',[53] and when
Kingsley published the essay *Phaethon; or, Loose Thoughts for Loose
Thinkers* (1852) the reviewers seized on his subtitle with glee. In each
case they were fair criticisms. The only surprise was that his writing
was not even more disjointed, given that the sudden enthusiasms of
his mind were compounded by a method of composition in which he
would assemble each paragraph in his head, while pacing up and
down in the open air, before rushing indoors to commit it to paper.
Even within the confines of a letter he was capable of disconcerting
swerves of direction. 'Mrs Marx is certainly one of the most clever,
agreeable, well-read women I have ever met,' he concludes in one
typical letter to Fanny, before pirouetting on his full stop and adding
'But she weighs 16 stone and has a moustache like a man.'[54]

  Kingsley recognized his weathercock tendencies, and although he
once tried to distinguish between changeable 'opinions' and settled
'convictions',[55] and defended the 'fragmentary and unconnected form'
of *Yeast* by suggesting that it was somehow bound up with his subject
matter,[56] he was fully aware of the need to balance his pleasure in the
moment with the sort of continuity required to turn a series of narrative snapshots into a novel. Revising *The Water-Babies* between its

[51] *Varieties of Parable* (Cambridge: Cambridge University Press, 1965), 83.

[52] *National Review*, 10 (Jan. 1860), 18–19.

[53] *Westminster Review*, 68 (July 1857), 307.

[54] Unpublished letter (1862), cited in Chitty, *The Beast and the Monk*, 175.

[55] See C. N. Manlove, *Modern Fantasy: Five Studies* (Cambridge: Cambridge
University Press, 1975), 15.

[56] 'Readers will probably complain of the fragmentary and unconnected form of the
book. Let them first be sure that that is not an integral feature of the subject itself, and
therefore the very form the book should take. Do not young men think, speak, act, just
now, in this very incoherent, fragmentary way; without methodic education or habits of
thought; with the various stereotyped systems which they have received by tradition,
breaking up under them like ice in a thaw; with a thousand facts and notions, which they
know not how to classify, pouring in on them like a flood?', *Yeast* ('Epilogue').

serialization in *Macmillan's* and its republication as a separate volume, he made some efforts to increase the story's coherence, making several alterations of 'and' to 'so', and introducing the figure of the mysterious Irishwoman at strategic moments in the story, thereby hinting at an overseeing intelligence in his novel as well as in the world. Some oddities and contradictions remained. Kingsley's New Testament theology continued to sit awkwardly with his unapologetically Old Testament love of violence, reflected in the brisk and often brutal deaths of many of the creatures Tom encounters. The narrative continued to switch unpredictably between the excited perspective of a child and a more measured adult consciousness. Even Tom's body was reluctant to stay the same: as a water-baby, there are times when he actually seems to be made out of water, as when he is pelted with stones which pass through his body without damaging it (p. 168), although only a few pages later he has somehow become a 'great man of science' who plans steam engines and electric telegraphs (p. 179). However, what the revised text successfully captures is a remarkable mixture of psychology and ethics. Just as Tom's sense of being overwhelmed by new experiences is reflected in a form of narrative excess, as sentence after sentence is barnacled with superfluous detail, so Kingsley's style offers glimpses of the hidden order that Tom eventually discovers.

Whenever Kingsley's writing seems to be veering off in a new direction, often it is merely looping back on itself to develop an underlying pattern. At the start of the story, Tom is discovered with half a brick in his hand, ready to heave it at a horse's legs; soon afterwards, one of the first creatures he encounters underwater is a 'wonderful little fellow' (p. 49) who makes bricks for his house wall. When Tom gets to know the caddis flies he longs 'to have wings like them some day' (p. 53); in the next chapter the fairies bring Ellie 'such a pretty pair of wings, that she could not help putting them on' (p. 86). Ellie herself is first encountered as a sleeping vision of loveliness, shortly after the earth at dawn is personified as a woman who 'looked still prettier asleep than awake' (p. 9). Such writing works like the waves Tom sees playing out at sea, which 'broke themselves all to pieces, and never minded it a bit, but mended themselves and jumped up again' (p. 73). It captures not only the inextricably interconnected nature of life, but also Tom's developing consciousness that these connections include him. Just as Kingsley could sense a divine purpose behind apparently random natural forces, so *The Water-Babies* delights in revealing that what might at first look like narrative digressions or cul-de-sacs are in fact part of a meaningful structure. Even when Kingsley slips into a form of prose poetry, such as his description of how the sea 'rolled and roared over the rocks in winter nights, and lay still in the bright summer days, for the children to bathe and play in' (pp. 9–10), it reflects his desire for writing that would echo the rhythms of the natural world. 'I do feel like a different being when I get into metre,' he once explained, 'like an otter in the water, rather than an otter ashore.'[57] The prose he deployed in *The Water-Babies* may have put up more resistance than verse, but never before had he found a subject in which he could immerse himself with so much joy. Every sentence he wrote was like a fresh channel of water flushing the dirt away.

### *'Come away, O human child!'*

Kingsley was aware that the style of *The Water-Babies* might not suit all readers—his descriptions of Harthover House's jumbled architecture (p. 14) and the caddis fly's patchwork appearance (pp. 48–9) sound suspiciously like a defence of his own way of assembling his materials—so he was probably not surprised by the work's mixed critical reception. While *The Times* admired his attempt to reconcile faith and science as a 'fine' goal,[58] other reviewers suspected that it was only in Kingsley's head that so many different ideas could be brought together without strain. The lolloping energy that led Thomas Hughes to characterize him as a Newfoundland dog struck others as excessive and aimless when translated on to the page; reviewing *The Water-Babies* in *The Spectator*, R. H. Hutton observed that it was 'like a dog which constantly loses the scent by turning aside to

---

[57] Martin, *The Dust of Combat*, 157.

[58] See Liza Marz Harper, 'Children's Literature, Science and Faith: *The Water-Babies*', in Karin Lesnik-Oberstein (ed.), *Children's Literature: New Approaches* (Basingstoke: Macmillan, 2004), 121.

worry cats, bark at ill-looking beggars, or simply to play with a bone with his four legs in the air'.[59] However impressive particular episodes may have been, as a novel it risked adding up to less than the sum of its parts. Yet if *The Water-Babies* is a fable about physical evolution, it is also one which brilliantly captures the branching life of the imagination, as individual words and sentences are both nurtured by and press back against the environment in which they find themselves. Like Mother Carey's creations (p. 146), Kingsley's story is one that seems to be making itself up as it goes along.

In these circumstances, perhaps it is not surprising that far more people know about *The Water-Babies* than have ever read Kingsley's original version. Its fragmentary form has encouraged dozens of allusions and echoes, particularly in later writers concerned with the question of how—or whether—children should develop. The most famous example is probably Lewis Carroll, whose *Alice's Adventures in Wonderland* (1865), published two years later, is in part an answer to Kingsley's question about whether man might undergo 'much more wonderful' changes than other animals 'as the Great Exhibition is more wonderful than a rabbit-burrow' (p. 42). On a more local level, the otter in *The Water-Babies* who is seen 'grinning like a Cheshire cat' (p. 58) may have planted the seed in Carroll's mind that would later develop into one of his most famous characters. His sequel *Through the Looking-Glass* (1871) is even closer in spirit to Kingsley's story, beginning with a scene in which Alice passes through a mirror, rather as Tom penetrates the surface of the river, before discovering a previously hidden world of marvels. Other echoes are fainter but no less enticing. The children who become water-babies after they have 'come to grief by ill-usage or ignorance or neglect' (p. 104) are close literary relatives of the Lost Boys in J. M. Barrie's *Peter Pan* (1904), who have ended up in Neverland after falling out of their prams. (Kingsley is more vicious than Barrie's gentle slapstick—his fictional children tend to die after falling into the fire rather than out of their prams—but also more egalitarian in allowing girls as well as boys to enjoy this fantasy afterlife.)

---

[59] *A Victorian Spectator: Uncollected Writings of R. H. Hutton*, ed. Robert H. Tener and Malcolm Woodfield (Bristol: Bristol Press, 1989), 70.

Kingsley's story may even have seeped into W. B. Yeats's poem 'The Stolen Child': when Yeats's fairies sing 'Come away, O human child! | To the waters and the wild', it is hard not to hear echoes of the water-babies dancing around Tom on the sand and crying out 'we must come away home, we must come away home, or the tide will leave us dry' (p. 100).

But it is not only Kingsley's fragmentary style that has encouraged later writers to borrow narrative odds and ends from him. Equally significant is the fact that *The Water-Babies* has long been known primarily through second-hand accounts. Abridged versions for children, in particular, have filed away the unruly outcrops of Kingsley's obsessions and tidied up the imaginative sprawl of his writing. Yet while such versions respond to perfectly legitimate concerns about what is comprehensible to a child, who might well feel 'squashed by the words and strangled by the sentence' (p. 87) when faced by some of Kingsley's more rococo passages, the result has usually been a literary version of the rock pools described by Edmund Gosse in *Father and Son*. Once swarming with colourful life, Gosse reports, the collectors quickly stripped them bare, leaving behind only a shadow of what had been there before. Too often *The Water-Babies* has suffered a similar fate at the hands of well-meaning adapters. Writing that was full of unruly energy has been turned into a straightforward moral fable, and a story that could be enjoyed because nobody—not even Kingsley himself—could be sure what would happen next, has been repackaged as one that generates pleasure through sheer predictability. Critics, similarly, have often been tempted to ignore Kingsley's contradictions and trim his excesses. Whether interpreting *The Water-Babies* as an early ecological fable (the term 'ecology' was coined in 1866),[60] or as a projection of Kingsley's own sexual anxieties (one critic is convinced that Tom is 'at one and the same time the questing penis and the unborn foetus in its amniotic fluid'[61]), the result has been the same: a playfully plural narrative has been turned into something more manageably singular.

[60] Naomi Wood, 'A (Sea) Green Victorian: Charles Kingsley and *The Water-Babies*', *The Lion and the Unicorn: A Critical Journal of Children's Literature*, 19/2 (1995), 233–52.
[61] Maureen Duffy, *The Erotic World of Faery* (London: Hodder and Stoughton, 1972), 313.

The most successful attempts to interpret *The Water-Babies* have been visual rather than verbal. Kingsley's 1863 edition of the story added two illustrations by Noel Paton to the magazine version, in addition to some illuminated capital letters, and these images would have a large influence on the story's later public reception. In some ways the artistic choices made by Paton were shrewd. One plate (p. l) depicts a set of water-babies surrounding Mrs Doasyouwouldbedoneby, sucking their thumbs while her hair billows out like seaweed; the other (p. 76) shows more water-babies slipping through the water like soft white eels. Both lithographs employ the circular tondo form made famous by artists such as Michelangelo and Botticelli, and therefore bring together modern science—the pictures resemble a microscope being lowered into the water—with traditional religious iconography. While many of the sea creatures in these pictures are drawn with the same realism as Kingsley's illustrations to *Glaucus*, the water-babies are depicted as little aquatic cherubs, who are as podgy and pouting as anything to be found in Renaissance art. However, the influence of Paton's plates on later illustrators was not altogether a positive one. Too often, in editions illustrated by artists like Jessie Wilcox Smith (1910) or Mabel Lucie Attwell (1915), Kingsley's water-babies degenerated from the sweetly cherubic to the merely sentimental; only in rare cases, such as the editions copiously illustrated by Linley Sambourne (1886) or W. Heath Robinson (1915), did anyone seek to capture Kingsley's wit rather than preferring to dissolve it into whimsy.

Yet while illustrations of *The Water-Babies* respond to Kingsley's keen visual sense, what they cannot do is capture the swirling energy of his writing. Film fares rather better in this respect: cinema adaptations include a 1935 Walt Disney cartoon, originally intended as an experiment in animation techniques, and a 1978 version starring James Mason and Bernard Cribbins which cleverly shifts from live action to fairy-tale animation once Tom jumps into the river. But the real influence of the story is far more diffuse than this. Search for 'water-babies' on an Internet search engine, and the results include everything from boat hire to swimming lessons. There are photographers such as Zena Holloway, who specializes in recreating real-life versions of Kingsley's story by taking photographs of young children underwater; in 1998 an Evian advertisement saw swimming babies perform an updated Esther Williams routine; strange echoes of Kingsley's fears about degeneration can even be traced forward to the 'Sea Monkeys' (actually brine shrimp) that generations of American children have been seduced into buying by advertisements in comic books that promise to turn every owner into a miniature Mother Carey: 'they keep their water so clean . . . they LOVE attention'. Indeed, although *The Water-Babies* sets out to describe a model of physical and moral progress, it has come to embody a rather different kind of evolution. Like all the best stories, it has survived by adapting to changed circumstances, becoming a modern myth that is every bit as diverse and surprising as the man who wrote it.

One Cambridge undergraduate who attended Kingsley's lectures in 1862–3 recalled how he was walking along by the river with a group of friends one evening, when out of the twilight emerged a tall figure in a white scarf 'slinging along at a great pace' on the towpath:

He passes down a little below us, and returns smoking a cigar, and goes a little above us and waits. Then the sound of the thrashing oars—up comes the boat—. . . As she passes him he throws his cigar into the river, and begins to run too. I shall never forget it. The crew are tired and row badly . . . He ran with us to Grassy Corner. I remember the boat stopped there for an 'Easy all,' and his short comment, 'I'm afraid that won't do, gentlemen.'[62]

It is hard to conjure up a better image of Kingsley's life, in which he fought to make his various obsessions work smoothly together— religion and science, sex and purity, history and legend—even as he came to realize that all too often the solutions he came up with just wouldn't do. (The pun lurking in 'row', meaning to pick a fight rather than pull an oar, was recognized by Richard Monckton Milnes who, on hearing that Kingsley had died, remarked of his quarrelsome friend that he had 'literally *rowed* himself to death'.[63]) Yet what might have crippled Kingsley as a person energized him as a writer, and

[62] Quoted in J. M. I. Klaver, *The Apostle of the Flesh: A Critical Life of Charles Kingsley* (Leiden: Brill, 2006), 524–5.
[63] Martin, *The Dust of Combat*, 122.

nothing he wrote better illustrates this than *The Water-Babies*. There is a moment near the beginning of Tom's underwater adventures when he sees a ball of glossy fur tumbling towards him: 'sometimes it broke up and streamed away in pieces,' the narrator reports, 'and then it joined again; and all the while the noise came out of it louder and louder'. Deciding to investigate more closely, Tom discovers that it is a bundle of otters 'rolling, and diving, and twisting, and wrestling, and cuddling, and kissing, and biting, and scratching, in the most charming fashion that ever was seen' (p. 57). That is an excellent description of otters at play. It is an equally good description of Kingsley himself at work.

# NOTE ON THE TEXT

*The Water-Babies* was first published, one chapter per month, in *Macmillan's Magazine* from August 1862 to March 1863. An edition in volume form must have been decided upon during this period, and Kingsley worked hard on his text to prepare it for a more permanent life. Many small changes and several large additions were made to the story, which was first published as a book in the summer of 1863. Although often reprinted, Kingsley did not make any further significant changes, and the present edition therefore follows the text of the first edition, including 'L'Envoi', which was cancelled during the press run, and the wood-engraved initial letters printed at the start of each chapter. Although it preserves Kingsley's inconsistent spelling, obvious printing errors have been silently corrected; misquotations—particularly of the poems Kingsley adopted for his chapter epigraphs—are pointed out in the Explanatory Notes. Appendix I shows all the substantive variations in text that occurred in the development from magazine to book publication. For further details about the first edition and illustrations see the Select Bibliography and Introduction, p. xxxvii.

# SELECT BIBLIOGRAPHY

### Editions of The Water-Babies

The first edition of *The Water-Babies* in book form was published by Macmillan in London and Cambridge in the summer of 1863. It collates as follows:

Pot 4°. [A]⁴B⁸(±B1) C–Z⁸. 180 (179) leaves. Pp. [i–viii] [1–3] or [3] 4–350 [2].

It had a tinted lithograph frontispiece and one tinted lithograph illustration after drawings by J. Noel Paton, and eight wood-engraved chapter initials by Robert (?) Dudley. The printing was by R. Clay, Son, and Taylor of Bread Street Hill. The 'Envoi' leaf (B1) was cancelled during the print run. The book was bound in dark green glazed cloth with a triple rule frame and a cartouche by Dudley on the front in gilt, gilt-lettered spine, and triple rule in blind on the back.

This heads a succession of Macmillan editions throughout the copyright period, published in various formats and with various illustrations. The most widely disseminated was the edition illustrated by Linley Sambourne, first published in 1886. The first American edition was based on the first English one and was published in Boston by T. O. P. Burnham in 1864.

After the copyright period ended, a multiplicity of full editions was (and continues to be) published, along with a large number of abridgements and adaptations. The most distinguished of these is the abridgement by Kathleen Lines, illustrated by Harold Jones, published in London by Victor Gollancz in 1961. Many independent editions have been published in the USA.

### Biographies and General Works

Chitty, Susan, *The Beast and the Monk: A Life of Charles Kingsley* (London: Hodder & Stoughton, 1974).

——, *Charles Kingsley's Landscape* (Newton Abbot: David & Charles, 1976).

Colloms, Brenda, *Charles Kingsley: The Lion of Eversley* (London: Constable, 1975).

Harris, Styron, *Charles Kingsley: A Reference Guide* (Boston: G. K. Hall, 1981).

Kingsley, Frances E. (ed.), *Charles Kingsley: His Letters and Memories of His Life*, 2 vols. (1877; London: Macmillan, 1910).

Klaver, J. M. I., *The Apostle of the Flesh: A Critical Life of Charles Kingsley* (Leiden: Brill, 2006).

Martin, R. B., *The Dust of Combat: A Life of Charles Kingsley* (London: Faber & Faber, 1959).

Pope-Hennessy, Una, *Canon Charles Kingsley: A Biography* (London: Chatto & Windus, 1948).

Rapple, Brendan A., *The Rev. Charles Kingsley: An Annotated Bibliography of Secondary Criticism, 1900–2006* (Lanham, Md.; Plymouth: Scarecrow, 2008).

Uffelman, Larry K., *Charles Kingsley* (Boston: Twayne, 1979).

### Critical Studies of The Water-Babies

Beer, Gillian, *Darwin's Plots: Evolutionary Narrative in Darwin, George Eliot and Nineteenth-Century Fiction* (London: Routledge & Kegan Paul, 1983), 133–9.

Carpenter, Humphrey, 'Parson Lot Takes a Cold Bath', in *Secret Gardens: A Study of the Golden Age of Children's Literature* (London: G. Allen & Unwin, 1985), 23–43.

Coleman, Dorothy, 'Rabelais and *The Water-Babies*', *Modern Language Review*, 66/3 (1971), 511–21.

Cunningham, Valentine, 'Soiled Fairy: *The Water-Babies* in Its Time', *Essays in Criticism*, 35/2 (1985), 131–48.

Harper, Lila Marz, 'Children's Literature, Science and Faith: *The Water-Babies*', in Karin Lesnik-Oberstein (ed.), *Children's Literature: New Approaches* (Basingstoke: Macmillan, 2004), 118–43.

Hawley, John C., '*The Water-Babies* as Catechetical Paradigm', *Children's Literature Association Quarterly*, 14/1 (Spring 1989), 19–21.

Johnston, Arthur, '*The Water-Babies*: Kingsley's Debt to Darwin', *English*, 12 (Autumn 1959), 215–19.

Leavis, Q. D., 'The Water-Babies', *Children's Literature in Education*, 23 (Winter 1976), 155–63.

MacNeice, Louis, *Varieties of Parable* (Cambridge: Cambridge University Press, 1965), 76–101.

Manlove, C. N., 'Charles Kingsley (1819–75) and *The Water-Babies*', in *Modern Fantasy: Five Studies* (Cambridge: Cambridge UP, 1975), 13–54.

——, *Christian Fantasy: From 1200 to the Present* (Basingstoke: Macmillan, 1992), 183–208.

Muller, Charles H., 'The Water-Babies—Moral Lessons for Children', *Unisa English Studies: Journal of the Department of English*, 24/1 (May 1986), 12–17.

O'Gorman, Francis, '"More Interesting than All the Books, Save One": Charles Kingsley's Construction of Natural History', in Juliet John and

Alice Jenkins (eds.), *Rethinking Victorian Culture* (Basingstoke: Macmillan, 2000), 144–61.

Padley, Jonathan, 'Marginal(ized) Demarcator: (Mis)Reading *The Water-Babies*', *Children's Literature Association Quarterly*, 34/1 (Spring 2009), 51–64.

Paradis, James G., 'Satire and Science in Victorian Culture', in Bernard Lightman (ed.), *Victorian Science in Context* (Chicago: University of Chicago Press, 1997), 143–75.

Prickett, Stephen, *Victorian Fantasy*, 2nd edn. (Waco, Tex.: Baylor University Press, 2005), 139–171.

Rapple, Brendan A., 'The Motif of Water in Charles Kingsley's *The Water-Babies*', *University of Mississippi Studies in English*, 11–12 (1993–95), 259–71.

Uffelman, Larry, and Scott, Patrick, 'Kingsley's Serial Novels II: *The Water-Babies*', *Victorian Periodicals Review*, 19/4 (Winter 1986), 122–31.

Wallace, Jo-Ann, 'De-Scribing *The Water-Babies*: The Child in Post-Colonial Theory', in Chris Tiffin and Alan Lawson (eds.), *De-Scribing Empire: Post-Colonialism and Textuality* (London: Routledge, 1994), 171–84.

Wilson, A. N., *The Victorians* (London: Arrow, 2003), 295–304.

Wood, Naomi, 'A (Sea) Green Victorian: Charles Kingsley and *The Water-Babies*', *The Lion and the Unicorn: A Critical Journal of Children's Literature*, 19/2 (Dec. 1995), 233–52.

# A CHRONOLOGY OF CHARLES KINGSLEY

| *Life* | *Historical and Cultural Background* |
|---|---|
| 1837 Attends King's College, London, as a day boy. | Queen Victoria succeeds William IV. Carlyle, *The French Revolution*. Dickens begins *Oliver Twist*. |
| 1838–41 Undergraduate at Magdalene College, Cambridge, where he leads a rather unstable life until meeting and falling in love with Frances Eliza Grenfell (1814–91) in the summer of 1839. Under her influence, and that of F. D. Maurice, he decides to enter the Church. | |
| 1838 | Irish Poor Law. People's Charter advocates universal suffrage. |
| 1839 | Chartist riots. Carlyle, *Chartism*; Darwin, *Voyage of the Beagle*. |
| 1841 | Peel becomes PM. |
| 1842 Ordained. Appointed curate in the parish of Eversley, Hampshire. | Chartist riots. Chadwick, *Report on the Sanitary Condition of the Labouring Population of Great Britain*. |
| 1843 | Thomas Hood, 'Song of the Shirt'; Dickens, 'A Christmas Carol'. |
| 1844 (10 Jan.) Marries FEG at Trinity church, Bath, and is appointed to the rectorship of Eversley, where he remains (with some intermissions) until his death. (Nov.) First daughter, Rose Georgiana, born. | Factory Act restricts the working hours of women and children. Ragged School Union. |
| 1845 Accepts the honorary canonry of Middleham in the North Riding and visits Yorkshire to attend service there. Deeply impressed with the scenery of the Dales. | Irish potato famine: 1 million die and 8 million emigrate. Disraeli, *Sybil*; Engels, *Condition of the Working Class in England*. |
| 1846 | Corn laws repealed. |
| 1847 (Feb.) First son, Maurice, born. During this period CK is working on his 'Life' of St Elizabeth of Hungary. | Factory Act limits working day for women and children to 10 hours. |

*Life*

1848   St Elizabeth emerges in his first book, a verse play, *The Saint's Tragedy*, published in London by John W. Parker, proprietor of *Fraser's Magazine* and publisher of serious works on education and religion. CK is also now involved with the Chartist movement and contributing to the news-sheet *Politics for the People*, which Parker published. (July–Dec.) *Fraser's* serializes CK's first novel, *Yeast: A Problem*, although its radicalism offends the publisher (John Parker).

Cholera outbreak in London. Public Health Act. 'The Year of Revolutions' in Europe. Marx and Engels, *Communist Manifesto*; J. S. Mill, *Principles of Political Economy*.

1849   Near collapse through overwork; recuperation at Ilfracombe, Lynmouth, and Clovelly (until Sept.).

Suppression of Communist riots in Paris. Charlotte Brontë, *Shirley*.

1849–50   Continuing involvement in the social reform and Christian Socialist movement, culminating in the anonymous publication by Chapman & Hall of his second novel *Alton Locke* (2 vols., 1850).

1850   (July) leaves for a tour of Germany with his parents and his brother Henry.

Factory Act limits the working week to 60 hours for women and young people. Death of Wordsworth.

1851   (May) *Yeast* reissued as a one-volume novel by Parker.

Great Exhibition in the Crystal Palace, Hyde Park.

1852   (Jan. 1852–Apr. 1853) *Hypatia* serialized in *Fraser's*. (4 June) Second daughter, Mary St Léger, born.

Harriet Beecher Stowe, *Uncle Tom's Cabin*; Dickens begins *Bleak House*.

1853   (Apr.) *Hypatia; or, New Foes with an Old Face* published as a two-volume novel by Parker. (Autumn) FEK has a serious miscarriage and goes to Torquay to recuperate. She is later joined by CK, who delights in the opportunity for some amateur zoology on the seashore. He begins correspondence with the naturalist P. H. Gosse.

First public aquarium opens at London's Zoological Gardens. (Oct.) Crimean War begins with Ottoman Empire declaring war on Russia.

1854   (Feb.) Visits Edinburgh to give four lectures at the Philosophical Institute on 'The Schools of Alexandria'. (June) Moves with his family to Bideford where he writes *Westward Ho!*. (Nov.) Publishes 'The Wonders of the Shore' in the *North British Review*, an article later expanded as *Glaucus* (1855).

(Mar.) Britain and France declare war on Russia. Dickens, *Hard Times*.

*Life*

1855 (Mar.) *Westward Ho!* (3 vols.) published, the start of CK's publishing association with Macmillan. (May) Returns to duties at Eversley, but moves temporarily out of the valley to Farley Court, Swallowfield. Writes the 'old Greek fairy tales' for his children, published at the end of the year as *The Heroes* (dated 1856), with CK's own illustrations.

Gaskell, *North and South.*

1856 Returns from Farley Court to Eversley. (Aug.) Fishing trip to North Wales with Thomas Hughes and Tom Taylor.

End of Crimean War. Mulock, *John Halifax, Gentleman*; Flaubert, *Madame Bovary.*

1857 (Mar.) *Two Years Ago* (3 vols.) published by Macmillan. (Apr.) Reviews Hughes's *Tom Brown's Schooldays* for the *Saturday Review* with great enthusiasm. Elected Fellow of the Linnean Society.

E. B. Browning, *Aurora Leigh*; Dickens, *Little Dorrit*; Livingstone, *Missionary Travels.*

1858 (Spring) Second son, Grenville Arthur, dedicatee of *The Water-Babies*, born. *Andromeda and Other Poems* published by Parker. (July) Visits Yorkshire to collect material for a proposed novel on the Pilgrimage of Grace.

Indian Mutiny suppressed. Clough, *Amours de Voyage.*

1859 (Apr.) Appointed Chaplain in Ordinary to the Queen. Receives an advance copy of Charles Darwin's *Origin of Species* and praises it in a letter Darwin later includes in the second edition.

J. S. Mill, *On Liberty*; Tennyson, *Idylls of the King*; Samuel Smiles, *Self-Help.*

1860 (May) Accepts the Regius professorship of history at Cambridge. (June) Leaves for Ireland on a fishing holiday with his recently widowed brother-in-law James Anthony Froude.

*Essays and Reviews.*

1861 Appointed tutor to the Prince of Wales at Cambridge.

Outbreak of American Civil War. Serfdom abolished in Russia. Vols. i–iii of Henry Mayhew's *London Labour and the London Poor*; Mrs Beeton, *Book of Household Management*; Eliot, *Silas Marner.*

| *Life* | *Historical and Cultural Background* |
|---|---|
| 1862 (Spring) Begins to write *The Water-Babies*, which is serialized in *Macmillan's Magazine* over the eight months Aug. 1862–Mar. 1863. | Henry Mayhew, vol. iv of *London Labour and the London Poor*. Famine among Lancashire cotton workers. Hugo, *Les Misérables*; C. G. Rossetti, *Goblin Market*. |
| 1863 (May) *The Water-Babies* published as a book by Macmillan. Elected Fellow of the Geological Society. (Dec.) Review written for the Jan. 1864 issue of *Macmillan's Magazine* sparks the quarrel with John Henry Newman which results in the latter's *Apologia pro vita sua*, published in weekly parts in 1864. | Beginning of work on London underground railway. Emancipation of US slaves. |
| 1864 (Mar.) Travels to the South of France with J. A. Froude. | Chimney-Sweepers' Act. Marx organizes first Socialist International in London. |
| 1865 (Jan.–Dec.) *Hereward the Wake* serialized in *Good Words*. | William Booth founds Christian Mission in Whitechapel, known from 1878 as the Salvation Army. Dickens, *Our Mutual Friend*; Lewis Carroll, *Alice's Adventures in Wonderland*. |
| 1866 (Mar.) *Hereward* published as a two-volume novel by Macmillan. | Second Reform Bill. Dr Barnado opens home for destitute children in London's East End. Eliot, *Felix Holt, the Radical*. Hyde Park riots. |
| 1867 | Factory Act. Marx, *Das Kapital*. |
| 1868 | Trades Union Congress founded. |
| 1869 (Apr.) Resigns chair at Cambridge. (Aug.) Appointed canon of Chester. (Dec.) Voyages to the West Indies, accompanied by his daughter Rose (returns Feb. 1870). (Nov. 1868–Dec. 1869) *Madam How and Lady Why* serialized in *Good Words for the Young*. | Arnold, *Culture and Anarchy*; J. S. Mill, *On the Subjection of Women*. |

| Life | Historical and Cultural Background |
|---|---|
| 1870 *Madam How* published as a book by Bell & Daldy. | Elementary Education Act. Death of Dickens. |
| 1871 *At Last: A Christmas in the West Indies* (2 vols.) published by Macmillan. | Legalization of trade unions. Eliot begins *Middlemarch*. Carroll, *Through the Looking-Glass*. |
| 1872 *Town Geology*, based upon a course given at Chester, published by Strahan & Co. | Licensing Act. |
| 1873 Appointed canon of Westminster. | |
| 1874 (Jan.–Aug.) Visits North America, travelling with his daughter Rose. Falls ill with pleurisy. | Factory Act establishes a 56-hour working week. Strike of agricultural workers. |
| 1875 (23 Jan.) Dies and is buried in Eversley churchyard. | Public Health Act. Trollope, *The Way We Live Now*. |

Water-Babies

*THE*

# WATER-BABIES:

A

𝔉airy 𝔗ale for a 𝔏and-𝔅aby.

BY

## THE REV. CHARLES KINGSLEY.

WITH TWO ILLUSTRATIONS BY J. NOEL PATON, R.S.A.

𝔏ondon & 𝔆ambridge :

MACMILLAN AND CO.

1863.

TO MY YOUNGEST SON,*

GRENVILLE ARTHUR,

AND TO

ALL OTHER GOOD LITTLE BOYS.

Come read me my riddle, each good little man:
If you cannot read it, no grown-up folk can.*

## L'ENVOI*

HENCE, unbelieving Sadducees,
And less believing Pharisees,
With dull conventionalities;
And leave a country muse at ease
To play at leap-frog, if she please,
With children and realities.

# CHAPTER I

I HEARD a thousand blended notes,
　　While in a grove I sate reclined;
In that sweet mood when pleasant thoughts
　　Bring sad thoughts to the mind.

To her fair works did Nature link
　　The human soul that through me ran;
And much it grieved my heart to think,
　　What man has made of man.*

WORDSWORTH.

NCE upon a time there was a little chimney-sweep, and his name was Tom. That is a short name, and you have heard it before,* so you will not have much trouble in remembering it. He lived in a great town in the North country,* where there were plenty of chimneys to sweep, and plenty of money for Tom to earn and his master to spend. He could not read nor write, and did not care to do either; and he never washed himself, for there was no water up the court where he lived. He had never been taught to say his prayers. He never had heard of God, or of Christ, except in words which you never have heard, and which it would have been well if he had never heard. He cried half his time, and laughed the other half. He cried when he had to climb the dark flues, rubbing his poor knees and elbows raw; and when the soot got into his eyes, which it did every day in the week; and when his master beat him, which he did every day in the week; and when he had not enough to eat, which happened every day in the week likewise. And he laughed the other half of the day, when he was tossing half-pennies with the other boys, or playing leap-frog over the posts, or bowling stones at the horses' legs as they trotted by, which last was excellent fun, when there was a wall at hand behind which to hide. As for chimney-sweeping, and being hungry, and being beaten, he took all that for the way of the world, like the rain and snow and thunder, and stood manfully with his back to it till it was over, as his old donkey did to a hailstorm; and then shook his ears and was as jolly as ever; and thought of the fine times coming, when he would be a man, and a master sweep, and sit in the public-house with a quart of beer and a long pipe, and play cards for silver money, and wear velveteens* and ankle-jacks,* and keep a white bull-dog with one grey ear, and carry her puppies in his pocket, just like a man. And he would have apprentices, one, two, three, if he could. How he would bully them, and knock them about, just as his master did to him; and make them carry home the soot sacks, while he rode before them on his donkey, with a pipe in his mouth and a flower in his button-hole, like a king at the head of his army. Yes, there were good times coming; and, when his master let him have a pull at the leavings of his beer, Tom was the jolliest boy in the whole town.

One day a smart little groom rode into the court where Tom lived. Tom was just hiding behind a wall, to heave half a brick at his horse's legs, as is the custom of that country when they welcome strangers; but the groom saw him, and hallooed to him to know where Mr Grimes, the chimney-sweep, lived. Now, Mr Grimes was Tom's own master, and Tom was a good man of business, and always civil to customers, so he put the half-brick down quietly behind the wall, and proceeded to take orders.

Mr Grimes was to come up next morning to Sir John Harthover's, at the Place, for his old chimney-sweep was gone to prison, and the chimneys wanted sweeping. And so he rode away, not giving Tom time to ask what the sweep had gone to prison for, which was a matter of interest to Tom, as he had been in prison once or twice himself. Moreover, the groom looked so very neat and clean, with his drab* gaiters, drab breeches, drab jacket, snow-white tie with a smart pin in it, and clean round ruddy face, that Tom was offended and disgusted at his appearance, and considered him a stuck-up fellow, who gave himself airs because he wore smart clothes, and other people paid for them; and went behind the wall to fetch the half-brick after all: but did not, remembering that he had come in the way of business, and was, as it were, under a flag of truce.

His master was so delighted at his new customer that he knocked Tom down out of hand, and drank more beer that night than he usually did in two, in order to be sure of getting up in time next morning; for the more a man's head aches when he wakes, the more glad he is to turn out, and have a breath of fresh air. And, when he did get up at four the next morning, he knocked Tom down again, in order to teach him (as young gentlemen used to be taught at public schools) that he must be an extra good boy that day, as they were going to a very great house, and might make a very good thing of it, if they could but give satisfaction.

And Tom thought so likewise, and, indeed, would have done and behaved his best, even without being knocked down. For, of all places upon earth, Harthover Place (which he had never seen) was the most wonderful; and, of all men on earth, Sir John (whom he had seen, having been sent to gaol by him twice) was the most awful.

Harthover Place was really a grand place, even for the rich North country; with a house so large that in the frame-breaking riots,* which Tom could just remember, the Duke of Wellington, with ten thousand soldiers and cannon to match, were easily housed therein; at least, so Tom believed; with a park full of deer, which Tom believed to be monsters who were in the habit of eating children; with miles of game-preserves, in which Mr Grimes and the collier-lads poached at times, on which occasions Tom saw pheasants, and wondered what they tasted like; with a noble salmon-river, in which Mr Grimes and his friends would have liked to poach; but then they must have got into cold water, and that they did not like at all. In short, Harthover was a grand place, and Sir John a grand old man,* whom even Mr Grimes respected, for not only could he send Mr Grimes to prison when he deserved it, as he did once or twice a week; not only did he own all the land about for miles; not only was he a jolly, honest, sensible squire as ever kept a pack of hounds, who would do what he thought right by his neighbours, as well as get what he thought right for himself, but, what was more, he weighed full fifteen stone, was nobody knew how many inches round the chest, and could have thrashed Mr Grimes himself in fair fight, which very few folk round there could do, and which, my dear little boy, would not have been right for him to do, as a great many things are not which one both can do, and would like very much to do. So Mr Grimes touched his hat to him when he rode through the town, and called him a 'buirdly* awd chap', and his young ladies 'gradely* lasses', which are two high compliments in the North country; and thought that that made up for his poaching Sir John's pheasants; whereby you may perceive that Mr Grimes had not been to a properly-inspected Government National School.*

Now, I dare say, you never got up at three o'clock on a midsummer morning. Some people get up then because they want to catch salmon; and some, because they want to climb Alps; and a great many more, because they must, like Tom. But, I assure you, that three o'clock on a midsummer morning is the pleasantest time of all the twenty-four hours, and all the three hundred and sixty-five days; and why every one does not get up then, I never could tell, save that they are all determined to spoil their nerves and their complexions, by doing all night, what they might just as well do all day. But Tom, instead of going out to dinner at half-past eight at night, and to a ball at ten, and finishing off somewhere between twelve and four, went to bed at seven, when his master went to the public-house, and slept like a dead pig: for which reason he was as piert* as a game-cock (who always gets up early to wake the maids), and just ready to get up when the fine gentlemen and ladies were just ready to go to bed.

So he and his master set out; Grimes rode the donkey in front, and Tom and the brushes walked behind; out of the court, and up the street, past the closed window-shutters, and the winking weary policemen, and the roofs all shining grey in the grey dawn.

They passed through the pitmen's village, all shut up and silent now; and through the turnpike; and then they were out in the real country, and plodding along the black dusty road, between black slag walls, with no sound but the groaning and thumping of the pit-engine in the next field. But soon the road grew white, and the walls likewise; and at the wall's foot grew long grass and gay flowers, all drenched with dew; and instead of the groaning of the pit-engine, they heard

the skylark saying his matins high up in the air, and the pit-bird*
warbling in the sedges, as he had warbled all night long.

All else was silent. For old Mrs Earth was still fast asleep; and, like
many pretty people, she looked still prettier asleep than awake. The
great elm-trees in the gold-green meadows were fast asleep above,
and the cows fast asleep beneath them; nay, the few clouds which
were about were fast asleep likewise, and so tired that they had lain
down on the earth to rest, in long white flakes and bars, among the
stems of the elm-trees, and along the tops of the alders by the stream,
waiting for the sun to bid them rise and go about their day's business
in the clear blue overhead.

On they went; and Tom looked, and looked, for he never had been
so far into the country before; and longed to get over a gate, and pick
buttercups, and look for birds' nests in the hedge; but Mr Grimes
was a man of business, and would not have heard of that.

Soon they came up with* a poor Irishwoman, trudging along with
a bundle at her back. She had a grey shawl over her head, and a crimson madder* petticoat; so you may be sure she came from Galway.
She had neither shoes nor stockings, and limped along as if she were
tired and footsore: but she was a very tall handsome woman, with
bright grey eyes, and heavy black hair hanging about her cheeks. And
she took Mr Grimes's fancy so much, that when he came alongside he
called out to her:

'This is a hard road for a gradely foot like that. Will ye up, lass, and
ride behind me?'

But, perhaps, she did not admire Mr Grimes's look and voice; for
she answered quietly:

'No, thank you; I'd sooner walk with your little lad here.'

'You may please yourself,' growled Grimes, and went on smoking.

So she walked beside Tom, and talked to him, and asked him
where he lived, and what he knew, and all about himself, till Tom
thought he had never met such a pleasant spoken woman. And she
asked him, at last, whether he said his prayers; and seemed sad when
he told her that he knew no prayers to say.

Then he asked her where she lived; and she said far away by the
sea. And Tom asked her about the sea; and she told him how it rolled

and roared over the rocks in winter nights, and lay still in the bright summer days, for the children to bathe and play in it; and many a story more, till Tom longed to go and see the sea, and bathe in it likewise.

At last, at the bottom of a hill, they came to a spring: not such a spring as you see here,* which soaks up out of a white gravel in the bog, among red fly-catchers, and pink bottle-heath, and sweet white orchis; nor such a one as you may see, too, here, which bubbles up under the warm sand-bank in the hollow lane, by the great tuft of lady ferns, and makes the sand dance reels at the bottom, day and night, all the year round; not such a spring as either of those: but a real North country limestone fountain, like one of those in Sicily or Greece, where the old heathen fancied the nymphs sat cooling themselves the hot summer's day, while the shepherds peeped at them from behind the bushes. Out of a low cave of rock, at the foot of a limestone crag, the great fountain rose, quelling and bubbling, and gurgling, so clear that you could not tell where the water ended and the air began; and ran away under the road, a stream large enough to turn a mill; among blue geranium, and golden globe-flower, and wild raspberry, and the bird-cherry with its tassels of snow.

And there Grimes stopped, and looked; and Tom looked too. Tom was wondering whether anything lived in that dark cave, and came out at night to fly in the meadows. But Grimes was not wondering at all. Without a word, he got off his donkey, and clambered over the low road wall, and knelt down, and began dipping his ugly head into the spring—and very dirty he made it.

Tom was picking the flowers as fast as he could. The Irishwoman helped him, and showed him how to tie them up; and a very pretty nosegay they had made between them. But when he saw Grimes actually wash, he stopped, quite astonished; and when Grimes had finished, and began shaking his ears to dry them, he said:

'Why, master, I never saw you do that before.'

'Nor will again, most likely. 'Twasn't for cleanliness I did it, but for coolness. I'd be ashamed to want washing every week or so, like any smutty collier-lad.'

'I wish I might go and dip my head in,' said poor little Tom.

'It must be as good as putting it under the town-pump; and there is no beadle here to drive a chap away.'

'Thou come along,' said Grimes, 'what dost want with washing thyself? Thou did not drink half a gallon of beer last night, like me.'

'I don't care for you,' said naughty Tom, and ran down to the stream, and began washing his face.

Grimes was very sulky, because the woman preferred Tom's company to his; so he dashed at him with horrid words, and tore him up from his knees, and began beating him. But Tom was accustomed to that, and got his head safe between Mr Grimes's legs, and kicked his shins with all his might.

'Are you not ashamed of yourself, Thomas Grimes?' cried the Irishwoman over the wall.

Grimes looked up, startled at her knowing his name; but all he answered was, 'No: nor never was yet'; and went on beating Tom.

'True for you. If you ever had been ashamed of yourself, you would have gone over into Vendale* long ago.'

'What do you know about Vendale?' shouted Grimes; but he left off beating Tom.

'I know about Vendale, and about you, too. I know, for instance, what happened in Aldermire Copse, by night, two years ago come Martinmas.'*

'You do?' shouted Grimes; and leaving Tom, climbed up over the wall, and faced the woman. Tom thought he was going to strike her; but she looked him too full and fierce in the face for that.

'Yes; I was there,' said the Irishwoman, quietly.

'You are no Irishwoman, by your speech,' said Grimes, after many bad words.

'Never mind who I am. I saw what I saw; and if you strike that boy again, I can tell what I know.'

Grimes seemed quite cowed, and got on his donkey without another word.

'Stop!' said the Irishwoman. 'I have one more word for you both; for you will both see me again, before all is over. Those that wish to be clean, clean they will be; and those that wish to be foul, foul they will be. Remember.'

And she turned away, and through a gate into the meadow. Grimes stood still a moment, like a man who had been stunned. Then he rushed after her, shouting 'You come back.' But when he got into the meadow the woman was not there.

Had she hidden away? There was no place to hide in. But Grimes looked about, and Tom also, for he was as puzzled as Grimes himself, at her disappearing so suddenly; but look where they would, she was not there.

Grimes came back again, as silent as a post, for he was a little frightened; and getting on his donkey, filled a fresh pipe, and smoked away, leaving Tom in peace.

And now they had gone three miles and more, and came to Sir John's lodge-gates.

Very grand lodges they were, with very grand iron gates, and stone gate-posts, and on the top of each a most dreadful bogy, all teeth, horns, and tail, which was the crest which Sir John's ancestors wore in the Wars of the Roses; and very prudent men they were to wear it, for all their enemies must have run for their lives at the very first sight of them.

Grimes rang at the gate, and out came a keeper on the spot, and opened.

'I was told to expect thee,' he said. 'Now, thou'lt be so good as to keep to the main avenue, and not let me find a hare or a rabbit on thee when thou comest back. I shall look sharp for one, I tell thee.'

'Not if it's in the bottom of the soot-bag,' quoth Grimes, and at that he laughed; and the keeper laughed and said—

'If that's thy sort, I may as well walk up with thee to the hall.'

'I think thou best had. It's thy business to see after thy game, man, and not mine.'

So the keeper went with them; and to Tom's surprise, he and Grimes chatted together all the way quite pleasantly. He did not know that a keeper is only a poacher turned outside in, and a poacher a keeper turned inside out.

They walked up a great lime-avenue, a full mile long, and between their stems Tom peeped trembling at the horns of the sleeping deer, which stood up among the ferns. Tom had never seen such enormous trees, and as he looked up he fancied that the blue sky rested on their heads. But he was puzzled very much by a strange murmuring noise, which followed them all the way. So much puzzled, that at last he took courage to ask the keeper what it was.

He spoke very civilly, and called him Sir, for he was horribly afraid of him, which pleased the keeper, and he told him that they were the bees about the lime-flowers.

'What are bees?' asked Tom.

'What make honey.'

'What is honey?' asked Tom.

'Thou hold thy noise,' said Grimes.

'Let the boy be,' said the keeper. 'He's a civil young chap now, and that's more than he'll be long, if he bides with thee.'

Grimes laughed, for he took that for a compliment.

'I wish I were a keeper,' said Tom, 'to live in such a beautiful place, and wear green velveteens, and have a real dog-whistle at my button, like you.'

The keeper laughed; he was a kind-hearted fellow enough.

'Let well alone, lad, and ill too, at times. Thy life's safer than mine at all events, eh, Mr Grimes?'

And Grimes laughed again, and then the two men began talking quite low. Tom could hear, though, that it was about some poaching fight—and at last Grimes said surlily—

'Hast thou anything against me?'

'Not now.'

'Then don't ask me any questions till thou hast, for I am a man of honour.'

And at that they both laughed again, and thought it a very good joke.

And by this time they were come up to the great iron gates in front of the house; and Tom stared through them at the rhododendrons and azaleas, which were all in flower; and then at the house itself, and wondered how many chimneys there were in it, and how long ago it was built, and what was the man's name that built it, and whether he got much money for his job?

These last were very difficult questions to answer. For Harthover had been built at ninety different times, and in nineteen different styles, and looked as if somebody had built a whole street of houses of every imaginable shape, and then stirred them together with a spoon.

For the attics were Anglo-Saxon.

The third-floor Norman.

The second Cinque-cento.

The first-floor Elizabethan.

The right wing Pure Doric.

The centre Early English, with a huge portico, copied from the Parthenon.

The left wing Pure Bœotian, which the country folk admired most of all, because it was just like the new barracks in the town, only three times as big.

The grand staircase was copied from the Catacombs at Rome.

The back staircase from the Tajmahal at Agra. This was built by Sir John's great-great-great-uncle, who won, in Lord Clive's Indian wars,* plenty of money, plenty of wounds, and no more taste than his betters.

The cellars were copied from the caves of Elephanta.*

The offices from the Pavilion at Brighton.

And the rest from nothing in heaven, or earth, or under the earth.*

So that Harthover House was a great puzzle to antiquarians, and a thorough Naboth's vineyard to critics, and architects,* and all persons who like meddling with other men's business, and spending other men's money. So they all were setting upon poor Sir John, year after year, and trying to talk him into spending a hundred thousand pounds or so, in building to please them and not himself. But he always put them off, like a canny North-countryman as he was. One wanted him to build a Gothic house, but he said he was no Goth; and another to build an Elizabethan, but he said he lived under good Queen Victoria, and not good Queen Bess; and another was bold enough to tell him that his house was ugly, but he said he lived inside it, and not outside; and another, that there was no unity in it; but he said that that was just why he liked the old place. For he liked to see how each Sir John, and Sir Hugh, and Sir Ralph, and Sir Randal, had left his mark upon the place, each after his own taste; and he had no more notion of disturbing his ancestors' work than of disturbing their graves. For now the house looked like a real live house, that had a history, and had grown and grown as the world grew; and that it was only an upstart fellow who did not know who his own grandfather was, who would change it for some spick and span new Gothic or Elizabethan thing, which looked as if it had been all spawned in a night, as mushrooms are. From which you may collect (if you have wit enough), that Sir John was a very sound-headed, sound-hearted squire, and just the man to keep the country side in order, and show good sport with his hounds.

But Tom and his master did not go in through the great iron gates, as if they had been Dukes or Bishops, but round the back way, and a very long way round it was; and into a little back-door, where the ash-boy* let them in, yawning horribly; and then in a passage the housekeeper met them, in such a flowered chintz dressing-gown, that Tom mistook her for My Lady herself, and she gave Grimes solemn orders about 'You will take care of this, and take care of that,' as if he was going up the chimneys, and not Tom. And Grimes listened, and said every now and then, under his voice, 'You'll mind that, you little beggar?' and Tom did mind, all at least that he could. And then the housekeeper turned them into a grand room, all covered up in sheets of brown paper, and bade them begin, in a lofty and tremendous voice; and so after a whimper or two, and a kick from his master, into the grate Tom went, and up the chimney, while a housemaid stayed in the room to watch the furniture; to whom Mr Grimes paid many playful and chivalrous compliments, but met with very slight encouragement in return.

How many chimneys he swept I cannot say: but he swept so many that he got quite tired, and puzzled too, for they were not like the town flues to which he was accustomed, but such as you would find— if you would only get up them and look, which perhaps you would not like to do—in old country-houses, large and crooked chimneys, which had been altered again and again, till they ran one into another, anastomosing* (as Professor Owen would say) considerably. So Tom fairly lost his way in them; not that he cared much for that, though he was in pitchy darkness, for he was as much at home in a chimney as a mole is underground; but at last, coming down as he thought the right chimney, he came down the wrong one, and found himself standing on the hearthrug in a room the like of which he had never seen before.

Tom had never seen the like. He had never been in gentlefolks' rooms but when the carpets were all up, and the curtains down, and the furniture huddled together under a cloth, and the pictures covered with aprons and dusters; and he had often enough wondered what the rooms were like when they were all ready for the quality to sit in. And now he saw, and he thought the sight very pretty.

The room was all dressed in white; white window curtains, white bed curtains, white furniture, and white walls, with just a few lines of pink here and there. The carpet was all over gay little flowers; and the walls were hung with pictures in gilt frames, which amused Tom very much. There were pictures of ladies and gentlemen, and pictures of horses and dogs. The horses he liked; but the dogs he did not care for much, for there were no bull-dogs among them, not even a terrier. But the two pictures which took his fancy most were, one a man in long garments, with little children and their mothers round him, who was laying his hand upon the children's heads. That was a very pretty picture, Tom thought, to hang in a lady's room. For he could see that it was a lady's room by the dresses which lay about.

The other picture was that of a man nailed to a cross, which surprised Tom much. He fancied that he had seen something like it in a shop window. But why was it there? 'Poor man,' thought Tom, 'and he looks so kind and quiet. But why should the lady have such a sad picture as that in her room? Perhaps it was some kinsman of hers, who had been murdered by the savages in foreign parts, and she kept it there for a remembrance.' And Tom felt sad, and awed, and turned to look at something else.

The next thing he saw, and that too puzzled him, was a washing-stand, with ewers and basons,* and soap and brushes, and towels; and a large bath, full of clean water—what a heap of things all for washing! 'She must be a very dirty lady,' thought Tom, 'by my master's rule, to want as much scrubbing as all that. But she must be very cunning to put the dirt out of the way so well afterwards, for I don't see a speck about the room, not even on the very towels.'

And then, looking toward the bed, he saw that dirty lady, and held his breath with astonishment.

Under the snow-white coverlet, upon the snow-white pillow, lay the most beautiful little girl that Tom had ever seen. Her cheeks were almost as white as the pillow, and her hair was like threads of gold spread all about over the bed. She might have been as old as Tom, or maybe a year or two older; but Tom did not think of that. He thought only of her delicate skin and golden hair, and wondered whether she were a real live person, or one of the wax dolls he had seen in the shops. But when he saw her breathe, he made up his mind that she was alive, and stood staring at her, as if she had been an angel out of heaven.

No. She cannot be dirty. She never could have been dirty, thought Tom to himself. And then he thought, 'And are all people like that when they are washed?' And he looked at his own wrist, and tried to rub the soot off, and wondered whether it ever would come off. 'Certainly I should look much prettier then, if I grew at all like her.'

And looking round, he suddenly saw, standing close to him, a little ugly, black, ragged figure, with bleared eyes and grinning white teeth. He turned on it angrily. What did such a little black ape want in that sweet young lady's room? And behold, it was himself, reflected in a great mirror, the like of which Tom had never seen before.

And Tom, for the first time in his life, found out that he was dirty; and burst into tears with shame and anger; and turned to sneak up the chimney again and hide, and upset the fender, and threw the fire-irons down, with a noise as of ten thousand tin kettles tied to ten thousand mad dogs' tails.

Up jumped the little white lady in her bed, and, seeing Tom, screamed as shrill as any peacock. In rushed a stout old nurse from the next room, and seeing Tom likewise, made up her mind that he had come to rob, plunder, destroy, and burn; and dashed at him, as he lay over the fender, so fast that she caught him by the jacket.

But she did not hold him. Tom had been in a policeman's hands many a time, and out of them too, what is more; and he would have been ashamed to face his friends for ever if he had been stupid enough to be caught by an old woman: so he doubled under the good lady's arm, across the room, and out of the window in a moment.

He did not need to drop out, though he would have done so bravely enough. Nor even to let himself down a spout, which would have been an old game to him; for once he got up by a spout to the church roof, he said to take jackdaws' eggs, but the policemen said to steal lead; and when he was seen on high, sat there till the sun got too hot, and came down by another spout, leaving the policemen to go back to the station-house and eat their dinners.

But all under the window spread a tree, with great leaves, and sweet white flowers, almost as big as his head. It was a magnolia, I suppose; but Tom knew nothing about that, and cared less; for down the tree he went, like a cat, and across the garden lawn, and over the iron-railings, and up the park towards the wood, leaving the old nurse to scream murder and fire at the window.

The under gardener, mowing, saw Tom, and threw down his scythe; caught his leg in it, and cut his shin open, whereby he kept his bed for a week: but in his hurry he never knew it, and gave chase to poor Tom. The dairymaid heard the noise, got the churn between her knees, and tumbled over it, spilling all the cream; and yet she jumped up, and gave chase to Tom. A groom cleaning Sir John's hack at the stables let him go loose, whereby he kicked himself lame in five minutes; but he ran out, and gave chase to Tom. Grimes upset the soot-sack in the new-gravelled yard, and spoilt it all utterly; but, he ran out and gave chase to Tom. The old steward opened the park gate in such a hurry; that he hung up his pony's chin upon the spikes, and for aught I know it hangs there still; but he jumped off, and gave chase to Tom. The ploughman left his horses at the headland,* and one jumped over the fence, and pulled the other into the ditch, plough and all; but he ran on, and gave chase to Tom. The keeper, who was taking a stoat out of a trap, let the stoat go, and caught his own finger; but he jumped up and ran after Tom, and considering what he said, and how he looked, I should have been sorry for Tom if he had caught him. Sir John looked out of his study window (for he was an early old gentleman), and up at the nurse, and a marten dropt mud in his eye, so that he had at last to send for the doctor; and yet he ran out and gave chase to Tom. The Irishwoman, too, was walking up to the house to beg—she must have got round by some byway: but she threw away her bundle, and gave chase to Tom likewise. Only my lady did not give chase; for when she had put her head out of the window, her night-wig fell into the garden, and she had to ring up her lady's-maid, and send her down for it privately; which quite put her out of the running, so that she came in nowhere, and is consequently not placed.

In a word, never was there heard at Hall Place, not even when the fox was killed in the conservatory, among acres of broken glass, and tons of smashed flower-pots, such a noise, row, hubbub, babel, shindy, hullabaloo, stramash, charivari,* and total contempt of dignity, repose, and order, as that day, when Grimes, gardener, the groom, the dairymaid, Sir John, the steward, the ploughman, the keeper, and the Irishwoman, all ran up the park, shouting 'Stop thief', in the belief that Tom had at least a thousand pounds' worth of jewels in his empty pockets; and the very magpies and jays followed Tom up, screaking* and screaming, as if he were a hunted fox, beginning to droop his brush.

And all the while poor Tom paddled up the park with his little bare feet, like a small black gorilla* fleeing to the forest. Alas for him! there was no big father gorilla therein to take his part; to scratch out the gardener's inside with one paw, toss the dairymaid into a tree with another, and wrench off Sir John's head with a third, while he cracked the keeper's skull with his teeth, as easily as if it had been a cocoa-nut or a paving-stone.

However, Tom did not remember ever having had a father; so he did not look for one, and expected to have to take care of himself; while as for running, he could keep up for a couple of miles with any stagecoach, if there was the chance of a copper or a cigar-end, and turn coach wheels on his hands and feet ten times following, which is more than you can do. Wherefore his pursuers found it very difficult to catch him; and we will hope that they did not catch him at all.

Tom, of course, made for the woods. He had never been in a wood in his life: but he was sharp enough to know that he might hide in a bush, or swarm up a tree, and, altogether, had more chance there than in the open. If he had not known that, he would have been foolisher than a mouse or a minnow.

But when he got into the wood, he found it a very different sort of place from what he had fancied. He pushed into a thick cover of rhododendrons, and found himself at once caught in a trap. The boughs laid hold of his legs and arms, poked him in his face and his stomach, made him shut his eyes tight (though that was no great loss, for he could not see at best a yard before his nose); and when he got through the rhododendrons, the hassock-grass* and sedges tumbled him over, and cut his poor little fingers afterwards most spitefully; the birches birched him as soundly as if he had been a nobleman at Eton, and over the face too (which is not fair swishing, as all brave boys will agree); and the lawyers* tripped him up, and tore his shins as if they had sharks' teeth—which lawyers are likely enough to have.

'I must get out of this,' thought Tom, 'or I shall stay here till somebody comes to help me—which is just what I don't want.'

But how to get out was the difficult matter. And indeed I don't think he would ever have got out at all, but have staid there till the cock-robins covered him with leaves,* if he had not suddenly run his head against a wall.

Now running your head against a wall is not pleasant, especially if it is a loose wall, with the stones all set on edge, and a sharp-cornered one hits you between the eyes, and makes you see all manner of beautiful stars. The stars are very beautiful, certainly: but unfortunately they go in the twenty-thousandth part of a split second, and the pain which comes after them does not. And so Tom hurt his head; but he was a brave boy, and did not mind that a penny. He guessed that over the wall the cover would end; and up it he went, and over like a squirrel.

And there he was, out on the great grouse-moors, which the country folk called Harthover Fell—heather and bog and rock, stretching away and up, up to the very sky.

Now, Tom was a cunning little fellow—as cunning as an old Exmoor stag. Why not? Though he was but ten years old, he had lived longer than most stags, and had more wits to start with into the bargain.

He knew as well as a stag, that if he backed* he might throw the hounds out. So the first thing he did when he was over the wall, was to make the neatest double sharp to his right, and run along under the wall for nearly half a mile.

Whereby Sir John, and the keeper, and the steward, and the gardener, and the ploughman, and the dairymaid, and all the hue-and-cry together, went on ahead half a mile in the very opposite direction, and inside the wall, leaving him a mile off on the outside, while Tom heard their shouts die away in the wood, and chuckled to himself merrily.

At last he came to a dip in the land, and went to the bottom of it, and then he turned bravely away from the wall, and up the moor; for he knew that he had put a hill between him and his enemies, and could go on without their seeing him.

But the Irishwoman, alone of them all, had seen which way Tom went. She had kept ahead of every one the whole time: and yet she neither walked or ran. She went along quite smoothly and gracefully, while her feet twinkled past each other so fast, that you could not see which was foremost; till every one asked the other who the strange woman was? and all agreed, for want of anything better to say, that she must be in league with Tom.

But when she came to the plantation they lost sight of her; and they could do no less. For she went quietly over the wall after Tom, and followed him wherever he went. Sir John and the rest saw no more of her; and out of sight was out of mind.

And now Tom was right away into the heather, over just such a moor* as those in which you have been bred, except that there were rocks and stones lying about everywhere; and that instead of the moor growing flat as he went upwards, it grew more and more broken and hilly: but not so rough but that little Tom could jog along well enough, and find time, too, to stare about at the strange place, which was like a new world to him.

He saw great spiders there, with crowns and crosses marked on their backs, who sat in the middle of their webs, and when they saw

Tom coming, shook them so fast that they became invisible. Then he saw lizards, brown, and grey, and green, and thought they were snakes, and would sting him: but they were as much frightened as he, and shot away into the heath. And then, under a rock, he saw a pretty sight—a great brown sharpnosed creature, with a white tag to her brush, and round her, four or five smutty little cubs, the funniest fellows Tom ever saw. She lay on her back, rolling about, and stretching out her legs, and head, and tail in the bright sunshine; and the cubs jumped over her, and ran round her, and nibbled her paws, and lugged her about by the tail; and she seemed to enjoy it mightily. But one selfish little fellow stole away from the rest to a dead crow close by, and dragged it off to hide it, though it was nearly as big as he was. Whereat all his little brothers set off after him in full cry, and saw Tom; and then all ran back, and up jumped Mrs Vixen, and caught one up in her mouth, and the rest toddled after her, and into a dark crack in the rocks; and there was an end of the show.

And next he had a fright; for as he scrambled up a sandy brow—whirr-poof-poof-cock-cock-kick—something went off in his face, with a most horrid noise. He thought the ground had blown up, and the end of the world come.

And when he opened his eyes (for he shut them very tight), it was only an old cock-grouse, who had been washing himself in sand, like an Arab, for want of water; and who, when Tom had all but trodden on him, jumped up, with a noise like the express train, leaving his wife and children to shift for themselves, like an old coward, and went off, screaming 'Cur-ru-u-uck, cur-ru-u-uck—murder, thieves, fire—cur-u-uck-cock-kick—the end of the world is come—kick-kick-cock-kick.' He was always fancying that the end of the world was come, when anything happened which was farther off than the end of his own nose. But the end of the world was not come, any more than the twelfth of August* was; though the old grouse-cock was quite certain of it.

So the old grouse came back to his wife and family an hour afterwards, and said solemnly, 'Cock-cock-kick; my dears, the end of the world is not quite come; but I assure you it is coming the day after to-morrow—cock.' But his wife had heard that so often, that she knew all about it, and a little more. And, beside, she was the mother of a family, and had seven little poults* to wash and feed every day; and that made her very practical, and a little sharp-tempered; so all she answered was: 'Kick-kick-kick—go and catch spiders, go and catch spiders—kick.'

So Tom went on, and on, he hardly knew why: but he liked the great, wide, strange place, and the cool, fresh, bracing air. But he went more and more slowly as he got higher up the hill; for now the ground grew very bad indeed. Instead of soft turf and springy heather, he met great patches of flat limestone rock, just like ill-made pavements, with deep cracks between the stones and ledges, filled with ferns; so he had to hop from stone to stone, and now and then he slipped in between, and hurt his little bare toes, though they were tolerably tough ones: but still he would go on and up, he could not tell why.

What would Tom have said, if he had seen, walking over the moor behind him, the very same Irishwoman who had taken his part upon the road? But whether it was that he looked too little behind him, or whether it was that she kept out of sight behind the rocks and knolls, he never saw her, though she saw him.

And now he began to get a little hungry, and very thirsty; for he had run a long way, and the sun had risen high in heaven, and the rock was as hot as an oven, and the air danced reels over it, as it does over a limekiln, till everything round seemed quivering and melting in the glare.

But he could see nothing to eat anywhere, and still less to drink.

The heath was full of bilberries and whimberries:* but they were only in flower yet, for it was June. And as for water, who can find that on the top of a limestone rock? Now and then he passed by a deep dark swallow-hole,* going down into the earth, as if it was the chimney of some dwarf's house underground; and more than once, as he passed, he could hear water falling, trickling, tinkling, many many feet below. How he longed to get down to it, and cool his poor baked lips! But, brave little chimney-sweep as he was, he dared not climb down such chimneys as those.

So he went on, and on, till his head spun round with the heat, and he thought he heard church-bells ringing, a long way off.

'Ah!' he thought, 'where there is a church, there will be houses and people; and, perhaps, some one will give me a bit and a sup.'* So he set off again, to look for the church; for he was sure that he heard the bells quite plain.

And in a minute more, when he looked round, he stopped again, and said, 'Why, what a big place the world is!'

And so it was; for, from the top of the mountain, he could see—what could he not see?

Behind him, far below,* was Harthover, and the dark woods, and the shining salmon river; and on his left, far below, was the town, and the smoking chimneys of the collieries; and far, far away, the river widened to the shining sea; and little white specks, which were ships, lay on its bosom. Before him lay, spread out like a map, great plains, and farms, and villages, amid dark knots of trees. They all seemed at his very feet; but he had sense to see that they were long miles away.

And to his right rose moor after moor, hill after hill, till they faded away, blue into blue sky. But between him and those moors, and really at his very feet, lay something, to which, as soon as Tom saw it, he determined to go, for that was the place for him.

A deep, deep green and rocky valley, very narrow, and filled with wood: but through the wood, hundreds of feet below him, he could see a clear stream glance. Oh, if he could but get down to that stream! Then, by the stream, he saw the roof of a little cottage, and a little garden, set out in squares and beds. And there was a tiny little red thing moving in the garden, no bigger than a fly. As Tom looked down, he saw that it was a woman in a red petticoat. Ah! perhaps she would give him something to eat. And there were the church-bells ringing again. Surely there must be a village down there. Well, nobody would know him, or what had happened at the Place. The news could not have got there yet, even if Sir John had set all the policemen in the county after him; and he could get down there in five minutes.

Tom was quite right about the hue-and-cry not having got thither; for he had come, without knowing it, the best part of ten miles from Harthover: but he was wrong about getting down in five minutes, for the cottage was more than a mile off, and a good thousand feet below.

However, down he went, like a brave little man as he was, though he was very footsore, and tired, and hungry, and thirsty; while the church-bells rang so loud, he began to think that they must be inside his own head, and the river chimed and tinkled far below; and this was the song which it sang: —

> Clear and cool, clear and cool,
> By laughing shallow, and dreaming pool;
> Cool and clear, cool and clear,
> By shining shingle, and foaming wear;
> Under the crag where the ouzel sings,
> And the ivied wall where the church-bell rings,
> Undefiled, for the undefiled;
> Play by me, bathe in me, mother and child.
>
> Dank and foul, dank and foul,
> By the smoky town in its murky cowl;
> Foul and dank, foul and dank,
> By wharf and sewer and slimy bank;
> Darker and darker the further I go,
> Baser and baser the richer I grow;
> Who dare sport with the sin-defiled?
> Shrink from me, turn from me, mother and child.
>
> Strong and free, strong and free,
> The floodgates are open, away to the sea.
> Free and strong, free and strong,
> Cleansing my streams as I hurry along,
> To the golden sands, and the leaping bar,
> And the taintless tide that awaits me afar,
> As I lose myself in the infinite main,
> Like a soul that has sinned and is pardoned again.
> Undefiled, for the undefiled,
> Play by me, bathe in me, mother and child.

So Tom went down; and all the while he never saw the Irishwoman going down behind him.

# CHAPTER II

AND is there care in heaven? and is there love
In heavenly spirits to these creatures base
That may compassion of their evils move?
There is:—else much more wretched were the case
Of men than beasts: But oh! the exceeding grace
Of Highest God that loves His creatures so,
And all His works with mercy doth embrace,
That blessed Angels He sends to and fro,
To serve to wicked man, to serve His wicked foe!*

SPENSER.

 MILE off, and a thousand feet down. So Tom found it; though it seemed as if he could have chucked a pebble on to the back of the woman in the red petticoat who was weeding in the garden, or even across the dale to the rocks beyond.

For the bottom of the valley was just one field broad, and on the other side ran the stream; and above it, grey crag, grey down, grey stair, grey moor, walled up to heaven.

A quiet, silent, rich, happy place; a narrow crack cut deep into the earth; so deep, and so out of the way, that the bad bogies can hardly find it out. The name of the place is Vendale; and if you want to see it for yourself, you must go up into the High Craven,* and search from Bolland Forest north by Ingleborough, to the Nine Standards and Cross Fell; and if you have not found it, you must turn south, and search the Lake Mountains, down to Scaw Fell and the sea; and then if you have not found it, you must go northward again by merry Carlisle, and search the Cheviots all across, from Annan Water to Berwick Law; and then, whether you have found Vendale or not, you will have found such a country, and such a people, as ought to make you proud of being a British boy.

So Tom went to go down; and first he went down three hundred feet of steep heather, mixed up with loose brown gritstone, as rough as a file; which was not pleasant to his poor little heels, as he came bump, stump, jump, down the steep. And still he thought he could throw a stone into the garden.

Then he went down three hundred feet of limestone terraces, one below the other, as straight as if Mr George White* had ruled them with his ruler and then cut them out with his chisel. There was no heath there, but—

First, a little grass slope, covered with the prettiest flowers, rock-rose and saxifrage, and thyme and basil, and all sorts of sweet herbs.

Then bump down a two-foot step of limestone.

Then another bit of grass and flowers.

Then bump down a one-foot step.

Then another bit of grass and flowers for fifty yards, as steep as the house-roof, where he had to slide down on his dear little tail.

Then another step of stone, ten feet high; and there he had to stop himself, and crawl along the edge to find a crack; for if he had rolled over, he would have rolled right into the old woman's garden, and frightened her out of her wits.

Then, when he had found a dark narrow crack, full of green-stalked fern, such as hangs in the basket in the drawing-room, and had crawled down through it, with knees and elbows, as he would down a chimney, there was another grass slope, and another step, and so on, till—oh, dear me! I wish it was all over; and so did he. And yet he thought he could throw a stone into the old woman's garden.

At last he came to a bank of beautiful shrubs; whitebeam with its great silver-backed leaves, and mountain-ash, and oak; and below them cliff and crag, cliff and crag, with great beds of crown-ferns and wood-sedge; while through the shrubs he could see the stream sparkling, and hear it murmur on the white pebbles. He did not know that it was three hundred feet below.

You would have been giddy, perhaps, at looking down: but Tom was not. He was a brave little chimney-sweep; and when he found himself on the top of a high cliff, instead of sitting down and crying for his baba* (though he never had had any baba to cry for), he said—'Ah, this will just suit me!' though he was very tired; and down he went, by stock and stone, sedge and ledge, bush and rush, as if he had been born a jolly little black ape, with four hands instead of two.

And all the while, he never saw the Irishwoman coming down behind him.

But he was getting terribly tired now. The burning sun on the fells had sucked him up; but the damp heat of the woody crag sucked him up still more; and the perspiration ran out of the ends of his fingers and toes, and washed him cleaner than he had been for a whole year. But, of course, he dirtied everything terribly as he went. There has been a great black smudge* all down the crag ever since. And there have been more black beetles in Vendale since than ever were known before; all, of course, owing to Tom's having blacked the original papa of them all, just as he was setting off to be married, with a sky-blue coat and scarlet leggings, as smart as a gardener's dog with a polyanthus in his mouth.

At last he got to the bottom. But, behold, it was not the bottom—as people usually find when they are coming down a mountain. For at the foot of the crag were heaps and heaps of fallen limestone of every size from that of your head to that of a stage-waggon, with holes between them full of sweet heath-fern; and before Tom got through them, he was out in the bright sunshine again; and then he felt, once for all and suddenly, as people generally do, that he was b-e-a-t, beat.

You must expect to be beat a few times in your life, little man, if you live such a life as a man ought to live, let you be as strong and healthy as you may: and when you are, you will find it a very ugly feeling. I hope that that day you may have a stout staunch friend by you who is not beat; for if you have not, you had best lie where you are, and wait for better times, as poor Tom did.

He could not get on. The sun was burning, and yet he felt chill all over. He was quite empty, and yet he felt quite sick. There was but two hundred yards of smooth pasture between him and the cottage, and yet he could not walk down it. He could hear the stream murmuring only one field beyond it, and yet it seemed to him as if it was a hundred miles off.

He lay down on the grass till the beetles ran over him, and the flies settled on his nose. I don't know when he would have got up again, if the gnats and the midges had not taken compassion on him. But the gnats blew their trumpets so loud in his ear, and the midges nibbled so at his hands and face wherever they could find a place free from soot, that at last he woke up, and stumbled away, down over a low wall, and into a narrow road, and up to the cottage door.

And a neat pretty cottage it was, with clipt yew hedges all round the garden, and yews inside too, cut into peacocks and trumpets and teapots and all kinds of queer shapes. And out of the open door came a noise like that of the frogs on the Great-A,* when they know that it is going to be scorching hot to-morrow—and how they know that I don't know, and you don't know, and nobody knows.

He came slowly up to the open door, which was all hung round with clematis and roses; and then peeped in, half afraid.

And there sat by the empty fire-place, which was filled with a pot of sweet herbs, the nicest old woman that ever was seen, in her red petticoat, and short dimity* bedgown, and clean white cap, with a black silk handkerchief over it, tied under her chin. At her feet sat the grandfather of all the cats; and opposite her sat, on two benches, twelve or fourteen neat rosy chubby little children, learning their Chris-cross-row;* and gabble enough they made about it.

Such a pleasant cottage it was, with a shiny clean stone floor, and curious old prints on the walls, and an old black oak sideboard full of bright pewter and brass dishes, and a cuckoo clock in the corner, which began shouting as soon as Tom appeared: not that it was frightened at Tom, but that it was just eleven o'clock.

All the children started at Tom's dirty black figure; the girls began to cry, and the boys began to laugh, and all pointed at him rudely enough: but Tom was too tired to care for that.

'What art thou, and what dost want?' cried the old dame.* 'A chimney-sweep! Away with thee. I'll have no sweeps here.'

'Water,' said poor little Tom, quite faint.

'Water? There's plenty i' the beck,' she said, quite sharply.

'But I can't get there; I'm most clemmed with hunger and drought.'* And Tom sank down upon the door-step, and laid his head against the post.

And the old dame looked at him through her spectacles one minute, and two, and three; and then she said, 'He's sick; and a bairn's a bairn, sweep or none.'

'Water,' said Tom.

'God forgive me!' and she put by her spectacles, and rose, and came to Tom. 'Water's bad for thee; I'll give thee milk.' And she toddled off into the next room, and brought a cup of milk and a bit of bread.

Tom drank the milk off at one draught, and then looked up, revived.

'Where didst come from?' said the dame.

'Over Fell, there,' said Tom, and pointed up into the sky.

'Over Harthover? and down Lewthwaite Crag? Art sure thou art not lying?'

'Why should I?' said Tom, and leant his head against the post.

'And how got ye up there?'

'I came over from the Place,' and Tom was so tired and desperate he had no heart or time to think of a story, so he told all the truth in a few words.

'Bless thy little heart! And thou hast not been stealing, then?'

'No.'

'Bless thy little heart! and I'll warrant not. Why, God's guided the bairn, because he was innocent! Away from the Place, and over Harthover Fell, and down Lewthwaite Crag! Who ever heard the like, if God hadn't led him? Why dost not eat thy bread?'

'I can't.'

'It's good enough, for I made it myself.'

'I can't,' said Tom, and he laid his head on his knees, and then asked—

'Is it Sunday?'

'No, then; why should it be?'

'Because I hear the church bells ringing so.'

'Bless thy pretty heart! The bairn's sick. Come wi' me, and I'll hap thee up somewhere. If thou wert a bit cleaner I'd put thee in my own bed, for the Lord's sake. But come along here.'

But when Tom tried to get up, he was so tired and giddy that she had to help him and lead him.

She put him in an outhouse upon soft sweet hay and an old rug, and bade him sleep off his walk, and she would come to him when school was over, in an hour's time.

And so she went in again, expecting Tom to fall fast asleep at once.

But Tom did not fall asleep.

Instead of it he turned and tossed and kicked about in the strangest way, and felt so hot all over that he longed to get into the river and cool himself; and then he fell half asleep, and dreamt that he heard the little white lady crying to him, 'Oh, you're so dirty; go and be washed'; and then that he heard the Irishwoman saying, 'Those that wish to be clean, clean they will be.' And then he heard the church bells ring so loud, close to him, too, that he was sure it must be Sunday, in spite of what the old dame had said; and he would go to church, and see what a church was like inside, for he had never been in one, poor little fellow, in all his life. But the people would never let him come in, all over soot and dirt like that. He must go to the river and wash first. And he said out loud again and again, though being half asleep he did not know it, 'I must be clean, I must be clean.'

And all of a sudden he found himself, not in the outhouse on the hay, but in the middle of a meadow, over the road, with the stream just before him, saying continually, 'I must be clean, I must be clean.' He had got there on his own legs, between sleep and awake, as children will often get out of bed, and go about the room, when they are not quite well. But he was not a bit surprised, and went on to the bank of the brook, and lay down on the grass, and looked into the clear clear limestone water, with every pebble at the bottom bright and clean, while the little silver trout dashed about in fright at the sight of his black face; and he dipped his hand in and found it so cool, cool, cool; and he said, 'I will be a fish; I will swim in the water; I must be clean, I must be clean.'

So he pulled off all his clothes in such haste that he tore some of them, which was easy enough with such ragged old things. And he put his poor hot sore feet into the water; and then his legs; and the further he went in, the more the church bells rang in his head.

'Ah,' said Tom, 'I must be quick and wash myself; the bells are ringing quite loud now: and they will stop soon, and then the door will be shut, and I shall never be able to get in at all.'

Tom was mistaken: for in England the church doors are left open all service time, for everybody who likes to come in, Churchman or Dissenter; ay, even if he were a Turk or a Heathen; and if any man dared to turn him out, as long as he behaved quietly, the good old English law would punish that man, as he deserved, for ordering any peaceable person out of God's house, which belongs to all alike. But Tom did not know that, any more than he knew a great deal more which people ought to know.

And all the while he never saw the Irishwoman: not behind him this time, but before.

For just before he came to the river side, she had stept down into the cool clear water; and her shawl and her petticoat floated off her, and the green water-weeds floated round her sides, and the white water-lilies floated round her head, and the fairies of the stream came up from the bottom, and bore her away and down upon their arms; for she was the Queen of them all; and perhaps of more besides.

'Where have you been?' they asked her.

'I have been smoothing sick folk's pillows, and whispering sweet dreams into their ears; opening cottage casements, to let out the stifling air; coaxing little children away from gutters, and foul pools where fever breeds; turning women from the gin-shop door, and staying men's hands as they were going to strike their wives; doing all I can to help those who will not help themselves: and little enough that is, and weary work for me. But I have brought you a new little brother, and watched him safe all the way here.'

Then all the fairies laughed for joy at the thought that they had a little brother coming.

'But mind, maidens, he must not see you, or know that you are here. He is but a savage now, and like the beasts which perish; and from the beasts which perish he must learn. So you must not play with him, or speak to him, or let him see you: but only keep him from being harmed.'

Then the fairies were sad, because they could not play with their new brother, but they always did what they were told.

And their Queen floated away down the river; and whither she went, thither she came. But all this Tom, of course, never saw or heard: and perhaps if he had, it would have made little difference in the story; for he was so hot and thirsty, and longed so to be clean for once, that he tumbled himself as quick as he could into the clear cool stream.

And he had not been in it two minutes before he fell fast asleep, into the quietest, sunniest, cosiest sleep that ever he had in his life; and he dreamt about the green meadows by which he had walked that morning, and the tall elm-trees, and the sleeping cows; and after that he dreamt of nothing at all.

The reason of his falling into such a delightful sleep is very simple; and yet hardly any one has found it out. It was merely that the fairies took him.

Some people think that there are no fairies. Cousin Cramchild tells little folks so in his Conversations.* Well, perhaps there are none—in Boston, US, where he was raised. There are only a clumsy lot of spirits there, who can't make people hear without thumping on the table:* but they get their living thereby, and I suppose that is all they want. And Aunt Agitate, in her Arguments on political economy,* says there are none. Well, perhaps there are none—in her political economy. But it is a wide world, my little man—and thank heaven for it, for else, between crinolines and theories, some of us would get squashed—and plenty of room in it for fairies, without people seeing them; unless, of course, they look in the right place. The most wonderful and the strongest things in the world, you know, are just the things which no one can see. There is life in you; and it is the life in you which makes you grow, and move, and think: and yet you can't see it. And there is steam in a steam-engine; and that is what makes it move: and yet you can't see it; and so there may be fairies in the world, and they may be just what makes the world go round to the old tune of

> C'est l'amour, l'amour, l'amour
> Qui fait la monde à la ronde:*

and yet no one may be able to see them except those whose hearts are going round to that same tune. At all events, we will make believe that there are fairies in the world. It will not be the last time by many a one that we shall have to make believe. And yet, after all, there is no need for that. There must be fairies; for this is a fairy tale: and how can one have a fairy tale if there are no fairies?

You don't see the logic of that? Perhaps not. Then please not to see the logic of a great many arguments exactly like it, which you will hear before your beard is grey.

The kind old dame came back at twelve, when school was over, to look at Tom: but there was no Tom there. She looked about for his footprints; but the ground was so hard that there was no slot,* as they say in dear old North Devon. And if you grow up to be a brave healthy man, you may know some day what no slot means, and know, too, I hope, what a slot does mean—a broad slot, with blunt claws, which makes a man put out his cigar, and set his teeth, and tighten his girths, when he sees it; and what his rights mean, if he has them, brow, bay, tray, and points;* and see something worth seeing between Haddon Wood and Countisbury Cliff,* with good Mr Palk Collyns* to show you the way, and mend your bones as fast as you smash them. Only when that jolly day comes, please don't break your neck: stogged* in a mire you never will be, I trust; for you are a heath-cropper* bred and born.

So the old dame went in again quite sulky, thinking that little Tom had tricked her with a false story, and shammed ill, and then run away again.

But she altered her mind the next day. For, when Sir John and the rest of them had run themselves out of breath, and lost Tom, they went back again, looking very foolish.

And they looked more foolish still when Sir John heard more of the story from the nurse; and more foolish still, again, when they heard the whole story from Miss Ellie, the little lady in white. All she had seen was a poor little black chimney-sweep, crying and sobbing, and going to get up the chimney again. Of course, she was very much frightened: and no wonder. But that was all. The boy had taken nothing in the room; by the mark of his little sooty feet, they could see that he had never been off the hearth-rug till the nurse caught hold of him. It was all a mistake.

So Sir John told Grimes to go home, and promised him five shillings if he would bring the boy quietly up to him, without beating him, that he might be sure of the truth. For he took for granted, and Grimes, too, that Tom had made his way home.

But no Tom came back to Mr Grimes that evening; and he went to the police-office, to tell them to look out for the boy. But no Tom was heard of. As for his having gone over those great fells to Vendale, they no more dreamed of that than of his having gone to the moon.

So Mr Grimes came up to Harthover next day with a very sour face; but when he got there, Sir John was over the hills and far away; and Mr Grimes had to sit in the outer servants' hall all day, and drink strong ale to wash away his sorrows; and they were washed away, long before Sir John came back.

For good Sir John had slept very badly that night; and he said to his lady, 'My dear, the boy must have got over into the grouse-moors, and lost himself; and he lies very heavily on my conscience, poor little lad. But I know what I will do.'

So, at five the next morning up he got, and into his bath, and into his shooting-jacket and gaiters, and into the stable-yard, like a fine old English gentleman, with a face as red as a rose, and a hand as hard as a table, and a back as broad as a bullock's; and bade them bring his shooting pony, and the keeper to come on his pony, and the huntsman, and the first whip, and the second whip,* and the under-keeper with the bloodhound in a leash—a great dog as tall as a calf, of the colour of a gravel walk, with mahogany ears and nose, and a throat like a church bell. They took him up to the place where Tom had gone into the wood; and there the hound lifted up his mighty voice, and told them all he knew.

Then he took them to the place where Tom had climbed the wall; and they shoved it down, and all got through.

And then the wise dog took them over the moor, and over the fells, step by step, very slowly; for the scent was a day old, you know, and very light from the heat and drought. But that was why cunning old Sir John started at five in the morning.

And at last he came to the top of Lewthwaite Crag, and there he bayed, and looked up in their faces, as much as to say, 'I tell you he is gone down here!'

They could hardly believe that Tom would have gone so far; and when they looked at that awful cliff, they could never believe that he would have dared to face it. But if the dog said so, it must be true.

'Heaven forgive us!' said Sir John. 'If we find him at all, we shall find him lying at the bottom.' And he slapped his great hand upon his great thigh, and said—

'Who will go down over Lewthwaite Crag, and see if that boy is alive? Oh that I were twenty years younger, and I would go down myself!' And so he would have done, as well as any sweep in the county. Then he said—

'Twenty pounds to the man who brings me that boy alive!' and as was his way, what he said he meant.

Now among the lot was a little groom-boy, a very little groom indeed; and he was the same who had ridden up the court, and told Tom to come to the Hall; and he said—

'Twenty pounds or none, I will go down over Lewthwaite Crag, if it's only for the poor boy's sake. For he was as civil a spoken little chap as ever climbed a flue.'

So down over Lewthwaite Crag he went: a very smart groom he was at the top, and a very shabby one at the bottom; for he tore his gaiters, and he tore his breeches, and he tore his jacket, and he burst his braces, and he burst his boots, and he lost his hat, and what was worst of all, he lost his shirt pin, which he prized very much, for it was gold, and he had won it in a raffle at Malton,* and there was a figure at the top of it of t'ould mare, noble old Beeswing herself,* as natural as life; so it was a really severe loss: but he never saw anything of Tom.

And all the while Sir John and the rest were riding round, full three miles to the right, and back again, to get into Vendale, and to the foot of the crag.

When they came to the old dame's school, all the children came out to see. And the old dame came out too; and when she saw Sir John she curtsied very low, for she was a tenant of his.

'Well, dame, and how are you?' said Sir John.

'Blessings on you as broad as your back, Harthover,' says she—she didn't call him Sir John, but only Harthover, for that is the fashion in the North country—'and welcome into Vendale: but you're no hunting the fox this time of year?'

'I am hunting, and strange game too,' said he.

'Blessings on your heart, and what makes you look so sad the morn?'

'I'm looking for a lost child, a chimney-sweep, that is run away.'

'Oh Harthover, Harthover,' says she, 'ye were always a just man and a merciful; and ye'll no harm the poor little lad if I give you tidings of him?'

'Not I, not I, dame. I'm afraid we hunted him out of the house all on a miserable mistake, and the hound has brought him to the top of Lewthwaite Crag, and—'

Whereat the old dame broke out crying, without letting him finish his story.

'So he told me the truth after all, poor little dear! Ah, first thoughts are best, and a body's heart'll guide them right, if they will but hearken to it.' And then she told Sir John all.

'Bring the dog here, and lay him on,' said Sir John, without another word, and he set his teeth very hard.

And the dog opened at once; and went away at the back of the cottage, over the road, and over the meadow, and through a bit of alder copse; and there, upon an alder stump, they saw Tom's clothes lying. And then they knew as much about it all as there was any need to know.

And Tom?

Ah, now comes the most wonderful part of this wonderful story. Tom, when he woke, for of course he woke—children always wake after they have slept exactly as long as is good for them—found himself swimming about in the stream, being about four inches, or—that I may be accurate—3.87902 inches long, and having round the parotid region of his fauces* a set of external gills (I hope you understand all the big words) just like those of a sucking eft,* which he mistook for a lace frill, till he pulled at them, found he hurt himself, and made up his mind that they were part of himself, and best left alone.

In fact, the fairies had turned him into a water-baby.

A water-baby? You never heard of a water-baby. Perhaps not. That is the very reason why this story was written. There are a great many things in the world which you never heard of; and a great many more which nobody ever heard of; and a great many things, too, which nobody will ever hear of, at least until the coming of the Cocqcigrues,* when man shall be the measure of all things.

'But there are no such things as water-babies.'

How do you know that? Have you been there to see? And if you had been there to see, and had seen none, that would not prove that there were none. If Mr Garth* does not find a fox in Eversley Wood— as folks sometimes fear he never will—that does not prove that there are no such things as foxes. And as is Eversley Wood to all the woods in England, so are the waters we know to all the waters in the world. And no one has a right to say that no water-babies exist, till they have seen no water-babies existing; which is quite a different thing, mind, from not seeing water-babies; and a thing which nobody ever did, or perhaps ever will do.

'But surely if there were water-babies, somebody would have caught one at least?'

Well. How do you know that somebody has not?

'But they would have put it into spirits, or into the Illustrated News,* or perhaps cut it into two halves, poor dear little thing, and sent one to Professor Owen, and one to Professor Huxley,* to see what they would each say about it.'

Ah, my dear little man! that does not follow at all, as you will see before the end of the story.

'But a water-baby is contrary to nature.'

Well, but, my dear little man, you must learn to talk about such things, when you grow older, in a very different way from that. You must not talk about 'ain't' and 'can't' when you speak of this great wonderful world round you, of which the wisest man knows only the very smallest corner, and is, as the great Sir Isaac Newton said, only a child picking up pebbles on the shore of a boundless ocean.*

You must not say that this cannot be, or that that is contrary to nature. You do not know what nature is, or what she can do; and nobody knows; not even Sir Roderick Murchison, or Professor Owen, or Professor Sedgwick, or Professor Huxley, or Mr Darwin, or Professor Faraday, or Mr Grove,* or any other of the great men whom good boys are taught to respect. They are very wise men; and you must listen respectfully to all they say: but even if they should say, which I am sure they never would, 'That cannot exist. That is contrary to nature,' you must wait a little, and see; for perhaps even they may be wrong. It is only children who read Aunt Agitate's Arguments, or Cousin Cramchild's Conversations; or lads who go to popular lectures, and see a man pointing at a few big ugly pictures on the wall, or making nasty smells with bottles and squirts, for an hour or two, and calling that anatomy or chemistry—who talk about 'cannot exist', and 'contrary to nature'. Wise men are afraid to say that there is anything contrary to nature, except what is contrary to mathematical truth; for two and two cannot make five, and two straight lines cannot join twice, and a part cannot be as great as the whole, and so on (at least, so it seems at present): but the wiser men are, the less they talk about 'cannot'. That is a very rash, dangerous word, that 'cannot'; and if people use it too often, the Queen of all the Fairies, who makes the clouds thunder and the fleas bite, and takes just as much trouble about one as about the other, is apt to astonish them suddenly by showing them, that though they say she cannot, yet she can, and what is more, will, whether they approve or not.

And therefore it is, that there are dozens and hundreds of things in the world which we should certainly have said were contrary to nature, if we did not see them going on under our eyes all day long. If people had never seen little seeds grow into great plants and trees, of quite different shape from themselves, and these trees again produce fresh seeds, to grow into fresh trees, they would have said, 'The thing cannot be; it is contrary to nature.' And they would have been quite as right in saying so, as in saying that most other things cannot be.

Or suppose again, that you had come, like M. Du Chaillu,* a traveller from unknown parts; and that no human being had ever seen or heard of an elephant. And suppose that you described him to people, and said, 'This is the shape, and plan, and anatomy of the beast, and of his feet, and of his trunk and of his grinders, and of his tusks, though they are not tusks at all, but two fore teeth run mad; and this is the section of his skull, more like a mushroom than a reasonable skull of a reasonable or unreasonable beast; and so forth, and so forth; and though the beast (which I assure you I have seen and shot) is first cousin to the little hairy coney of Scripture, second cousin to a pig, and (I suspect) thirteenth or fourteenth cousin to a rabbit, yet he is the wisest of all beasts, and can do everything save read write and cast accounts.' People would surely have said, 'Nonsense; your elephant is contrary to nature'; and have thought you were telling stories— as the French thought of Le Vaillant* when he came back to Paris and said that he had shot a giraffe; and as the king of the Cannibal Islands* thought of the English sailor, when he said that in his country water turned to marble, and rain fell as feathers. They would tell you, the more they knew of science, 'Your elephant is an impossible monster, contrary to the laws of comparative anatomy, as far as yet known.' To which you would answer the less, the more you thought.

Did not learned men, too, hold, till within the last twenty-five years, that a flying dragon was an impossible monster? And do we not now know that there are hundreds of them found fossil up and down the world? People call them Pterodactyles:* but that is only because they are ashamed to call them flying dragons, after denying so long that flying dragons could exist. And has not a German, only lately discovered, what is most monstrous of all, that some of these flying dragons, lizards though they are, had feathers? And if that last is not contrary to what people mean by nature now-a-days, one hardly knows what is.*

The truth is, that folks' fancy that such and such things cannot be, simply because they have not seen them, is worth no more than a savage's fancy that there cannot be such a thing as a locomotive, because he never saw one running wild in the forest. Wise men know that their business is to examine what is, and not to settle what is not. They know that there are elephants; they know that there have been flying dragons; and the wiser they are, the less inclined they will be to say positively that there are no water-babies.

No water-babies, indeed? Why, wise men of old said that everything on earth had its double in the water; and you may see that

that is, if not quite true, still quite as true as most other theories which you are likely to hear for many a day. There are land-babies—then why not water-babies? Are there not water-rats, water-flies, water-crickets, water-crabs, water-tortoises, water-scorpions, water-tigers and water-hogs, water-cats and water-dogs, sea-lions and sea-bears, sea-horses and sea-elephants, sea-mice and sea-urchins, sea-razors and sea-pens, sea-combs and sea-fans; and of plants, are there not water-grass, and water-crowfoot, water-milfoil, and so on, without end?

'But all these things are only nicknames; the water things are not really akin to the land things.'

That's not always true. They are, in millions of cases, not only of the same family, but actually the same individual creatures. Do not even you know that a green drake,* and an alder-fly, and a dragon-fly, live under water till they change their skins, just as Tom changed his? And if a water animal can continually change into a land animal, why should not a land animal sometimes change into a water animal? Don't be put down by any of Cousin Cramchild's arguments, but stand up to him like a man, and answer him (quite respectfully, of course) thus:—

If Cousin Cramchild says, that if there are water-babies, they must grow into water men, ask him how he knows that they do not? and then, how he knows that they must, any more than the Proteus of the Adelsberg caverns* grows into a perfect newt?

If he says that it is too strange a transformation for a land-baby to turn into a water-baby, ask him if he ever heard of the transformation of Syllis, or the Distomas, or the common jelly-fish, of which M. Quatrefages* says excellently well—'who would not exclaim that a miracle had come to pass, if he saw a reptile come out of the egg dropped by the hen in his poultry-yard, and the reptile give birth at once to an indefinite number of fishes and birds? Yet the history of the jelly-fish is quite as wonderful as that would be.' Ask him if he knows about all this; and if he does not, tell him to go and look for himself; and advise him (very respectfully, of course) to settle no more what strange things cannot happen, till he has seen what strange things do happen every day.

If he says that things cannot degrade, that is, change downwards into lower forms, ask him, who told him that water-babies were lower than land-babies? But even if they were, does he know about the strange degradation of the common goose-barnacles,* which one finds sticking on ships' bottoms; or the still stranger degradation of some cousins of theirs, of which one hardly likes to talk, so shocking and ugly it is?

And, lastly, if he says (as he most certainly will) that these trans-formations only take place in the lower animals, and not in the higher, say that that seems to little boys, and to some grown people, a very strange fancy. For if the changes of the lower animals are so wonder-ful, and so difficult to discover, why should not there be changes in the higher animals far more wonderful, and far more difficult to dis-cover? And may not man, the crown and flower of all things, undergo some change as much more wonderful than all the rest, as the Great Exhibition* is more wonderful than a rabbit-burrow? Let him answer that. And if he says (as he will) that not having seen such a change in his experience, he is not bound to believe it, ask him respectfully where his microscope has been? Does not each of us, in coming into this world, go through a transformation just as wonderful as that of a sea-egg, or a butterfly? and does not reason and analogy, as well as Scripture, tell us that that transformation is not the last? and that, though what we shall be, we know not, yet we are here but as the crawling caterpillar, and shall be hereafter as the perfect fly. The old Greeks, heathens as they were, saw as much as that two thousand years ago; and I care very little for Cousin Cramchild, if he sees even less than they. And so forth, and so forth, till he is quite cross. And then tell him that if there are no water-babies, at least, there ought to be; and that, at least, he cannot answer.

And meanwhile, my dear little man, till you know a great deal more about nature than Professor Owen and Professor Huxley, put together, don't tell me about what cannot be, or fancy that anything is too wonderful to be true. 'We are fearfully and wonderfully made,'* said old David; and so we are; and so is every thing around us, down to the very deal table. Yes; much more fearfully and wonderfully made, already, is the table, as it stands now, nothing but a piece of dead deal wood, than if, as foxes say, and geese believe, spirits could make it dance, or talk to you by rapping on it.*

Am I in earnest? Oh dear no. Don't you know that this is a fairy tale, and all fun and pretence; and that you are not to believe one word of it, even if it is true?

But at all events, so it happened to Tom. And, therefore, the keeper, and the groom, and Sir John, made a great mistake, and were very unhappy (Sir John, at least) without any reason, when they found a black thing in the water, and said it was Tom's body, and that he had been drowned. They were utterly mistaken. Tom was quite alive; and cleaner, and merrier, than he ever had been. The fairies had washed him, you see, in the swift river, so thoroughly, that not only his dirt, but his whole husk and shell had been washed quite off him, and the pretty little real Tom was washed out of the inside of it, and swam away, as a caddis* does when its case of stones and silk is bored through, and away it goes on its back, paddling to the shore, there to split its skin, and fly away as a caperer, on four fawn-coloured wings, with long legs and horns. They are foolish fellows, the caperers, and fly into the candle at night, if you leave the door open. We will hope Tom will be wiser, now he has got safe out of his sooty old shell.

But good Sir John did not understand all this, not being a fellow of the Linnæan Society;* and he took it into his head that Tom was drowned. When they looked into the empty pockets of his shell, and found no jewels there, nor money—nothing but three marbles, and a brass button with a string to it—then Sir John did something as like crying as ever he did in his life, and blamed himself more bitterly than he need have done. So he cried, and the groom-boy cried, and the huntsman cried, and the dame cried, and the little girl cried, and the dairymaid cried, and the old nurse cried (for it was somewhat her fault), and my lady cried, for though people have wigs, that is no reason why they should not have hearts: but the keeper did not cry, though he had been so good-natured to Tom the morning before; for he was so dried up with running after poachers, that you could no more get tears out of him than milk out of leather: and Grimes did not cry, for Sir John gave him ten pounds, and he drank it all in a week.

Sir John sent, far and wide, to find Tom's father and mother: but he might have looked till Doomsday for them, for one was dead, and the other was in Botany Bay.* And the little girl would not play with her dolls for a whole week, and never forgot poor little Tom. And soon my lady put a pretty little tombstone over Tom's shell in the little churchyard in Vendale, where the old dalesmen all sleep side by side between the limestone crags. And the dame decked it with garlands every Sunday, till she grew so old that she could not stir abroad; then the little children decked it for her. And always she sung an old old song, as she sat spinning what she called her wedding-dress. The children could not understand it, but they liked it none the less for that; for it was very sweet, and very sad; and that was enough for them. And these are the words of it—

> When all the world is young, lad,
>   And all the trees are green;
> And every goose a swan, lad,
>   And every lass a queen;
> Then hey for boot and horse, lad,
>   And round the world away:
> Young blood must have its course, lad,
>   And every dog his day.
>
> When all the world is old, lad,
>   And all the trees are brown;
> And all the sport is stale, lad,
>   And all the wheels run down;
> Creep home, and take your place there,
>   The spent and maimed among:
> God grant you find one face there,
>   You loved when all was young.

Those are the words: but they are only the body of it: the soul of the song was the dear old woman's sweet face, and sweet voice, and the sweet old air to which she sang; and that, alas! one cannot put on paper. And at last she grew so stiff and lame, that the angels were forced to carry her; and they helped her on with her wedding-dress, and carried her up over Harthover Fells, and a long way beyond that too; and there was a new schoolmistress in Vendale, and we will hope that she was not certificated.*

And all the while Tom was swimming about in the river, with a pretty little lace-collar of gills about his neck, as lively as a grig,* and as clean as a fresh-run salmon.

Now if you don't like my story, then go to the schoolroom and learn your multiplication-table, and see if you like that better. Some people, no doubt, would do so. So much the better for us, if not for them. It takes all sorts, they say, to make a world.

# CHAPTER III

HE prayeth well who loveth well,
Both man and bird and beast;
He prayeth best who loveth best,
All things both great and small:
For the dear God who loveth us,
He made and loveth all.*

COLERIDGE.

 OM was now quite amphibious. You do not know what that means? You had better, then, ask the nearest Government pupil-teacher, who may possibly answer you smartly enough, thus—

'Amphibious.* Adjective, derived from two Greek words, *amphi*, a fish, and *bios*, a beast. An animal supposed by our ignorant ancestors to be compounded of a fish and a beast; which therefore, like the hippopotamus, can't live on the land, and dies in the water.'

However that may be, Tom was amphibious; and what is better still, he was clean. For the first time in his life, he felt how comfortable it was to have nothing on him but himself. But he only enjoyed it: he did not know it, or think about it; just as you enjoy life and health, and yet never think about being alive and healthy: and may it be long before you have to think about it!

He did not remember having ever been dirty. Indeed, he did not remember any of his old troubles, being tired, or hungry, or beaten, or sent up dark chimneys. Since that sweet sleep, he had forgotten all about his master, and Harthover Place, and the little white girl, and in a word, all that had happened to him when he lived before; and what was best of all, he had forgotten all the bad words which he had learnt from Grimes, and the rude boys with whom he used to play.

That is not strange: for you know, when you came into this world, and became a land-baby, you remembered nothing. So why should he, when he became a water-baby?

Then have you lived before?

My dear child, who can tell? One can only tell that, by remembering something which happened where we lived before; and as we remember nothing, we know nothing about it; and no book, and no man, can ever tell us certainly.

There was a wise man once,* a very wise man, and a very good man, who wrote a poem about the feelings which some children have about having lived before; and this is what he said—

> Our birth is but a sleep and a forgetting:
> The soul that rises with us, our life's Star,
>     Hath had elsewhere its setting,
>     And cometh from afar:
>     Not in entire forgetfulness,
>     And not in utter nakedness,
> But trailing clouds of glory, do we come
>     From God, who is our home.

There, you can know no more than that. But if I was you, I would believe that. For then the great fairy Science, who is likely to be queen of all the fairies for many a year to come, can only do you good, and never do you harm; and instead of fancying, with some people, that your body makes your soul, as if a steam-engine could make its own coke; or, with some other people, that your soul has nothing to do with your body, but is only stuck into it like a pin into a pincushion, to fall out with the first shake;—you will believe the one true,

> orthodox,
> rational,
> philosophical,
> logical,
> irrefragable,
> nominalistic,
> realistic,
> inductive,
> deductive,

seductive,
productive,
salutary,
comfortable,
and on-all-accounts-to-be-received*

doctrine of this wonderful fairy tale; which is, that your soul makes your body, just as a snail makes his shell. For the rest, it is enough for us to be sure that whether or not we lived before, we shall live again; though not, I hope, as poor little heathen Tom did. For he went downward into the water: but we, I hope, shall go upward to a very different place.

But Tom was very happy in the water. He had been sadly over-worked in the land-world; and so now, to make up for that, he had nothing but holidays in the water-world for a long, long time to come. He had nothing to do now but enjoy himself, and look at all the pretty things which are to be seen in the cool clear water-world, where the sun is never too hot, and the frost is never too cold.

And what did he live on? Water-cresses, perhaps; or perhaps water-gruel, and water-milk: too many land-babies do so likewise. But we do not know what one-tenth of the water things eat; so we are not answerable for the water-babies.

Sometimes he went along the smooth gravel waterways, looking at the crickets which ran in and out among the stones, as rabbits do on land; or he climbed over the ledges of rock, and saw the sand-pipes* hanging in thousands, with every one of them a pretty little head and legs peeping out; or he went into a still corner, and watched the cad-dises eating dead sticks as greedily as you would eat plum-pudding, and building their houses with silk and glue. Very fanciful ladies they were; none of them would keep to the same materials for a day. One would begin with some pebbles; then she would stick on a piece of green weed; then she found a shell, and stuck it on too; and the poor shell was alive, and did not like at all being taken to build houses with: but the caddis did not let him have any voice in the matter, being rude and selfish, as vain people are apt to be; then she stuck on a piece of rotten wood, then a very smart pink stone, and so on, till she was patched all over like an Irishman's coat. Then she found a long straw, five times as long as herself, and said, 'Hurrah! my sister has a tail, and I'll have one too'; and she stuck it on her back, and marched about with it quite proud, though it was very inconvenient indeed. And, at that, tails became all the fashion among the caddis-baits in that pool, as they were at the end of the Long Pond* last May, and they all toddled about with long straws sticking out behind, getting between each other's legs, and tumbling over each other, and looking so ridiculous, that Tom laughed at them till he cried, as we did. But they were quite right, you know; for people must always follow the fashion, even if it be spoon-bonnets.*

Then sometimes he came to a deep still reach; and there he saw the water-forests. They would have looked to you only little weeds: but Tom, you must remember, was so little that everything looked a hundred times as big to him as it does to you, just as things do to a minnow, who sees and catches the little water-creatures which you can only see in a microscope.

And in the water-forest he saw the water-monkeys and water-squirrels (they had all six legs, though; every thing almost has six legs in the water, except efts and water-babies); and nimbly enough they ran among the branches. There were water-flowers there, too, in thousands; and Tom tried to pick them: but as soon as he touched them, they drew themselves in and turned into knots of jelly; and then Tom saw that they were all alive—bells, and stars, and wheels, and flowers, of all beautiful shapes and colours; and all alive and busy, just as Tom was. So now he found that there was a great deal more in the world than he had fancied at first sight.

There was one wonderful little fellow,* too, who peeped out of the top of a house built of round bricks. He had two big wheels, and one little one, all over teeth, spinning round and round like the wheels in a thrashing-machine; and Tom stood and stared at him, to see what he was going to make with his machinery. And what do you think he was doing? Brick-making. With his two big wheels he swept together all the mud which floated in the water: all that was nice in it he put into his stomach and ate; and all the mud he put into the little wheel on his breast, which really was a round hole set with teeth; and there he spun it into a neat hard round brick; and then he took it and stuck it on the top of his house-wall, and set to work to make another. Now was not he a clever little fellow?

Tom thought so: but when he wanted to talk to him, the brick-maker was much too busy and proud of his work to take notice of him.

Now you must know that all the things under the water talk: only not such a language as ours; but such as horses, and dogs, and cows, and birds talk to each other; and Tom soon learned to understand them and talk to them; so that he might have had very pleasant company if he had only been a good boy. But I am sorry to say, he was too like some other little boys, very fond of hunting and tormenting creatures for mere sport. Some people say that boys cannot help it; that it is nature, and only a proof that we are all originally descended from beasts of prey. But whether it is nature or not, little boys can help it, and must help it. For if they have naughty, low, mischievous tricks in their nature, as monkeys have, that is no reason why they should give way to those tricks like monkeys, who know no better. And therefore they must not torment dumb creatures; for if they do, a certain old lady who is coming will surely give them exactly what they deserve.

But Tom did not know that; and he pecked and howked* the poor water things about sadly, till they were all afraid of him, and got out of his way, or crept into their shells; so he had no one to speak to or play with.

The water-fairies, of course, were very sorry to see him so unhappy, and longed to take him, and tell him how naughty he was, and teach him to be good, and to play and romp with him too: but they had been forbidden to do that. Tom had to learn his lesson for himself by sound and sharp experience, as many another foolish person has to do, though there may be many a kind heart yearning over them all the while, and longing to teach them what they can only teach themselves.

At last one day he found a caddis, and wanted it to peep out of its house: but its house-door was shut. He had never seen a caddis with a house-door before: so what must he do, the meddlesome little fellow, but pull it open, to see what the poor lady was doing inside. What a shame! How should you like to have any one breaking your bedroom-door in, to see how you looked when you were in bed? So Tom broke to pieces the door, which was the prettiest little grating of silk, stuck all over with shining bits of crystal; and when he looked in, the caddis poked out her head, and it had turned into just the shape of a bird's. But when Tom spoke to her she could not answer; for her mouth and face were tight tied up in a new nightcap of neat pink skin. However, if she didn't answer, all the other caddises did; for they held up their hands and shrieked like the cats in Struwelpeter:* 'Oh, you nasty horrid boy; there you are at it again! And she had just laid herself up for a fortnight's sleep, and then she would have come out with such beautiful wings, and flown about, and laid such lots of eggs: and now you have broken her door, and she can't mend it because her mouth is tied up for a fortnight, and she will die. Who sent you here to worry us out of our lives?'

So Tom swam away. He was very much ashamed of himself, and felt all the naughtier; as little boys do when they have done wrong, and won't say so.

Then he came to a pool full of little trout, and began tormenting them, and trying to catch them: but they slipt through his fingers, and jumped clean out of water in their fright. But as Tom chased them, he came close to a great dark hover* under an alder root, and out floushed* a huge old brown trout ten times as big as he was, and ran right against him, and knocked all the breath out of his body; and I don't know which was the more frightened of the two.

Then he went on sulky and lonely, as he deserved to be; and under a bank he saw a very ugly dirty creature sitting, about half as big as himself; which had six legs, and a big stomach, and a most ridiculous head with two great eyes and a face just like a donkey's.

'Oh,' said Tom, 'you are an ugly fellow to be sure!' and he began making faces at him; and put his nose close to him, and hallooed at him, like a very rude boy.

When, hey presto! all the thing's donkey-face came off in a moment, and out popped a long arm with a pair of pincers at the end of it, and caught Tom by the nose. It did not hurt him much; but it held him quite tight.

'Yah, ah! Oh, let me go!' cried Tom.

'Then let me go,' said the creature. 'I want to be quiet. I want to split.'

Tom promised to let him alone, and he let go. 'Why do you want to split?' said Tom.

'Because my brothers and sisters have all split, and turned into beautiful creatures with wings; and I want to split too. Don't speak to me. I am sure I shall split. I will split!'

Tom stood still, and watched him. And he swelled himself, and puffed, and stretched himself out stiff, and at last—crack, puff, bang—he opened all down his back, and then up to the top of his head.

And out of his inside came the most slender, elegant, soft creature, as soft and smooth as Tom: but very pale and weak, like a little child who has been ill a long time in a dark room. It moved its legs very feebly; and looked about it half ashamed, like a girl when she goes for the first time into a ballroom; and then it began walking slowly up a grass stem to the top of the water.

Tom was so astonished that he never said a word: but he stared with all his eyes. And he went up to the top of the water too, and peeped out to see what would happen.

And as the creature sat in the warm bright sun, a wonderful change came over it. It grew strong and firm; the most lovely colours began to show on its body, blue and yellow and black, spots and bars and rings; out of its back rose four great wings of bright brown gauze; and its eyes grew so large that they filled all its head, and shone like ten thousand diamonds.

'Oh, you beautiful creature!' said Tom; and he put out his hand to catch it.

But the thing whirred up into the air, and hung poised on its wings a moment, and then settled down again by Tom quite fearless.

'No!' it said, 'you cannot catch me. I am a dragon-fly now, the king of all the flies; and I shall dance in the sunshine, and hawk over the river, and catch gnats, and have a beautiful wife like myself. I know what I shall do. Hurrah!' And he flew away into the air, and began catching gnats.

'Oh! come back, come back,' cried Tom, 'you beautiful creature.

I have no one to play with, and I am so lonely here. If you will but come back I will never try to catch you.'

'I don't care whether you do or not,' said the dragon-fly; 'for you can't. But when I have had my dinner, and looked a little about this pretty place, I will come back; and have a little chat about all I have seen in my travels. Why, what a huge tree this is! and what huge leaves on it!'

It was only a big dock: but you know the dragon-fly had never seen any but little water-trees; starwort, and milfoil, and water-crowfoot, and such like; so it did look very big to him. Besides, he was very short-sighted, as all dragon-flies are; and never could see a yard before his nose; any more than a great many other folks, who are not half as handsome as he.

The dragon-fly did come back, and chatted away with Tom. He was a little conceited about his fine colours and his large wings; but you know, he had been a poor dirty ugly creature all his life before; so there were great excuses for him. He was very fond of talking about all the wonderful things he saw in the trees and the meadows; and Tom liked to listen to him, for he had forgotten all about them. So in a little while they became great friends.

And I am very glad to say, that Tom learnt such a lesson that day, that he did not torment creatures for a long time after. And then the caddises grew quite tame, and used to tell him strange stories about the way they built their houses, and changed their skins, and turned at last into winged flies; till Tom began to long to change his skin, and have wings like them some day.

And the trout and he made it up (for trout very soon forget, if they have been frightened and hurt). So Tom used to play with them at hare and hounds,* and great fun they had; and he used to try to leap out of the water, head over heels, as they did before a shower came on: but somehow he never could manage it. He liked most, though, to see them rising at the flies, as they sailed round and round under the shadow of the great oak, where the beetles fell flop into the water, and the green caterpillars let themselves down* from the boughs by silk ropes for no reason at all; and then changed their foolish minds for no reason at all either; and hauled themselves up again into the tree, rolling up the rope in a ball between their paws; which is a very clever rope-dancer's trick, and neither Blondin nor Leotard* could do it: but why they should take so much trouble about it no one can tell; for they cannot get their living, as Blondin and Leotard do, by trying to break their necks on a string.

And very often Tom caught them just as they touched the water; and caught the alder flies, and the caperers, and the cock-tailed duns and spinners,* yellow, and brown, and claret, and grey, and gave them to his friends the trout. Perhaps he was not quite kind to the flies; but one must do a good turn to one's friends when one can.

And at last he gave up catching even the flies; for he made acquaintance with one by accident, and found him a very merry little fellow. And this was the way it happened; and it is all quite true.

He was basking at the top of the water one hot day in July, catching duns and feeding the trout, when he saw a new sort, a dark grey little fellow with a brown head. He was a very little fellow indeed: but he made the most of himself, as people ought to do. He cocked up his head, and he cocked up his wings, and he cocked up his tail, and he cocked up the two whisks at his tail-end, and, in short, he looked the cockiest little man of all little men. And so he proved to be; for instead of getting away, he hopped upon Tom's finger, and sat there as bold as nine tailors;* and he cried out in the tiniest, shrillest, squeakiest little voice you ever heard.

'Much obliged to you, indeed; but I don't want it yet.'

'Want what?' said Tom, quite taken aback by his impudence.

'Your leg, which you are kind enough to hold out for me to sit on. I must just go and see after my wife for a few minutes. Dear me! what a troublesome business a family is!' (though the idle little rogue did nothing at all, but left his poor wife to lay all the eggs by herself). 'When I come back, I shall be glad of it, if you'll be so good as to keep it sticking out just so'; and off he flew.

Tom thought him a very cool sort of personage; and still more so, when in five minutes he came back, and said—'Ah, you were tired waiting? Well, your other leg will do as well.'

And he popped himself down on Tom's knee, and began chatting away in his squeaking voice.

'So you live under the water? It's a low place. I lived there for some time; and was very shabby and dirty. But I didn't choose that that should last. So I turned respectable, and came up to the top, and put on this grey suit. It's a very business-like suit, you think, don't you?'

'Very neat and quiet indeed,' said Tom.

'Yes, one must be quiet, and neat, and respectable, and all that sort of thing for a little, when one becomes a family man. But I'm tired of it, that's the truth. I've done quite enough business, I consider, in the last week, to last me my life. So I shall put on a ball-dress, and go out and be a smart man, and see the gay world, and have a dance or two. Why shouldn't one be jolly if one can?'

'And what will become of your wife?'

'Oh! she is a very plain stupid creature, and that's the truth; and thinks about nothing but eggs. If she chooses to come, why she may; and if not, why I go without her;—and here I go.'

And, as he spoke, he turned quite pale, and then quite white.

'Why, you're ill!' said Tom. But he did not answer.

'You're dead,' said Tom, looking at him as he stood on his knee as white as a ghost.

'No I ain't!' answered a little squeaking voice over his head. 'This is me up here, in my ball-dress: and that's my skin. Ha, ha! you could not do such a trick as that!'

And no more Tom could, nor Houdin, nor Robin, nor Frikell,* nor all the conjurors in the world. For the little rogue had jumped clean out of his own skin, and left it standing on Tom's knee, eyes, wings, legs, tails, exactly as if it had been alive.

'Ha, ha!' he said, and he jerked and skipped up and down, never stopping an instant, just as if he had St Vitus's dance. 'Ain't I a pretty fellow now?'

And so he was; for his body was white, and his tail orange, and his eyes all the colours of a peacock's tail. And what was the oddest of all, the whisks at the end of his tail had grown five times as long as they were before.

'Ah!' said he, 'now I will see the gay world. My living won't cost me much, for I have no mouth, you see, and no inside; so I can never be hungry, nor have the stomach-ache neither.'

No more he had. He had grown as dry and hard and empty as a quill, as such silly shallow-hearted fellows deserve to grow.

But, instead of being ashamed of his emptiness, he was quite proud of it, as a good many fine gentlemen are, and began flirting and flipping up and down, and singing—

> My wife shall dance, and I shall sing,
>   So merrily pass the day;
> For I hold it one of the wisest things,
>   To drive dull care away.*

And he danced up and down for three days and three nights, till he grew so tired, that he tumbled into the water, and floated down. But what became of him Tom never knew, and he himself never minded; for Tom heard him singing to the last, as he floated down—

> To drive dull care away-ay-ay!

And if he did not care, why nobody else cared either.

But one day Tom had a new adventure. He was sitting on a water-lily leaf, he and his friend the dragon-fly, watching the gnats dance. The dragon-fly had eaten as many as he wanted, and was sitting quite still and sleepy, for it was very hot and bright. The gnats (who did not care the least for their poor brothers' death), danced a foot over his head quite happily, and a large black fly settled within an inch of his nose, and began washing his own face and combing his hair with his paws: but the dragon-fly never stirred, and kept on chatting to Tom about the times when he lived under the water.

Suddenly, Tom heard the strangest noise up the stream; cooing, and grunting, and whining, and squeaking, as if you had put into a bag two stock-doves, nine mice, three guinea-pigs, and a blind puppy, and left them there to settle themselves and make music.

He looked up the water, and there he saw a sight as strange as the noise; a great ball rolling over and over down the stream, seeming one moment of soft brown fur, and the next of shining glass: and yet it was not a ball; for sometimes it broke up and streamed away in pieces, and then it joined again; and all the while the noise came out of it louder and louder.

Tom asked the dragon-fly what it could be: but, of course, with his short sight, he could not even see it, though it was not ten yards away. So he took the neatest little header into the water, and started off to see for himself; and, when he came near, the ball turned out to be four or five beautiful creatures, many times larger than Tom, who were swimming about, and rolling, and diving, and twisting, and wrestling, and cuddling, and kissing, and biting, and scratching, in the most charming fashion that ever was seen. And if you don't believe me, you may go to the Zoological Gardens* (for I am afraid that you won't see it nearer, unless, perhaps, you get up at five in the morning, and go down to Cordery's Moor,* and watch by the great withy pollard which hangs over the backwater, where the otters breed sometimes), and then say, if otters at play in the water are not the merriest, lithest, gracefullest creatures you ever saw.

But, when the biggest of them saw Tom, she darted out from the rest, and cried in the water-language sharply enough, 'Quick, children, here is something to eat, indeed!' and came at poor Tom, showing such a wicked pair of eyes, and such a set of sharp teeth in a grinning mouth, that Tom, who had thought her very handsome, said to himself, Handsome is that handsome does, and slipt in between the water-lily roots as fast as he could, and then turned round and made faces at her.

'Come out,' said the wicked old otter, 'or it will be worse for you.'

But Tom looked at her from between two thick roots, and shook them with all his might, making horrible faces all the while, just as he used to grin through the railings at the old women, when he lived before. It was not quite well-bred, no doubt; but you know, Tom had not finished his education yet.

'Come away, children,' said the otter in disgust, 'it is not worth eating, after all. It is only a nasty eft, which nothing eats, not even those vulgar pike in the pond.'

'I am not an eft!' said Tom; 'efts have tails.'

'You are an eft,' said the otter, very positively; 'I see your two hands quite plain, and I know you have a tail.'

'I tell you I have not,' said Tom. 'Look here!' and he turned his pretty little self quite round; and, sure enough, he had no more tail than you.

The otter might have got out of it by saying that Tom was a frog: but, like a great many other people, when she had once said a thing, she stood to it, right or wrong; so she answered:

'I say you are an eft, and therefore you are, and not fit food for gentlefolk like me and my children. You may stay there till the salmon eat you (she knew the salmon would not, but she wanted to frighten poor Tom). Ha! ha! they will eat you, and we will eat them'; and the otter laughed such a wicked cruel laugh—as you may hear them do sometimes; and the first time that you hear it you will probably think it is bogies.*

'What are salmon?' asked Tom.

'Fish, you eft, great fish, nice fish to eat. They are the lords of the fish, and we are the lords of the salmon'; and she laughed again. 'We hunt them up and down the pools, and drive them up into a corner, the silly things; they are so proud, and bully the little trout, and the minnows, till they see us coming, and then they are so meek all at once; and we catch them, but we disdain to eat them all; we just bite out their soft throats and suck their sweet juice—Oh, so good!'— (and she licked her wicked lips)—'and then throw them away, and go and catch another. They are coming soon, children, coming soon; I can smell the rain coming up off the sea, and then hurrah for a fresh,* and salmon, and plenty of eating all day long.'

And the otter grew so proud that she turned head over heels twice, and then stood upright half out of the water, grinning like a Cheshire cat.*

'And where do they come from?' asked Tom, who kept himself very close, for he was considerably frightened.

'Out of the sea, eft, the great wide sea, where they might stay and be safe if they liked. But out of the sea the silly things come, into the great river down below, and we come up to watch for them; and when they go down again we go down and follow them. And there we fish for the bass and the pollock, and have jolly days along the shore, and toss and roll in the breakers, and sleep snug in the warm dry crags. Ah, that is a merry life too, children, if it were not for those horrid men.'

'What are men?' asked Tom; but somehow he seemed to know before he asked.

'Two-legged things, eft: and, now I come to look at you, they are actually something like you, if you had not a tail' (she was determined that Tom should have a tail), 'only a great deal bigger, worse luck for us; and they catch the fish with hooks and lines, which get into our feet sometimes, and set pots along the rocks to catch lobsters. They speared my poor dear husband as he went out to find something for me to eat. I was laid up among the crags then, and we were very low in the world, for the sea was so rough that no fish would come in shore. But they speared him, poor fellow, and I saw them carrying him away upon a pole. Ah, he lost his life for your sakes, my children, poor dear obedient creature that he was.'

And the otter grew so sentimental (for otters can be very sentimental when they choose, like a good many people who are both cruel and greedy, and no good to anybody at all) that she sailed solemnly away down the burn, and Tom saw her no more for that time. And lucky it was for her that she did so; for no sooner was she gone, than down the bank came seven little rough terrier dogs, snuffing and yapping, and grubbing and splashing, in full cry after the otter. Tom hid among the water-lilies till they were gone; for he could not guess that they were the water-fairies come to help him.

But *He* could not help thinking of what the otter had said about the great river and the broad sea. And, as he thought, he longed to go and see them. He could not tell why; but the more he thought, the more he grew discontented with the narrow little stream in which he lived, and all his companions there; and wanted to get out into the wide wide world, and enjoy all the wonderful sights of which he was sure it was full.

And once he set off to go down the stream. But the stream was very low; and when he came to the shallows he could not keep under water, for there was no water left to keep under. So the sun burnt his back and made him sick; and he went back again and lay quiet in the pool for a whole week more.

And then, on the evening of a very hot day, he saw a sight.

He had been very stupid all day, and so had the trout; for they would not move an inch to take a fly, though there were thousands on the water, but lay dozing at the bottom under the shade of the stones;

and Tom lay dozing too, and was glad to cuddle their smooth cool sides, for the water was quite warm and unpleasant.

But toward evening it grew suddenly dark, and Tom looked up and saw a blanket of black clouds lying right across the valley above his head, resting on the crags right and left. He felt not quite frightened, but very still; for everything was still. There was not a whisper of wind, nor a chirp of a bird to be heard; and next a few great drops of rain fell plop into the water, and one hit Tom on the nose and made him pop his head down quickly enough.

And then the thunder roared, and the lightning flashed, and leapt across Vendale and back again, from cloud to cloud, and cliff to cliff, till the very rocks in the stream seemed to shake; and Tom looked up at it through the water, and thought it the finest thing he ever saw in his life.

But out of the water he dared not put his head; for the rain came down by bucketsful, and the hail hammered like shot on the stream, and churned it into foam; and soon the stream rose, and rushed down, higher and higher, and fouler and fouler, full of beetles, and sticks, and straws, and worms, and addle-eggs, and wood-lice, and leeches, and odds and ends, and omnium-gatherums,* and this, that, and the other, enough to fill nine museums.

Tom could hardly stand against the stream, and hid behind a rock. But the trout did not; for out they rushed from among the stones, and began gobbling the beetles and leeches in the most greedy and quarrelsome way, and swimming about with great worms hanging out of their mouths, tugging and kicking to get them away from each other.

And now, by the flashes of the lightning, Tom saw a new sight—all the bottom of the stream alive with great eels, turning and twisting along, all down stream and away. They had been hiding for weeks past in the cracks of the rocks, and in burrows in the mud; and Tom had hardly ever seen them, except now and then at night: but now they were all out, and went hurrying past him so fiercely and wildly that he was quite frightened. And as they hurried past he could hear them say to each other, 'We must run, we must run. What a jolly thunderstorm! Down to the sea, down to the sea!'

And then the otter came by with all her brood, twining and

sweeping along as fast as the eels themselves; and she spied Tom as she came by, and said:—

'Now is your time, eft, if you want to see the world. Come along, children, never mind those nasty eels: we shall breakfast on salmon to-morrow. Down to the sea, down to the sea!'

Then came a flash brighter than all the rest, and by the light of it—in the thousandth part of a second they were gone again—but he had seen them, he was certain of it—Three beautiful little white girls, with their arms twined round each other's necks, floating down the torrent, as they sang, 'Down to the sea, down to the sea!'

'Oh stay! Wait for me!' cried Tom; but they were gone: yet he could hear their voices clear and sweet through the roar of thunder and water and wind, singing as they died away, 'Down to the sea!'

'Down to the sea?' said Tom; 'everything is going to the sea, and I will go too. Good-bye, trout.' But the trout were so busy gobbling worms that they never turned to answer him; so that Tom was spared the pain of bidding them farewell.

And now, down the rushing stream, guided by the bright flashes of the storm; past tall birch-fringed rocks, which shone out one moment as clear as day, and the next were dark as night; past dark hovers under swirling banks, from which great trout rushed out on Tom, thinking him to be good to eat, and turned back sulkily, for the fairies sent them home again with a tremendous scolding, for daring to meddle with a water-baby; on through narrow strids* and roaring cataracts, where Tom was deafened and blinded for a moment by the rushing waters; along deep reaches, where the white water-lilies tossed and flapped beneath the wind and hail; past sleeping villages; under dark bridge-arches, and away and away to the sea. And Tom could not stop, and did not care to stop; he would see the great world below, and the salmon, and the breakers, and the wide, wide sea.

And when the daylight came, Tom found himself out in the salmon river.

And what sort of a river was it? Was it like an Irish stream, winding through the brown bogs, where the wild ducks squatter up* from among the white water-lilies, and the curlews flit to and fro, crying 'Tullie-wheep, mind your sheep'; and Dennis* tells you strange

stories of the Peishtamore, the great bogy-snake which lies in the
black peat pools, among the old pine stems, and puts his head out at
night to snap at the cattle as they come down to drink?—But you
must not believe all that Dennis tells you, mind; for if you ask him,

'Is there a salmon here, do you think, Dennis?'

'Is it salmon, thin, your honour manes? Salmon? Cartloads it is of
thim, thin, an' ridgmens, shouldthering ache other out of water, av'
ye'd but the luck to see thim.'

Then you fish the pool all over, and never get a rise.

'But there can't be a salmon here, Dennis! and, if you'll but think,
if one had come up last tide, he'd be gone to the higher pools by now.'

'Shure thin, and your honour's the thrue fisherman, and understands it all like a book. Why, ye spake as if ye'd known the wather a
thousand years! As I said, how could there be a fish here at all, just
now?'

'But you said just now they were shouldering each other out of
water?'

And then Dennis will look up at you with his handsome, sly, soft,
sleepy, good-natured, untrustable, Irish grey eye, and answer with
the prettiest smile:

'Shure, and didn't I think your honour would like a pleasant
answer?'

So you must not trust Dennis, because he is in the habit of giving
pleasant answers: but, instead of being angry with him, you must
remember that he is a poor Paddy, and knows no better; so you must
just burst out laughing; and then he will burst out laughing too, and
slave for you, and trot about after you, and show you good sport if he
can—for he is an affectionate fellow, and as fond of sport as you
are—and if he can't, tell you fibs instead, a hundred an hour; and
wonder all the while why poor ould Ireland does not prosper like
England and Scotland, and some other places, where folk have taken
up a ridiculous fancy that honesty is the best policy.

Or was it like a Welsh salmon river, which is remarkable chiefly (at
least, till this last year) for containing no salmon, as they have been all
poached out by the enlightened peasantry, to prevent the Cythrawl
Sassenach (which means you, my little dear, your kith and kin, and

signifies much the same as the Chinese Fan Quei)* from coming bothering into Wales, with good tackle, and ready money, and civilization, and common honesty, and other like things of which the Cymry stand in no need whatsoever?

Or was it such a salmon stream as I trust you will see among the Hampshire water-meadows before your hairs are grey, under the wise new fishing laws?*—when Winchester apprentices shall covenant, as they did three hundred years ago, not to be made to eat salmon more than three days a week; and fresh-run fish shall be as plentiful under Salisbury spire as they are in Hollyhole at Christchurch; in the good time coming,* when folks shall see that, of all Heaven's gifts of food, the one to be protected most carefully is that worthy gentleman salmon, who is generous enough to go down to the sea weighing five ounces, and to come back next year weighing five pounds, without having cost the soil or the state one farthing?

Or was it like a Scotch stream, such as Arthur Clough drew in his 'Bothie':*—

Where over a ledge of granite

Into a granite bason the amber torrent descended . . .
Beautiful there for the colour derived from green rocks under;
Beautiful most of all, where beads of foam uprising
Mingle their clouds of white with the delicate hue of the stillness . . .
Cliff over cliff for its sides, with rowan and pendant birch boughs . . .

Ah, my little man, when you are a big man, and fish such a stream as that, you will hardly care, I think, whether she be roaring down in full spate, like coffee covered with scald cream,* while the fish are swirling at your fly as an oar-blade swirls in a boat-race, or flashing up the cataract like silver arrows, out of the fiercest of the foam; or whether the fall be dwindled to a single thread, and the shingle below be as white and dusty as a turnpike road, while the salmon huddle together in one dark cloud in the clear amber pool, sleeping away their time till the rain creeps back again off the sea. You will not care much, if you have eyes and brains; for you will lay down your rod contentedly, and drink in at your eyes the beauty of that glorious place; and listen to the water-ouzel piping on the stones,* and watch the yellow roes come down to drink, and look up at you with their great soft trustful eyes, as much as to say, 'You could not have the heart to shoot at us?' And then, if you have sense, you will turn and talk to the great giant of a gilly* who lies basking on the stone beside you. He will tell you no fibs, my little man; for he is a Scotchman, and fears God, and not the priest; and, as you talk with him, you will be surprised more and more at his knowledge, his sense, his humour, his courtesy; and you will find out—unless you have found it out before—that a man may learn from his Bible to be a more thorough gentleman than if he had been brought up in all the drawing-rooms in London.

No. It was none of these, the salmon stream at Harthover. It was such a stream as you see in dear old Bewick;* Bewick, who was born and bred upon them. A full hundred yards broad it was, sliding on from broad pool to broad shallow, and broad shallow to broad pool, over great fields of shingle, under oak and ash coverts, past low cliffs of sandstone, past green meadows, and fair parks, and a great house of grey stone, and brown moors above, and here and there against the sky the smoking chimney of a colliery. You must look at Bewick to see just what it was like, for he has drawn it a hundred times with the care and the love of a true north countryman; and, even if you do not care about the salmon river, you ought, like all good boys, to know your Bewick.

At least, so old Sir John used to say, and very sensibly he put it too, as he was wont to do—

'If they want to describe a finished young gentleman in France, I hear, they say of him, "Il sait son Rabelais." But if I want to describe one in England, I say, "He knows his Bewick." And I think that is the higher compliment.'

But Tom thought nothing about what the river was like. All his fancy was, to get down to the wide wide sea.

And after a while he came to a place where the river spread out into broad still shallow reaches, so wide that little Tom, as he put his head out of the water, could hardly see across.

And there he stopped. He got a little frightened. 'This must be the sea,' he thought. 'What a wide place it is. If I go on into it I shall surely lose my way, or some strange thing will bite me. I will stop here and look out for the otter, or the eels, or some one to tell me where I shall go.'

So he went back a little way, and crept into a crack of the rock, just where the river opened out into the wide shallows, and watched for some one to tell him his way: but the otter and the eels were gone on miles and miles down the stream.

There he waited, and slept too, for he was quite tired with his night's journey; and, when he woke, the stream was clearing to a beautiful amber hue, though it was still very high. And after a while he saw a sight which made him jump up; for he knew in a moment it was one of the things which he had come to look for.

Such a fish! ten times as big as the biggest trout, and a hundred times as big as Tom, sculling up the stream past him, as easily as Tom had sculled down.

Such a fish! shining silver from head to tail, and here and there a crimson dot; with a grand hooked nose, and grand curling lip, and a grand bright eye, looking round him as proudly as a king, and survey-ing the water right and left as if it all belonged to him. Surely he must be the salmon, the king of all the fish.

Tom was so frightened that he longed to creep into a hole; but he need not have been; for salmon are all true gentlemen, and, like true gentlemen, they look noble and proud enough, and yet, like true gen-tlemen, they never harm or quarrel with any one, but go about their own business, and leave rude fellows to themselves.

The salmon looked him full in the face, and then went on without minding him, with a swish or two of his tail which made the stream boil again. And in a few minutes came another, and then four or five, and so on; and all passed Tom, rushing and plunging up the cataract with strong strokes of their silver tails, now and then leaping clean out of water and up over a rock, shining gloriously for a moment in the bright sun; while Tom was so delighted that he could have watched them all day long.

And at last one came up bigger than all the rest; but he came slowly, and stopped, and looked back, and seemed very anxious and busy. And Tom saw that he was helping another salmon, an especially handsome one, who had not a single spot upon it, but was clothed in pure silver from nose to tail.

'My dear,' said the great fish to his companion, 'you really look dreadfully tired, and you must not over-exert yourself at first. Do rest yourself behind this rock'; and he shoved her gently with his nose, to the rock where Tom sat.

You must know that this was the salmon's wife. For salmon, like other true gentlemen, always choose their lady, and love her, and are true to her, and take care of her, and work for her, and fight for her, as every true gentleman ought; and are not like vulgar chub and roach and pike, who have no high feelings, and take no care of their wives.

Then he saw Tom, and looked at him very fiercely one moment, as if he was going to bite him.

'What do you want here?' he said, very fiercely.

'Oh, don't hurt me!' cried Tom. 'I only want to look at you; you are so handsome.'

'Ah?' said the salmon, very stately but very civilly. 'I really beg your pardon; I see what you are, my little dear. I have met one or two creatures like you before, and found them very agreeable and well-behaved. Indeed, one of them showed me a great kindness lately, which I hope to be able to repay. I hope we shall not be in your way here. As soon as this lady is rested, we shall proceed on our journey.'

What a well-bred old salmon he was!

'So you have seen things like me before?' asked Tom.

'Several times, my dear. Indeed, it was only last night that one at the river's mouth came and warned me and my wife of some new stake-nets* which had got into the stream, I cannot tell how, since last winter, and showed us the way round them, in the most charmingly obliging way.'

'So there are babies in the sea?' cried Tom, and clapped his little hands. 'Then I shall have some one to play with there? How delightful!'

'Were there no babies up this stream?' asked the lady salmon.

'No; and I grew so lonely. I thought I saw three last night: but they were gone in an instant, down to the sea. So I went too; for I had nothing to play with but caddises and dragon-flies and trout.'

'Ugh!' cried the lady, 'what low company!'

'My dear, if he has been in low company, he has certainly not learnt their low manners,' said the salmon.

'No, indeed, poor little dear: but how sad for him to live among such people as caddises, who have actually six legs, the nasty things; and dragon-flies, too! why they are not even good to eat; for I tried them once, and they are all hard and empty; and, as for trout, every one knows what they are.' Whereon she curled up her lip, and looked dreadfully scornful, while her husband curled up his too, till he looked as proud as Alcibiades.*

'Why do you dislike the trout so?' asked Tom.

'My dear, we do not even mention them, if we can help it; for I am sorry to say they are relations of ours who do us no credit. A great many years ago they were just like us: but they were so lazy, and cowardly, and greedy, that instead of going down to the sea every year to see the world and grow strong and fat, they chose to stay and poke about in the little streams and eat worms and grubs: and they are very properly punished for it; for they have grown ugly and brown and spotted and small; and are actually so degraded in their tastes, that they will eat our children.'

'And then they pretend to scrape acquaintance with us again,' said the lady. 'Why, I have actually known one of them propose to a lady salmon, the little impudent little creature.'

'I should hope,' said the gentleman, 'that there are very few ladies of our race who would degrade themselves by listening to such a creature for an instant. If I saw such a thing happen, I should consider it my duty to put them both to death upon the spot.' So the old salmon said, like an old blue-blooded hidalgo* of Spain: and what is more, he would have done it too. For you must know, no enemies are so bitter against each other as those who are of the same race; and a salmon looks on a trout, as some great folks look on some little folks, as something just too much like himself to be tolerated.

# CHAPTER IV

SWEET is the lore which Nature brings;
Our meddling intellect
Mis-shapes the beauteous forms of things;
We murder to dissect.

Enough of science and of art;
Close up these barren leaves;
Come forth, and bring with you a heart
That watches and receives.*

WORDSWORTH.

o the salmon went up, after Tom had warned them of the wicked old otter; and Tom went down, but slowly and cautiously, coasting along the shore. He was many days about it, for it was many miles down to the sea; and perhaps he would never have found his way, if the fairies had not guided him, without his seeing their fair faces, or feeling their gentle hands.

And, as he went, he had a very strange adventure. It was a clear still September night, and the moon shone so brightly down through the water, that he could not sleep, though he shut his eyes as tight as possible. So at last he came up to the top, and sat upon a little point of rock, and looked up at the broad yellow moon, and wondered what she was, and thought that she looked at him. And he watched the moonlight on the rippling river, and the black heads of the firs, and the silver-frosted lawns, and listened to the owl's hoot, and the snipe's bleat, and the fox's bark, and the otter's laugh; and smelt the soft perfume of the birches, and the wafts of heather honey off the grouse-moor far above; and felt very happy, though he could not well tell why. You, of course, would have been very cold sitting there on a September night, without the least bit of clothes on your wet back; but Tom was a water-baby, and therefore felt cold no more than a fish.

Suddenly, he saw a beautiful sight. A bright red light moved along the river side, and threw down into the water a long taproot of flame. Tom, curious little rogue that he was, must needs go and see what it was; so he swam to the shore, and met the light as it stopped over a shallow run at the edge of a low rock.

And there, underneath the light, lay five or six great salmon, looking up at the flame with their great goggle eyes, and wagging their tails, as if they were very much pleased at it.

Tom came to the top, to look at this wonderful light nearer, and made a splash.

And he heard a voice say:—

'There was a fish rose.'

He did not know what the words meant: but he seemed to know the sound of them, and to know the voice which spoke them; and he saw on the bank three great two-legged creatures, one of whom held the light, flaring and sputtering, and another a long pole. And he knew that they were men, and was frightened, and crept into a hole in the rock, from which he could see what went on.

The man with the torch bent down over the water, and looked earnestly in; and then he said:

'Tak that muckle* fellow, lad; he's ower fifteen punds; and haud your hand steady.'

Tom felt that there was some danger coming, and longed to warn the foolish salmon, who kept staring up at the light as if he was bewitched. But, before he could make up his mind, down came the pole through the water; there was a fearful splash and struggle, and Tom saw that the poor salmon was speared right through, and was lifted out of the water.

And then, from behind, there sprung on these three men three other men; and there were shouts, and blows, and words which Tom recollected to have heard before; and he shuddered and turned sick at them now, for he felt somehow that they were strange, and ugly, and wrong, and horrible. And it all began to come back to him. They were men; and they were fighting; savage, desperate, up-and-down fighting, such as Tom had seen too many times before.

And he stopped his little ears, and longed to swim away; and was very glad that he was a water-baby, and had nothing to do any more with horrid dirty men, with foul clothes on their backs, and foul words on their lips: but he dared not stir out of his hole; while the rock shook over his head with the trampling and struggling of the keepers and the poachers.

All of a sudden there was a tremendous splash, and a frightful flash, and a hissing, and all was still.

For into the water, close to Tom, fell one of the men; he who held the light in his hand. Into the swift river he sank, and rolled over and over in the current. Tom heard the men above run along, seemingly looking for him: but he drifted down into the deep hole below, and there lay quite still, and they could not find him.

Tom waited a long time, till all was quiet; and then he peeped out, and saw the man lying. At last he screwed up his courage, and swam down to him. 'Perhaps', he thought, 'the water has made him fall asleep, as it did me.'

Then he went nearer. He grew more and more curious, he could not tell why. He must go and look at him. He would go very quietly, of course; so he swam round and round him, closer and closer; and, as he did not stir, at last he came quite close and looked him in the face.

The moon shone so bright that Tom could see every feature; and, as he saw, he recollected, bit by bit. It was his old master, Grimes.

Tom turned tail, and swam away as fast as he could.

'Oh dear me!' he thought, 'now he will turn into a water-baby. What a nasty troublesome one he will be! And perhaps he will find me out, and beat me again.'

So he went up the river again a little way, and lay there the rest of the night under an alder root; but, when morning came, he longed to go down again to the big pool, and see whether Mr Grimes had turned into a water-baby yet.

So he went very carefully, peeping round all the rocks, and hiding under all the roots. Mr Grimes lay there still; he had not turned into a water-baby. In the afternoon Tom went back again. He could not rest till he had found out what had become of Mr Grimes. But this time Mr Grimes was gone; and Tom made up his mind that he was turned into a water-baby.

He might have made himself easy, poor little man; Mr Grimes did not turn into a water-baby, or anything like one at all. But he did not make himself easy; and a long time he was fearful lest he should meet Grimes suddenly in some deep pool. He could not know that the fairies had carried him away, and put him, where they put everything which falls into the water, exactly where it ought to be. But, do you know, what had happened to Mr Grimes had such an effect on him, that he never poached salmon any more. And it is quite certain that, when a man becomes a confirmed poacher, the only way to cure him is to put him under water for twenty-four hours, like Grimes. So, when you grow to be a big man, do you behave as all honest fellows should; and never touch a fish or a head of game which belongs to another man without his express leave; and then people will call you a gentleman, and treat you like one; and perhaps give you good sport: instead of hitting you into the river, or calling you a poaching snob.*

Then Tom went on down, for he was afraid of staying near Grimes; and as he went, all the vale looked sad. The red and yellow leaves showered down into the river; the flies and beetles were all dead and gone; the chill autumn fog lay low upon the hills, and sometimes spread itself so thickly on the river, that he could not see his way. But he felt his way instead, following the flow of the stream, day after day, past great bridges, past boats and barges, past the great town, with its wharfs, and mills, and tall smoking chimneys, and ships which rode at anchor in the stream; and now and then he ran against their hawsers, and wondered what they were, and peeped out, and saw the sailors lounging on board, smoking their pipes; and ducked under again, for he was terribly afraid of being caught by man and turned into a chimney-sweep once more. He did not know that the fairies were close to him always, shutting the sailors' eyes lest they should see him, and turning him aside from millraces,* and sewer-mouths, and all foul and dangerous things. Poor little fellow, it was a dreary journey for him; and more than once he longed to be back in Vendale, playing with the trout in the bright summer sun.

But it could not be. What has been once can never come over again. And people can be little babies, even water-babies, only once in their lives.

Besides, people who make up their minds to go and see the world, as Tom did, must needs find it a weary journey. Lucky for them if they do not lose heart and stop halfway, instead of going on bravely to the end as Tom did. For then they will remain neither boys nor men, neither fish, flesh, nor good red herring; having learnt a great deal too much, and yet not enough; and sown their wild oats, without having the advantage of reaping them.

But Tom was always a brave, determined little English bulldog, who never knew when he was beaten; and on and on he held, till he saw a long way off the red buoy through the fog. And then he found, to his surprise, the stream turned round, and running up inland.

It was the tide, of course: but Tom knew nothing of the tide. He only knew that in a minute more the water, which had been fresh, turned salt all round him. And then there came a change over him. He felt as strong, and light, and fresh, as if his veins had run champagne; and gave, he did not know why, three skips out of the water, a yard high, and head over heels, just as the salmon do when they first touch the noble rich salt water, which, as some wise men tell us,* is the mother of all living things.

He did not care now for the tide being against him. The red buoy was in sight, dancing in the open sea; and to the buoy he would go, and to it he went. He passed great shoals of bass and mullet, leaping and rushing in after the shrimps, but he never heeded them, or they him; and once he passed a great black shining seal, who was coming in after the mullet. The seal put his head and shoulders out of water, and stared at him, looking exactly like a fat old greasy negro with a grey pate. And Tom, instead of being frightened, said, 'How d'ye do, sir; what a beautiful place the sea is!' And the old seal, instead of trying to bite him, looked at him with his soft sleepy winking eyes, and said, 'Good tide to you, my little man; are you looking for your brothers and sisters? I passed them all at play outside.'

'Oh, then,' said Tom, 'I shall have playfellows at last!' and he swam on to the buoy, and got upon it (for he was quite out of breath) and sat there, and looked round for water-babies: but there were none to be seen.

The sea-breeze came in freshly with the tide, and blew the fog away; and the little waves danced for joy around the buoy, and the old buoy danced with them. The shadows of the clouds ran races over the bright blue bay, and yet never caught each other up; and the breakers plunged merrily upon the wide white sands, and jumped up over the rocks, to see what the green fields inside were like, and tumbled down and broke themselves all to pieces, and never minded it a bit, but mended themselves and jumped up again. And the terns hovered over Tom like huge white dragon-flies with black heads, and the gulls laughed like girls at play, and the sea-pies,* with their red bills and legs, flew to and fro from shore to shore, and whistled sweet and wild. And Tom looked and looked, and listened; and he would have been very happy, if he could only have seen the water-babies. Then, when the tide turned, he left the buoy, and swam round and round in search of them: but in vain. Sometimes he thought he heard them laughing: but it was only the laughter of the ripples. And sometimes he thought he saw them at the bottom: but it was only white and pink shells. And once he was sure he had found one, for he saw two bright eyes peeping out of the sand. So he dived down, and began scraping the sand away, and cried, 'Don't hide; I do want some one to play with so much!' And out jumped a great turbot, with his ugly eyes and mouth all awry, and flopped away along the bottom, knocking poor Tom over. And he sat down at the bottom of the sea, and cried salt tears from sheer disappointment.

To have come all this way, and faced so many dangers, and yet to find no water-babies! How hard! Well, it did seem hard: but people, even little babies, cannot have all they want without waiting for it, and working for it too, my little man, as you will find out some day.

And Tom sat upon the buoy long days, long weeks, looking out to sea, and wondering when the water-babies would come back; and yet they never came.

Then he began to ask all the strange things which came in out of the sea if they had seen any; and some said 'Yes,' and some said nothing at all.

He asked the bass and the pollock; but they were so greedy after the shrimps that they did not care to answer him a word.

Then there came in a whole fleet of purple sea-snails, floating along each on a sponge full of foam, and Tom said, 'Where do you come from, you pretty creatures? and have you seen the water-babies?'

And the sea-snails answered, 'Whence we come we know not; and whither we are going, who can tell? We float out our little life in the mid-ocean, with the warm sunshine above our heads, and the warm gulf stream below; and that is enough for us. Yes, perhaps we have seen the water-babies. We have seen many strange things as we sailed along.' And they floated away, the happy stupid things, and all went ashore upon the sands.

Then there came in a great lazy sunfish,* as big as a fat pig cut in half; and he seemed to have been cut in half too, and squeezed in a clothes-press till he was flat; but to all his big body and big fins he had only a little rabbit's mouth, no bigger than Tom's; and, when Tom questioned him, he answered in a little squeaky, feeble voice:

'I'm sure I don't know, I've lost my way. I meant to go to the Chesapeake,* and I'm afraid I've got wrong, somehow. Dear me! it was all by following that pleasant warm water. I'm sure I've lost my way.'

And, when Tom asked him again, he could only answer, 'I've lost my way. Don't talk to me, I want to think.'

But, like a good many other people, the more he tried to think the less he could think; and Tom saw him blundering about all day, till the coast-guardsmen saw his big fin above the water, and rowed out, and struck a boat-hook into him, and took him away. They took him up to the town and showed him for a penny a head, and made a good day's work of it. But of course Tom did not know that.

Then there came by a shoal of porpoises, rolling as they went— papas, and mammas, and little children—and all quite smooth and shiny, because the fairies French-polish them every morning; and they sighed so softly as they came by, that Tom took courage to speak to them: but all they answered was, 'Hush, hush, hush'; for that was all they had learnt to say.

And then there came a shoal of basking sharks, some of them as long as a boat, and Tom was frightened at them. But they were very lazy, good-natured fellows, not greedy tyrants, like white sharks and blue sharks and ground sharks and hammer-heads, who eat men, or saw-fish and threshers* and ice-sharks, who hunt the poor old whales. They came and rubbed their great sides against the buoy, and lay basking in the sun with their backfins out of water; and winked at Tom: but he never could get them to speak. They had eaten so many herrings that they were quite stupid; and Tom was glad when a collier brig* came by, and frightened them all away; for they did smell most horribly, certainly, and he had to hold his nose tight as long as they were there.

And then there came by a beautiful creature, like a ribbon of pure silver* with a sharp head and very long teeth: but it seemed very sick and sad. Sometimes it rolled helpless on its side; and then it dashed away glittering like white fire; and then it lay sick again and motionless.

'Where do you come from?' asked Tom. 'And why are you so sick and sad?'

'I come from the warm Carolinas, and the sand-banks fringed with pines; where the great owl-rays* leap and flap, like giant bats, upon the tide. But I wandered north and north, upon the treacherous warm gulf stream, till I met with the cold icebergs, afloat in the mid-ocean. So I got tangled among the icebergs, and chilled with their frozen breath. But the water-babies helped me from among them, and set me free again. And now I am mending every day; but I am very sick and sad; and perhaps I shall never get home again to play with the owl-rays any more.'

'Oh!' cried Tom. 'And you have seen water-babies? Have you seen any near here?'

'Yes; they helped me again last night, or I should have been eaten by a great black porpoise.'

How vexatious! The water-babies close to him, and yet he could not find one.

And then he left the buoy, and used to go along the sands and round the rocks, and come out in the night—like the forsaken Merman* in Mr Arnold's beautiful, beautiful poem, which you

Water-Babies

must learn by heart some day—and sit upon a point of rock, among the shining sea-weeds, in the low October tides, and cry and call for the water-babies: but he never heard a voice call in return. And, at last, with his fretting and crying, he grew quite lean and thin.

But one day among the rocks he found a playfellow. It was not a water-baby, alas! but it was a lobster; and a very distinguished lobster he was; for he had live barnacles on his claws, which is a great mark of distinction in lobsterdom, and no more to be bought for money than a good conscience or the Victoria Cross.*

Tom had never seen a lobster before; and he was mightily taken with this one; for he thought him the most curious, odd, ridiculous creature he had ever seen; and there he was not far wrong; for all the ingenious men, and all the scientific men, and all the fanciful men, in the world, with all the old German bogy-painters* into the bargain, could never invent, if all their wits were boiled into one, anything so curious, and so ridiculous, as a lobster.

He had one claw knobbed and the other jagged; and Tom delighted in watching him hold on to the sea-weed with his knobbed claw, while he cut up salads with his jagged one, and then put them into his mouth, after smelling at them, like a monkey. And always the little barnacles threw out their casting nets and swept the water, and came in for their share of whatever there was for dinner.

But Tom was most astonished to see how he fired himself off—snap! like the leap-frogs* which you make out of a goose's breast-bone. Certainly he took the most wonderful shots, and backwards, too. For, if he wanted to go into a narrow crack ten yards off, what do you think he did? If he had gone in head foremost, of course he could not have turned round. So he used to turn his tail to it, and lay his long horns, which carry his sixth sense in their tips (and nobody knows what that sixth sense is), straight down his back to guide him, and twist his eyes back till they almost came out of their sockets, and then make ready, present, fire, snap!—and away he went, pop into the hole; and peeped out and twiddled his whiskers, as much as to say, 'You couldn't do that.'

Tom asked him about water-babies. 'Yes,' he said. He had seen them often. But he did not think much of them. They were meddlesome little creatures, that went about helping fish and shells which got into scrapes. Well, for his part, he should be ashamed to be helped by little soft creatures that had not even a shell on their backs. He had lived quite long enough in the world to take care of himself.

He was a conceited fellow, the old lobster, and not very civil to Tom; and you will hear how he had to alter his mind before he was done, as conceited people generally have. But he was so funny, and Tom so lonely, that he could not quarrel with him; and they used to sit in holes in the rocks, and chat for hours.

And about this time there happened to Tom a very strange and important adventure—so important, indeed, that he was very near never finding the water-babies at all; and I am sure you would have been sorry for that.

I hope that you have not forgotten the little white lady all this while. At least, here she comes, looking like a clean white good little darling, as she always was, and always will be. For it befel in the pleasant short December days, when the wind always blows from the south-west, till Old Father Christmas comes and spreads the great white table-cloth, ready for little boys and girls to give the birds their Christmas dinner of crumbs—it befel (to go on) in the pleasant December days, that Sir John was so busy hunting that nobody at home could get a word out of him. Four days a week he hunted, and very good sport he had; and the other two he went to the bench and the board of guardians,* and very good justice he did; and, when he got home in time, he dined at five; for he hated this absurd new fashion of dining at eight in the hunting season, which forces a man to make interest with the footman for cold beef and beer as soon as he comes in, and so spoil his appetite, and then sleep in an arm-chair in his bed-room, all stiff and tired, for two or three hours before he can get his dinner like a gentleman. And do you be like Sir John, my dear little man, when you are your own master; and, if you want either to read hard or ride hard, stick to the good old Cambridge hours of breakfast at eight and dinner at five, by which you may get two days' work out of one. But, of course, if you find a fox at three in the afternoon and run him till dark, and leave off twenty miles from home, why you must wait for your dinner till you can get it, as better men than you have done. Only see that, if you go hungry, your horse does not: but give him his warm gruel and beer, and take him gently home, remembering that good horses don't grow on the hedge like blackberries.

It befel (to go on a second time) that Sir John, hunting all day and dining at five, fell asleep every evening, and snored so terribly that all the windows in Harthover shook, and the soot fell down the chimneys. Whereon My Lady, being no more able to get conversation out of him than a song out of a dead nightingale, determined to go off and leave him, and the doctor, and Captain Swinger the agent, to snore in concert every evening to their hearts' content. So she started for the sea-side with all the children, in order to put herself and them into condition by mild applications of iodine. She might as well have stayed at home and used Parry's liquid horse-blister,* for there was plenty of it in the stables; and then she would have saved her money, and saved the chance, also, of making all the children ill instead of well (as hundreds are made), by taking them to some nasty smelling undrained lodging, and then wondering how they caught scarlatina and diphtheria: but people won't be wise enough to understand that till they are all dead of bad smells,* and then it will be too late: besides, you see, Sir John did certainly snore very loud.

But where she went to nobody must know, for fear young ladies should begin to fancy that there are water-babies there; and so hunt and howk after them (besides raising the price of lodgings), and keep them in aquariums, as the ladies at Pompeii (as you may see by the paintings) used to keep Cupids in cages. But nobody ever heard that they starved the Cupids, or let them die of dirt and neglect, as English young ladies do by the poor sea-beasts. So nobody must know where My Lady went. Letting water-babies die is as bad as taking singing-birds' eggs; for, though there are thousands, ay, millions, of both of them in the world, yet there is not one too many.

Now it befel that, on the very shore, and over the very rocks, where Tom was sitting with his friend the lobster, there walked one day the little white lady, Ellie herself, and with her a very wise man indeed—Professor Ptthmllnsprts.*

His mother was a Dutchwoman, and therefore he was born at

Curacao (of course you have learnt your geography, and therefore
know why); and his father a Pole, and therefore he was brought up
at Petropaulowski (of course you have learnt your modern politics,
and therefore know why):* but for all that he was as thorough an
Englishman as ever coveted his neighbour's goods. And his name, as
I said, was Professor Ptthmllnsprts, which is a very ancient and noble
Polish name.

He was, as I said, a very great naturalist, and chief professor of
Necrobioneopalæonthydrochthonanthropopithekology in the new
university which the king of the Cannibal Islands had founded; and,
being a member of the Acclimatisation Society,* he had come here to
collect all the nasty things which he could find on the coast of England,
and turn them loose round the Cannibal Islands, because they had
not nasty things enough there to eat what they left.

But he was a very worthy kind good-natured little old gentleman;
and very fond of children (for he was not the least a cannibal himself); and very good to all the world as long as it was good to him.
Only one fault he had, which cock-robins have likewise, as you may
see if you will look out of the nursery-window—that, when any one
else found a curious worm, he would hop round them, and peck
them, and set up his tail, and bristle up his feathers, just as a cock-
robin would; and declare that he found the worm first; and that it was
his worm: and, if not, that then it was not a worm at all.

He had met Sir John at Scarborough, or Fleetwood, or somewhere
or other (if you don't care where, nobody else does), and had made
acquaintance with him, and become very fond of his children. Now,
Sir John knew nothing about sea-cockyolybirds,* and cared less, provided the fishmonger sent him good fish for dinner; and My Lady
knew as little: but she thought it proper that the children should
know something. For in the stupid old times, you must understand,
children were taught to know one thing, and to know it well: but in
these enlightened new times they are taught to know a little about
everything, and to know it all ill; which is a great deal pleasanter and
easier, and therefore quite right.

So Ellie and he were walking on the rocks, and he was showing her
about one in ten thousand of all the beautiful and curious things

which are to be seen there. But little Ellie was not satisfied with them
at all. She liked much better to play with live children, or even with
dolls, which she could pretend were alive; and at last she said honestly, 'I don't care about all these things, because they can't play with
me, or talk to me. If there were little children now in the water, as
there used to be, and I could see them, I should like that.'

'Children in the water, you strange little duck?' said the professor.

'Yes,' said Ellie. 'I know there used to be children in the water, and
mermaids too, and mermen. I saw them all in a picture at home, of a
beautiful lady sailing in a car drawn by dolphins, and babies flying
round her, and one sitting in her lap; and the mermaids swimming
and playing, and the mermen trumpeting on conch-shells; and it is
called "The Triumph of Galatea";* and there is a burning mountain
in the picture behind. It hangs on the great staircase, and I have
looked at it ever since I was a baby, and dreamt about it a hundred
times; and it is so beautiful, that it must be true.'

Ah, you dear little Ellie, fresh out of heaven! when will people
understand that one of the deepest and wisest speeches which can
come out of a human mouth is that—'It is so beautiful that it must
be true.'

Not till they give up believing that Mr John Locke (good man and
honest though he was) was the wisest man that ever lived on earth:
and recollect that a wiser man than he lived long before him; and that
his name was Plato* the son of Ariston.

But the professor was not in the least of that opinion. He held very
strange theories about a good many things. He had even got up once
at the British Association, and declared that apes had hippopotamus
majors* in their brains just as men have. Which was a shocking thing
to say; for, if it were so, what would become of the faith, hope, and
charity* of immortal millions? You may think that there are other
more important differences between you and an ape, such as being
able to speak, and make machines, and know right from wrong, and
say your prayers, and other little matters of that kind: but that is a
child's fancy, my dear. Nothing is to be depended on but the great
hippopotamus test. If you have a hippopotamus major in your brain,
you are no ape, though you had four hands, no feet, and were more

apish than the apes of all aperies. But, if a hippopotamus major is ever discovered in one single ape's brain, nothing will save your great-great-great-great-great-great-great-great-great-great-great-greater-greatest-grandmother from having been an ape too. No, my dear little man; always remember that the one true, certain, final, and all-important difference between you and an ape is, that you have a hippopotamus major in your brain, and it has none; and that, therefore, to discover one in its brain will be a very wrong and dangerous thing, at which every one will be very much shocked, as we may suppose they were at the professor.—Though really, after all, it don't much matter: because—as Lord Dundreary* and others would put it—nobody but men have hippopotamuses in their brains; so, if a hippopotamus was discovered in an ape's brain, why it would not be one, you know, but something else.

But the professor had gone, I am sorry to say, even further than that; for he had read at the British Association at Melbourne,* Australia, in the year 1999, a paper, in which he assured every one who found himself the better or wiser for the news, that there were not, never had been, and could not be, any rational or half-rational beings except men, anywhere, anywhen, or anyhow; that nymphs, satyrs, fauns, inui, dwarfs, trolls, elves, gnomes, fairies, brownies, nixes, wilis, kobolds, leprechaunes, cluricaunes, banshees, will-o'-the-wisps, follets, lutins, magots, goblins, afrits, marids, jinns, ghouls, peris, deevs, angels, archangels, imps, bogies, or worse,* were nothing at all, and pure bosh and wind.* And he had to get up very early in the morning to prove that, and to eat his breakfast overnight: but he did it, at least to his own satisfaction. Whereon a certain great divine, and a very clever divine was he, called him a regular Sadducee; and probably he was quite right. Whereon the professor, in return, called him a regular Pharisee;* and probably he was quite right too. But they did not quarrel in the least; for, when men are men of the world, hard words run off them like water off a duck's back. So the professor and the divine met at dinner that evening, and sat together on the sofa afterwards for an hour, and talked over the state of female labour on the antarctic continent (for nobody talks shop after his claret), and each vowed that the other was the best company he ever met in his life. What an advantage it is to be men of the world!

From all which you may guess that the professor was not the least of little Ellie's opinion. So he gave her a succinct compendium of his famous paper at the British Association, in a form suited for the youthful mind. But, as we have gone over his arguments against water-babies once already, which is once too often, we will not repeat them here.

Now little Ellie was, I suppose, a stupid little girl; for, instead of being convinced by Professor Ptthmllnsprts' arguments, she only asked the same question over again.

'But why are there not water-babies?'

I trust and hope that it was because the professor trod at that moment on the edge of a very sharp mussel, and hurt one of his corns sadly, that he answered quite sharply, forgetting that he was a scientific man, and therefore ought to have known that he couldn't know; and that he was a logician, and therefore ought to have known that he could not prove an universal negative—I say, I trust and hope it was because the mussel hurt his corn, that the professor answered quite sharply—

'Because there ain't.'

Which was not even good English, my dear little boy; for, as you must know from Aunt Agitate's Arguments, the professor ought to have said, if he was so angry as to say anything of the kind—Because there are not: or are none: or are none of them; or (if he had been reading Aunt Agitate too), because they do not exist.

And he groped with his net under the weeds so violently, that, as it befel, he caught poor little Tom.

He felt the net very heavy; and lifted it out quickly, with Tom all entangled in the meshes.

'Dear me!' he cried. 'What a large pink Holothurian; with hands, too! It must be connected with Synapta.'

And he took him out.

'It has actually eyes!' he cried. 'Why, it must be a Cephalopod!* This is most extraordinary!'

'No, I ain't!' cried Tom, as loud as he could; for he did not like to be called bad names.

'It is a water-baby!' cried Ellie; and of course it was.

'Water-fiddlesticks, my dear!' said the professor; and he turned away sharply.

There was no denying it. It was a water-baby: and he had said a moment ago that there were none. What was he to do?

He would have liked, of course, to have taken Tom home in a bucket. He would not have put him in spirits. Of course not. He would have kept him alive, and petted him (for he was a very kind old gentleman), and written a book about him, and given him two long names, of which the first would have said a little about Tom, and the second all about himself; for of course he would have called him Hydrotecnon Ptthmllnsprtsianum, or some other long name like that; for they are forced to call everything by long names now, because they have used up all the short ones, ever since they took to making nine species out of one. But—what would all the learned men say to him after his speech at the British Association? And what would Ellie say, after what he had just told her?

There was a wise old heathen* once, who said, 'Maxima debetur pueris reverentia'—The greatest reverence is due to children; that is, that grown people should never say or do anything wrong before children, lest they should set them a bad example.—Cousin Cramchild says it means, 'The greatest respectfulness is expected from little boys.' But he was raised in a country where little boys are not expected to be respectful, because all of them are as good as the President:— Well, every one knows his own concerns best; so perhaps they are. But poor Cousin Cramchild, to do him justice, not being of that opinion, and having a moral mission, and being no scholar to speak of, and hard up for an authority—why, it was a very great temptation for him. But some people, and I am afraid the professor was one of them, interpret that in a more strange, curious, one-sided, left-handed, topsy-turvy, inside-out, behind-before fashion, than even Cousin Cramchild; for they make it mean, that you must show your respect for children, by never confessing yourself in the wrong to them, even if you know that you are so, lest they should lose confidence in their elders.

Now, if the professor had said to Ellie, 'Yes, my darling, it is a water-baby, and a very wonderful thing it is; and it shows how little I know of the wonders of nature, in spite of forty years' honest labour. I was just telling you that there could be no such creatures: and, behold! here is one come to confound my conceit, and show me that Nature can do, and has done, beyond all that man's poor fancy can imagine. So, let us thank the Maker, and Inspirer, and Lord of Nature for all His wonderful and glorious works, and try and find out something about this one':—I think that, if the professor had said that, little Ellie would have believed him more firmly, and respected him more deeply, and loved him better, than ever she had done before. But he was of a different opinion. He hesitated a moment. He longed to keep Tom, and yet he half wished he never had caught him; and, at last, he quite longed to get rid of him. So he turned away, and poked Tom with his finger, for want of anything better to do; and said carelessly, 'My dear little maid, you must have dreamt of water-babies last night, your head is so full of them.'

Now Tom had been in the most horrible and unspeakable fright all the while; and had kept as quiet as he could, though he was called a Holothurian and a Cephalopod; for it was fixed in his little head that if a man with clothes on caught him, he might put clothes on him too, and make a dirty black chimney-sweep of him again. But when the professor poked him, it was more than he could bear; and, between fright and rage, he turned to bay as valiantly as a mouse in a corner, and bit the professor's finger till it bled.

'Oh! ah! yah!' cried he; and glad of an excuse to be rid of Tom, dropped him on to the sea-weed, and thence he dived into the water, and was gone in a moment.

'But it was a water-baby, and I heard it speak!' cried Ellie. 'Ah, it is gone!' And she jumped down off the rock to try and catch Tom before he slipt into the sea.

Too late! and what was worse, as she sprang down, she slipped, and fell some six feet, with her head on a sharp rock, and lay quite still.

The professor picked her up, and tried to waken her, and called to her, and cried over her, for he loved her very much: but she would not waken at all. So he took her up in his arms, and carried her to her governess, and they all went home; and little Ellie was put to bed, and lay there quite still; only now and then she woke up, and called out about the water-baby: but no one knew what she meant, and the professor did not tell, for he was ashamed to tell.

And, after a week, one moonlight night, the fairies came flying in at the window, and brought her such a pretty pair of wings, that she could not help putting them on; and she flew with them out of the window, and over the land, and over the sea, and up through the clouds, and nobody heard or saw anything of her for a very long while.

And this is why they say that no one has ever yet seen a water-baby. For my part, I believe that the naturalists get dozens of them when they are out dredging: but they say nothing about them, and throw them overboard again, for fear of spoiling their theories. But, you see the professor was found out, as every one is in due time. A very terrible old fairy* found the professor out; she felt his bumps, and cast his nativity, and took the lunars of him carefully inside and out; and so she knew what he would do as well as if she had seen it in a print book, as they say in the dear old west country; and he did it; and so he was found out beforehand, as everybody always is; and the old fairy will find out the naturalists some day, and put them in the Times; and then on whose side will the laugh be?

So the old fairy took him in hand very severely there and then. But she says she is always most severe with the best people, because there is most chance of curing them, and therefore they are the patients who pay her best; for she has to work on the same salary as the Emperor of China's physicians (it is a pity that all do not), no cure, no pay.

So she took the poor professor in hand: and because he was not content with things as they are, she filled his head with things as they are not, to try if he would like them better; and because he did not choose to believe in a water-baby when he saw it, she made him believe in worse things than water-babies—in unicorns, firedrakes, manticoras, basilisks, amphisbœnas, griffins, phœnixes, rocs, orcs, dogheaded men, three-headed dogs, three-bodied geryons,* and other pleasant creatures, which folks think never existed yet, and which folks hope never will exist, though they know nothing about the matter, and never will; and these creatures so upset, terrified, flustered, aggravated, confused, astounded, horrified, and totally flabbergasted the poor professor, that the doctors said that he was out of his wits for three months; and, perhaps, they were right, as they are now and then.

So all the doctors in the county were called in, to make a report on his case; and of course every one of them flatly contradicted the other: else what use is there in being men of science? But at last the majority agreed on a report, in the true medical language, one half bad Latin, the other half worse Greek, and the rest what might have been English, if they had only learnt to write it. And this is the beginning thereof—*

'The subanhypaposupernal anastomoses of peritomic diacellurite in the encephalo digital region of the distinguished individual of whose symptomatic phænomena we had the melancholy honour (subsequently to a preliminary diagnostic inspection) of making an inspectorial diagnosis, presenting the interexclusively quadrilateral and anti-nomian that diathesis known as Bumpsterhausen's blue follicles, we proceeded'—

But what they proceeded to do my lady never knew; for she was so frightened at the long words that she ran for her life, and locked herself into her bedroom, for fear of being squashed by the words and strangled by the sentence. A boa constrictor, she said, was bad company enough: but what was a boa constrictor made of paving-stones?

'It was quite shocking! What can they think is the matter with him?' said she to the old nurse.

'That his wit's just addled; may be wi' unbelief and heathenry,' quoth she.

'Then why can't they say so?'

And the heaven, and the sea, and the rocks, and the vales re-echoed—'Why indeed?' But the doctors never heard them.

So she made Sir John write to the Times to command the Chancellor of the Exchequer for the time being to put a tax on long words;—

A light tax on words over three syllables, which are necessary evils, like rats: but like them, must be kept down judiciously.

A heavy tax on words over four syllables, as heterodoxy, spontaneity, spiritualism, spuriosity, etc.

And on words over five syllables (of which I hope no one will wish to see any examples), a totally prohibitory tax.

And a similar prohibitory tax on words derived from three or more languages at once; words derived from two languages having become so common, that there was no more hope of rooting out them than of rooting out peth-winds.*

The Chancellor of the Exchequer, being a scholar and a man of sense, jumped at the notion; for he saw in it the one and only plan for abolishing Schedule D:* but when he brought in his bill, most of the Irish members, and (I am sorry to say) some of the Scotch likewise, opposed it most strongly, on the ground that in a free country no man was bound either to understand himself or to let others understand him. So the bill fell through on the first reading; and the Chancellor, being a philosopher, comforted himself with the thought, that it was not the first time that a woman had hit off a grand idea, and the men turned up their stupid noses thereat.

Now the doctors had it all their own way; and to work they went in earnest, and they gave the poor Professor divers and sundry medicines, as prescribed by the ancients and moderns, from Hippocrates* to Feuchtersleben,* as below, viz.:—

1. Hellebore,* to wit—

   Hellebore of Æta.

   Hellebore of Galatia.

   Hellebore of Sicily.

   And all other Hellebores, after the method of the Helleborizing Helleborists of the Helleboric era. But that would not do. Bumpsterhausen's blue follicles would not stir an inch out of his encephalo digital region.

2. Trying to find out what was the matter with him; after the method of—

   Hippocrates.

   Aretæus.*

   Celsus.*

Cœlius Aurelianus,*

And Galen:* but they found that a great deal too much trouble, as
most people have since; and so had recourse to—

3. Borage.*

Cauteries.*

Boring a hole in his head to let out fumes, which (says Gordonius*)
'will, without doubt, do much good'. But it didn't.

Bezoar stone.*

Diamargaritum.*

A ram's brain boiled in spice.

Oil of wormwood.

Water of Nile.

Capers.

Good wine (but there was none to be got).

The water of a smith's forge.

Hops.

Ambergris.*

Mandrake pillows.

Dormouse' fat.*

Hares' ears.

Starvation.

Camphor.

Salts and Senna.

Musk.

Opium.

Strait-waistcoats.

Bullyings.

Bumpings.

Blisterings.

Bleedings.

Bucketings with cold water.

Knockings down.

Kneeling on his chest till they broke it in, etc. etc.; after the
mediæval or monkish method: but that would not do. Bumpsterhausen's blue follicles stuck there still.

Then—

4. Coaxing.

Kissing.

Champagne and turtle.

Red herrings and soda water.

Good advice.

Gardening.

Croquet.*

Musical soirées.

Aunt Sally.*

Mild tobacco.

The Saturday Review.*

A carriage with outriders,* etc. etc. after the modern method. But that would not do.

And if he had but been a convict lunatic, and had shot at the Queen, killed all his creditors to avoid paying them, or indulged in any other little amiable eccentricity of that kind, they would have given him in addition—

The healthiest situation in England, on Easthampstead Plain.*

Free run of Windsor Forest.

the Times every morning.

A double-barrelled gun and pointers, and leave to shoot three Wellington College* boys a week (not more) in case black game* were scarce.

But as he was neither mad enough nor bad enough to be allowed such luxuries, they grew desperate, and fell into bad ways, viz.:—

5. Suffumigations* of sulphur.

Heerwiggius* his 'Incomparable drink for madmen': only they could not find out what it was.

Suffumigation of the liver of the fish * * * only they had forgotten its name, so Dr Gray* could not well procure them a specimen.

Metallic tractors.*

Holloway's Ointment.*

Electro-biology.*

Valentine Greatrakes* his Stroking Cure.

Spirit-rapping.

Holloway's Pills.*

Table-turning.

Morrison's Pills.

Homœopathy.

Parr's Life Pills.*

Mesmerism.*

Pure Bosh.

Exorcisms, for which they read Malleus Maleficarum, Nideri Formicarium, Delrio, Wierus,* etc., but could not get one that mentioned water-babies.

Hydropathy.*

Madame Rachel's Elixir of Youth.*

The Poughkeepsie Seer his Prophecies.*

The distilled liquor of addle eggs.*

Pyropathy,* as successfully employed by the old inquisitors to cure the malady of thought, and now by the Persian Mollahs to cure that of rheumatism.

Geopathy, or burying him.

Atmopathy, or steaming him.

Sympathy, after the method of Basil Valentine* his Triumph of Antimony, and Kenelm Digby his Weapon-salve,* which some call a hair of the dog that bit him.

Hermopathy, or pouring mercury down his throat, to move the animal spirits.

Meteoropathy, or going up to the moon to look for his lost wits, as Ruggiero* did for Orlando Furioso's: only, having no hippogriff,* they were forced to use a balloon; and, falling into the North Sea, were picked up by a Yarmouth herring-boat, and came home much the wiser, and all over scales.

Antipathy, or using him like 'a man and a brother'.*

Apathy, or doing nothing at all.

With all other ipathies and opathies which Noodle has invented, and Foodle* tried, since black-fellows chipped flints at Abbeville*—which is a considerable time ago, to judge by the Great Exhibition.

But nothing would do; for he screamed and cried all day for a water-baby, to come and drive away the monsters; and of course they did not try to find one, because they did not believe in them, and were thinking of nothing but Bumpsterhausen's blue follicles; having, as usual, set the cart before the horse, and taken the effect for the cause.

So they were forced at last to let the poor professor ease his mind by writing a great book, exactly contrary to all his old opinions; in which he proved that the moon was made of green cheese, and that all the mites in it (which you may see sometimes quite plain through a telescope, if you will only keep the lens dirty enough, as Mr Weekes* kept his voltaic battery) are nothing in the world but little babies, who are hatching and swarming up there in millions, ready to come down into this world whenever children want a new little brother or sister.

Which must be a mistake, for this one reason: that, there being no atmosphere round the moon (though some one or other says there is, at least on the other side, and that he has been round at the back of it to see, and found that the moon was just the shape of a Bath bun, and so wet that the man in the moon went about on Midsummer-day in Macintoshes and Cording's boots,* spearing eels and sneezing); that therefore, I say, there being no atmosphere, there can be no evaporation; and, therefore, the dew-point can never fall below 71.5 below zero of Fahrenheit; and, therefore, it cannot be cold enough there about four o'clock in the morning to condense the babies' mesenteric apophthegms into their left ventricles;* and, therefore, they can never catch the hooping-cough; and if they do not have hooping-cough, they cannot be babies at all; and, therefore, there are no babies in the moon.—Q.E.D.

Which may seem a roundabout reason; and so, perhaps, it is: but you will have heard worse ones in your time, and from better men than you are.

But one thing is certain; that, when the good old doctor got his book written, he felt considerably relieved from Bumpsterhausen's blue follicles, and a few things infinitely worse; to wit, from pride and vain-glory, and from blindness and hardness of heart; which are the true causes of Bumpsterhausen's blue follicles, and of a good many other ugly things beside. Whereon the foul flood-water in his brains ran down, and cleared to a fine coffee colour, such as fish like to rise in, till very fine clean fresh-run fish did begin to rise in his brains; and he caught two or three of them (which is exceedingly fine sport, for brain rivers), and anatomized them carefully, and never mentioned what he found out from them, except to little children; and became ever after a sadder and a wiser man; which is a very good thing to become, my dear little boy, even though one has to pay a heavy price for the blessing.

# CHAPTER V

STERN Lawgiver! yet thou dost wear
The Godhead's most benignant grace;
Nor know we anything so fair
As is the smile upon thy face:
Flowers laugh before thee on their beds
And fragrance in thy footing treads;
Thou dost preserve the stars from wrong;
And the most ancient heavens, through Thee,
    are fresh and strong.

WORDSWORTH.—*Ode to Duty.**

UT what became of little Tom?

He slipt away off the rocks into the water, as I said before. But he could not help thinking of little Ellie. He did not remember who she was; but he knew that she was a little girl, though she was a hundred times as big as he. That is not surprising: size has nothing to do with kindred. A tiny weed may be first cousin to a great tree; and a little dog like Vick knows that Lioness* is a dog too, though she is twenty times larger than herself. So Tom knew that Ellie was a little girl, and thought about her all that day, and longed to have had her to play with; but he had very soon to think of something else. And here is the account of what happened to him, as it was published next morning in the Waterproof Gazette, on the finest watered paper, for the use of the great fairy, Mrs Bedonebyasyoudid, who reads the news very carefully every morning, and especially the police cases, as you will hear very soon.

He was going along the rocks in three-fathom water, watching the pollock catch prawns, and the wrasses nibble barnacles off the rocks, shells and all, when he saw a round cage of green withes;* and inside it, looking very much ashamed of himself, sat his friend the lobster, twiddling his horns, instead of thumbs.

'What, have you been naughty, and have they put you in the lock-up?' asked Tom.

The lobster felt a little indignant at such a notion, but he was too much depressed in spirits to argue; so he only said, 'I can't get out.'*

'Why did you get in?'

'After that nasty piece of dead fish.' He had thought it looked and smelt very nice when he was outside, and so it did, for a lobster: but now he turned round and abused it because he was angry with himself.

'Where did you get in?'

'Through that round hole at the top.'

'Then why don't you get out through it?'

'Because I can't'; and the lobster twiddled his horns more fiercely than ever, but he was forced to confess.

'I have jumped upwards, downwards, backwards, and sideways, at least four thousand times; and I can't get out: I always get up underneath there, and can't find the hole.'

Tom looked at the trap, and having more wit than the lobster, he saw plainly enough what was the matter; as you may if you will look at a lobster-pot.

'Stop a bit,' said Tom. 'Turn your tail up to me, and I'll pull you through hindforemost, and then you won't stick in the spikes.'

But the lobster was so stupid and clumsy that he couldn't hit the hole. Like a great many fox-hunters, he was very sharp as long as he was in his own country: but as soon as they get out of it they lose their heads; and so the lobster, so to speak, lost his tail.

Tom reached and clawed down the hole after him, till he caught hold of him; and then, as was to be expected, the clumsy lobster pulled him in head foremost.

'Hullo! here is a pretty business,' said Tom. 'Now take your great claws, and break the points off those spikes, and then we shall both get out easily.'

'Dear me, I never thought of that,' said the lobster; 'and after all the experience of life that I have had!'

You see, experience is of very little good unless a man, or a lobster, has wit enough to make use of it. For a good many people, like old Polonius,* have seen all the world, and yet remain little better than children after all.

But they had not got half the spikes away, when they saw a great dark cloud over them; and lo and behold, it was the otter.

How she did grin and girn* when she saw Tom. 'Yar!' said she, 'you little meddlesome wretch, I have you now! I will serve you out for telling the salmon where I was!' And she crawled all over the pot to get in.

Tom was horribly frightened, and still more frightened when she found the hole in the top, and squeezed herself right down through it, all eyes and teeth. But no sooner was her head inside than valiant Mr Lobster caught her by the nose, and held on.

And there they were all three in the pot, rolling over and over, and very tight packing it was. And the lobster tore at the otter, and the otter tore at the lobster, and both squeezed and thumped poor Tom till he had no breath left in his body; and I don't know what would have happened to him if he had not at last got on the otter's back, and safe out of the hole.

He was right glad when he got out: but he would not desert his friend who had saved him; and the first time he saw his tail uppermost he caught hold of it, and pulled with all his might.

But the lobster would not let go.

'Come along,' said Tom; 'don't you see she is dead?' And so she was, quite drowned and dead.

And that was the end of the wicked otter.

But the lobster would not let go.

'Come along, you stupid old stick-in-the-mud,' cried Tom, 'or the fisherman will catch you!' And that was true, for Tom felt some one above beginning to haul up the pot.

But the lobster would not let go.

Tom saw the fisherman haul him up to the boatside, and thought it was all up with him. But when Mr Lobster saw the fisherman, he gave such a furious and tremendous snap, that he snapped out of his hand, and out of the pot, and safe into the sea. But he left his knobbed claw behind him; for it never came into his stupid head to let go after all, so he just shook his claw off as the easier method. It was something of a bull, that;* but you must know the lobster was an Irish lobster, and was hatched off Island Magee at the mouth of Belfast Lough.

Tom asked the lobster why he never thought of letting go. He said very determinedly that it was a point of honour among lobsters. And so it is, as the mayor of Plymouth found out once to his cost— eight or nine hundred years ago, of course; for if it had happened lately it would be personal to mention it.

For one day he was so tired with sitting on a hard chair, in a grand furred gown, with a gold chain round his neck, hearing one policeman after another come in and sing, 'What shall we do with the drunken sailor, so early in the morning?'* and answering them each exactly alike—

'Put him in the round house till he gets sober, so early in the morning'—

That, when it was over, he jumped up, and played leap-frog with the town-clerk till he burst his buttons, and then had his luncheon, and burst some more buttons, and then said: 'It is a low spring tide; I shall go out this afternoon and cut my capers.'*

Now he did not mean to cut such capers as you eat with boiled mutton. It was the commandant of artillery at Valetta who used to amuse himself with cutting them, and who stuck upon one of the bastions a notice, 'No one allowed to cut capers here but me,' which greatly edified the midshipmen in port, and the Maltese on the Nix Mangiare stairs. But all that the mayor meant was that he would go and have an afternoon's fun, like any school-boy, and catch lobsters with an iron hook.

So to the Mewstone* he went, and for lobsters he looked. And, when he came to a certain crack in the rocks, he was so excited, that, instead of putting in his hook, he put in his hand; and Mr Lobster was at home, and caught him by the finger, and held on.

'Yah!' said the mayor, and pulled as hard as he dared: but the more he pulled the more the lobster pinched, till he was forced to be quiet.

Then he tried to get his hook in with his other hand; but the hole was too narrow.

Then he pulled again; but he could not stand the pain.

Then he shouted and bawled for help: but there was no one nearer him than the men-of-war inside the breakwater.

Then he began to turn a little pale; for the tide flowed, and still the lobster held on.

Then he turned quite white; for the tide was up to his knees, and still the lobster held on.

Then he thought of cutting off his finger; but he wanted two things to do it with—courage and a knife; and he had got neither.

Then he turned quite yellow; for the tide was up to his waist, and still the lobster held on.

Then he thought over all the naughty things he ever had done: all the sand which he had put in the sugar, and the sloe-leaves in the tea, and the water in the treacle, and the salt in the tobacco* (because his brother was a brewer, and a man must help his own kin).

Then he turned quite blue; for the tide was up to his breast, and still the lobster held on.

Then, I have no doubt, he repented fully of all the said naughty things which he had done, and promised to mend his life, as too many do when they think they have no life left to mend. Whereby, as they fancy, they make a very cheap bargain. But the old fairy with the birch rod soon undeceives them.

And then he grew all colours at once, and turned up his eyes like a duck in thunder; for the water was up to his chin, and still the lobster held on.

And then came a man-of-war's boat round the Mewstone, and saw his head sticking up out of the water. One said it was a keg of brandy, and another that it was a cocoanut, and another that it was a buoy loose, and another that it was a black diver,* and wanted to fire at it, which would not have been pleasant for the mayor: but just then such a yell came out of a great hole in the middle of it that the midshipman in charge guessed what it was, and bade pull up to it as fast as they could. So somehow or other the Jack-tars got the lobster out, and set the mayor free, and put him ashore at the Barbican. He never went lobster-catching again; and we will hope he put no more salt in the tobacco, not even to sell his brother's beer.

And that is the story of the Mayor of Plymouth, which has two advantages—first, that of being quite true; and second, that of having (as folks say all good stories ought to have) no moral whatsoever: no more, indeed, has any part of this book, because it is a fairy tale, you know.

And now happened to Tom a most wonderful thing; for he had not left the lobster five minutes before he came upon a water-baby.

A real live water-baby, sitting on the white sand, very busy about a little point of rock. And when it saw Tom it looked up for a moment, and then cried, 'Why, you are not one of us. You are a new baby! Oh, how delightful!'

And it ran to Tom, and Tom ran to it, and they hugged and kissed each other for ever so long, they did not know why. But they did not want any introductions there under the water.

At last Tom said, 'Oh, where have you been all this while? I have been looking for you so long, and I have been so lonely.'

'We have been here for days and days. There are hundreds of us about the rocks. How was it you did not see us, or hear us when we sing and romp every evening before we go home?'

Tom looked at the baby again, and then he said:

'Well, this is wonderful! I have seen things just like you again and again, but I thought you were shells, or sea-creatures. I never took you for water-babies like myself.'

Now, was not that very odd? So odd, indeed, that you will, no doubt, want to know how it happened, and why Tom could never find a water-baby till after he had got the lobster out of the pot. And, if you will read this story nine times over, and then think for yourself, you will find out why. It is not good for little boys to be told everything, and never to be forced to use their own wits. They would learn, then, no more than they do at Dr Dulcimer's famous suburban establishment for the idler members of the youthful aristocracy, where the masters learn the lessons, and the boys hear them—which saves a great deal of trouble—for the time being.

'Now,' said the baby, 'come and help me, or I shall not have finished before my brothers and sisters come, and it is time to go home.'

'What shall I help you at?'

'At this poor dear little rock; a great clumsy boulder came rolling by in the last storm, and knocked all its head off, and rubbed off all its flowers. And now I must plant it again with sea-weeds, and coralline, and anemones, and I will make it the prettiest little rock-garden on all the shore.'

So they worked away at the rock, and planted it, and smoothed the sand down round it, and capital fun they had till the tide began to turn. And then Tom heard all the other babies coming, laughing and singing and shouting and romping; and the noise they made was just like the noise of the ripple. So he knew that he had been hearing and seeing the water-babies all along; only he did not know them, because his eyes and ears were not opened.

And in they came, dozens and dozens of them, some bigger than Tom and some smaller, all in the neatest little white bathing dresses; and when they found that he was a new baby they hugged him and kissed him, and then put him in the middle and danced round him on the sand, and there was no one ever so happy as poor little Tom.

'Now then,' they cried all at once, 'we must come away home, we must come away home, or the tide will leave us dry. We have mended all the broken sea-weed, and put all the rock pools in order, and planted all the shells again in the sand, and nobody will see where the ugly storm swept in last week.'

And this is the reason why the rock pools are always so neat and clean; because the water-babies come in shore after every storm, to sweep them out, and comb them down, and put them all to rights again.

Only where men are wasteful and dirty, and let sewers run into the sea, instead of putting the stuff upon the fields like thrifty reasonable souls; or throw herrings' heads, and dead dog-fish, or any other refuse, into the water; or in any way make a mess upon the clean shore, there the water-babies will not come, sometimes not for hundreds of years (for they cannot abide anything smelly or foul): but leave the sea-anemones and the crabs to clear away everything, till the good tidy sea has covered up all the dirt in soft mud and clean sand, where the water-babies can plant live cockles and whelks and razor shells and sea-cucumbers and golden-combs, and make a pretty live garden again, after man's dirt is cleared away. And that, I suppose, is the reason why there are no water-babies at any watering-place which I have ever seen.

And where is the home of the water-babies? In St Brandan's fairy isle.*

Did you never hear of the blessed St Brandan, how he preached to the wild Irish, on the wild wild Kerry coast; he and five other hermits, till they were weary, and longed to rest? For the wild Irish would not listen to them, or come to confession and to mass, but liked better to brew potheen,* and dance the pater o'pee,* and knock each other over the head with shillelaghs, and shoot each other from behind turf-dykes, and steal each other's cattle, and burn each other's homes; till St Brandan and his friends were weary of them, for they would not learn to be peaceable Christians at all.

So St Brandan went out to the point of old Dunmore,* and looked over the tide-way roaring round the Blasquets, at the end of all the world, and away into the ocean, and sighed—'Ah that I had wings as a dove!'* And far away, before the setting sun, he saw a blue fairy sea, and golden fairy islands, and he said, 'Those are the islands of the blest.' Then he and his friends got into a hooker,* and sailed away and away to the westward, and were never heard of more. But the people who would not hear him were changed into gorillas, and gorillas they are until this day.

And when St Brandan and the hermits came to that fairy isle, they found it overgrown with cedars, and full of beautiful birds; and he sat down under the cedars, and preached to all the birds in the air. And they liked his sermons so well that they told the fishes in the sea; and they came, and St Brandan preached to them; and the fishes told the water-babies, who live in the caves under the isle; and they came up by hundreds every Sunday, and St Brandan got quite a neat little Sunday-school. And there he taught the water-babies for a great many hundred years, till his eyes grew too dim to see, and his beard grew so long that he dared not walk for fear of treading on it, and then he might have tumbled down. And at last he and the five hermits fell fast asleep under the cedar shades, and there they sleep unto this day. But the fairies took to the water-babies, and taught them their lessons themselves.

And some say that St Brandan will awake, and begin to teach the babies once more: but some think that he will sleep on, for better for worse, till the coming of the Cocqcigrues. But, on still clear summer evenings, when the sun sinks down into the sea, among golden cloud-capes and cloud-islands, and locks and friths* of azure sky, the sailors fancy that they see, away to westward, St Brandan's fairy isle.

But whether men can see it or not, St Brandan's Isle once actually stood there; a great land out in the ocean, which has sunk and sunk beneath the waves. Old Plato called it Atlantis,* and told strange tales of the wise men who lived therein, and of the wars they fought in the old times. And from off that island came strange flowers, which linger still about this land:—the Cornish heath, and Cornish moneywort, and the delicate Venus's hair, and the London-pride which covers the Kerry mountains, and the little pink butterwort of Devon, and the great blue butterwort of Ireland, and the Connemara heath, and the bristle-fern of the Turk waterfall, and many a strange plant more; all fairy tokens left for wise men and good children from off St Brandan's Isle.

Now when Tom got there, he found that the isle stood all on pillars, and that its roots were full of caves. There were pillars of black basalt, like Staffa; and pillars of green and crimson serpentine, like Kynance; and pillars ribboned with red and white and yellow sandstone, like Livermead; and there were blue grottoes, like Capri; and white grottoes, like Adelsberg; all curtained and draped with seaweeds, purple and crimson, green and brown; and strewn with soft white sand, on which the water-babies sleep every night. But, to keep the place clean and sweet, the crabs picked up all the scraps off the floor, and ate them like so many monkeys; while the rocks were covered with ten thousand sea-anemones, and corals and madrepores, who scavenged the water all day long, and kept it nice and pure. But, to make up to them for having to do such nasty work, they were not left black and dirty, as poor chimney-sweeps and dustmen are. No; the fairies are more considerate and just than that; and have dressed them all in the most beautiful colours and patterns, till they look like vast flower-beds of gay blossoms. If you think I am talking nonsense, I can only say that it is true; and that an old gentleman named Fourier* used to say that we ought to do the same by chimney-sweeps and dustmen, and honour them instead of despising them; and he was a very clever old gentleman: but unfortunately for him and the world, as mad as a March hare.

And, instead of watchmen and policemen to keep out nasty things at night, there were thousands and thousands of water-snakes, and most wonderful creatures they were. They were all named after the Nereids,* the sea fairies who took care of them, Eunice and Polynoe, Phyllodoce and Psamathe, and all the rest of the pretty darlings who swim round their Queen Amphitrite, and her car of cameo shell. They were dressed in green velvet, and black velvet, and purple velvet; and were all jointed in rings; and some of them had three hundred brains apiece, so that they must have been uncommonly shrewd detectives; and some had eyes in their tails; and some had eyes in every joint, so that they kept a very sharp look-out; and when they wanted a baby-snake, they just grew one at the end of their own tails, and when it was able to take care of itself it dropped off; so that they brought up their families very cheaply. But if any nasty thing came by, out they rushed upon it; and then out of each of their hundreds of feet there sprang a whole cutler's shop of

| | |
|---|---|
| Scythes, | Yataghans, |
| Billhooks, | Creeses, |
| Pickaxes, | Ghoorka swords, |
| Forks, | Tucks, |
| Penknives, | Javelins, |
| Rapiers, | Lances, |
| Sabres, | Halberts, |
| Gisarines, | Gimblets, |
| Poleaxes, | Corkscrews, |
| Fishhooks, | Pins, |
| Bradawls, | Needles,* |

And so forth,

which stabbed, shot, poked, pricked, scratched, ripped, pinked, and crimped those naughty beasts so terribly, that they had to run for their lives, or else be chopped into small pieces and be eaten afterwards. And, if that is not all, every word, true, then there is no faith in microscopes, and all is over with the Linnæan Society.

And there were the water-babies in thousands, more than Tom, or you either, could count.—All the little children whom the good fairies take to, because their cruel mothers and fathers will not; all who are untaught and brought up heathens, and all who come to grief by ill-usage or ignorance or neglect; all the little children who are overlaid,* or given gin when they are young, or are let to drink out of hot kettles, or to fall into the fire; all the little children in alleys and courts, and tumble-down cottages, who die by fever, and cholera, and measles, and scarlatina, and nasty complaints which no one has any business to have, and which no one will have some day, when folks have common sense; and all the little children who have been killed by cruel masters, and wicked soldiers; they were all there, except, of course, the babes of Bethlehem who were killed by wicked King Herod; for they were taken straight to heaven long ago, as everybody knows, and we call them the Holy Innocents.

But I wish Tom had given up all his naughty tricks, and left off tormenting dumb animals, now that he had plenty of playfellows to amuse him. Instead of that, I am sorry to say, he would meddle with the creatures, all but the water-snakes, for they would stand no nonsense. So he tickled the madrepores, to make them shut up; and frightened the crabs, to make them hide in the sand and peep out at him with the tips of their eyes; and put stones into the anemones' mouths to make them fancy that their dinner was coming.

The other children warned him, and said, 'Take care what you are at. Mrs Bedonebyasyoudid is coming.' But Tom never heeded them, being quite riotous with high spirits and good luck, till, one Friday morning early, Mrs Bedonebyasyoudid came indeed.

A very tremendous lady she was; and when the children saw her, they all stood in a row, very upright indeed, and smoothed down their bathing dresses, and put their hands behind them, just as if they were going to be examined by the inspector.

And she had on a black bonnet, and a black shawl, and no crinoline at all; and a pair of large green spectacles, and a great hooked nose, hooked so much that the bridge of it stood quite up above her eyebrows; and under her arm she carried a great birch-rod. Indeed, she was so ugly, that Tom was tempted to make faces at her: but did not; for he did not admire the look of the birch-rod under her arm.

And she looked at the children one by one, and seemed very much pleased with them, though she never asked them one question about how they were behaving; and then began giving them all sorts of nice sea-things—sea-cakes, sea-apples, sea-oranges, sea-bullseyes, sea-toffee; and to the very best of all she gave sea-ices, made out of sea-cows' cream, which never melt under water.

And, if you don't quite believe me, then just think—What is more cheap and plentiful than sea-rock? Then why should there not be sea-toffee as well? And every one can find sea-lemons (ready quartered too) if they will look for them at low tide; and sea-grapes too sometimes, hanging in bunches; and, if you will go to Nice, you will find the fish-market full of sea-fruit, which they call 'frutta di mare': though I suppose they call them 'fruits de mer' now, out of compliment to that most successful, and therefore most immaculate, potentate* who is seemingly desirous of inheriting the blessing pronounced on those who remove their neighbours' landmark. And, perhaps, that is the very reason why the place is called Nice, because there are so many nice things in the sea there: at least, if it is not, it ought to be.

Now little Tom watched all these sweet things given away, till his mouth watered, and his eyes grew as round as an owl's. For he hoped that his turn would come at last; and so it did. For the lady called him up, and held out her fingers with something in them, and popped it into his mouth; and, lo and behold, it was a nasty cold hard pebble.

'You are a very cruel woman,' said he, and began to whimper.

'And you are a very cruel boy, who puts pebbles into the sea-anemones' mouths, to take them in, and make them fancy that they had caught a good dinner? As you did to them, so I must do to you.'

'Who told you that?' said Tom.

'You did yourself, this very minute.'

Tom had never opened his lips; so he was very much taken aback indeed.

'Yes; every one tells me exactly what they have done wrong; and that without knowing it themselves. So there is no use trying to hide anything from me. Now go, and be a good boy, and I will put no more pebbles in your mouth, if you put none in other creatures'.'

'I did not know there was any harm in it,' said Tom.

'Then you know now. People continually say that to me: but I tell them, if you don't know that fire burns, that is no reason that it should not burn you; and if you don't know that dirt breeds fever, that is no reason why the fevers should not kill you. The lobster did not know that there was any harm in getting into the lobster pot; but it caught him all the same.'

'Dear me,' thought Tom, 'she knows everything!' And so she did, indeed.

'And so, if you do not know that things are wrong, that is no reason why you should not be punished for them; though not as much, not as much, my little man' (and, the lady looked very kindly, after all), 'as if you did know.'

'Well, you are a little hard on a poor lad,' said Tom.

'Not at all; I am the best friend you ever had in all your life. But I will tell you; I cannot help punishing people when they do wrong. I like it no more than they do; I am often very, very sorry for them, poor things: but I cannot help it. If I tried not to do it, I should do it all the same. For I work by machinery, just like an engine; and am full of wheels and springs inside; and am wound up very carefully, so that I cannot help going.'

'Was it long ago since they wound you up?' asked Tom. For he thought, the cunning little fellow, 'She will run down some day: or they may forget to wind her up, as old Grimes used to forget to wind up his watch when he came in from the public-house: and then I shall be safe.'

'I was wound up once and for all, so long ago that I forget all about it.'

'Dear me,' said Tom, 'you must have been made a long time!'

'I never was made, my child; and I shall go for ever and ever; for I am as old as Eternity, and yet as young as Time.'

And there came over the lady's face a very curious expression— very solemn, and very sad; and yet very, very sweet. And she looked up and away, as if she were gazing through the sea, and through the sky, at something far, far off; and as she did so, there came such a quiet, tender, patient, hopeful smile over her face, that Tom thought for the moment that she did not look ugly at all. And no more she did; for she was like a great many people who have not a pretty feature in their faces, and yet are lovely to behold, and draw little children's hearts to them at once; because, though the house is plain enough, yet from the windows a beautiful and good spirit is looking forth.

And Tom smiled in her face, she looked so pleasant for the moment. And the strange fairy smiled too, and said:

'Yes. You thought me very ugly just now, did you not?'

Tom hung down his head, and got very red about the ears.

'And I am very ugly. I am the ugliest fairy in the world; and I shall be, till people behave themselves as they ought to do. And then I shall grow as handsome as my sister, who is the loveliest fairy in the world; and her name is Mrs Doasyouwouldbedoneby. So she begins where I end, and I begin where she ends; and those who will not listen to her must listen to me, as you will see. Now, all of you run away, except Tom; and he may stay and see what I am going to do. It will be a very good warning for him to begin with, before he goes to school.

'Now, Tom, every Friday I come down here and call up all who have ill-used little children, and serve them as they served the children.'

And at that Tom was frightened, and crept under a stone; which made the two crabs who lived there very angry, and frightened their friend the butter-fish into flapping hysterics: but he would not move for them.

And first she called up all the doctors who give little children so much physic (they were most of them old ones; for the young ones have learnt better, all but a few army surgeons, who still fancy that a baby's inside is much like a Scotch grenadier's), and she set them all in a row; and very rueful they looked; for they knew what was coming.

And first she pulled all their teeth out; and then she bled them all round; and then she dosed them with calomel,* and jalap,* and salts and senna, and brimstone and treacle; and horrible faces they made; and then she gave them a great emetic of mustard and water, and no basons; and began all over again; and that was the way she spent the morning.

And then she called up a whole troop of foolish ladies, who pinch up their children's waists and toes; and she laced them all up in tight stays, so that they were choked and sick, and their noses grew red, and their hands and feet swelled; and then she crammed their poor feet into the most dreadfully tight boots, and made them all dance, which they did most clumsily indeed; and then she asked them how they liked it; and when they said not at all, she let them go: because they had only done it out of foolish fashion, fancying it was for their children's good, as if wasps' waists and pigs' toes could be pretty, or wholesome, or of any use to anybody.

Then she called up all the careless nurserymaids, and stuck pins into them all over, and wheeled them about in perambulators with tight straps across their stomachs and their heads and arms hanging over the side, till they were quite sick and stupid, and would have had sun-strokes: but, being under the water, they could only have water-strokes; which, I assure you, are nearly as bad, as you will find if you try to sit under a mill wheel. And mind—when you hear a rumbling at the bottom of the sea, sailors will tell you that it is a ground-swell: but now you know better. It is the old lady wheeling the maids about in perambulators.

And by that time she was so tired, she had to go to luncheon.

And after luncheon she set to work again, and called up all the cruel schoolmasters—whole regiments and brigades of them; and, when she saw them, she frowned most terribly, and set to work in earnest, as if the best part of the day's work was to come. More than half of them were nasty, dirty, frowzy, grubby, smelly old monks, who, because they dare not hit a man of their own size, amused themselves with beating little children instead; as you may see in the picture of old Pope Gregory (good man and true though he was, when he meddled with things which he did understand), teaching children to sing their fa-fa-mi-fa with a cat-o'-nine tails under his chair:* but, because they never had any children of their own, they took into their heads (as some folks do still) that they were the only people in the world who knew how to manage children; and they first brought into England, in the old Anglo-Saxon times, the fashion of treating free boys, and girls too, worse than you would treat a dog or a horse: but Mrs Bedonebyasyoudid has caught them all long ago; and given them many a taste of their own rods; and much good may it do them.

And she boxed their ears, and thumped them over the head with rulers, and pandied their hands with canes, and told them that they told stories, and were this and that bad sort of people; and the more they were very indignant, and stood upon their honour, and declared they told the truth, the more she declared they were not, and that they were only telling lies; and at last she birched them all round soundly with her great birch rod, and set them each an imposition of three hundred thousand lines of Hebrew to learn by heart before she came back next Friday. And at that they all cried and howled so, that their breaths came all up through the sea like bubbles out of soda-water; and that is one reason of the bubbles in the sea. There are others: but that is the one which principally concerns little boys. And by that time she was so tired that she was glad to stop; and, indeed, she had done a very good day's work.

Tom did not quite dislike the old lady: but he could not help thinking her a little spiteful—and no wonder if she was, poor old soul; for, if she has to wait to grow handsome till people do as they would be done by, she will have to wait a very long time.

Poor old Mrs Bedonebyasyoudid! she has a great deal of hard work before her, and had better have been born a washerwoman, and stood over a tub all day: but, you see, people cannot always choose their own profession.

But Tom longed to ask her one question; and after all, whenever she looked at him, she did not look cross at all; and now and then there was a funny smile in her face, and she chuckled to herself in a way which gave Tom courage, and at last he said:

'Pray, ma'am, may I ask you a question?'

'Certainly, my little dear.'

'Why don't you bring all the bad masters here, and serve them out too? The butties* that knock about the poor collier-boys; and the nailers that file off their lads' noses and hammer their fingers; and all the master sweeps, like my master Grimes? I saw him fall into the water long ago; so I surely expected he would have been here. I'm sure he was bad enough to me.'

Then the old lady looked so very stern that Tom was quite frightened, and sorry that he had been so bold. But she was not angry with him. She only answered, 'I look after them all the week round; and they are in a very different place from this, because they knew that they were doing wrong.'

She spoke very quietly; but there was something in her voice which made Tom tingle from head to foot, as if he had got into a shoal of sea-nettles.

'But these people', she went on, 'did not know that they were doing wrong: they were only stupid and impatient; and therefore I only punish them till they become patient, and learn to use their common sense like reasonable beings. But as for chimney-sweeps, and collier-boys, and nailer lads, my sister has set good people to stop all that sort of thing; and very much obliged to her I am; for if she could only stop the cruel masters from ill-using poor children, I should grow handsome at least a thousand years sooner. And now do you be a good boy, and do as you would be done by, which they did not; and then, when my sister, Madame Doasyouwouldbedoneby, comes on Sunday, perhaps she will take notice of you, and teach you how to behave. She understands that better than I do.' And so she went.

Tom was very glad to hear that there was no chance of meeting Grimes again, though he was a little sorry for him, considering that he used sometimes to give him the leavings of the beer: but he determined to be a very good boy all Saturday; and he was; for he never frightened one crab, nor tickled any live corals, nor put stones into the sea-anemones' mouths, to make them fancy they had got a dinner; and, when Sunday morning came, sure enough, Mrs Doasyouwouldbedoneby came too. Whereat all the little children began dancing and clapping their hands, and Tom danced too with all his might.

And as for the pretty lady, I cannot tell you what the colour of her hair was, or of her eyes; no more could Tom; for, when any one looks at her, all they can think of is, that she has the sweetest, kindest, tenderest, funniest, merriest face they ever saw, or want to see. But Tom saw that she was a very tall woman, as tall as her sister: but instead of being gnarly, and horny, and scaly, and prickly, like her, she was the most nice, soft, fat, smooth, pussy, cuddly, delicious creature who ever nursed a baby; and she understood babies thoroughly, for she had plenty of her own, whole rows and regiments of them, and has to this day. And all her delight was, whenever she had a spare moment, to play with babies, in which she showed herself a woman of sense; for babies are the best company, and the pleasantest playfellows, in the world; at least, so all the wise people in the world think. And therefore when the children saw her, they naturally all caught hold of her, and pulled her till she sat down on a stone, and climbed into her lap, and clung round her neck, and caught hold of her hands; and then they all put their thumbs into their mouths, and began cuddling and purring like so many kittens, as they ought to have done. While those who could get nowhere else sat down on the sand, and cuddled her feet—for no one, you know, wears shoes in the water, except horrid old bathing-women,* who are afraid of the water-babies pinching their horny toes. And Tom stood staring at them; for he could not understand what it was all about.

'And who are you, you little darling?' she said.

'Oh, that is the new baby!' they all cried, pulling their thumbs out of their mouths; 'and he never had any mother,' and they all put their thumbs back again, for they did not wish to lose any time.

'Then I will be his mother, and he shall have the very best place; so get out all of you, this moment.'

And she took up two great armfuls of babies—nine hundred under one arm, and thirteen hundred under the other—and threw them away, right and left, into the water. But they minded it no more than the naughty boys in Struwelpeter* minded when St Nicholas dipped them in his inkstand; and did not even take their thumbs out of their mouths, but came paddling and wriggling back to her like so many tadpoles, till you could see nothing of her from head to foot for the swarm of little babies.

But she took Tom in her arms, and laid him in the softest place of all, and kissed him, and patted him, and talked to him, tenderly and low, such things as he had never heard before in his life; and Tom looked up into her eyes, and loved her, and loved, till he fell fast asleep from pure love.

And when he woke, she was telling the children a story. And what story did she tell them? One story she told them, which begins every Christmas Eve, and yet never ends at all for ever and ever; and, as she went on, the children took their thumbs out of their mouths, and listened quite seriously; but not sadly at all; for she never told them anything sad; and Tom listened too, and never grew tired of listening. And he listened so long that he fell fast asleep again, and, when he woke, the lady was nursing him still.

'Don't go away,' said little Tom. 'This is so nice. I never had anyone to cuddle me before.'

'Don't go away,' said all the children; 'you have not sung us one song.'

'Well, I have time for only one. So what shall it be?'

'The doll you lost! The doll you lost!' cried all the babies at once.

So the strange fairy sang: —

> I once had a sweet little doll, dears,
>    The prettiest doll in the world;
> Her cheeks were so red and so white, dears,
>    And her hair was so charmingly curled.
> But I lost my poor little doll, dears,
>    As I played in the heath one day;
> And I cried for her more than a week, dears;
>    But I never could find where she lay.
>
> I found my poor little doll, dears,
>    As I played in the heath one day:
> Folks say she is terribly changed, dears,
>    For her paint is all washed away,
> And her arm trodden off by the cows, dears,
>    And her hair not the least bit curled:
> Yet for old sakes' sake she is still, dears,
>    The prettiest doll in the world.

What a silly song for a fairy to sing!

And what silly water-babies to be quite delighted at it!

Well, but you see they have not the advantage of Aunt Agitate's Arguments in the sea-land down below.

'Now,' said the fairy to Tom, 'will you be a good boy for my sake, and torment no more sea-beasts, till I come back?'

'And you will cuddle me again?' said poor little Tom.

'Of course I will, you little duck. I should like to take you with me, and cuddle you all the way, only I must not'; and away she went.

So Tom really tried to be a good boy, and tormented no sea-beasts after that, as long as he lived; and he is quite alive, I assure you, still.

Oh, how good little boys ought to be, who have kind pussy mammas to cuddle them and tell them stories; and how afraid they ought to be of growing naughty, and bringing tears into their mammas' pretty eyes!

# CHAPTER VI

Thou little child, yet glorious in the might
Of heaven-born freedom on thy Being's height,
Why with such earnest pains dost thou provoke
The Years to bring the inevitable yoke—
Thus blindly with thy blessedness at strife?
Full soon thy soul shall have her earthly freight,
And custom lie upon thee with a weight
Heavy as frost, and deep almost as life.*

Wordsworth.

 ere I come to the very saddest part of all my story. I know some people will only laugh at it, and call it much ado about nothing. But I know one man who would not; and he was an officer with a pair of grey moustaches as long as your arm, who said once in company, that two of the most heart-rending sights in the world, which moved him most to tears, which he would do anything to prevent or remedy, were a child over a broken toy, and a child stealing sweets.

The company did not laugh at him; his moustaches were too long and too grey for that: but, after he was gone, they called him sentimental, and so forth, all but one dear little old quaker lady with a soul as white as her cap, who was not, of course, generally partial to soldiers; and she said—very quietly, like a quaker:

'Friends, it is borne upon my mind that that is a truly brave man.'

Now you may fancy that Tom was quite good, when he had everything that he could want or wish: but you would be very much mistaken. Being quite comfortable is a very good thing; but it does not make people good. Indeed, it sometimes makes them naughty, as it has made the people in America; and as it made the people in the

Bible,* who waxed fat and kicked, like horses overfed and underworked. And I am very sorry to say that this happened to little Tom. For he grew so fond of the sea-bull's-eyes and sea-lollipops, that his foolish little head could think of nothing else: and he was always longing for more, and wondering when the strange lady would come again and give him some, and what she would give him, and how much, and whether she would give him more than the others. And he thought of nothing but lollipops by day, and dreamt of nothing else by night—and what happened then?

That he began to watch the lady to see where she kept the sweet things; and began hiding, and sneaking, and following her about, and pretending to be looking the other way, or going after something else, till he found out that she kept them in a beautiful mother-of-pearl cabinet, away in a deep crack of the rocks.

And he longed to go to the cabinet, and yet he was afraid; and then he longed again, and was less afraid; and at last, by continual thinking about it, he longed so violently, that he was not afraid at all. And one night, when all the other children were asleep, and he could not sleep for thinking of lollipops, he crept away among the rocks, and got to the cabinet, and behold! it was open.

But, when he saw all the nice things inside, instead of being delighted, he was quite frightened, and wished he had never come there. And then he would only touch them, and he did; and then he would only taste one, and he did; and then he would only eat one, and he did; and then he would only eat two, and then three, and so on; and then he was terrified lest she should come and catch him, and began gobbling them down so fast that he did not taste them, or have any pleasure in them; and then he felt sick, and would have only one more; and then only one more again; and so on till he had eaten them all up.

And all the while, close behind him, stood Mrs Bedonebyasyoudid.

Some people may say, But why did she not keep her cupboard locked? Well, I know.—It may seem a very strange thing, but she never does keep her cupboard locked; every one may go and taste for themselves, and fare accordingly. It is very odd, but so it is; and I am quite sure that she knows best. Perhaps she wishes people to keep their fingers out of the fire, by having them burnt.

She took off her spectacles, because she did not like to see too much; and in her pity she arched up her eyebrows into her very hair, and her eyes grew so wide that they would have taken, in all the sorrows of the world, and filled with great big tears, as they too often do.

But all she said was:

'Ah, you poor little dear! you are just like all the rest.'

But she said it to herself, and Tom neither heard nor saw her. Now, you must not fancy that she was sentimental at all. If you do, and think that she is going to let off you, or me, or any human being when we do wrong, because she is too tender-hearted to punish us, then you will find yourself very much mistaken, as many a man does every year and every day.

But what did the strange fairy do when she saw all her lollipops eaten?

Did she fly at Tom, catch him by the scruff of the neck, hold him, howk him, hump him,* hurry him, hit him, poke him, pull him, pinch him, pound him, put him in the corner, shake him, slap him, set him on a cold stone to reconsider himself, and so forth?

Not a bit. You may watch her at work, if you know where to find her. But you will never see her do that. For, if she had, she knew quite well, Tom would have fought, and kicked, and bit, and said bad words, and turned again that moment into a naughty little heathen chimney-sweep, with his hand, like Ishmael's* of old, against every man, and every man's hand against him.

Did she question him, hurry him, frighten him, threaten him, to make him confess? Not a bit. You may see her, as I said, at her work often enough, if you know where to look for her: but you will never see her do that. For if she had, she would have tempted him to tell lies in his fright; and that would have been worse for him, if possible, than even becoming a heathen chimney-sweep again.

No. She leaves that for anxious parents and teachers (lazy ones, some call them), who, instead of giving children a fair trial, such as they would expect and demand for themselves, force them by fright to confess their own faults—which is so cruel and unfair, that no judge on the bench dare do it to the wickedest thief or murderer, for the good British law forbids it—ay, and even punish them to make them confess, which is so detestable a crime, that it is never committed now, save by Inquisitors, and Kings of Naples,* and a few other wretched people of whom the world is weary. And then they say, 'We have trained up the child in the way he should go, and when he grew up he has departed from it. Why then did Solomon* say that he would not depart from it?' But perhaps the way of beating, and hurrying, and frightening, and questioning, was not the way that the child should go; for it is not even the way in which a colt should go, if you want to break it in, and make it a quiet serviceable horse.

Some folks may say, 'Ah! but the Fairy does not need to do that, if she knows everything already.' True. But if she did not know, she would not surely behave worse than a British judge and jury; and no more should parents and teachers either.

So she just said nothing at all about the matter, not even when Tom came next day with the rest for sweet things. He was horribly afraid of coming: but he was still more afraid of staying away, lest any one should suspect him. He was dreadfully afraid, too, lest there should be no sweets—as was to be expected, he having eaten them all—and lest then the fairy should inquire who had taken them. But, behold! she pulled out just as many as ever, which astonished Tom, and frightened him still more.

And, when the fairy looked him full in the face, he shook from head to foot: however, she gave him his share like the rest, and he thought within himself that she could not have found him out.

But, when he put the sweets into his mouth, he hated the taste of them; and they made him so sick, that he had to get away as fast as he could; and terribly sick he was, and very cross and unhappy, all the week after.

Then, when next week came, he had his share again; and again the fairy looked him full in the face; but more sadly than she had ever looked. And he could not bear the sweets: but took them again in spite of himself.

And, when Mrs Doasyouwouldbedoneby came, he wanted to be cuddled like the rest; but she said very seriously:

'I should like to cuddle you; but I cannot, you are so horny and prickly.'

And Tom looked at himself: and he was all over prickles, just like a sea-egg.*

Which was quite natural; for you must know and believe that people's souls make their bodies, just as a snail makes its shell* (I am not joking, my little man; I am in serious, solemn earnest). And, therefore, when Tom's soul grew all prickly with naughty tempers, his body could not help growing prickly too, so that nobody would cuddle him, or play with him, or even like to look at him.

What could Tom do now, but go away and hide in a corner, and cry? For nobody would play with him, and he knew full well why.

And he was so miserable all that week that, when the ugly fairy came, and looked at him once more full in the face, more seriously and sadly than ever, he could stand it no longer, and thrust the sweetmeats away, saying, 'No, I don't want any; I can't bear them now,' and then burst out crying, poor little man, and told Mrs Bedonebyasyoudid every word as it happened.

He was horribly frightened when he had done so; for he expected her to punish him very severely. But, instead, she only took him up and kissed him, which was not quite pleasant, for her chin was very bristly indeed; but he was so lonely-hearted, he thought that rough kissing was better than none.

'I will forgive you, little man,' she said. 'I always forgive every one the moment they tell me the truth of their own accord.'

'Then you will take away all these nasty prickles?'

'That is a very different matter. You put them there yourself, and only you can take them away.'

'But how can I do that?' asked Tom, crying afresh.

'Well, I think it is time for you to go to school; so I shall fetch you a schoolmistress, who will teach you how to get rid of your prickles.' And so she went away.

Tom was frightened at the notion of a schoolmistress; for he thought she would certainly come with a birch-rod or a cane; but he comforted himself, at last, that she might be something like the old woman in Vendale—which she was not in the least; for, when the fairy brought her, she was the most beautiful little girl that ever was seen, with long curls floating behind her like a golden cloud, and long robes floating all round her like a silver one.

'There he is,' said the fairy; 'and you must teach him to be good, whether you like or not.'

'I know,' said the little girl; but she did not seem quite to like, for she put her finger in her mouth, and looked at Tom under her brows; and Tom put his finger in his mouth, and looked at her under his brows, for he was horribly ashamed of himself.

The little girl seemed hardly to know how to begin; and perhaps she would never have begun at all, if poor Tom had not burst out crying, and begged her to teach him to be good, and help him to cure his prickles; and at that she grew so tender-hearted, that she began teaching him as prettily as ever child was taught in the world.

And what did the little girl teach Tom? She taught him, first, what you have been taught ever since you said your first prayers at your mother's knees; but she taught him much more simply. For the lessons in that world, my child, have no such hard words in them as the lessons in this, and therefore the water-babies like them better than you like your lessons, and long to learn them more and more; and grown men cannot puzzle nor quarrel over their meaning, as they do here on land; for those lessons all rise clear and pure, like the Test out of Overton Pool,* out of the everlasting ground of all life and truth.

So she taught Tom every day in the week; only on Sundays she always went away home, and the kind fairy took her place. And, before she had taught Tom many Sundays, his prickles had vanished quite away, and his skin was smooth and clean again.

'Dear me!' said the little girl; 'why, I know you now. You are the very same little chimney-sweep who came into my bedroom.'

'Dear me!' cried Tom. 'And I know you, too, now. You are the very little white lady whom I saw in bed.' And he jumped at her, and longed to hug and kiss her; but did not, remembering that she was a lady born; so he only jumped round and round her, till he was quite tired.

And then they began telling each other all their story—how he had got into the water, and she had fallen over the rock; and how he had swam down to the sea, and how she had flown out of the window; and how this, that, and the other, till it was all talked out: and then they both began over again, and I can't say which of the two talked fastest.

And then they set to work at their lessons again, and both liked them so well, that they went on well till seven full years were past and gone.

You may fancy that Tom was quite content and happy all those seven years; but the truth is, he was not. He had always one thing on his mind, and that was—where little Ellie went, when she went home on Sundays.

To a very beautiful place, she said.

But what was the beautiful place like, and where was it?

Ah! that is just what she could not say. And it is strange, but true, that no one can say; and that those who have been oftenest in it, or even nearest to it, can say least about it, and make people understand least what it is like. There are a good many folks about the Other-end-of-Nowhere (where Tom went afterwards), who pretend to know it from north to south as well as if they had been penny postmen there; but, as they are safe at the Other-end-of-Nowhere, nine hundred and ninety-nine million miles away, what they say cannot concern us.

But the dear, sweet, loving, wise, good, self-sacrificing people, who really go there, can never tell you anything about it, save that it is the most beautiful place in all the world; and, if you ask them more, they grow modest, and hold their peace, for fear of being laughed at; and quite right they are.

So all that good little Ellie could say was, that it was worth all the rest of the world put together. And of course that only made Tom the more anxious to go likewise.

'Miss Ellie,' he said, at last, 'I will know why I cannot go with you when you go home, on Sundays, or I shall have no peace, and give you none either.'

'You must ask the fairies that.'

So when the fairy, Mrs Bedonebyasyoudid, came next, Tom asked her.

'Little boys who are only fit to play with sea-beasts cannot go there,' she said. 'Those who go there must go first where they do not like, and do what they do not like, and help somebody they do not like.'

'Why, did Ellie do that?'

'Ask her.'

And Ellie blushed, and said, 'Yes, Tom; I did not like coming here at first; I was so much happier at home, where it is always Sunday. And I was afraid of you, Tom, at first, because—because—'

'Because I was all over prickles? But I am not prickly now, am I, Miss Ellie?'

'No,' said Ellie. 'I like you very much now; and I like coming here, too.'

'And perhaps,' said the fairy, 'you will learn to like going where you don't like, and helping some one that you don't like, as Ellie has.'

But Tom put his finger in his mouth, and hung his head down; for he did not see that at all.

So when Mrs Doasyouwouldbedoneby came, Tom asked her; for he thought in his little head, She is not so strict as her sister, and perhaps she may let me off more easily.

Ah, Tom, Tom, silly fellow! and yet I don't know why I should blame you, while so many grown people have got the very same notion in their heads.

But, when they try it, they get just the same answer as Tom did. For, when he asked the second fairy, she told him just what the first did, and in the very same words.

Tom was very unhappy at that. And, when Ellie went home on Sunday, he fretted and cried all day, and did not care to listen to the fairy's stories about good children, though they were prettier than ever. Indeed, the more he overheard of them, the less he liked to listen, because they were all about children who did what they did not like, and took trouble for other people, and worked to feed their little brothers and sisters, instead of caring only for their play. And, when she began to tell a story about a holy child in old times, who was martyred by the heathen because it would not worship idols,* Tom could bear no more, and ran away and hid among the rocks.

And, when Ellie came back, he was shy with her, because he fancied she looked down on him, and thought him a coward. And then he grew quite cross with her, because she was superior to him, and did what he could not do. And poor Ellie was quite surprised and sad; and at last Tom burst out crying; but he would not tell her what was really in his mind.

And all the while he was eaten up with curiosity to know where Ellie went to; so that he began not to care for his playmates, or for the sea-palace, or anything else. But perhaps that made matters all the easier for him; for he grew so discontented with everything round him, that he did not care to stay, and did not care where he went.

'Well,' he said, at last, 'I am so miserable here, I'll go; if only you will go with me?'

'Ah!' said Ellie, 'I wish I might; but the worst of it is, that the fairy says, that you must go alone, if you go at all. Now don't poke that poor crab about, Tom (for he was feeling very naughty and mischievous), or the fairy will have to punish you.'

Tom was very nearly saying, 'I don't care if she does'; but he stopped himself in time.

'I know what she wants me to do,' he said, whining most dolefully. 'She wants me to go after that horrid old Grimes. I don't like him, that's certain. And if I find him, he will turn me into a chimney-sweep again, I know. That's what I have been afraid of all along.'

'No, he won't—I know as much as that. Nobody can turn water-babies into sweeps, or hurt them at all, as long as they are good.'

'Ah,' said naughty Tom, 'I see what you want; you are persuading me all along to go, because you are tired of me, and want to get rid of me.'

Little Ellie opened her eyes very wide at that, and they were all brimming over with tears.

'Oh, Tom, Tom!' she said, very mournfully—and then she cried, 'Oh, Tom! where are you?'

And Tom cried, 'Oh, Ellie, where are you?'

For neither of them could see each other—not the least. Little Ellie vanished quite away, and Tom heard her voice calling him, and growing smaller and smaller, and fainter and fainter, till all was silent.

Who was frightened then but Tom? He swam up and down among the rocks, into all the halls and chambers, faster than ever he swam before, but could not find her. He shouted after her, but she did not answer; he asked all the other children, but they had not seen her; and at last he went up to the top of the water and began crying and screaming for Mrs Doasyouwouldbedoneby, but she did not come. Then he began crying and screaming for Mrs Bedonebyasyoudid— which perhaps was the best thing to do—for she came in a moment.

'Oh!' said Tom. 'Oh dear, oh dear! I have been naughty to Ellie, and I have killed her—I know I have killed her.'

'Not quite that,' said the fairy; 'but I have sent her away home, and she will not come back again for I do not know how long.'

And at that Tom cried so bitterly, that the salt sea was swelled with his tears, and the tide was: .3,954,620,819 of an inch higher than it had been the day before: but perhaps that was owing to the waxing of the moon. It may have been so; but it is considered right in the new philosophy,* you know, to give spiritual causes for physical phenomena—especially in parlour-tables; and, of course, physical causes for spiritual ones, like thinking, and praying, and knowing right from wrong. And so they odds it till it comes even, as folks say down in Berkshire.

'How cruel of you to send Ellie away!' sobbed Tom. 'However, I will find her again, if I go to the world's end to look for her.'

The fairy did not slap Tom, and tell him to hold his tongue: but she took him on her lap very kindly, just as her sister would have done; and put him in mind how it was not her fault, because she was wound up inside, like watches, and could not help doing things whether she liked or not. And then she told him how he had been in the nursery long enough, and must go out now and see the world, if he intended ever to be a man; and how he must go all alone by himself, as every one else that ever was born has to go, and see with his own eyes, and smell with his own nose, and make his own bed and lie on it, and burn his own fingers if he put them into the fire. And then she told him how many fine things there were to be seen in the world, and what an odd, curious, pleasant, orderly, respectable, well-managed, and, on the whole, successful (as, indeed, might have been expected) sort of a place it was, if people would only be tolerably brave and honest and good in it; and then she told him not to be afraid of anything he met, for nothing would harm him if he remembered all his lessons, and did what he knew was right. And at last she comforted poor little Tom so much, that he was quite eager to go, and wanted to set out that minute. 'Only,' he said, 'if I might see Ellie once before I went!'

'Why do you want that?'

'Because—because I should be so much happier if I thought she had forgiven me.'

And in the twinkling of an eye* there stood Ellie, smiling, and looking so happy that Tom longed to kiss her; but was still afraid it would not be respectful, because she was a lady born.

'I am going, Ellie!' said Tom. 'I am going, if it is to the world's end. But I don't like going at all, and that's the truth.'

'Pooh! pooh! pooh!' said the fairy. 'You will like it very well indeed, you little rogue, and you know that at the bottom of your heart. But if you don't, I will make you like it. Come here, and see what happens to people who do only what is pleasant.'

And she took out of one of her cupboards (she had all sorts of mysterious cupboards in the cracks of the rocks) the most wonderful waterproof book, full of such photographs* as never were seen. For she had found out photography (and this is a fact) more than 13,598,000 years before anybody was born; and, what is more, her photographs did not merely represent light and shade, as ours do, but colour also, and all colours, as you may see if you look at a black cock's tail, or a butterfly's wing, or, indeed, most things that are or can be, so to speak. And, therefore, her photographs were very curious and famous, and the children looked with great delight for the opening of the book.

And on the title-page was written, 'The History of the great and famous nation of the Doasyoulikes,* who came away from the country of Hardwork, because they wanted to play on the Jews'-harp* all day long.'

In the first picture they saw these Doasyoulikes living in the land of Readymade, at the foot of the Happygolucky Mountains, where flapdoodle grows wild; and if you want to know what that is, you must read Peter Simple.*

They lived very much such a life as those jolly old Greeks in Sicily, whom you may see painted on the ancient vases, and really there seemed to be great excuses for them, for they had no need to work.

Instead of houses, they lived in the beautiful caves of tufa,* and bathed in the warm springs three times a day; and, as for clothes, it was so warm there that the gentlemen walked about in little beside a cocked hat and a pair of straps, or some light summer tackle of that kind; and the ladies all gathered gossamer in autumn (when they were not too lazy) to make their winter dresses.

They were very fond of music, but it was too much trouble to learn the piano or the violin; and, as for dancing, that would have been too great an exertion. So they sat on ant-hills all day long, and played on the Jews'-harp; and, if the ants bit them, why they just got up and went to the next ant-hill, till they were bitten there likewise.

And they sat under the flapdoodle-trees, and let the flapdoodle drop into their mouths; and under the vines, and squeezed the grape-juice down their throats; and, if any little pigs ran about ready roasted, crying, 'Come and eat me,' as was their fashion in that country, they waited till the pigs ran against their mouths, and then took a bite, and were content, just as so many oysters would have been.

They needed no weapons, for no enemies ever came near their land; and no tools, for everything was ready-made to their hand; and the stern old fairy Necessity never came near them, to hunt them up, and make them use their wits, or die.

And so on, and so on, and so on, till there were never such comfortable, easy-going, happy-go-lucky people in the world.

'Well, that is a jolly life,' said Tom.

'You think so?' said the fairy. 'Do you see that great peaked mountain there behind,' said the fairy, 'with smoke coming out of its top?'

'Yes.'

'And do you see all those ashes, and slag, and cinders, lying about?'

'Yes.'

'Then turn over the next five hundred years, and you will see what happens next.'

And behold the mountain had blown up like a barrel of gunpowder, and then boiled over like a kettle; whereby one-third of the Doasyoulikes were blown into the air, and another third were smothered in ashes; so that there was only one-third left.

'You see', said the fairy, 'what comes of living on a burning mountain.'

'Oh, why did you not warn them?' said little Ellie.

'I did warn them all that I could. I let the smoke come out of the mountain; and wherever there is smoke there is fire. And I laid the ashes and cinders all about; and wherever there are cinders, cinders may be again. But they did not like to face facts, my dears, as very few people do; and so they invented a cock-and-bull story, which, I am sure, I never told them, that the smoke was the breath of a giant, whom some gods or other had buried under the mountain; and that the cinders were what the dwarfs roasted the little pigs whole with; and other nonsense of that kind. And, when folks are in that humour, I cannot teach them, save by the good old birch-rod.'

And then she turned over the next five hundred years: and there were the remnant of the Doasyoulikes, doing as they liked, as before. They were too lazy to move away from the mountain; so they said, If it has blown up once, that is all the more reason that it should not blow up again. And they were few in number: but they only said, The more the merrier, but the fewer the better fare. However, that was not quite true; for all the flapdoodle-trees were killed by the volcano, and they had eaten all the roast pigs, who, of course, could not be expected to have little ones. So they had to live very hard, on nuts and roots which they scratched out of the ground with sticks. Some of them talked of sowing corn, as their ancestors used to do, before they came into the land of Readymade; but they had forgotten how to make ploughs (they had forgotten even how to make Jews'-harps by this time), and had eaten all the seed-corn which they brought out of the land of Hardwork years since; and of course it was too much trouble to go away and find more. So they lived miserably on roots and nuts, and all the weakly little children had great stomachs, and then died.

'Why,' said Tom, 'they are growing no better than savages.'

'And look how ugly they are all getting,' said Ellie.

'Yes; when people live on poor vegetables instead of roast beef and plum-pudding, their jaws grow large, and their lips grow coarse, like the poor Paddies who eat potatoes.'

And she turned over the next five hundred years. And there they were all living up in trees, and making nests to keep off the rain. And underneath the trees lions were prowling about.

'Why,' said Ellie, 'the lions seem to have eaten a good many of them, for there are very few left now.'

'Yes,' said the fairy; 'you see it was only the strongest and most active ones who could climb the trees, and so escape.'

'But what great, hulking, broad-shouldered chaps they are,' said Tom; 'they are a rough lot as ever I saw.'

'Yes, they are getting very strong now; for the ladies will not marry any but the very strongest and fiercest gentlemen, who can help them up the trees out of the lions' way.'

And she turned over the next five hundred years. And in that they were fewer still, and stronger, and fiercer; but their feet had changed shape very oddly, for they laid hold of the branches with their great toes, as if they had been thumbs, just as a Hindoo tailor uses his toes to thread his needle.

The children were very much surprised, and asked the fairy whether that was her doing.

'Yes, and no,' she said, smiling. 'It was only those who could use their feet as well as their hands who could get a good living: or, indeed, get married; so that they got the best of everything, and starved out all the rest; and those who are left keep up a regular breed of toe-thumb-men, as a breed of shorthorns, or skye-terriers, or fancy pigeons is kept up,'

'But there is a hairy one among them,' said Ellie.

'Ah!' said the fairy, 'that will be a great man in his time, and chief of all the tribe.'

And, when she turned over the next five hundred years, it was true.

For this hairy chief had had hairy children, and they hairier children still; and every one wished to marry hairy husbands, and have hairy children too; for the climate was growing so damp that none but the hairy ones could live: all the rest coughed and sneezed, and had sore throats, and went into consumptions, before they could grow up to be men and women.

Then the fairy turned over the next five hundred years. And they were fewer still.

'Why, there is one on the ground picking up roots,' said Ellie, 'and he cannot walk upright.'

No more he could; for in the same way that the shape of their feet had altered, the shape of their backs had altered also.

'Why,' cried Tom, 'I declare they are all apes.'

'Something fearfully like it, poor foolish creatures,' said the fairy. 'They are grown so stupid now, that they can hardly think: for none of them have used their wits for many hundred years. They have almost forgotten, too, how to talk. For each stupid child forgot some of the words it heard from its stupid parents, and had not wits enough to make fresh words for itself. Beside, they are grown so fierce and suspicious and brutal that they keep out of each other's way, and mope and sulk in the dark forests, never hearing each other's voice, till they have forgotten almost what speech is like. I am afraid they will all be apes very soon, and all by doing only what they liked.'

And in the next five hundred years they were all dead and gone, by bad food and wild beasts and hunters; all except one tremendous old fellow with jaws like a jack, who stood full seven feet high; and M. Du Chaillu* came up to him, and shot him, as he stood roaring and thumping his breast. And he remembered that his ancestors had once been men, and tried to say, 'Am I not a man and a brother?'* but had forgotten how to use his tongue; and then he had tried to call for a doctor, but he had forgotten the word for one. So all he said was, 'Ubboboo!' and died.

And that was the end of the great and jolly nation of the Doasyoulikes. And, when Tom and Ellie came to the end of the book, they looked very sad and solemn; and they had good reason so to do, for they really fancied that the men were apes, and never thought, in their simplicity, of asking whether the creatures had hippopotamus majors in their brains or not; in which case, as you have been told already, they could not possibly have been apes, though they were more apish than the apes of all aperies.

'But could you not have saved them from becoming apes?' said little Ellie, at last.

'At first, my dear; if only they would have behaved like men, and set to work to do what they did not like. But the longer they waited, and behaved like the dumb beasts, who only do what they like, the stupider and clumsier they grew; till at last they were past all cure, for they had thrown their own wits away. It is such things as this that help to make me so ugly, that I know not when I shall grow fair.'

'And where are they all now?' asked Ellie.

'Exactly where they ought to be, my dear.'

'Yes!' said the fairy, solemnly, half to herself, as she closed the wonderful book. 'Folks say now that I can make beasts into men, by circumstance, and selection, and competition, and so forth. Well, perhaps they are right; and perhaps, again, they are wrong. That is one of the seven things which I am forbidden to tell, till the coming of the Cocqcigrues; and, at all events, it is no concern of theirs. Whatever their ancestors were, men they are; and I advise them to behave as such, and act accordingly. But let them recollect this, that there are two sides to every question, and a downhill as well as an uphill road; and, if I can turn beasts into men, I can, by the same laws of circumstance, and selection, and competition, turn men into beasts. You were very near being turned into a beast once or twice, little Tom. Indeed, if you had not made up your mind to go on this journey, and see the world, like an Englishman, I am not sure but that you would have ended as an eft in a pond.'

'Oh, dear me!' said Tom; 'sooner than that, and be all over slime, I'll go this minute, if it is to the world's end.'

# CHAPTER VII

AND Nature, the old Nurse, took
    The child upon her knee,
Saying 'Here is a story book
    Thy father hath written for thee.

'Come wander with me' she said,
    'Into regions yet untrod,
And read what is still unread
    In the Manuscripts of God.'

And he wandered away and away
    With Nature, the dear old Nurse,
Who sang to him night and day
    The rhymes of the universe.*

                 LONGFELLOW.

ow,' said Tom, 'I am ready to be off, if it's to the world's end.'

'Ah!' said the fairy, 'that is a brave, good boy. But you must go further than the world's end, if you want to find Mr Grimes; for he is at the Other-end-of-Nowhere. You must go to Shiny Wall, and through the white gate that never was opened; and then you will come to Peacepool, and Mother Carey's Haven, where the good whales go when they die. And there Mother Carey will tell you the way to the Other-end-of-Nowhere, and there you will find Mr Grimes.'

'Oh, dear!' said Tom. 'But I do not know my way to Shiny Wall, or where it is at all.'

'Little boys must take the trouble to find out things for themselves, or they will never grow to be men; so that you must ask all the beasts in the sea and the birds in the air, and if you have been good to them, some of them will tell you the way to Shiny Wall.'

. 'Well,' said Tom, 'it will be a long journey, so I had better start at once. Good-bye, Miss Ellie; you know I am getting a big boy, and I must go out and see the world.'

'I know you must,' said Ellie; 'but you will not forget me, Tom. I shall wait here till you come.'

And she shook hands with him, and bade him good-bye. Tom longed very much again to kiss her; but he thought it would not be respectful, considering she was a lady born; so he promised not to forget her: but his little whirl-about of a head was so full of the notion of going out to see the world, that it forgot her in five minutes: however, though his head forgot her, I am glad to say his heart did not.

So he asked all the beasts in the sea, and all the birds in the air, but none of them knew the way to Shiny Wall. For why? He was still too far down south.

Then he met a ship, far larger than he had ever seen—a gallant ocean-steamer, with a long cloud of smoke trailing behind; and he wondered how she went on without sails, and swam up to her to see. A school of dolphins were running races round and round her, going three feet for her one, and Tom asked them the way to Shiny Wall: but they did not know. Then he tried to find out how she moved, and at last he saw her screw, and was so delighted with it that he played under her quarter* all day, till he nearly had his nose knocked off by the fans, and thought it time to move. Then he watched the sailors upon deck, and the ladies, with their bonnets and parasols: but none of them could see him, because their eyes were not opened—as, indeed, most people's eyes are not.

At last there came out into the quarter-gallery* a very pretty lady, in deep black widow's weeds, and in her arms a baby. She leaned over the quarter-gallery, and looked back and back toward England far away; and as she looked she sang:

I.

Soft soft wind, from out the sweet south sliding,
Waft thy silver cloud-webs athwart the summer sea;

Thin thin threads of mist on dewy fingers twining
Weave a veil of dappled gauze to shade my babe and me.

II.

Deep deep Love, within thine own abyss abiding,
Pour Thyself abroad, O Lord, on earth and air and sea;
Worn weary hearts within Thy holy temple hiding,
Shield from sorrow, sin, and shame my helpless babe and me.

Her voice was so soft and low,* and the music of the air so sweet, that Tom could have listened to it all day. But as she held the baby over the gallery-rail, to show it the dolphins leaping and the water gurgling in the ship's wake, lo! and behold, the baby saw Tom.

He was quite sure of that; for when their eyes met, the baby smiled and held out its hands; and Tom smiled and held out his hands too; and the baby kicked and leaped, as if it wanted to jump overboard to him.

'What do you see, my darling?' said the lady; and her eyes followed the baby's till she too caught sight of Tom, swimming about among the foam-beads below.

She gave a little shriek and start; and then she said, quite quietly, 'Babies in the sea? Well, perhaps it is the happiest place for them,' and waved her hand to Tom, and cried, 'Wait a little, darling, only a little: and perhaps we shall go with you and be at rest.'

And at that an old nurse, all in black, came out and talked to her, and drew her in. And Tom turned away northward, sad and wondering; and watched the great steamer slide away into the dusk, and the lights on board peep out one by one, and die out again, and the long bar of smoke fade away into the evening mist, till all was out of sight.

And he swam northward again, day after day, till at last he met the King of the Herrings, with a curry-comb growing out of his nose, and a sprat in his mouth for a cigar, and asked him the way to Shiny Wall; so he bolted his sprat head foremost, and said:

'If I were you, young gentleman, I should go to the Allalonestone, and ask the last of the Gairfowl.* She is of a very ancient clan, very nearly as ancient as my own; and knows a good deal which these modern upstarts don't, as ladies of old houses are likely to do.'

Tom asked his way to her, and the King of the Herrings told him very kindly; for he was a courteous old gentleman of the old school, though he was horribly ugly, and strangely bedizened too, like the old dandies who lounge in the clubhouse windows.

But just as Tom had thanked him and set off, he called after him: 'Hi! I say, can you fly?'

'I never tried,' says Tom. 'Why?'

'Because, if you can, I should advise you to say nothing to the old lady about it. There; take a hint. Good-bye.'

And away Tom went for seven days and seven nights due north-west, till he came to a great codbank, the like of which he never saw before. The great cod lay below in tens of thousands, and gobbled shellfish all day long; and the blue sharks roved above in hundreds, and gobbled them when they came up. So they ate, and ate, and ate each other, as they had done since the making of the world; for no man had come here yet to catch them, and find out how rich old Mother Carey is.

And there he saw the last of the Gairfowl, standing up on the Allalonestone, all alone. And a very grand old lady she was, full three feet high, and bolt upright, like some old Highland chieftainess. She had on a black velvet gown, and a white pinner and apron, and a very high bridge to her nose (which is a sure mark of high breeding), and a large pair of white spectacles on it, which made her look rather odd: but it was the ancient fashion of her house.

And instead of wings, she had two little feathery arms, with which she fanned herself, and complained of the dreadful heat; and she kept on crooning an old song to herself, which she learnt when she was a little baby-bird, long ago—

> Two little birds, they sat on a stone,
> One swam away, and then there was one;
>     With a fal-lal-la-lady.

> The other swam after, and then there was none,
> And so the poor stone was left all alone;
>     With a fal-lal-la-lady.*

It was 'flew' away, properly, and not 'swam' away: but, as she could not fly, she had a right to alter it. However, it was a very fit song for her to sing, because she was a lady herself.

Tom came up to her very humbly, and made his bow; and the first thing she said was—

'Have you wings? Can you fly?'

'Oh dear, no, ma'am; I should not think of such a thing,' said cunning little Tom.

'Then I shall have great pleasure in talking to you, my dear. It is quite refreshing nowadays to see anything without wings. They must all have wings, forsooth, now, every new upstart sort of bird, and fly. What can they want with flying, and raising themselves above their proper station in life? In the days of my ancestors no birds ever thought of having wings, and did very well without; and now they all laugh at me because I keep to the good old fashion. Why, the very marrocks* and dovekies* have got wings, the vulgar creatures, and poor little ones enough they are; and my own cousins too, the razorbills, who are gentlefolk born, and ought to know better than to ape their inferiors.'

And so she was running on, while Tom tried to get in a word edgeways; and at last he did, when the old lady got out of breath, and began fanning herself again; and then he asked if she knew the way to Shiny Wall.

'Shiny Wall? Who should know better than I? We all came from Shiny Wall, thousands of years ago, when it was decently cold, and the climate was fit for gentlefolk; but now, what with the heat, and what with these vulgar-winged things who fly up and down and eat everything, so that gentlepeople's hunting is all spoilt, and one really cannot get one's living, or hardly venture off the rock for fear of being flown against by some creature that would not have dared to come within a mile of one a thousand years ago—what was I saying? Why, we have quite gone down in the world, my dear, and have nothing left but our honour. And I am the last of my family. A friend of mine and I came and settled on this rock when we were young, to be out of the way of low people. Once we were a great nation, and spread over all the Northern Isles. But men shot us so, and knocked us on the head, and took our eggs—why, if you will believe it, they say that on the coast of Labrador the sailors used to lay a plank from the rock on board the thing they called their ship, and drive us along the plank by hundreds, till we tumbled down into the ship's waist in heaps; and then, I suppose, they ate us, the nasty fellows! Well—but—what was I saying? At last there were none of us left, except on the old Gairfowlskerry,* just off the Iceland coast, up which no man could climb. Even there we had no peace; for one day, when I was quite a young girl, the land rocked, and the sea boiled, and the sky grew dark, and all the air was filled with smoke and dust, and down tumbled the old Gairfowlskerry into the sea. The dovekies and marrocks, of course, all flew away; but we were too proud to do that. Some of us were dashed to pieces, and some drowned; and those who were left got away to Eldey, and the dovekies tell me they are all dead now, and that another Gairfowlskerry has risen out of the sea close to the old one, but that it is such a poor flat place that it is not safe to live on: and so here I am left alone.'

This was the Gairfowl's story, and, strange as it may seem, it is every word of it true.

'If you only had had wings!' said Tom; 'then you might all have flown away too.'

'Yes, young gentleman: and if people are not gentlemen and ladies, and forget that *noblesse oblige*, they will find it as easy to get on in the world as other people who don't care what they do. Why, if I had not recollected that *noblesse oblige*, I should not have been all alone now.' And the poor old lady sighed.

'How was that, ma'am?'

'Why, my dear, a gentleman came hither with me, and after we had been here some time, he wanted to marry—in fact, he actually proposed to me. Well, I can't blame him; I was young, and very handsome then, I don't deny: but you see, I could not hear of such a thing, because he was my deceased sister's husband,* you see?'

'Of course not, ma'am,' said Tom; though, of course, he knew nothing about it. 'She was very much diseased, I suppose?'

'You do not understand me, my dear. I mean, that being a lady, and with right and honourable feelings, as our house always has had, I felt it my duty to snub him, and howk him, and peck him continually, to keep him at his proper distance; and, to tell the truth, I once pecked him a little too hard, poor fellow, and he tumbled backwards off the rock, and—really, it was very unfortunate, but it was not my fault—a shark coming by saw him flapping, and snapped him up. And since then I have lived all alone—

> With a fal-lal-la-lady.

And soon I shall be gone, my little dear, and nobody will miss me; and then the poor stone will be left all alone.'

'But, please, which is the way to Shiny Wall?' said Tom.

'Oh, you must go, my little dear—you must go. Let me see—I am sure—that is—really, my poor old brains are getting quite puzzled. Do you know, my little dear, I am afraid, if you want to know, you must ask some of these vulgar birds about, for I have quite forgotten.'

And the poor old Gairfowl began to cry tears of pure oil; and Tom was quite sorry for her; and for himself too, for he was at his wit's end whom to ask.

But by there came a flock of petrels, who are Mother Carey's own chickens; and Tom thought them much prettier than Lady Gairfowl, and so perhaps they were; for Mother Carey had had a great deal of fresh experience between the time that she invented the Gairfowl and the time that she invented them. They flitted along like a flock of black swallows, and hopped and skipped from wave to wave, lifting up their little feet behind them so daintily, and whistling to each other so tenderly, that Tom fell in love with them at once, and called them to know the way to Shiny Wall.

'Shiny Wall? Do you want Shiny Wall? Then come with us, and we will show you. We are Mother Carey's own chickens, and she sends us out over all the seas, to show the good birds the way home.'

Tom was delighted, and swam off to them, after he had made his bow to the Gairfowl. But she would not return his bow: but held herself bolt upright, and wept tears of oil as she sang:

> And so the poor stone was left all alone;
> With a fal-lal-la-lady.

But she was wrong there; for the stone was not left all alone: and the next time that Tom goes by it, he will see a sight worth seeing.

The old Gairfowl is gone already: but there are better things come in her place; and when Tom comes he will see the fishing-smacks anchored there in hundreds, from Scotland, and from Ireland, and from the Orkneys, and the Shetlands, and from all the Northern ports, full of the children of the old Norse Vikings, the masters of the sea. And the men will be hauling in the great cod by thousands, till their hands are sore from the lines; and they will be making cod-liver oil and guano, and salting down the fish; and there will be a man-of-war steamer there to protect them, and a lighthouse to show them the way; and you and I, perhaps, shall go some day to the Allalonestone to the great summer sea-fair, and dredge strange creatures such as man never saw before; and we shall hear the sailors boast that it is not the worst jewel in Queen Victoria's crown, for there are eighty miles of codbank, and food for all the poor folk in the land. That is what Tom will see, and perhaps you and I shall see it too. And then we shall not be sorry because we cannot get a Gairfowl to stuff, much less find gairfowl enough to drive them into stone pens and slaughter them, as the old Norsemen did, or drive them on board along a plank till the ship was victualled with them, as the old English and French rovers used to do, of whom dear old Hakluyt* tells: but we shall remember what Mr Tennyson* says, how

> The old order changeth, giving place to the new,
> And God fulfils Himself in many ways.

And now Tom was all agog to start for Shiny Wall; but the petrels said no. They must go first to Allfowlsness, and wait there for the great gathering of all the seabirds, before they start for their summer breeding-places far away in the Northern isles; and there they would be sure to find some birds which were going to Shiny Wall: but where Allfowlsness was, he must promise never to tell, lest men should go there and shoot the birds, and stuff them, and put them into stupid museums, instead of leaving them to play and breed and work in Mother Carey's water-garden, where they ought to be.

So where Allfowlsness is nobody must know; and all that is to be said about it is, that Tom waited there many days; and as he waited, he saw a very curious sight. On the rabbit burrows on the shore there gathered hundreds and hundreds of hoodiecrows, such as you see in Cambridgeshire. And they made such a noise, that Tom came on shore and went up to see what was the matter.

And there he found them holding their great caucus, which they hold every year in the North; and all their stump-orators* were speechifying; and for a tribune, the speaker stood on an old sheep's skull.

And they cawed and cawed, and boasted of all the clever things they had done; how many lambs' eyes they had picked out, and how many dead bullocks they had eaten, and how many young grouse they had swallowed whole, and how many grouse-eggs they had flown away with, stuck on the point of their bills, which is the hoodiecrow's particularly clever feat, of which he is as proud as a gipsy is of doing the hokany-baro;* and what that is, I won't tell you.

And at last they brought out the prettiest, neatest young lady-crow that ever was seen, and set her in the middle, and all began abusing and vilifying, and rating, and bullyragging at her, because she had stolen no grouse-eggs, and had actually dared to say that she would not steal any. So she was to be tried publicly by their laws (for the hoodies always try some offenders in their great yearly parliament). And there she stood in the middle, in her black gown and grey hood, looking as meek and as neat as a quakeress, and they all bawled at her at once—

And it was in vain that she pleaded

That she did not like grouse-eggs;
That she could get her living very well without them;
That she was afraid to eat them, for fear of the gamekeepers;
That she had not the heart to eat them, because the grouse were such
   pretty, kind, jolly birds;
And a dozen reasons more.

For all the other scaul-crows set upon her, and pecked her to death there and then, before Tom could come to help her; and then flew away, very proud of what they had done.

Now, was not this a scandalous transaction?

But they are true republicans, these hoodies, who do every one just what he likes, and make other people do so too; so that, for any freedom of speech, thought, or action, which is allowed among them, they might as well be American citizens of the new school.

But the fairies took the good crow, and gave her nine new sets of feathers running, and turned her at last into the most beautiful bird of paradise with a green velvet suit and a long tail, and sent her to eat fruit in the Spice Islands, where cloves and nutmegs grow.

And Mrs Bedonebyasyoudid settled her account with the wicked hoodies. For, as they flew away, what should they find but a nasty dead dog?—on which they all set to work, pecking and gobbling and cawing and quarrelling, to their hearts' content. But the moment afterwards, they all threw up their bills into the air, and gave one screech; and then turned head over heels backward, and fell down dead, one hundred and twenty-three of them at once. For why? The fairy had told the gamekeeper in a dream, to fill the dead dog full of strychnine; and so he did.

And after a while the birds began to gather at Allfowlsness, in thousands and tens of thousands, blackening all the air; swans and brant geese, harlequins and eiders, harelds and garganeys, smews and goosanders, divers and loons, grebes and dovekies, auks and razor-bills, gannets and petrels, skuas and terns, with gulls beyond all naming or numbering; and they paddled and washed and splashed and combed and brushed themselves on the sand, till the shore was white with feathers; and they quacked and clucked and gabbled and chattered and screamed and whooped as they talked over matters with their friends, and settled where they were to go and breed that summer, till you might have heard them ten miles off; and lucky it was for them that there was no one to hear them but the old keeper, who lived all alone upon the Ness, in a turf hut thatched with heather and fringed round with great stones slung across the roof by bent-ropes,* lest the winter gales should blow the hut right away. But he never minded the birds nor hurt them, because they were not in season: indeed, he minded but two things in the whole world, and those were, his Bible and his grouse; for he was as good an old Scotchman as ever knit stockings on a winter's night: only, when all the birds were going, he toddled out, and took off his cap to them, and wished them a merry journey and a safe return; and then gathered up all the feathers which they had left, and cleaned them to sell down south, and make feather-beds for stuffy people to lie on.

Then the petrels asked this bird and that whether they would take Tom to Shiny Wall: but one set was going to Sutherland, and one to the Shetlands, and one to Norway, and one to Spitzbergen, and one to Iceland, and one to Greenland: but none would go to Shiny Wall. So the good-natured petrels said that they would show him part of the way themselves, but they were only going as far as Jan Mayen's land;* and after that he must shift for himself.

And then all the birds rose up, and streamed away in long black lines, north, and north-east, and north-west, across the bright blue summer sky; and their cry was like ten thousand packs of hounds, and ten thousand peals of bells. Only the puffins stayed behind, and killed the young rabbits, and laid their eggs in the rabbit-burrows; which was rough practice, certainly: but a man must see to his own family.

And, as Tom and the petrels went north-eastward, it began to blow right hard; for the old gentleman in the grey greatcoat, who looks after the big copper boiler in the gulf of Mexico, had got behind-hand with his work; so Mother Carey had sent an electric message to him for more steam; and now the steam was coming, as much in an hour as ought to have come in a week, puffing and roaring and swishing and swirling, till you could not see where the sky ended and the sea began. But Tom and the petrels never cared, for the gale was right abaft, and away they went over the crests of the billows, as merry as so many flying-fish.

And at last they saw an ugly sight—the black side of a great ship, water-logged in the trough of the sea. Her funnel and her masts were overboard, and swayed and surged under her lee; her decks were swept as clean as a barn floor, and there was no living soul on board.

The petrels flew up to her, and wailed round her; for they were very sorry indeed, and also they expected to find some salt pork; and Tom scrambled on board of her and looked round, frightened and sad.

And there, in a little cot, lashed tight under the bulwark, lay a baby fast asleep; the very same baby, Tom saw at once, which he had seen in the singing lady's arms.

He went up to it, and wanted to wake it: but behold, from under the cot out jumped a little black and tan terrier dog, and began barking and snapping at Tom, and would not let him touch the cot.

Tom knew the dog's teeth could not hurt him: but at least it could shove him away, and did; and he and the dog fought and struggled, for he wanted to help the baby, and did not want to throw the poor dog overboard: but, as they were struggling, there came a tall green sea, and walked in over the weather side of the ship, and swept them all into the waves.

'Oh, the baby, the baby!' screamed Tom: but the next moment he did not scream at all; for he saw the cot settling down through the green water, with the baby smiling in it, fast asleep; and he saw the fairies come up from below, and carry baby and cradle gently down in their soft arms; and then he knew it was all right, and that there would be a new water-baby in St Brandan's Isle.

And the poor little dog?

Why, after he had kicked and coughed a little, he sneezed so hard, that he sneezed himself clean out of his skin, and turned into a waterdog, and jumped and danced round Tom, and ran over the crests of the waves, and snapped at the jelly-fish and the mackarel, and followed Tom the whole way to the Other-end-of-Nowhere.

Then they went on again, till they began to see the peak of Jan Mayen's Land, standing up like a white sugar-loaf, two miles above the clouds.

And there they fell in with a whole flock of molly-mocks,* who were feeding on a dead whale.

'These are the fellows to show you the way,' said Mother Carey's chickens; 'we cannot help you further north. We don't like to get among the ice pack, for fear it should nip our toes; but the mollys dare fly anywhere.'

So the petrels called to the mollys: but they were so busy and greedy, gobbling and pecking and spluttering and fighting over the blubber, that they did not take the least notice.

'Come, come,' said the petrels, 'you lazy greedy lubbers,* this young gentleman is going to Mother Carey, and if you don't attend on him, you won't earn your discharge from her, you know.'

'Greedy we are,' says a great fat old molly, 'but lazy we ain't; and, as for lubbers, we're no more lubbers than you. Let's have a look at the lad.'

And he flapped right into Tom's face, and stared at him in the most impudent way (for the mollys are audacious fellows, as all whalers know), and then asked him where he hailed from, and what land he sighted last.

And, when Tom told him, he seemed pleased, and said he was a good plucked* one to have got so far.

'Come along, lads,' he said to the rest, 'and give this little chap a cast over the pack, for Mother Carey's sake. We've eaten blubber enough for to-day, and we'll e'en work out a bit of our time by helping the lad.'

So the mollys took Tom up on their backs, and flew off with him, laughing and joking—and oh, how they did smell of train oil!

'Who are you, you jolly birds?' asked Tom.

'We are the spirits of the old Greenland skippers (as every sailor knows), who hunted here, right whales and horse-whales,* full hundreds of years agone. But, because we were saucy and greedy, we were all turned into mollys, to eat whale's blubber all our days. But lubbers we are none, and could sail a ship now against any man in the North Seas, though we don't hold with this new-fangled steam. And it's a shame of those black imps of petrels to call us so; but because they're her grace's pets, they think they may say anything they like.'

'And who are you?' asked Tom of him, for he saw that he was the king of all the birds.

'My name is Hendrick Hudson,* and a right good skipper was I; and my name will last to the world's end, in spite of all the wrong I did. For I discovered Hudson River, and I named Hudson's Bay; and many have come in my wake that dared not have shown me the way. But I was a hard man in my time, that's truth, and stole the poor Indians off the coast of Maine, and sold them for slaves down in Virginia; and at last I was so cruel to my sailors, here in these very seas, that they set me adrift in an open boat, and I never was heard of more. So now I'm the king of all the mollys, till I've worked out my time.'

And now they came to the edge of the pack, and beyond it they could see Shiny Wall looming, through mist, and snow, and storm. But the pack rolled horribly upon the swell, and the ice giants fought and roared, and leapt upon each other's backs, and ground each other to powder, so that Tom was afraid to venture among them, lest he should be ground to powder too. And he was the more afraid, when he saw lying among the ice pack the wrecks of many a gallant ship; some with masts and yards all standing, some with the seamen frozen fast on board. Alas, alas, for them! They were all true English hearts; and they came to their end like good knights-errant, in searching for the white gate that never was opened yet.*

But the good mollys took Tom and his dog up, and flew with them safe over the pack and the roaring ice giants, and set them down at the foot of Shiny Wall.

'And where is the gate?' asked Tom.

'There is no gate,' said the mollys.

'No gate?' cried Tom aghast.

'None; never a crack of one, and that's the whole of the secret, as better fellows, lad, than you have found to their cost; and if there had been, they'd have killed by now every right whale that swims the sea.'

'What am I to do, then?'

'Dive under the floe, to be sure, if you have pluck.'

'I've not come so far to turn now,' said Tom; 'so here goes for a header.'

'A lucky voyage to you, lad,' said the mollys; 'we knew you were one of the right sort. So good-bye.'

'Why don't you come too?' asked Tom.

But the mollys only wailed sadly, 'We can't go yet, we can't go yet,' and flew away over the pack.

So Tom dived under the great white gate which never was opened yet, and went on in black darkness, at the bottom of the sea, for seven days and seven nights. And yet he was not a bit frightened. Why should he be? He was a brave English lad, whose business is to go out and see all the world.

And at last he saw the light, and clear clear water overhead; and up he came a thousand fathoms, among clouds of sea-moths,* which fluttered round his head. There were moths with pink heads and wings and opal bodies, that flapped about slowly; moths with brown wings that flapped about quickly; yellow shrimps that hopped and skipped most quickly of all; and jellies of all the colours in the world, that neither hopped nor skipped, but only dawdled and yawned, and would not get out of his way. The dog snapped at them till his jaws were tired: but Tom hardly minded them at all, he was so eager to get to the top of the water, and see the pool where the good whales go.

And a very large pool it was, miles and miles across, though the air was so clear that the ice cliffs on the opposite side looked as if they were close at hand. All round it the ice cliffs rose, in walls and spires and battlements, and caves and bridges, and stories and galleries, in which the ice-fairies live, and drive away the storms and clouds, that Mother Carey's pool may lie calm from year's end to year's end. And the sun acted policeman, and walked round outside every day, peeping just over the top of the ice wall, to see that all went right; and now and then he played conjuring tricks, or had an exhibition of fireworks, to amuse the ice-fairies. For he would make himself into four or five suns at once, or paint the sky with rings and crosses and crescents of white fire, and stick himself in the middle of them, and wink at the fairies; and I dare say they were very much amused; for anything's fun in the country.

And there the good whales lay, the happy sleepy beasts, upon the still oily sea. They were all right whales, you must know, and finners, and razor-backs, and bottle-noses, and spotted sea-unicorns with long ivory horns. But the sperm whales are such raging, ramping, roaring, rumbustious fellows, that, if Mother Carey let them in, there would be no more peace in Peacepool. So she packs them away in a great pond by themselves at the South Pole, two hundred and sixty-three miles south-south east of Mount Erebus,* the great volcano in the ice; and there they butt each other with their ugly noses, day and night from year's end to year's end. And if they think that sport—why, so do their American cousins.

But here there were only good quiet beasts, lying about like the black hulls of sloops, and blowing every now and then jets of white steam, or sculling round with their huge mouths open, for the sea-moths to swim down their throats. There were no threshers there to thresh their poor old backs, or sword-fish to stab their stomachs, or saw-fish to rip them up, or ice-sharks to bite lumps out of their sides, or whalers to harpoon and lance them. They were quite safe and happy there; and all they had to do was to wait quietly in Peacepool, till Mother Carey sent for them to make them out of old beasts into new.

Tom swam up to the nearest whale, and asked the way to Mother Carey.

'There she sits in the middle,' said the whale.

Tom looked; but he could see nothing in the middle of the pool, but one peaked iceberg: and he said so.

'That's Mother Carey,' said the whale, 'as you will find when you get to her. There she sits making old beasts into new all the year round.'

'How does she do that?'

'That's her concern, not mine,' said the old whale; and yawned so wide (for he was very large) that there swam into his mouth 943 sea-moths, 13,846 jelly-fish no bigger than pins' heads, a string of salpæ* nine yards long, and forty-three little ice-crabs, who gave each other a parting pinch all round, tucked their legs under their stomachs, and determined to die decently, like Julius Cæsar.

'I suppose', said Tom, 'she cuts up a great whale like you into a whole shoal of porpoises?'

At which the old whale laughed so violently that he coughed up all the creatures; who swam away again very thankful at having escaped out of that terrible whalebone net of his, from which bourne no traveller returns;* and Tom went on to the iceberg, wondering.

And, when he came near it, it took the form of the grandest old lady he had ever seen—a white marble lady, sitting on a white marble throne. And from the foot of the throne there swum away, out and out into the sea, millions of new-born creatures, of more shapes and colours than man ever dreamed. And they were Mother Carey's children, whom she makes out of the sea-water all day long.

He expected, of course—like some grown people who ought to

know better—to find her snipping, piecing, fitting, stitching, cobbling, basting, filing, planing, hammering, turning, polishing, moulding, measuring, chiselling, clipping, and so forth, as men do when they go to work to make anything.

But, instead of that, she sat quite still with her chin upon her hand, looking down into the sea with two great grand blue eyes, as blue as the sea itself. Her hair was as white as the snow—for she was very very old—in fact, as old as any thing which you are likely to come across, except the difference between right and wrong.

And, when she saw Tom, she looked at him very kindly.

'What do you want, my little man? It is long since I have seen a water-baby here.'

Tom told her his errand, and asked the way to the Other-end-of-Nowhere.

'You ought to know yourself, for you have been there already.'

'Have I, ma'am? I'm sure I forget all about it.'

'Then look at me.'

And, as Tom looked into her great blue eyes, he recollected the way perfectly.

Now, was not that strange?

'Thank you, ma'am,' said Tom. 'Then I won't trouble your ladyship any more; I hear you are very busy.'

'I am never more busy than I am now,' she said, without stirring a finger.

'I heard, ma'am, that you were always making new beasts out of old.'

'So people fancy. But I am not going to trouble myself to make things, my little dear. I sit here and make them make themselves.'

'You are a clever fairy, indeed,' thought Tom. And he was quite right.

That is a grand trick of good old Mother Carey's, and a grand answer,* which she has had occasion to make several times to impertinent people.

There was once, for instance, a fairy who was so clever that she found out how to make butterflies. I don't mean sham ones; no: but real live ones, which would fly, and eat, and lay eggs, and do everything that they ought; and she was so proud of her skill that she went flying straight off to the North Pole, to boast to Mother Carey how she could make butterflies.

But Mother Carey laughed.

'Know, silly child,' she said, 'that any one can make things, if they will take time and trouble enough: but it is not every one who, like me, can make things make themselves.'

But people do not yet believe that Mother Carey is as clever as all that comes to; and they will not till they, too, go the journey to the Other-end-of-Nowhere.

'And now, my pretty little man,' said Mother Carey, 'you are sure you know the way to the Other-end-of-Nowhere?'

Tom thought; and behold, he had forgotten it utterly.

'That is because you took your eyes off me.'

Tom looked at her again, and recollected; and then looked away, and forgot in an instant.

'But what am I to do, ma'am? For I can't keep looking at you when I am somewhere else.'

'You must do without me, as most people have to do, for nine hundred and ninety-nine thousandths of their lives; and look at the dog instead; for he knows the way well enough, and will not forget it. Besides, you may meet some very queer-tempered people there, who will not let you pass without this passport of mine, which you must hang round your neck and take care of; and, of course, as the dog will always go behind you, you must go the whole way backward.'

'Backward!' cried Tom. 'Then I shall not be able to see my way.'

'On the contrary, if you look forward, you will not see a step before you, and be certain to go wrong; but, if you look behind you, and watch carefully whatever you have passed, and especially keep your eye on the dog, who goes by instinct, and therefore can't go wrong, then you will know what is coming next as plainly as if you saw it in a looking-glass.'

Tom was very much astonished: but he obeyed her, for he had learnt always to believe what the fairies told him.

'So it is, my dear child,' said Mother Carey; 'and I will tell you a story, which will show you that I am perfectly right, as it is my custom to be.'

'Once on a time, there were two brothers. One was called Prometheus, because he always looked before him, and boasted that he was wise beforehand. The other was called Epimetheus,* because he always looked behind him, and did not boast at all; but said humbly, like the Irishman, that he had sooner prophesy after the event.

'Well, Prometheus was a very clever fellow, of course, and invented all sorts of wonderful things. But, unfortunately, when they were set to work, to work was just what they would not do: wherefore very little has come of them, and very little is left of them; and now nobody knows what they were, save a few archæological old gentlemen who scratch in queer corners, and find little there save Ptinum Furem, Blaptem Mortisagam, Acarum Horridum, and Tineam Laciniarum.*

'But Epimetheus was a very slow fellow, certainly, and went among men for a clod, and a muff, and a milksop, and a slowcoach, and a bloke, and a boodle, and so forth. And very little he did, for many years: but what he did, he never had to do over again.

'And what happened at last? There came to the two brothers the most beautiful creature that ever was seen, Pandora by name; which means, All the gifts of the Gods. But because she had a strange box in her hand, this fanciful, forecasting, suspicious, prudential, theoretical, deductive, prophesying Prometheus, who was always settling what was going to happen, would have nothing to do with pretty Pandora and her box.

'But Epimetheus took her and it, as he took everything that came; and married her for better for worse, as every man ought, whenever he has even the chance of a good wife. And they opened the box between them, of course, to see what was inside: for, else, of what possible use could it have been to them?

'And out flew all the ills which flesh is heir to;* all the children of the four great bogies, Self-will, Ignorance, Fear, and Dirt—for instance:

Measles,
Monks,

Scarlatina,
Idols,
Hooping-coughs,
Popes,
Wars,
Peacemongers,
Famines,
Quacks,
Unpaid bills,
Tight stays,
Potatoes,
Bad Wine,
Despots,
Demagogues,

And, worst of all, Naughty Boys and Girls:

But one thing remained at the bottom of the box, and that was, Hope.

'So Epimetheus got a great deal of trouble, as most men do in this world: but he got the three best things in the world into the bargain—a good wife, and experience, and hope: while Prometheus had just as much trouble, and a great deal more (as you will hear), of his own making; with nothing beside, save fancies spun out of his own brain, as a spider spins her web out of her stomach.

'And Prometheus kept on looking before him so far ahead, that as he was running about with a box of lucifers* (which were the only useful things he ever invented, and do as much harm as good), he trod on his own nose, and tumbled down (as most deductive philosophers do), whereby he set the Thames on fire; and they have hardly put it out again yet. So he had to be chained to the top of a mountain, with a vulture by him to give him a peck whenever he stirred, lest he should turn the whole world upside down with his prophecies and his theories.

'But stupid old Epimetheus went working and grubbing on, with the help of his wife Pandora, always looking behind him to see what had happened, till he really learnt to know now and then what would

happen next; and understood so well which side his bread was but-
tered, and which way the cat jumped, that he began to make things
which would work, and go on working, too; to till and drain the
ground, and to make looms, and ships, and railroads, and steam
ploughs, and electric telegraphs, and all the things which you see in
the Great Exhibition; and to foretel famine, and bad weather, and the
price of stocks, and the end of President Lincoln's policy;* till at last
he grew as rich as a Jew, and as fat as a farmer; and people thought
twice before they meddled with him, but only once before they asked
him to help them; for, because he earned his money well, he could
afford to spend it well likewise.

  'And his children are the men of science, who get good lasting
work done in the world: but the children of Prometheus are the fanatics, and the theorists, and the bigots, and the bores, and the noisy
windy people, who go telling silly folk what will happen, instead of
looking to see what has happened already.'

  Now, was not Mother Carey's a wonderful story? And, I am happy
to say, Tom believed it every word.

  For so it happened to Tom likewise. He was very sorely tried; for
though, by keeping the dog to heels (or rather to toes, for he had to
walk backward), he could see pretty well which way the dog was
hunting, yet it was much slower work to go backwards than to go
forwards. But, what was more trying still, no sooner had he got out of
Peacepool, than there came running to him all the conjurors, fortune-
tellers, astrologers, prophesiers, projectors, prestigiators, as many
as were in those parts (and there are too many of them everywhere),
Old Mother Shipton on her broomstick, with Merlin, Thomas the
Rhymer, Gerbertus, Rabanus Maurus, Nostradamus, Zadkiel,
Raphael Moore, Old Nixon,* and a good many in black coats and
white ties who might have known better, considering in what century
they were born, all bawling and screaming at him, 'Look a-head, only
look a-head; and we will show you what man never saw before, and
right away to the end of the world!'

  But I am proud to say that, though Tom had not been at
Cambridge—for, if he had, he would have certainly been senior
wrangler*—he was such a little dogged, hard, gnarly, foursquare

brick of an English boy, that he never turned his head round once all the way from Peacepool to the Other-end-of-Nowhere: but kept his eye on the dog, and let him pick out the scent, hot or cold, straight or crooked, wet or dry, up hill or down dale; by which means he never made a single mistake, and saw all the wonderful and hitherto by-no-mortal-man-imagined things, which it is my duty to relate to you in the next chapter.

# CHAPTER VIII AND LAST

COME to me, O ye children!
　For I hear you at your play;
And the questions that perplexed me
　Have vanished quite away.

Ye open the Eastern windows,
　That look towards the sun,
Where thoughts are singing swallows,
　And the brooks of morning run.

\*　　\*　　\*　　\*　　\*

For what are all our contrivings
　And the wisdom of our books,
When compared with your caresses,
　And the gladness of your looks?.

Ye are better than all the ballads
　That ever were sung or said;
For ye are living poems,
　And all the rest are dead.\*

LONGFELLOW.

ERE begins the never-to-be-too-much-studied account of the nine-hundred-and-ninety-ninth part of the wonderful things which Tom saw, on his journey to the Other-end-of-Nowhere; which all good little children are requested to read; that, if ever they get to the Other-end-of-Nowhere, as they may very probably do, they may not burst out laughing, or try to run away, or do any other silly vulgar thing which may offend Mrs Bedonebyasyoudid.

Now, as soon as Tom had left Peacepool, he came to the white lap of the great sea-mother, ten thousand fathoms deep; where she makes world-pap all day long, for the steam-giants to knead, and the fire-giants to bake, till it has risen and hardened into mountain-loaves and island-cakes.

And there Tom was very near being kneaded up in the world-pap, and turned into a fossil water-baby; which would have astonished the Geological Society of New Zealand some hundreds of thousands of years hence.

For, as he walked along in the silence of the sea-twilight, on the soft white ocean floor, he was aware of a hissing, and a roaring, and a thumping, and a pumping, as of all the steam-engines in the world at once. And, when he came near, the water grew boiling hot; not that that hurt him in the least: but it also grew as foul as gruel; and every moment he stumbled over dead shells, and fish, and sharks, and seals, and whales, which had been killed by the hot water.

And at last he came to the great sea-serpent himself, lying dead at the bottom; and, as he was too thick to scramble over, Tom had to walk round him three-quarters of a mile and more, which put him out of his path sadly; and, when he had got round, he came to the place called Stop. And there he stopped, and just in time.

For he was on the edge of a vast hole in the bottom of the sea, up which was rushing and roaring clear steam enough to work all the engines in the world at once; so clear, indeed, that it was quite light at moments; and Tom could see almost up to the top of the water above, and down below into the pit for nobody knows how far.

But, as soon as he bent his head over the edge, he got such a rap on the nose from pebbles, that he jumped back again; for the steam, as it rushed up, rasped away the sides of the hole, and hurled it up into the sea in a shower of mud and gravel and ashes; and then it spread all around, and sank again, and covered in the dead fish so fast, that before Tom had stood there five minutes he was buried in silt up to his ancles, and began to be afraid that he should have been buried alive.

And perhaps he would have been, but that while he was thinking, the whole piece of ground on which he stood was torn off and blown upwards, and away flew Tom a mile up through the sea, wondering what was coming next.

At last he stopped—thump! and found himself tight in the legs of the most wonderful bogy which he had ever seen.

It had I don't know how many wings, as big as the sails of a windmill, and spread out in a ring like them; and with them it hovered over the steam which rushed up, as a ball hovers over the top of a fountain. And for every wing above it had a leg below, with a claw like a comb at the tip, and a nostril at the root; and in the middle it had no stomach and one eye; and as for its mouth, that was all on one side, as the madreporiform tubercle* in a star-fish is. Well, it was a very strange beast; but no stranger than some dozens which you may see.

'What do you want here,' it cried quite peevishly, 'getting in my way?' and it tried to drop Tom: but he held on tight to its claws, thinking himself safer where he was.

So Tom told him who he was, and what his errand was. And the thing winked its one eye, and sneered:

'I am too old to be taken in in that way. You are come after gold— I know you are.'

'Gold! What is gold?' And really Tom did not know; but the suspicious old bogy would not believe him.

But after a while Tom began to understand a little. For, as the vapours came up out of the hole, the bogy smelt them with his nostrils, and combed them and sorted them with his combs; and then, when they steamed up through them against his wings, they were changed into showers and streams of metal. From one wing fell gold-dust, and from another silver, and from another copper, and from another tin, and from another lead, and so on, and sank into the soft mud, into veins and cracks, and hardened there. Whereby it comes to pass that the rocks are full of metal.

But, all of a sudden, somebody shut off the steam below, and the hole was left empty in an instant: and then down rushed the water into the hole, in such a whirlpool that the bogy spun round and round as fast as a tee-totum. But that was all in his day's work, like a fair fall with the hounds; so all he did was to say to Tom—

'Now is your time, youngster, to get down, if you are in earnest, which I don't believe.'

'You'll soon see,' said Tom; and away he went, as bold as Baron

Munchausen,* and shot down the rushing cataract like a salmon at Ballisodare.*

And, when he got to the bottom, he swam till he was washed on shore safe upon the Other-end-of-Nowhere; and he found it, to his surprise, as most other people do, much more like This-End-of-Somewhere than he had been in the habit of expecting.

And first he went through Waste-paper-land, where all the stupid books lie in heaps, up hill and down dale, like leaves in a winter wood; and there he saw people digging and grubbing among them, to make worse books out of bad ones, and thrashing chaff to save the dust of it; and a very good trade they drove thereby, especially among children.

Then he went by the sea of slops, to the mountain of messes, and the territory of tuck, where the ground was very sticky, for it was all made of bad toffee (not Everton toffee,* of course), and full of deep cracks and holes choked with wind-fallen fruit, and green gooseberries, and sloes, and crabs, and whinberries, and hips and haws, and all the nasty things which little children will eat if they can get them. But the fairies hide them out of the way in that country as fast as they can, and very hard work they have, and of very little use it is. For as fast as they hide away the old trash, foolish and wicked people make fresh trash full of lime and poisonous paints, and actually go and steal receipts out of old Madame Science's big book to invent poisons for little children, and sell them at wakes and fairs and tuck-shops. Very well. Let them go on. Dr Letheby and Dr Hassall* cannot catch them, though they are setting traps for them all day long. But the Fairy with the birch-rod will catch them all in time, and make them begin at one corner of their shops, and eat their way out at the other: by which time they will have got such stomach-aches as will cure them of poisoning little children.

Next he saw all the little people in the world, writing all the little books in the world, about all the other little people in the world; probably because they had no great people to write about: and if the names of the books* were not Squeeky, nor the Pumplighter, nor the Narrow Narrow World, nor the Hills of the Chattermuch, nor the Children's Twaddeday, why then they were something else.

And all the rest of the little people in the world read the books, and thought themselves each as good as the President; and perhaps they were right, for every one knows his own business best. But Tom thought he would sooner have a jolly good fairy tale, about Jack the Giant-killer or Beauty and the Beast, which taught him something that he didn't know already.

And next he came to the centre of Creation (the hub, they call it there), which lies in latitude 42.21 south, and longitude 108.56 east.

And there he found all the wise people instructing mankind in the science of spirit-rapping,* while their house was burning over their heads: and when Tom told them of the fire, they held an indignation meeting forthwith, and unanimously determined to hang Tom's dog for coming into their country with gunpowder in his mouth. Tom couldn't help saying that though they did fancy they had carried all the wit away with them out of Lincolnshire two hundred years ago, yet if they had had one such Lincolnshire nobleman among them as good old Lord Yarborough,* he would have called for the fire-engines before he hanged other people's dogs. But it was of no use, and the dog was hanged: and Tom couldn't even have his carcase; for they had abolished the have-his-carcase act in that country, for fear lest when rogues fell out, honest men should come by their own. And so they would have succeeded perfectly, as they always do, only that (as they also always do) they failed in one little particular, viz. that the dog would not die, being a water-dog, but bit their fingers so abominably that they were forced to let him go, and Tom likewise, as British subjects. Whereon they recommenced rapping for the spirits of their fathers; and very much astonished the poor old spirits were when they came, and saw how, according to the laws of Mrs Bedonebyasyoudid, their descendants had weakened their constitution by hard living.

Then came Tom to the Island of Polupragmosyne,* which some call Rogues' Harbour (but they are wrong; for that is in the middle of Bramshill Bushes,* and the county police have cleared it out long ago). There everyone knows his neighbour's business better than his own; and a very noisy place it is, as might be expected, considering that all the inhabitants are ex-officio on the wrong side of the house in the 'Parliament of Man, and the Federation of the World';* and are always making wry mouths, and crying that the fairies' grapes were sour.

There Tom saw ploughs drawing horses, nails driving hammers, birds' nests taking boys, books making authors, bulls keeping china-shops, monkeys shaving cats, dead dogs drilling live lions, blind briga-diers shelfed as principals of colleges, play-actors not in the least shelfed as popular preachers; and, in short, every one set to do some-thing which he had not learnt, because in what he had learnt, or pre-tended to learn, he had failed.

There stands the Pantheon of the Great Unsuccessful, from the builders of the Tower of Babel to those of the Trafalgar Fountains;* in which politicians lecture on the constitutions which ought to have marched, conspirators on the revolutions which ought to have suc-ceeded, economists on the schemes which ought to have made every one's fortune, projectors on the discoveries which ought to have set the Thames on fire; and (in due time) presidents on the union which ought to have re-united, and secretaries of state on the greenbacks which ought to have done just as well as hard money. There cobblers lecture on orthopedy (whatsoever that may be) because they cannot sell their shoes; and poets on Æsthetics (whatsoever that may be) because they cannot sell their poetry. There philosophers demon-strate that England would be the freest and richest country in the world, if she would only turn Papist again; penny-a-liners abuse the Times, because they have not wit enough to get on its staff; and young ladies walk about with lockets of Charles the First's hair (or of some-body else's, when the Jews' genuine stock is used up), inscribed with the neat and appropriate legend—which indeed is popular through all that land, and which, I hope, you will learn to translate in due time and to perpend likewise:—

Victrix causa diis placuit, sed victa puellis.*

When he got into the middle of the town, they all set on him at once, to show him his way; or rather, to show him that he did not know his way; for as for asking him what way he wanted to go, no one ever thought of that.

But one pulled him hither, and another poked him thither, and a third cried—

'You mustn't go west, I tell you; it is destruction to go west.'

'But I am not going west, as you may see,' said Tom.

And another, 'The east lies here, my dear; I assure you this is the east.'

'But I don't want to go east,' said Tom.

'Well then at all events, whichever way you are going, you are going wrong,' cried they all with one voice—which was the only thing which they ever agreed about; and all pointed at once to all the thirty-and-two points of the compass, till Tom thought all the signposts in England had got together, and fallen fighting.

And whether he would have ever escaped out of the town, it is hard to say, if the dog had not taken it into his head that they were going to pull his master in pieces, and tackled them so sharply about the gastrocnemius muscle,* that he gave them some business of their own to think of at last; and while they were rubbing their bitten calves, Tom and the dog got safe away.

On the borders of that island he found Gotham,* where the wise men live; the same who dragged the pond because the moon had fallen into it, and planted a hedge round the cuckoo, to keep spring all the year. And he found them bricking up the town gate, because it was so wide that little folks could not get through. And, when he asked why, they told him they were expanding their liturgy.* So he went on; for it was no business of his: only he could not help saying that in his country, if the kitten could not get in at the same hole as the cat, she might stay outside and mew.

But he saw the end of such fellows, when he came to the island of the Golden Asses,* where nothing but thistles grow. For there they were all turned into mokes* with ears a yard long, for meddling with matters which they do not understand, as Lucius did in the story. And like him, mokes they must remain, till, by the laws of development, the thistles develop into roses. Till then, they must comfort themselves with the thought, that the longer their ears are, the thicker their hides; and so a good beating don't hurt them.

Then came Tom to the great land of Hearsay, in which are no less than thirty and odd kings, beside half a dozen Republics, and perhaps more by next mail.

And there he fell in with a deep, dark, deadly, and destructive war, waged by the princes and potentates of those parts, both spiritual and temporal, against what do you think? One thing I am sure of. That unless I told you, you would never know; nor how they waged that war either; for all their strategy and art military consisted in the safe and easy process of stopping their ears and screaming, 'Oh, don't tell us!' and then running away.

So when Tom came into that land, he found them all, high and low, man, woman and child, running for their lives day and night continually, and entreating not to be told they didn't know what: only the land being an island, and they having a dislike to the water (being a musty lot for the most part) they ran round and round the shore for ever, which (as the island was exactly of the same circumference as the planet on which we have the honour of living) was hard work, especially to those who had business to look after. But before them, as bandmaster and fugleman,* ran a gentleman shearing a pig; the melodious strains of which animal led them for ever, if not to conquest, still to flight; and kept up their spirits mightily with the thought that they would at least have the pig's wool for their pains.

And running after them, day and night, came such a poor, lean, seedy, hard-worked old giant, as ought to have been cockered up,* and had a good dinner given him, and a good wife found him, and been set to play with little children; and then he would have been a very presentable old fellow after all; for he had a heart, though it was considerably overgrown with brains.

He was made up principally of fish bones and parchment, put together with wire and Canada balsam;* and smelt strongly of spirits, though he never drank anything but water: but spirits he used somehow, there was no denying. He had a great pair of spectacles on his nose, and a butterfly-net in one hand, and a geological hammer in the other; and was hung all over with pockets, full of collecting boxes, bottles, microscopes, telescopes, barometers, ordnance maps, scalpels, forceps, photographic apparatus, and all other tackle for finding out everything about everything, and a little more too. And, most strange of all, he was running not forwards but backwards, as fast as he could.

Away all the good folks ran from him, except Tom, who stood his ground and dodged between his legs; and the giant, when he had passed him, looked down, and cried, as if he was quite pleased and comforted,—

'What? who are you? And you actually don't run away, like all the rest?' But he had to take his spectacles off, Tom remarked, in order to see him plainly.

Tom told him who he was; and the giant pulled out a bottle and a cork instantly, to collect him with.

But Tom was too sharp for that, and dodged between his legs and in front of him; and then the giant could not see him at all.

'No, no, no!' said Tom, 'I've not been round the world, and through the world, and up to Mother Carey's haven, beside being caught in a net and called a Holothurian and a Cephalopod, to be bottled up by any old giant like you.'

And when the giant understood what a great traveller Tom had been, he made a truce with him at once, and would have kept him there to this day to pick his brains, so delighted was he at finding any one to tell him what he did not know before.

'Ah, you lucky little dog!' said he at last, quite simply—for he was the simplest, pleasantest, honestest, kindliest old Dominie Sampson* of a giant that ever turned the world upside down without intending it—'Ah, you lucky little dog! If I had only been where you have been, to see what you have seen!'

'Well,' said Tom, 'if you want to do that, you had best put your head under water for a few hours, as I did, and turn into a water-baby, or some other baby, and then you might have a chance.'

'Turn into a baby, eh? If I could do that, and know what was happening to me for but one hour, I should know everything then, and be at rest. But I can't; I can't be a little child again; and I suppose if I could, it would be no use, because then I should know nothing about what was happening to me. Ah, you lucky little dog!' said the poor old giant.

'But why do you run after all these poor people?' said Tom, who liked the giant very much.

'My dear, it's they that have been running after me, father and son, for hundreds and hundreds of years, throwing stones at me till they have knocked off my spectacles fifty times, and calling me a malignant and a turbaned Turk,* who beat a Venetian and traduced the state—goodness only knows what they mean, for I never read poetry—and hunting me round and round—though catch me they can't, for every time I go over the same ground, I go the faster, and grow the bigger. While all I want is to be friends with them, and to tell them something to their advantage, like Mr Joseph Ady:* only somehow they are so strangely afraid of hearing it. But, I suppose I am not a man of the world, and have no tact.'

'But why don't you turn round and tell them so?'

'Because I can't. You see, I am one of the sons of Epimetheus,* and must go backwards, if I am to go at all.'

'But why don't you stop, and let them come up to you?'

'Why, my dear, only think. If I did, all the butterflies and cockyolybirds* would fly past me, and then I could catch no more new species, and should grow rusty and mouldy, and die. And I don't intend to do that, my dear; for I have a destiny before me, they say: though what it is I don't know, and don't care.'

'Don't care?' said Tom.

'No. Do the duty which lies nearest you, and catch the first beetle you come across, is my motto; and I have thriven by it for some hundred years. Now I must go on. Dear me, while I have been talking to you, at least nine new species have escaped me.'

And on went the giant, behind before, like a bull in a china shop, till he ran into the steeple of the great idol temple (for they are all idolaters in those parts, of course, else they would never be afraid of giants), and knocked the upper half clean off, hurting himself horribly about the small of the back.

But little he cared; for as soon as the ruins of the steeple were well between his legs, he poked and peered among the falling stones, and shifted his spectacles, and pulled out his pocket-magnifier, and cried—

'An entirely new Oniscus, and three obscure Podurellæ! Beside a moth which M. le Roi des Papillons* (though he, like all Frenchmen, is given to hasty inductions) says is confined to the limits of the Glacial Drift. This is most important!'

And down he sat on the nave of the temple (not being a man of the world) to examine his Podurellæ. Whereon (as was to be expected) the roof caved in bodily, smashing the idols, and sending the priests flying out of doors and windows, like rabbits out of a burrow when a ferret goes in.

But he never heeded; for out of the dust flew a bat, and the giant had him in a moment.

'Dear me! This is even more important! Here is a cognate species to that which Macgilliwaukie Brown insists is confined to the Buddhist Temples of Little Thibet; and now when I look at it, it may be only a variety produced by difference of climate!'

And having bagged his bat, up he got, and on he went; while all the people ran, being in none the better humour for having their temple smashed for the sake of three obscure species of Podurella, and a Buddhist bat.

'Well,' thought Tom; 'this is a very pretty quarrel, with a good deal to be said on both sides. But it is no business of mine.'

And no more it was; because he was a water-baby, and had the original sow by the right ear;* which you will never have, unless you be a baby, whether of the water, the land, or the air, matters not, provided you can only keep on continually being a baby.

So the giant ran round after the people, and the people ran round after the giant, and they are running unto this day for aught I know, or do not know; and will run till either he, or they, or both, turn into little children. And then, as Shakspeare says (and therefore it must be true)—

> Jack shall have Gill
> Nought shall go ill
> The man shall have his mare again, and all go well.*

Then Tom came to a very famous island, which was called, in the days of the great traveller Captain Gulliver, the Isle of Laputa.* But Mrs Bedonebyasyoudid has named it over again, the Isle of Tomtoddies, all heads and no bodies.

And when Tom came near it, he heard such a grumbling and grunting and growling and wailing and weeping and whining that he thought people must be ringing little pigs, or cropping puppies' ears, or drowning kittens: but when he came nearer still, he began to hear words among the noise; which was the Tomtoddies' song which they sing morning and evening, and all night too, to their great idol Examination—

> I can't learn my lesson: the examiner's coming!

And that was the only song which they knew.

And when Tom got on shore the first thing he saw was a great pillar, on one side of which was inscribed, 'Playthings not allowed here'; at which he was so shocked that he would not stay to see what was written on the other side. Then he looked round for the people of the island: but instead of men, women, and children, he found nothing but turnips and radishes, beet and mangold wurzel, without a single green leaf among them, and half of them burst and decayed, with toadstools growing out of them. Those which were left began crying to Tom, in half a dozen different languages at once, and all of them badly spoken, 'I can't learn my lesson; do come and help me!' And one cried, 'Can you show me how to extract this square-root?'

And another, 'Can you tell me the distance between α Lyræ and β Camelopardalis?'*

And another, 'What is the latitude and longitude of Snooksville, in Noman's County, Oregon, US?'

And another, 'What was the name of Mutius Scævola's* thirteenth cousin's grandmother's maid's cat?'

And another, 'How long would it take a school-inspector of average activity to tumble head over heels from London to York?'

And another, 'Can you tell me the name of a place that nobody ever heard of, where nothing ever happened, in a country which has not been discovered yet?'

And another, 'Can you show me how to correct this hopelessly corrupt passage of Graidiocolosyrtus Tabenniticus,* on the cause why crocodiles have no tongues?'

And so on, and so on, and so on, till one would have thought they were all trying for tide-waiters'* places, or cornetcies* in the heavy dragoons.

'And what good on earth will it do you if I did tell you?' quoth Tom.

Well, they didn't know that: all they knew was the examiner was coming.

Then Tom stumbled on the hugest and softest nimble-comequick* turnip you ever saw filling a hole in a crop of swedes, and it cried to him, 'Can you tell me anything at all about anything you like?'

'About what?' says Tom.

'About anything you like; for as fast as I learn things I forget them again. So my mamma says that my intellect is not adapted for methodic science, and says that I must go in for general information.'

Tom told him that he did not know general information, nor any officers in the army; only he had a friend once that went for a drummer: but he could tell him a great many strange things which he had seen in his travels.

So he told him prettily enough, while the poor turnip listened very carefully; and the more he listened, the more he forgot, and the more water ran out of him.

Tom thought he was crying: but it was only his poor brains running away, from being worked so hard; and as Tom talked, the unhappy turnip streamed down all over with juice, and split and shrank till nothing was left of him but rind and water; whereat Tom ran away in a fright, for he thought he might be taken up for killing the turnip.

But, on the contrary, the turnip's parents were highly delighted, and considered him a saint and a martyr, and put up a long inscription over his tomb about his wonderful talents, early development, and unparalleled precocity. Were they not a foolish couple? But there was a still more foolish couple next to them, who were beating a wretched little radish, no bigger than my thumb, for sullenness and obstinacy and wilful stupidity, and never knew that the reason why it couldn't learn or hardly even speak was, that there was a great worm inside it eating out all its brains. But even they are no foolisher than some hundred score of papas and mammas, who fetch the rod when they ought to fetch a new toy, and send to the dark cupboard instead of to the doctor.

Tom was so puzzled and frightened with all he saw, that he was longing to ask the meaning of it; and at last he stumbled over a respectable old stick lying half covered with earth. But a very stout and worthy stick it was, for it belonged to good Roger Ascham* in old time, and had carved on its head King Edward the Sixth, with the Bible in his hand.

'You see,' said the stick, 'there were as pretty little children once as you could wish to see, and might have been so still if they had been only left to grow up like human beings, and then handed over to me; but their foolish fathers and mothers, instead of letting them pick flowers, and make dirt-pies, and get birds' nests, and dance round the gooseberry bush,* as little children should, kept them always at lessons, working, working, working, learning weekday lesson all weekdays, and Sunday lessons all Sunday, and weekly examinations every Saturday, and monthly examinations every month, and yearly examinations every year, everything seven times over, as if once was not enough, and enough as good as a feast—till their brains grew big, and their bodies grew small, and they were all changed into turnips, with little but water inside; and still their foolish parents actually pick the leaves off them as fast as they grow, lest they should have anything green about them.'

'Ah!' said Tom, 'if dear Mrs Doasyouwouldbedoneby knew of it she would send them a lot of tops, and balls, and marbles, and ninepins, and make them all as jolly as sand-boys.'

'It would be no use,' said the stick. 'They can't play now, if they tried. Don't you see how their legs have turned to roots and grown into the ground, by never taking any exercise, but sapping and moping always in the same place? But here comes the Examiner-of-all-Examiners. So you had better get away, I warn you, or he will examine you and your dog into the bargain, and set him to examine all the other dogs, and you to examine all the other water-babies. There is no escaping out of his hands, for his nose is nine thousand miles long, and can go down chimneys and through keyholes, upstairs, downstairs, in my lady's chamber, examining all little boys, and the little boys' tutors likewise. But when he is thrashed—so Mrs Bedonebyasyoudid has promised me—I shall have the thrashing of him: and if I don't lay it on with a will it's a pity.'

Tom went off: but rather slowly and surlily; for he was somewhat minded to face this same Examiner-of-all-Examiners, who came striding among the poor turnips, binding heavy burdens and grievous to be borne, and laying them on little children's shoulders, like the Scribes and Pharisees of old,* and not touching the same with one of his fingers; for he had plenty of money, and a fine house to live in, and so forth; which was more than the poor little turnips had.

But when he got near, he looked so big and burly and dictatorial, and shouted so loud to Tom to come and be examined, that Tom ran for his life, and the dog too. And really it was time; for the poor turnips, in their hurry and fright, crammed themselves so fast to be ready for the Examiner, that they burst and popped by dozens all round him, till the place sounded like Aldershott* on a field-day, and Tom thought he should be blown into the air, dog and all.

As he went down to the shore he passed the poor turnip's new tomb. But Mrs Bedonebyasyoudid had taken away the epitaph about talents and precocity and development, and put up one of her own instead which Tom thought much more sensible:—

> Instruction sore long time I bore,
>     And cramming was in vain;
> Till Heaven did please my woes to ease,
>     By water on the brain.

So Tom jumped into the sea, and swam on his way, singing:—

> Farewell, Tomtoddies all; I thank my stars
> That nought I know save those three royal r's:
> Reading and riting sure, with rithmetick,
> Will help a lad of sense through thin and thick.

Whereby you may see that Tom was no poet: but no more was John Bunyan,* though he was as wise a man as you will meet in a month of Sundays.

And next he came to Oldwivesfabledom, where the folks were all heathens, and worshipped a howling ape.

And there he found a little boy sitting in the middle of the road, and crying bitterly.

'What are you crying for?' said Tom.

'Because I am not as frightened as I could wish to be.'

'Not frightened? You are a queer little chap: but, if you want to be frightened, here goes—Boo!'

'Ah,' said the little boy, 'that is very kind of you; but I don't feel that it has made any impression.'

Tom offered to upset him, punch him, stamp on him, fettle* him over the head with a brick, or anything else whatsoever which would give him the slightest comfort.

But he only thanked Tom very civilly, in fine long words which he had heard other folk use, and which, therefore, he thought were fit and proper to use himself; and cried on till his papa and mamma came, and sent off for the Powwow man immediately. And a very good-natured gentleman and lady they were, though they were heathens; and talked quite pleasantly to Tom about his travels, till the Powwow man arrived, with his thunderbox* under his arm.

And a well-fed, ill-favoured gentleman he was, as ever served her Majesty at Portland.* Tom was a little frightened at first; for he thought it was Grimes. But he soon saw his mistake: for Grimes always looked a man in the face; and this fellow never did. And when he spoke, it was fire and smoke; and when he sneezed, it was squibs and crackers; and when he cried (which he did whenever it paid him), it was boiling pitch; and some of it was sure to stick.

'Here we are again!'* cried he, like the clown in a pantomime. 'So you can't feel frightened, my little dear—eh? I'll do that for you. I'll make an impression on you! Yah! Boo! Whirroo! Hullabaloo!'

And he rattled, thumped, brandished his thunderbox, yelled, shouted, raved, roared, stamped, and danced corrobory* like any black fellow; and then he touched a spring in the thunderbox, and out popped turnip-ghosts and magic-lanthorns and pasteboard bogies and spring-heeled Jacks and sallabalas,* with such a horrid din, clatter, clank, roll, rattle, and roar, that the little boy turned up the whites of his eyes, and fainted right away.

And at that his poor heathen papa and mamma were as much

delighted as if they had found a gold mine; and fell down upon their knees before the Powwow man, and gave him a palanquin* with a pole of solid silver and curtains of cloth of gold; and carried him about in it on their own backs: but as soon as they had taken him up, the pole stuck to their shoulders, and they could not set him down any more, but carried him on willy-nilly, as Sinbad carried the old man of the sea:* which was a pitiable sight to see; for the father was a very brave officer, and wore two swords and a blue button; and the mother was as pretty a lady as ever had pinched feet like a Chinese. But you see, they had chosen to do a foolish thing just once too often; so by the laws of Mrs Bedonebyasyoudid, they had to go on doing it whether they chose or not, till the coming of the Cocqcigrues.

Ah! don't you wish that some one would go and convert those poor heathens, and teach them not to frighten their little children into fits?

'Now, then,' said the Powwow man to Tom, 'wouldn't you like to be frightened, my little dear? For I can see plainly that you are a very wicked, naughty, graceless, reprobate boy.'

'You're another,' quoth Tom, very sturdily. And when the man ran at him, and cried 'Boo!' Tom ran at him in return, and cried 'Boo!' likewise, right in his face, and set the little dog upon him; and at his legs the dog went.

At which, if you will believe it, the fellow turned tail, thunderbox and all, with a 'Woof!' like an old sow on the common; and ran for his life, screaming, 'Help! thieves! murder! fire! He is going to kill me! I am a ruined man! He will murder me; and break, burn, and destroy my precious and invaluable thunderbox; and then you will have no more thunder showers in the land. Help! help! help!'

At which the papa and mamma and all the people of Oldwivesfabledom, flew at Tom, shouting, 'Oh, the wicked, impudent, hard-hearted, graceless boy! Beat him, kick him, shoot him, drown him, hang him, burn him!' and so forth: but luckily they had nothing to shoot, hang, or burn him with, for the fairies had hid all the killing-tackle out of the way a little while before; so they could only pelt him with stones; and some of the stones went clean through him, and came out the other side. But he did not mind that a bit; for the holes closed up again as fast as they were made, because he was a water-baby. However, he was very glad when he was safe out of the country, for the noise there made him all but deaf.

Then he came to a very quiet place, called Leaveheavenalone. And there the sun was drawing water out of the sea to make steam-threads, and the wind was twisting them up to make cloud-patterns, till they had worked between them the loveliest wedding veil of Chantilly lace, and hung it up in their own Crystal Palace* for any one to buy who could afford it; while the good old sea never grudged, for she knew they would pay her back honestly. So the sun span, and the wind wove, and all went well with the great steam-loom; as is likely, considering—and considering—and considering—

And at last, after innumerable adventures, each more wonderful than the last, he saw before him a huge building, much bigger, and—what is most surprising—a little uglier than a certain new lunatic asylum,* but not built quite of the same materials. None of it, at least—or, indeed, for aught that I ever saw, any part of any other building whatsoever—is cased with nine-inch brick inside and out, and filled up with rubble between the walls, in order that any gentleman who has been confined during her Majesty's pleasure may be unconfined during his own pleasure, and take a walk in the neighbouring park to improve his spirits, after an hour's light and wholesome labour with his dinner-fork or one of the legs of his iron bedstead. No. The walls of this building were built on an entirely different principle, which need not be described, as it has not yet been discovered.

Tom walked towards this great building, wondering what it was, and having a strange fancy that he might find Mr Grimes inside it, till he saw running toward him, and shouting 'Stop!' three or four people, who, when they came nearer, were nothing else than policemen's truncheons, running along without legs or arms.

Tom was not astonished. He was long past that. Besides, he had seen the naviculæ* in the water move nobody knows how, a hundred times, without arms, or legs, or anything to stand in their stead. Neither was he frightened; for he had been doing no harm.

So he stopped; and, when the foremost truncheon came up and

asked his business, he showed Mother Carey's pass; and the truncheon looked at it in the oddest fashion; for he had one eye in the
middle of his upper end, so that when he looked at anything, being
quite stiff, he had to slope himself, and poke himself, till it was a
wonder why he did not tumble over; but, being quite full of the spirit
of justice (as all policemen, and their truncheons, ought to be), he
was always in a position of stable equilibrium, whichever way he put
himself.

'All right—pass on,' said he at last. And then he added: 'I had better go with you, young man.' And Tom had no objection, for such
company was both respectable and safe; so the truncheon coiled its
thong neatly round its handle, to prevent nipping itself up—for the
thong had got loose in running—and marched on by Tom's side.

'Why have you no policeman to carry you?' asked Tom, after a
while.

'Because we are not like those clumsy-made truncheons in the
land-world, which cannot go without having a whole man to carry
them about. We do our own work for ourselves; and do it very well,
though I say it who should not.'

'Then why have you a thong to your handle?' asked Tom.

'To hang ourselves up by, of course, when we are off duty.'

Tom had got his answer, and had no more to say, till they came up
to the great iron door of the prison. And there the truncheon knocked
twice, with its own head.

A wicket in the door opened, and out looked a tremendous old
brass blunderbuss charged up to the muzzle with slugs, who was the
porter; and Tom started back a little at the sight of him.

'What case is this?' he asked in a deep voice, out of his broad
bell-mouth.

'If you please, sir, it is no case; only a young gentleman from her
ladyship, who wants to see Grimes the master-sweep.'

'Grimes?' said the blunderbuss. And he pulled in his muzzle,
perhaps to look over his prison-lists.

'Grimes is up chimney No. 345,' he said from inside. 'So the young
gentleman had better go on to the roof.'

Tom looked up at the enormous wall, which seemed at least ninety miles high, and wondered how he should ever get up: but, when he hinted that to the truncheon, it settled the matter in a moment. For it whisked round, and gave him such a shove behind as sent him up to the roof in no time, with his little dog under his arm.

And there he walked along the leads, till he met another truncheon, and told him his errand.

'Very good,' it said. 'Come along: but it will be of no use. He is the most unremorseful, hard-hearted, foul-mouthed fellow I have in charge; and thinks about nothing but beer and pipes, which are not allowed here, of course.'

So they walked along over the leads, and very sooty they were, and Tom thought the chimneys must want sweeping very much. But he was surprised to see that the soot did not stick to his feet, or dirty them in the least. Neither did the live coals, which were lying about in plenty, burn him; for, being a water-baby, his radical humours were of a moist and cold nature, as you may read at large in Lemnius, Cardan, Van Helmont,* and other gentlemen, who knew as much as they could, and no man can know more.

And at last they came to chimney No. 345. Out of the top of it, his head and shoulders just showing, stuck poor Mr Grimes; so sooty, and bleared, and ugly, that Tom could hardly bear to look at him. And in his mouth was a pipe: but it was not a-light, though he was pulling at it with all his might.

'Attention, Mr Grimes,' said the truncheon; 'here is a gentleman come to see you.'

But Mr Grimes only said bad words; and kept grumbling, 'My pipe won't draw. My pipe won't draw.'

'Keep a civil tongue, and attend!' said the truncheon; and popped up just like Punch,* hitting Grimes such a crack over the head with itself, that his brains rattled inside like a dried walnut in its shell. He tried to get his hands out, and rub the place: but he could not, for they were stuck fast in the chimney.

Now he was forced to attend.

'Hey!' he said, 'why, it's Tom! I suppose you have come here to laugh at me, you spiteful little atomy?'*

Tom assured him he had not, but only wanted to help him.

'I don't want anything except beer, and that I can't get; and a light to this bothering pipe, and that I can't get either.'

'I'll get you one,' said Tom; and he took up a live coal (there were plenty lying about) and put it to Grimes's pipe: but it went out instantly.

'It's no use,' said the truncheon, leaning itself up against the chimney, and looking on. 'I tell you, it is no use. His heart is so cold that it freezes everything that comes near him. You will see that presently, plain enough.'

'Oh, of course, it's my fault. Everything's always my fault,' said Grimes. 'Now don't go to hit me again (for the truncheon started upright, and looked very wicked); you know, if my arms were only free, you daren't hit me then.'

The truncheon leant back against the chimney, and took no notice of the personal insult, like a well-trained policeman as it was, though he was ready enough to avenge any transgression against morality or order.

'But can't I help you in any other way? Can't I help you to get out of this chimney?' said Tom.

'No,' interposed the truncheon; 'he has come to the place where everybody must help themselves;* and he will find it out, I hope, before he is done with me.'

'Oh, yes,' said Grimes, 'of course it's me. Did I ask to be brought here into the prison? Did I ask to be set to sweep your foul chimneys? Did I ask to have lighted straw put under me to make me go up? Did I ask to stick fast in the very first chimney of all, because it was so shamefully clogged up with soot? Did I ask to stay here—I don't know how long—a hundred years, I do believe, and never get my pipe, nor my beer, nor nothing fit for a beast, let alone a man.'

'No,' answered a solemn voice behind. 'No more did Tom, when you behaved to him in the very same way.'

It was Mrs Bedonebyasyoudid. And, when the truncheon saw her, it started bolt upright—Attention!—and made such a low bow, that if it had not been full of the spirit of justice, it must have tumbled on its end, and probably hurt its one eye. And Tom made his bow too.

'Oh, ma'am,' he said, 'don't think about me; that's all past and gone, and good times and bad times and all times pass over. But may not I help poor Mr Grimes? Mayn't I try and get some of these bricks away, that he may move his arms?'

'You may try, of course,' she said.

So Tom pulled and tugged at the bricks: but he could not move one. And then he tried to wipe Mr Grimes's face: but the soot would not come off.

'Oh, dear!' he said, 'I have come all this way, through all these terrible places, to help you, and now I am of no use after all.'

'You had best leave me alone,' said Grimes; 'you are a good-natured forgiving little chap, and that's truth; but you'd best be off. The hail's coming on soon, and it will beat the eyes out of your little head.'

'What hail?'

'Why hail that falls every evening here; and, till it comes close to me, it's like so much warm rain: but then it turns to hail over my head, and knocks me about like small shot.'

'That hail will never come any more,' said the strange lady. 'I have told you before what it was. It was your mother's tears, those which she shed when she prayed for you by her bedside; but your cold heart froze it into hail. But she is gone to heaven now, and will weep no more for her graceless son.'

Then Grimes was silent a while; and then he looked very sad.

'So my old mother's gone, and I never there to speak to her! Ah! a good woman she was, and might have been a happy one, in her little school there in Vendale, if it hadn't been for me and my bad ways.'

'Did she keep the school in Vendale?' asked Tom. And then he told Grimes all the story of his going to her house, and how she could not abide the sight of a chimney-sweep, and then how kind she was, and how he turned into a water-baby.

'Ah!' said Grimes, 'good reason she had to hate the sight of a chimney-sweep. I ran away from her and took up with the sweeps, and never let her know where I was, nor sent her a penny to help her, and now it's too late—too late!' said Mr Grimes.

And he began crying and blubbering like a great baby, till his pipe dropped out of his mouth, and broke all to bits.

'Oh dear, if I was but a little chap in Vendale again, to see the clear beck, and the apple-orchard, and the yew-hedge, how different I would go on! But it's too late now. So you go along, you kind little chap, and don't stand to look at a man crying, that's old enough to be your father, and never feared the face of man, nor of worse neither. But I'm beat now, and beat I must be. I've made my bed, and I must lie on it. Foul I would be, and foul I am, as an Irishwoman said to me once; and little I heeded it. It's all my own fault: but it's too late.' And he cried so bitterly that Tom began crying too.

'Never too late,' said the fairy, in such a strange soft new voice that Tom looked up at her; and she was so beautiful for the moment, that Tom half fancied she was her sister.

No more was it too late. For, as poor Grimes cried and blubbered on, his own tears did what his mother's could not do, and Tom's could not do, and nobody's on earth could do for him; for they washed the soot off his face and off his clothes; and then they washed the mortar away from between the bricks; and the chimney crumbled down; and Grimes began to get out of it.

Up jumped the truncheon, and was going to hit him on the crown a tremendous thump, and drive him down again like a cork into a bottle. But the strange lady put it aside.

'Will you obey me if I give you a chance?'

'As you please, ma'am. You're stronger than me, that I know too well, and wiser than me, I know too well also. And, as for being my own master, I've fared ill enough with that as yet. So whatever your ladyship pleases to order me; for I'm beat, and that's the truth.'

'Be it so then—you may come out. But remember, disobey me again, and into a worse place still you go.'

'I beg pardon, ma'am, but I never disobeyed you that I know of. I never had the honour of setting eyes upon you till I came to these ugly quarters.'

'Never saw me? Who said to you, Those that will be foul, foul they will be?'

Grimes looked up; and Tom looked up too; for the voice was that of the Irishwoman who met them the day that they went out together to Harthover. 'I gave you your warning then: but you gave it yourself a thousand times before and since. Every bad word that you said—every cruel and mean thing that you did—every time that you got tipsy—every day that you went dirty—you were disobeying me, whether you knew it or not.'

'If I'd only known, ma'am—'

'You knew well enough that you were disobeying something, though you did not know it was me. But come out and take your chance. Perhaps it may be your last.'

So Grimes stept out of the chimney, and, really, if it had not been for the scars on his face, he looked as clean and respectable as a master-sweep need look.

'Take him away,' said she to the truncheon, 'and give him his ticket-of-leave.'*

'And what is he to do, ma'am?'

'Get him to sweep out the crater of Etna; he will find some very steady men working out their time there, who will teach him his business: but mind, if that crater gets choked again, and there is an earthquake in consequence, bring them all to me, and I shall investigate the case very severely.'

So the truncheon marched off Mr Grimes, looking as meek as a drowned worm.

And for aught I know, or do not know, he is sweeping the crater of Etna to this very day.

'And now', said the fairy to Tom, 'your work here is done. You may as well go back again.'

'I should be glad enough to go,' said Tom, 'but how am I to get up that great hole again, now the steam has stopped blowing?'

'I will take you up the backstairs: but I must bandage your eyes first; for I never allow anybody to see those backstairs of mine.'

'I am sure I shall not tell anybody about them, ma'am, if you bid me not.'

'Aha! So you think, my little man. But you would soon forget your promise if you got back into the land-world. For, if people only once found out that you had been up my backstairs, you would have all the fine ladies kneeling to you, and the rich men emptying their purses before you, and statesmen offering you place and power; and young

and old, rich and poor, crying to you, "Only tell us the great backstairs secret, and we will be your slaves; we will make you lord, king,
emperor, bishop, archbishop, pope, if you like—only tell us the
secret of the backstairs. For thousands of years we have been paying,
and petting, and obeying, and worshipping quacks who told us they
had the key of the backstairs, and could smuggle us up them; and in
spite of all our disappointments, we will honour, and glorify, and
adore, and beatify, and translate, and apotheotize you likewise, on the
chance of your knowing something about the backstairs, that we may
all go on pilgrimage to it; and, even if we cannot get up it, lie at the
foot of it, and cry—

> Oh backstairs,
> precious backstairs,
> invaluable backstairs,
> requisite backstairs,
> necessary backstairs,
> good-natured backstairs,
> cosmopolitan backstairs,
> comprehensive backstairs,
> accommodating backstairs,
> well-bred backstairs,
> comfortable backstairs,
> humane backstairs,
> reasonable backstairs,
> long-sought backstairs,
> coveted backstairs,
> aristocratic backstairs,
> respectable backstairs,
> gentlemanlike backstairs,
> ladylike backstairs,
> commercial backstairs,
> economical backstairs,
> practical backstairs,
> logical backstairs,
> deductive backstairs,

orthodox backstairs,
probable backstairs,
credible backstairs,
demonstrable backstairs,
irrefragable backstairs,
potent backstairs,
all-but-omnipotent backstairs,
etc.

Save us from the consequences of our own actions, and from the cruel fairy, Mrs Bedonebyasyoudid!" Do not you think that you would be a little tempted then to tell what you know, laddie?'

Tom thought so certainly. 'But why do they want so to know about the backstairs?' asked he, being a little frightened at the long words, and not understanding them the least; as, indeed, he was not meant to do, or you either.

'That I shall not tell you. I never put things into little folks' heads which are but too likely to come there of themselves. So come—now I must bandage your eyes.' So she tied the bandage on his eyes with one hand, and with the other she took it off.

'Now,' she said, 'you are safe up the stairs.' Tom opened his eyes very wide, and his mouth too; for he had not, as he thought, moved a single step. But, when he looked round him, there could be no doubt that he was safe up the backstairs, whatsoever they may be, which no man is going to tell you, for the plain reason that no man knows.

The first thing which Tom saw was the black cedars, high and sharp against the rosy dawn; and St Brandan's Isle reflected double in the still broad silver sea. The wind sang softly in the cedars, and the water sang among the caves; the sea-birds sang as they streamed out into the ocean, and the land-birds as they built among the boughs; and the air was so full of song that it stirred St Brandan and his hermits, as they slumbered in the shade; and they moved their good old lips, and sang their morning hymn amid their dreams. But among all the songs one came across the water more sweet and clear than all; for it was the song of a young girl's voice.

And what was the song which she sang? Ah, my little man, I am too old to sing that song, and you too young to understand it. But have patience, and keep your eye single, and your hands clean, and you will learn some day to sing it yourself, without needing any man to teach you.

And as Tom neared the island, there sat upon a rock the most graceful creature that ever was seen, looking down, with her chin upon her hand, and paddling with her feet in the water. And when they came to her she looked up, and behold it was Ellie.

'Oh, Miss Ellie,' said he, 'how you are grown!'

'Oh, Tom,' said she, 'how you are grown, too!'

And no wonder; they were both quite grown up—he into a tall man, and she into a beautiful woman.

'Perhaps I may be grown,' she said. 'I have had time enough; for I have been sitting here waiting for you many a hundred years, till I thought you were never coming.'

'Many a hundred years?' thought Tom; but he had seen so much in his travels that he had quite given up being astonished; and, indeed, he could think of nothing but Ellie. So he stood and looked at Ellie, and Ellie looked at him; and they liked the employment so much that they stood and looked for seven years more, and neither spoke or stirred.

At last they heard the fairy say: 'Attention, children! Are you never going to look at me again?'

'We have been looking at you all this while,' they said. And so they thought they had been.

'Then look at me once more,' said she.

They looked—and both of them cried out at once, 'Oh, who are you, after all?'

'You are our dear Mrs Doasyouwouldbedoneby.'

'No, you are good Mrs Bedonebyasyoudid; but you are grown quite beautiful now!'

'To you,' said the fairy. 'But look again.'

'You are Mother Carey,' said Tom, in a very low, solemn voice; for he had found out something which made him very happy, and yet frightened him more than all that he had ever seen.

'But you are grown quite young again.'

'To you,' said the fairy. 'Look again.'

'You are the Irishwoman who met me the day I went to Harthover!'

And when they looked she was neither of them, and yet all of them at once.

'My name is written in my eyes, if you have eyes to see it there.'

And they looked into her great, deep, soft eyes, and they changed again and again into every hue, as the light changes in a diamond.

'Now read my name,' said she, at last.

And her eyes flashed, for one moment, clear, white, blazing light:* but the children could not read her name; for they were dazzled, and hid their faces in their hands.

'Not yet, young things, not yet,' said she, smiling; and then she turned to Ellie.

'You may take him home with you now on Sundays, Ellie. He has won his spurs in the great battle, and become fit to go with you, and be a man; because he has done the thing he did not like.'

So Tom went home with Ellie on Sundays, and sometimes on week-days, too; and he is now a great man of science, and can plan railroads, and steam-engines, and electric telegraphs, and rifled guns, and so forth; and knows everything about everything, except why a hen's egg don't turn into a crocodile, and two or three other little things which no one will know till the coming of the Cocqcigrues. And all this from what he learnt when he was a water-baby, underneath the sea.

'And of course Tom married Ellie?'

My dear child, what a silly notion! Don't you know that no one ever marries in a fairy tale, under the rank of a prince or a princess?

'And Tom's dog?'

Oh, you may see him any clear night in July; for the old dog-star was so worn out by the last three hot summers that there have been no dog-days* since; so that they had to take him down and put Tom's dog up in his place. Therefore, as new brooms sweep clean, we may hope for some warm weather this year. And that is the end of my story.

## MORAL.

And now, my dear little man, what should we learn from this parable?

We should learn thirty-seven or thirty-nine things,* I am not exactly sure which: but one thing, at least, we may learn, and that is this—when we see efts in the ponds, never to throw stones at them, or catch them with crooked pins, or put them into vivariums* with sticklebacks, that the sticklebacks may prick them in their poor little stomachs, and make them jump out of the glass into somebody's workbox, and so come to a bad end. For these efts are nothing else but the water-babies who are stupid and dirty, and will not learn their lessons and keep themselves clean; and, therefore (as comparative anatomists will tell you fifty years hence, though they are not learned enough to tell you now), their skulls grow flat, their jaws grow out, and their brains grow small, and their tails grow long, and they lose all their ribs (which I am sure you would not like to do), and their skins grow dirty and spotted, and they never get into the clear rivers, much less into the great wide sea, but hang about in dirty ponds, and live in the mud, and eat worms, as they deserve to do.

But that is no reason why you should ill-use them: but only why you should pity them, and be kind to them, and hope that some day they will wake up, and be ashamed of their nasty, dirty, lazy, stupid life, and try to amend, and become something better once more. For, perhaps, if they do so, then after 379,423 years, nine months, thirteen days, two hours, and twenty-one minutes (for aught that appears to the contrary), if they work very hard and wash very hard all that time, their brains may grow bigger, and their jaws grow smaller, and their ribs come back, and their tails wither off, and they will turn into water-babies again, and, perhaps, after that into land-babies; and after that, perhaps, into grown men.

You know they won't? Very well, I dare say you know best. But, you see, some folks have a great liking for those poor little efts. They never did anybody any harm, or could if they tried; and their only fault is, that they do no good—any more than some thousands of their betters. But what with ducks, and what with pike, and what with sticklebacks, and what with water-beetles, and what with naughty boys, they are 'sae sair haddened doun',* as the Scotsmen say, that it is a wonder how they live; and some folks can't help hoping, with good Bishop Butler,* that they may have another chance, to make things fair and even, somewhere, somewhen, somehow.

Meanwhile, do you learn your lessons, and thank God that you have plenty of cold water to wash in; and wash in it too, like a true English man. And then, if my story is not true, something better is; and if I am not quite right, still you will be, as long as you stick to hard work and cold water.

But remember always, as I told you at first, that this is all a fairy tale, and only fun and pretence; and, therefore, you are not to believe a word of it, even if it is true.

# APPENDIX I

## TEXTUAL VARIANTS

THE following table sets out the chief changes in the text of *The Water-Babies* that took place between its original publication in *Macmillan's Magazine* (*MM*) and the first edition of 1863. A few verbal alterations of no significance have been omitted, as have many changes to punctuation (mostly the deletion of commas). References are to page and line number in the present edition; in each case the 1863 text is printed first, followed by the *MM* version.

7.15 Harthover Place] For Harthover Place

8.19 just as well do all day] just as well do by day

9.16–10.4 Soon they came up with . . . bathe in it likewise. Not in *MM*.

10.13 sat] satt

10.20 raspberry] raspberries

10.27–30 Tom was picking . . . he stopped] Tom was picking the flowers as fast as he could, and a very pretty nosegay he had made. But when he saw Grimes do that, he stopped

11.5–12.11 'I don't care for you' . . . leaving Tom in peace. Not in *MM*, where this lengthy passage is covered simply by: 'So little Tom was forced to come along, looking back wistfully at the cool clear spring.' [Probably not intended as a pre-echo of the now famous verses that end the chapter.]

12.32–3 outside in . . . inside out] inside out . . . outside in

16.20–1 one a man] one of a man

17.34 plunder, destroy] plunder, and destroy

18.25 Grimes] His master

18.32 he ran on, and gave chase to Tom] he ran after Tom

19.3–5 The Irishwoman . . . to Tom likewise. Not in *MM*.

19.15–16 when Grimes, gardener, the groom] when the gardener, the groom

19.17 and the Irishwoman. Not in *MM*.

19.29–31 However, Tom . . . while as for running] However, Tom had never had a father; so certainly he did not want one, and expected to have to take care of himself; and as for running

19.34 Wherefore] And so

21.17–27 But the Irishwoman . . . out of mind. Not in *MM*.

21.28 And now Tom] And now he

21.33 stare about at] stare about him at

22.27–8 went off, screaming . . . the end of the world is come] went off, screaming 'Tipsalteery, tipsalteery—murder, thieves, fire—tipsal-cock-cock-kick—the end of the world is come

23.15–19 What Tom would have said . . . she saw him. Not in *MM*.

24.13 Before him] And before him

24.23 Then] And now

24.25 As Tom looked] And as Tom looked

25.1 However] But

25.4 tinkled] trickled

25.15 smoky] smoke-grimed

25.32–3 So Tom went down . . . behind him. Not in *MM*.

27.11 saxifrage] saxifrages

27.30 while through] and through

28.4–5 And all the while . . . behind him. Not in *MM*.

28.27 I hope] And I hope

29.15 fire-place, which was filled with] fire-place, filled with

29.18 At her feet] And at her feet

29.27–8 the girls began to cry] and the girls began to cry

31.11–12 and then that he heard . . . they will be. Not in *MM*.

32.6–7 him . . . he . . . that man] them . . . they . . . him

32.11–33.6 And all the while . . . that he tumbled . . . into the clear cool stream. Not in *MM*, except: So he tumbled . . . into the clear cool water.

33.17–19 There are only a clumsy lot . . . all they want. Not in *MM*.

35.27 They took him up] And they took him up

36.33 When they came] And when they came

37.15 Whereat the old dame] And the old dame

38.41 *MM* did not place quotes around the sequence of interlocutory statements and questions as from Grenville.

40.22–3 only lately] this very year [see note to p. 40 for textual changes regarding Archaeopteryx here]

40.27 folks' fancy] people's fancy

43.1 as foxes say, and geese believe] as rogues say, and fools believe

43.6 But at all events] At all events

43.28 than he need have done] than he ought

44.14–29 Verses entitled SONG in *MM*.

44.30 but they are only the body of it] but they are but the body of it

45.4 Now if] And if

46.9 a fish and a beast] a beast and a fish

48.22 Sometimes] And sometimes

48.24 sand-pipes] sand-tubes

48.30–1 pebbles; then . . . weed; then] pebbles; and then . . . weed; and then

48.34–49.1 apt to be; then . . . rotten wood, then . . . Irishman's coat.

Then] apt to be; and then . . . rotten wood, and then . . . Irishman's coat. And then

49.6–9  as they were at the end of the Long Pond last May, [and] as we did. Not in *MM*.

49.26  So now he found] And now he found

49.28–9  There was one . . . fellow, too, who peeped . . . bricks. He had two big wheels] And there was one . . . fellow, who peeped . . . bricks; and he had two big wheels

49.35  all the mud he put into the little wheel] all the mud he swept together into the little wheel

50.21–2  out of his way, or crept] out of his way, and crept

50.24–31  The water-fairies . . . teach themselves. Paragraph not in *MM*.

50.34  house-door before: so] house-door before; and

51.1  in bed? So] in bed? But

51.7  However, if she didn't] But if she didn't

52.3  he let go] he left go

52.14  dark room. It moved] dark room. And it moved

52.22  strong and firm; the most lovely] strong and firm; and the most lovely

53.28  and hurt). So Tom] and hurt). And Tom

54.19  cocked up the two whisks] cocked up his two whisks

55.1  It's a low place] It's a dirty low place

56.2  such silly shallow-hearted] such empty shallow-hearted

56.16  But one day] And one day

58.17–18  we just bite out their soft throats and suck their sweet juice] we just bite out the back of their heads and suck their sweet brains—

59.8  so rough that no fish] so rough no fish

59.15–20  And lucky it was for her . . . come to help him. Not in *MM*.

59.21  But *He* could not help] But Tom could not help

61.6–13  Then came a flash . . . 'Down to the sea!' Two paragraphs not in *MM*.

61.22–4  sulkily, for the fairies . . . meddle with a water-baby;] sulkily, for nothing dare eat water-babies:

62.7  ridgmens] ridgments

62.25–6  knows no better; so you must just] knows no better, and you must just

62.33–4  (at least, till this last year). Not in *MM*.

64.14  A full hundred yards broad it was, sliding] A full hundred yards broad, sliding

65.11  jump up; for he knew] jump up; and he knew

66.33–4  I thought I saw three . . . So I went too; for. Not in *MM*.

67.30  as some great folks look on some little folks] as a Yankee looks on a nigger

68.13 shore. He was] shore; and was

68.15–17 and perhaps he would never . . . their gentle hands. Not in *MM*.

68.20–1 as tight as possible. So at last] as tight as he could. So, at last,

70.20 of course; so he swam] of course; and he swam

71.31–4 once more] again. Followed by: He did not know . . . dangerous
things. Not in *MM*.

72.5 as Tom did, must needs] as Tom had, must needs

72.28 mullet. The seal] mullet. And the seal

72.33–4 looking for your brothers and sisters? I passed them] looking for
your brothers? I past [*sic*] them

74.15 he was flat; but to all] he was flat; and to all

74.18–20 to go to the Chesapeake . . . pleasant warm water] to go to New
York . . . nice warm water

78.33 dinner at five] dinner at half-past five

78.36 wait for your dinner till you can get it] wait for your victuals till you
can get them

79.9 a song out of a dead nightingale] a bray out of a dead donkey

79.20 too late: besides] too late; and besides

79.34 the little white lady, Ellie herself] the white girl, little Ellie herself

80.12–13 England, and turn them loose] England, to turn them loose

80.24 Scarborough, or Fleetwood] Scarborough, or Filey

81.21–2 good man and honest] good man and true

82.7 and it has none] and he has none. The following 'in its brain' omitted in *MM*.

82.20–4 The following sprites in K's list were not present in *MM*: brownies, wilis, follets, lutins, magots, goblins.

85.1 and it shows] and shows

86.5 the fairies came flying] the angels came flying

87.6–88.19–20 So all the doctors . . . they went in earnest. These thirteen
paragraphs not in *MM*.

88.20 and they gave the poor Professor] And they gave him [new paragraph]

88.29–30 Bumpsterhausen's . . . digital region. Not in *MM*.

89.34–5 Bumpsterhausen's . . . still. Not in *MM*.

90.18 The healthiest . . . Easthampstead Plain. This phrase is shorn of its
last three words and placed after 'Windsor Forest' in *MM*.

90.31 name, so Dr Gray] name, and so Dr Gray

92.4–6 and were thinking . . . effect for the cause. Not in *MM*.

92.13–14 to come down into this world whenever] for the doctors to bring
them in band-boxes at night, when

92.16–17 (though some one or other says there is, at least] (though a certain gentleman, who is no fool, says there is

92.20 Macintoshes] Macintosh

92.22  71.5 below] 17.5 above

92.33  considerably relieved] considerably relieved all over. The lines
        immediately following ['from Bumpsterhausen's . . . Whereon']
        not in *MM*; replaced by 'and'.

93.2–3  rise in, till very fine] rise in; and very fine

93.5–6  and never mentioned what he found out from them, except to
        little children;] and kept what he learned to himself;

94.11  Initial 'But'] And

96.3–4  little better than children] little better than blokes and boodles

96.21  He was right glad] How glad he was

96.27  And that was the end of the wicked otter. Found after 'Belfast
        Lough' in *MM*.

97.13  come in and sing] come in and say

98.24–5  and bade pull up . . . they could. So] and bid pull up . . . they
        could. And

99.32–3  suburban establishment . . . aristocracy. *MM* sets this in quotes.

100.32–3  any other refuse . . . make a mess upon] any refuse . . . make a
        dirt upon

101.10  wild wild Kerry coast] wild Connemara coast

101.18–21  So St Brandan went out to the point . . . And far away, before]
        So St Brandan went to the top of old Kylemore, and looked out
        over the Atlantic far away. And there, before

101.22–3  the blest.' Then] the blest.' And

102.6–9  But, on still clear . . . fairy isle. Moved down in *MM* to form a
        paragraph after '. . . in the old times'.

102.18–19  Connemara heath, and the] Connemara heath which grows in
        the garden, and the

102.22  Now when Tom] But when Tom

102.28  brown; and strewn with] brown. And all were strewn with

102.29  But, to keep] And, to keep

102.31  monkeys; while the] monkeys; and the

102.33–4  pure. But, to make] pure. And, to make

103.2  blossoms. If you think] blossoms. But if you think

103.11–12  Polynoe, Phyllodoce] Polynoe and Phyllodoce

103.20  it was able to take care of itself] it was full-grown

104.12  fire; all] fire; and all

104.20  . . . the Holy Innocents. [*MM* continues with the following para-
        graph] But the poor little children were there whom King Darius,
        like a passionate old heathen sultan as he was, threw into the lion's
        den along with their fathers (though he was quite right in throwing
        their fathers in, for that was according to the laws of the great fairy
        Madam Bedonebyasyoudid, which alter no more than the laws of

the Medes and Persians). And the forty and two little boys were there whom the bears ate for mocking Elijah; but, because they were heathens and knew no better, the fairies took to them, and taught them; and they were growing to be the civillest boys in all the sea. And, when Tom heard their story, he was quite frightened, and determined never to grin at old women through the railings, or heave half-bricks at people any more, lest the sea-bears should eat him, as the land-bears had eaten them, [then] But I wish Tom] But I wish he

105.5–6  but did not; for he] but he did not, recollecting the forty-two boys and the bears. Besides he

105.17  go to Nice, you will] go to Nice in Italy, you will

105.19–22  compliment to that most successful . . . neighbours' landmark] compliment to that sweet saint who has just taken the place under his gracious protection

105.26  as an owl's. For] as an owl's. And

106.5  from me. Now] from me. So now

107.10  lovely to behold] lovely to see

107.11–12  yet from the windows . . . is looking forth] yet out of the windows . . . is looking.

108.23  mill wheel. And mind—when] mill wheel; and when

108.35–6  (good man . . . understand). Omitted in *MM*.

110.34  came too. Whereat] came too. And

111.3  funniest, merriest] funniest, jolliest

111.17  as they ought to have done. While] as they ought to do. And

112.5  . . . from pure love. *MM* adds: for not being accustomed to it, it tired him very soon.

114.10  Here I come] And now I come

114.23  as her cap, who] as her cap, and who

115.21–3  But, when . . . never come there] And, when . . . never come here

115.32  Well, I know.—It may] Well, I know. But—it may

116.14  the strange fairy] the strange lady

117.3  save by Inquisitors] but by Inquisitors

117.6  Why then] And why

117.12  Ah! but the fairy] Ah! but she

117.25  however, she gave him] but she gave him

121.10–11  am I, Miss Ellie?] am I, Ellie?

123.16  It may have been so] It may be so

123.20  as folks say] as we say

124.26  if you look] if you will look

125.28–9  never such comfortable] never such jolly, comfortable

126.4–7  blown up like a barrel . . . boiled over like a kettle; whereby one-
   third . . . in ashes; so that] blown up, bang, like a barrel . . . boiled
   over, fizz, like a kettle; and one-third . . . in ashes, and

126.29  So they had to live] So that they had to live

128.2  every one wished to marry] every one tried to marry

128.7  Then the fairy] And the fairy

128.14  Something fearfully like it] Something very like it

128.16–17  hundred years. They . . . forgotten, too, how to talk] hundred
   years, and . . . forgotten how to talk

128.19  Beside, they are grown] And beside they are grown

128.29–30  but had forgotten] but he had forgotten

129.2–3  as you have been told already] as you know

129.8–9  the longer they waited, and behaved like] the longer they waited
   and cried like

131.12–13  five minutes: however] five minutes: but

132.6  my helpless babe] my seely babe

132.18–21  She gave a little shriek and start . . . be at rest. This paragraph
   given in *MM* as: She gave a little shriek, and a start; and then she
   said quietly, 'Yes, it is your little brother's spirit,' and waved her
   hand to Tom, and cried, 'Wait a little longer, darling, only a little
   longer: and we shall be all together once more.'

133.2–3  like the old dandies] like the old bucks

133.31  The other swam after] The other swam away

136.22–3  called them] called to them

138.35  American citizens of the new school] American citizens, sir!

139.14  gather at] gather to

140.27  her lee; her decks] her lee; and her decks

141.19–20  followed Tom] ran after Tom

141.24  molly-mocks] mollys

142.16–17  (as every sailor knows). Not in *MM*.

142.27  my name will last] my fame will last

144.1–6  moths with pink heads . . . quickly; yellow . . . out of his way. The
   dog] moths with red heads . . . quickly; and yellow . . . out of his
   way: and the dog

147.4–5  But Mother Carey . . . silly child] And Mother Carey . . . silly girl

147.13–22  Tom thought . . . Besides, you may meet. These paragraphs
   omitted from *MM*, replaced by: 'I recollect now, ma'am, every
   step,' said Tom. 'But it is not as easy to get there as you think. In
   the first place, you may meet

147.22–3  people there] people on the road

147.24–5  of course, as the dog will always go behind you] in the next place

148.5  beforehand. The] beforehand; and the

148.32 In *MM* 'the four great bogies' etc. are confusingly included as part of the list.

149.14 Demagogues] Democrats

149.22 making; with nothing] making; and nothing

149.28 whereby he set] and he set

149.28–9 Nostradamus, Zadkiel, Raphael Moore. Not in *MM*.

152.19 the nine-hundred] the one nine-hundred

154.9 star-fish] sea-egg

155.14–15 for it was all made . . . of course). Not in *MM*.

155.33–156.1 and if the names . . . something else. And all] and the names of the books were 'Squeeky', and the 'Pumplighter', and the 'Narrow, Narrow World', and the 'Hills of the Chattermuch', and the 'Children's Twaddeday'. And all

156.31–166.34 Then came Tom . . . month of Sundays. Almost the whole of this lengthy satirical passage did not occur in *MM*. The exceptions are the two paragraphs describing Tom's visit to Gotham and the island of the Golden Asses, which appear in *MM* in reverse order and with minor textual variations.

168.4–7 on their own backs: but as soon . . . of the sea: which was] on their own backs for the rest of their lives: which was

168.9–12 as ever had pinched feet . . . Cocqcigrues. Not in *MM*, where the paragraph ends 'as ever you saw in your life'.

169.4 Then he came] And then he came

169.9 afford it; while] afford it. And

174.5 of man, nor of worse neither] of man, or horse neither

174.7–8 Foul I would be . . . heeded it. Not in *MM*.

174.32–175.1 Never saw me? . . . before and since. Not in *MM*.

176.12–177.7 *MM* economically abbreviates 'backstairs' to 'b' in this list.

178.1–5 And what was the song . . . to teach you. Not in *MM*.

179.3–4 'You are the Irishwoman . . . Harthover!' Not in *MM*.

179.35 for some warm] for some decently warm

180.14 grow flat, their jaws] grow flat, and their jaws

180.23 and try to amend] and repent, and try to amend

180.25–6 (for aught that appears to the contrary)] as far as I can calculate

180.31–181.5 Very well, I dare say . . . somewhen, somehow.] Very well then, be it so; it is their concern, and not ours. We did not make them, and we are not responsible for them.

181.9 and if I am not quite right, still you will be] and if I am quite right, you will be

# APPENDIX II

## 'THE WONDERS OF THE SHORE'

[KINGSLEY's essay 'The Wonders of the Shore' was originally written as
a review of several recent books on marine biology, and was published in
the November 1854 edition of the *North British Review* (vol. 22 no. 43,
pp. 2–56); it was subsequently revised and republished by Kingsley as
*Glaucus; or, The Wonders of the Shore* (Cambridge: Macmillan, 1855). This
appendix reprints the opening pages, in which Kingsley rehearses many of
the ideas that would later be developed in *The Water-Babies*.]

THE study of Natural History has become now-a-days an honourable one;
and the successful investigator of the minutest animals takes his place
unquestioned among the men of genius, and, like the philosopher of old
Greece,* is considered, by virtue of his science, fit company for dukes and
princes. Nay, the study is now more than honourable; it is even fashionable. Thanks to the works which head this Article,* and to innumerable
others on kindred branches of science which have appeared of late, every
well-educated person is bound to know somewhat, at least, of the wondrous organic forms which surround him in every sunbeam and every pebble; and if Mr Gosse's presages* be correct, a few years more will see every
clever young lady with her 'aquarium', and live sea-anemones and algæ
will supplant 'crochet' and Berlin wool. Happy consummation—when
women's imagination shall be content with admiring Nature's real beau-
ties, instead of concealing their own idleness.

What a change from the temper of two generations since, when the naturalist was looked on as a harmless enthusiast, who went 'bug-hunting',
simply because he had not spirit to follow a fox. There are those now alive
who can recollect an amiable man being literally bullied out of the New
Forest, because he dared to make a collection (now, we believe, in some
unknown abyss of that great Avernus, the British Museum) of fossil shells
from those very Hordle Cliffs, for exploring which there is now established
a society of subscribers and correspondents. They can remember, too,
when, on the first appearance of Bewick's 'British Birds'*, the excellent
sportsman who brought it down to the forest, was asked, Why on earth he
had bought a book about 'cock-sparrows'? and had to justify himself again
and again, simply by lending the book to his brother sportsmen, to con-
vince them that there were rather more than a dozen sorts of birds (as they
then held) indigenous to Hampshire. But the book, perhaps, which turned
the tide in favour of Natural History, among the higher classes at least in

the south of England, was White's 'History of Selbourne'*. A Hampshire gentleman and sportsman, whom everybody knew, had taken the trouble to write a book about the birds and the weeds in his own parish, and the everyday-things which went on under his eyes, and everyone else's. And all gentlemen, from the Weald of Kent to the Vale of Blackmoor, shrugged their shoulders mysteriously, and said, 'Poor fellow!' till they opened the book itself, and discovered to their surprise that it read like any novel. And then came a burst of confused, but honest admiration; from the young squire's 'Bless me! who would have thought that there were so many wonderful things to be seen in one's own park!' to the old squire's more morally valuable 'Bless me! why I have seen that and that a hundred times, and never thought till now how wonderful they were!'

There were great excuses, though, of old, for the contempt in which the naturalist was held; great excuses for the pitying tone of banter with which the Spectator talks of 'the ingenious' Don Saltero,* (as no doubt the Neapolitan gentlemen talked of Ferrante Imperato* the apothecary, and his museum;) great excuses for Voltaire, when he classes the collection of butterflies among the other 'bigarrures de l'esprit humain'.* For, in the last generation, the needs of the world were different. It had no time for butterflies and fossils. While Buonaparte was hovering on the Boulogne coast, the pursuits and the education which were needed were such as would raise up men to fight him; and the coarse, fierce, hardhanded training of our grandfathers came when it was wanted, and did the work which was required of it, else we had not been here now. Let us be thankful that we have had leisure for science; and shew now in war that our science has at least not unmanned us.

Moreover, Natural History, if not fifty years ago, certainly a hundred years ago, was hardly worthy of men of practical common sense. After, indeed, Linné,* by his invention of generic and specific names, had made classification possible, and by his own enormous labours had shewn how much could be done when once a method was established, the science has grown rapidly enough. But before him little or nothing had been put into form definite enough to allure those who (as the many always will) prefer to profit by others' discoveries, than to discover for themselves; and Natural History was attractive only to a few earnest seekers, who found too much trouble in disencumbering their own minds of the dreams of bygone generations, whether facts, like cockatrices, basilisks, and krakens, the breeding of bees out of a dead ox, and of geese from barnacles, or theories, like those of the four elements, the *vis plastrix** in Nature, animal spirits, and the other musty heirlooms of Aristotelism and Neo-platonism, to try to make a science popular, which as yet was not even a science at all. Honour to them, nevertheless. Honour to Ray* and his illustrious contemporaries in Holland and France. Honour to Seba and Aldrovandus; to Pomet,* with his 'Historie of Drugges'; even to the ingenious Don Saltero, and his tavern-museum in Cheyne Walk. Where all was chaos, every man was useful who could contribute a single spot of organized standing ground in the shape of a fact or a specimen. But it is a question whether Natural History would have ever attained its present honours, had not Geology arisen, to connect every other branch of Natural History with problems as vast and awful as they are captivating to the imagination. Nay, the very opposition with which Geology met was of as great benefit to the sister sciences as to itself. For, when questions belonging to the most sacred hereditary beliefs of Christendom were supposed to be affected by the verification of a fossil shell, or the proving that the Maestricht 'homo diluvii testis'* was, after all, a monstrous eft, it became necessary to work upon Conchology, Botany, and Comparative Anatomy, with a care and a reverence, a caution and a severe induction, which had been never before applied to them; and thus gradually, in the last half century, the whole quire of cosmical sciences have acquired a soundness, severity, and fulness, which render them, as mere intellectual exercises, as valuable to a manly mind as Mathematics and Metaphysics.

And how very lately have they attained that firm and honourable standing ground! It is a question, whether, even twenty years ago, Geology, as it then stood, was worth troubling one's head about, so little had been really proved. And heavy and uphill was the work, even within the last fifteen years, of those who steadfastly set themselves to the task of proving, and of asserting at all risks, that the Maker of the coal seam and the diluvial cave could not be a 'Deus quidam deceptor',* and that the facts which the rock and the silt revealed were sacred, not to be warped or trifled with, for the sake of any cowardly and hasty notion that they contradicted His other messages. When a few more years are past, Buckland and Sedgwick, Lyell and Jameson,* and the group of brave men who accompanied and followed them, will be looked back to as moral benefactors to their race, and almost as martyrs, also, when it is remembered how much misunderstanding, obloquy, and plausible folly they had to endure from well-meaning fanatics like Fairholme or Granville Penn,* and the respectable mob at their heels, who tried (as is the fashion in such cases) to make a hollow compromise between fact and the Bible, by twisting facts just enough to make them fit the fancied meaning of the Bible, and the Bible just enough to make them fit the fancied meaning of the facts. But there were a few who would have no compromise; who laboured on with a noble recklessness, determined to speak the thing which they had seen, and neither more nor less, sure that God could take better care than they of His own everlasting truth; and now they have conquered; and the facts which were twenty years ago denounced as contrary to Revelation, are now accepted not merely as consonant with, but as corroborative thereof; and sound practical geologists, like Hugh Miller,* in his 'Footprints of the Creator', and Professor Sedgwick, in the invaluable notes to his 'Discourse on the Studies of Cambridge', are wielding in defence of Christianity the very science which was faithlessly and cowardly expected to subvert it.

But of all the branches of cosmic science which owe a debt to geology, marine zoology and botany owe most; and the tiny zoophytes and microscopic animalcules which people every shore and every drop of water, have been now raised to a rank in the human mind, more important, perhaps, than even those gigantic monsters, whose models fill the lake at the New Crystal Palace.* The research which has been bestowed, for the last century, upon these once unnoticed atomies, has well repaid itself; for from no branch of physical science has more been learnt of the *scientia scientiarum*,* the priceless art of learning; no branch of science has more utterly confounded the wisdom of the wise, shattered to pieces systems and theories, and the idolatry of arbitrary names, and taught man to be silent while his Maker speaks, than this apparent pedantry of zoophytology,* in which our old distinctions of 'animal', 'vegetable', and 'mineral' are trembling in the balance, seemingly ready to vanish like their fellows, 'the four elements', of fire, air, earth, and water. No branch of science has helped so much to sweep away that sensuous idolatry of mere size, which tempts man to admire and respect objects in proportion to the number of feet or inches which they occupy in space. And no branch, moreover, has been more humbling to the boasted rapidity and omnipotence of the human reason, and taught those who have eyes to see, and hearts to understand,* how weak and wayward, staggering and slow, are the stops of our fallen race (rapid and triumphant enough in that broad road of theories which leads to intellectual destruction) whensoever they tread the narrow path of true science, which leads (if we may be allowed to transfer our Lord's great parable from moral to intellectual matters) to life; to the living and permanent knowledge of living things, and the laws of their existence. Humbling, truly, to one who, in this summer of 1854, the centenary year of British zoophytology, looks back to the summer of 1754, when good Mr Ellis,* the wise and benevolent West Indian merchant, read before the Royal Society his famous paper proving the animal nature of corals, and followed it up the year after by that famous 'Essay toward a Natural History of the Corallines, and other like marine productions of the British coasts', which forms the groundwork of all our knowledge on the subject to this day. The chapter in Dr G. Johnston's British Zoophytes,* p. 407, or the excellent little résumé thereof in Dr Landsborough's book on the same subject,* is really a saddening one, as one sees how loth were not merely dreamers like

Marsigli or Bonnet, but sound-headed men like Pallas* and Linné, to give
up the old sense-bound fancy, that these corals were vegetables, and their
polypes some sort of living flowers. Yet after all there are excuses for them.
Without our improved microscopes, and while the sciences of comparative
anatomy and chemistry were yet infantile, it was difficult to believe what
was the truth; and for this simple reason that, as usual, the truth, when
discovered, turned out far more startling and prodigious than the dreams
which men had hastily substituted for it; more strange than Ovid's old
story that the coral was soft under the sea, and hardened by exposure to air;
than Marsigli's notion, that the coral-polypes were its flowers; than
Dr Parsons'* contemptuous denial, that these complicated forms could be
'the operations of little, poor, helpless, jelly-like animals, and not the work
of more sure vegetation'; than Baker* the microscopist's detailed theory of
their being produced by the crystallization of the mineral salts in the sea-
water, just as he had seen 'the particles of mercury and copper in aquafor-
tis assume tree-like forms, or curious delineations of mosses and minute
shrubs on slates and stones, owing to the shooting of salts intermixed with
mineral particles';—one smiles at it now, yet these men were no less sensible than we of the year 1854, and if we know better, it is only because other
men, and those few and far between, have laboured amid disbelief, ridi-
cule, and error, having again and again to retrace their steps, and to unlearn
more than they learnt, seeming to go backwards when they were really
progressing most; and we have entered into their labours, and find them,
as we have just said, more wondrous than all the poetic dreams of a Bonnet
or a Darwin. For who, after all, to take a few broad instances, (not to enlarge
on the great root-wonder of a number of distinct individuals connected
by a common life, and forming a seeming plant invariable in each species,) would have dreamed of the 'bizarreries' which these very zoophytes
present in their classification? You go down to Leith* shore after a gale
of wind, and pick up a few of those delicate little sea-ferns. You have two
in your hand, which probably look to you, even under a good pocket magni-
fier, identical, or nearly so. You are told to your surprise, that however like
the dead horny polypidoms* which you hold may be, the two species
of animal which have formed them are at least as far apart in the scale of
creation as a quadruped is from a fish. You see in some Musselburgh*
dredger's boat the phosphorescent sea-pen, (unknown in England,) a living
feather, of the look and consistency of a cock's comb; or the still stranger
sea-rush, (*Virgularia mirabilis*,) a spine two feet long, with hundreds of
rosy flowerets arranged in half-rings round it from end to end; and you are
told that these are the congeners* of the great stony Venus's fan which
hangs in seamen's cottages, brought home from the West Indies. And ere
you have done wondering, you hear that all three are congeners of the ugly

shapeless white 'dead man's hand',* which you may pick up after a storm on any shore. You have a beautiful madrepore or brainstone* on your mantelpiece, brought home from some Pacific coral-reef. You are to believe that it has no more to do with the beautiful tubular corals among which it was growing, than a bird has with a worm, and that its first cousins are the soft slimy sea-anemones, which you see expanding their living flowers in every pool at the back of Musselburgh pier, bags of sea-water, without a trace of bone or stone. You must believe it; for in science, as in higher matters, he who will walk surely, must 'walk by faith and not by sight'.*

These are but a few of the wonders which the classification of marine animals afford; and only drawn from one class of them, though almost as common among every other family of that submarine world whereof Spenser sang—

> Oh, what an endless work have I in hand
>     To count the sea's abundant progeny!
> Whose fruitful seed far passeth those in land,
>     And also those which won in th' azure sky.
>     For much more eath to tell the stars on high,
> Albe they endless seem in estimation,
>     Than to recount the sea's posterity;
> So fertile be the flouds in generation,
> So huge their numbers, and so numberless their nation.*

But these few examples will be sufficient to account both for the slow pace at which the knowledge of sea-animals has progressed, and for the allurement which men of the highest attainments have found, and still find in it. And when to this we add the marvels which meet us at every step in the anatomy and the reproduction of these creatures, and in the chemical and mechanical functions which they fulfil in the great economy of our planet, we cannot wonder at finding that the books at the head of our article carry with them a certain charm of romance, and feed the play of fancy, and that love of the marvellous which is inherent in man, at the same time that they lead the reader to more solemn and lofty trains of thought, which can find their full satisfaction only in self-forgetful worship, and that hymn of praise which goes up ever from land and sea, as well as from saints and martyrs and the heavenly host, 'Oh, all ye works of the Lord, and ye, too, spirits and souls of the righteous, praise Him, and magnify Him for ever!'*

We have said, that there were excuses for the old contempt for the study of Natural History. We have said too, it may be hoped, enough to shew that contempt to have been ill-founded, at least as far as regards its effect on the feelings and the intellect. But still, there are those who regard it as

a mere amusement, and that at best as an effeminate one, and think that it
can at best help to while away a leisure hour harmlessly, and perhaps use-
fully, as a substitute for coarser sports, or the reading of novels. Those,
however, who have followed it out, especially on the sea-shore, know better, and can tell from experience, that over and above its accessory charms
of pure sea-breezes, and wild rambles by cliff and loch, the study itself has
had a weighty moral effect upon their hearts and spirits. There are those
who can well understand how the good and wise John Ellis, amid all his
philanthropic labours for the good of the West Indies, while he was spending his intellect and fortune in introducing into our tropic settlements the
bread fruit and mangosteen,* and every plant and seed which he hoped
might be useful for medicine, agriculture, and commerce, could yet feel
himself justified in devoting large portions of his ever well-spent time to
the fighting the battle of the corallines against Parsons and the rest, and
even measuring pens with Linné, the prince of naturalists. There are those
who can sympathize with the gallant old Scotch officer mentioned by some
writer on sea-weeds, who, desperately wounded in the breach at Badajos,
and a sharer in all the toils and triumphs of the Peninsular war, could in his
old age shew a rare sea-weed with as much triumph as his well-earned
medals, and talk over a tiny spore-capsule with as much zest as the records
of sieges and battles. Why not? That temper which made him a good soldier may very well have made him a good naturalist also. And certainly, the
best naturalist, as far as logical acumen, as well as earnest research, is concerned, whom England has ever seen, was the Devonshire squire, Colonel
George Montagu,* of whom Mr E. Forbes* well says, that 'had he been
educated a physiologist', (and not, as he was, a soldier and a sportsman,)
'and made the study of nature his aim and not his amusement, his would
have been one of the greatest names in the whole range of British science'.
We question, nevertheless, whether he would have not lost more than he
would have gained by a different training. It might have made him a more
learned systematizer; but would it have quickened in him that 'seeing eye'
of the true soldier and sportsman, which makes Montagu's descriptions
indelible word-pictures, instinct with life and truth? 'There is no question', says Professor E. Forbes, after bewailing the vagueness of most naturalists, 'about the identity of any animal Montagu described. . . . He was
a forward-looking philosopher; he spoke of every creature as if one exceeding like it, yet different from it, would be washed up by the waves next tide.
Consequently his descriptions are permanent.' Scientific men will recog-
nise in this the highest praise which can be bestowed, because it attributes
to him that highest faculty—*the Art of Seeing*: but the study and the book
would not have given that. It is God's gift, wheresoever educated: but its
true schoolroom is the camp and the ocean, the prairie and the forest;

active self-helping life, which can grapple with nature herself: not merely with printed books about her. Let no one think that this same natural history is a pursuit fitted only for effeminate or pedantic men. We should say rather, that the qualifications required for a perfect naturalist are as many and as lofty as were required, by old chivalrous writers, for the perfect knight-errant of the middle ages; for (to sketch an ideal, of which we are happy to say our race now affords many a fair realization) our perfect naturalist should be strong in body, able to haul a dredge, climb a rock, turn a boulder, walk all day, uncertain where he shall eat or rest; able to face sun and rain, wind and frost, and to eat and drink thankfully anything, however coarse or meagre; he should know how to swim for his life, to pull an oar, sail a boat, and ride the first horse which comes to hand; and, finally, he should be a thoroughly good shot, and a skilful fisherman; and if he go far abroad, be able on occasion to fight for his life.

For his moral character, he must, like a knight of old, be first of all gentle and courteous, ready and able to ingratiate himself with the poor, the ignorant, and the savage; not only because foreign travel will be often otherwise impossible, but because he knows how much invaluable local information can be only obtained from fishermen, miners, and tillers of the soil. Next, he should be brave and enterprising, and withal patient and undaunted, not merely in travel, but in investigation, knowing (as Lord Bacon* might have put it) that the kingdom of nature, like the kingdom of heaven, must be taken by violence, and that only to those who knock long and earnestly, does the great mother open the doors of her sanctuary. He must be of a reverent turn of mind also, not rashly discrediting any reports, however vague and fragmentary; giving man credit always for some germ of truth, and giving nature credit for an inexhaustible fertility and variety, which will keep him his life long always reverent, yet never superstitious; wondering at the commonest, but not surprised by the most strange; free from the idols of size and sensuous loveliness; able to see grandeur in the minutest objects, beauty in the most ungainly; estimating each thing not carnally, as the vulgar do, by its size or its pleasantness to the senses, but spiritually, by the amount of Divine thought revealed to him therein; holding every phenomenon worth the noting down; believing that every pebble holds a treasure, every bud a revelation; making it a point of conscience to pass over nothing through laziness or hastiness, lest the vision once offered and despised should be withdrawn, and looking at every object as if he were never to behold it again.

Moreover, he must keep himself free from all those perturbations of mind which not only weaken energy, but darken and confuse the inductive faculty; from haste and laziness, from melancholy, testiness, and pride, and all the passions which make men see only what they wish to see. Of solemn and scrupulous reverence for truth, of the habit of mind which regards each fact and discovery not as our own possession, but as the possession of its Creator, independent of us, our tastes, our needs, or our vain glory, we hardly need to speak; for it is the very essence of a naturalist's faculty, the very tenure of his existence; and without truthfulness, science would be as impossible now as chivalry would have been of old.

And last, but not least, the perfect naturalist should have in him the very essence of true chivalry, namely, self-devotion; the desire to advance, not himself and his own fame or wealth, but knowledge and mankind. He should have this great virtue; and in spite of many shortcomings, (for what man is there who liveth and sinneth not?) naturalists as a class have it, to a degree which makes them stand out most honourably in the midst of a self-seeking and mammonite generation, inclined to value everything by its money price, its private utility. The spirit which gives freely, because it knows that it has received freely; which communicates knowledge without hope of reward, without jealousy and mean rivalry, to fellow-students and to the world; which is content to delve and toil comparatively unknown, that from its obscure and seemingly worthless results others may derive pleasure, and even build up great fortunes, and change the very face of cities and lands, by the practical use of some stray talisman which the poor student has invented in his laboratory;—this is the spirit which is abroad among our scientific men, to a greater degree than it ever has been among any body of men, for many a century past; and might well be copied by those who profess deeper purposes and a more exalted calling, than the discovery of a new zoophyte, or the classification of a moorland crag.

And it is these qualities, however imperfectly they may be realized in any individual instance, which make our scientific men, as a class, the wholesomest and pleasantest of companions abroad, and at home the most blameless, simple, and cheerful, in all domestic relations; men for the most part, of manful heads, and yet of child-like hearts, turning to quiet study, in these late piping times of peace, an intellectual health and courage, which might have made them, in more fierce and troublous times, capable of doing good service with very different instruments than the scalpel and the microscope.

We have been sketching an ideal: but one which we seriously recommend to the consideration of all parents; for, though it be impossible, and absurd to wish, that every young man should grow up a naturalist by profession, yet this age offers no more wholesome training, both moral and intellectual, than that which is given by instilling into the young an early taste for out-door physical science. The education of our children is now more than ever a puzzling problem, if by education we mean the development of the whole humanity, not merely of some arbitrarily chosen part of it. How to feed the imagination with wholesome food, and teach it to despise French novels, and that sugared slough of sentimental poetry, in comparison with which the old fairy-tales and ballads were manful and rational; how to counteract the tendency to shallow and conceited sciolism,* engendered by hearing popular lectures on all manner of subjects, which can only be really learnt by stern methodic study; how to give habits of enterprise, patience, accurate observation, which the counting-house or the library will never bestow; above all, how to develop the physical powers, without engendering brutality and coarseness, are questions becoming daily more and more puzzling, while they need daily more and more to be solved, in an age of enterprise, travel, and emigration, like the present. For the truth must be told, that the great majority of men who are now distinguished by commercial success, have had a training the directly opposite to that which they are giving their sons. They are for the most part men who have migrated from the country to the town, and had in their youth all the advantages of a sturdy and manful hill-side or sea-side training, whose bodies were developed, and their lungs fed on pure breezes, long before they brought to work in the city the bodily and mental strength which they had gained by loch and moor. But it is not so with their sons. Their business habits are learnt in the counting-house; a good school, doubtless, as far as it goes: but one which will expand none but the lowest intellectual faculties; which will make them accurate accountants, shrewd computers, but never the originators of daring schemes, men able and willing to go forth to replenish the earth and subdue it. And in the hours of relaxation, how much of their time is thrown away for want of anything better, on frivolity, not to say secret profligacy, parents know too well; and often shut their eyes in very despair to evils which they know not how to cure. A frightful majority of our middle class young men are growing up effeminate, empty of all knowledge but what tends directly to the making of a fortune; or rather, to speak correctly, to the keeping up the fortunes which their fathers made for them; while of the minority, who are indeed thinking and reading men, how many women as well as men have we seen wearying their souls with study undirected, often misdirected study; craving to learn, yet not knowing how or what to learn; cultivating, with unwholesome energy, the head at the expense of body and of heart, catching up with the most capricious self-will one mania after another, and tossing it away again for some new phantom; gorging the memory with facts which no one has taught them to arrange, and the reason with problems which they have no method for solving, till they fret themselves into a chronic fever of the brain, which too often urges them on to plunge, as it were to cool the inward fire, into the ever restless sea of doubt and disbelief. It is a sad picture. There are many who may read these pages whose hearts will tell them that it is a true one. What is wanted in these cases is a methodic and scientific habit of mind; and a class of objects on which to exercise that habit, which will fever neither the speculative intellect nor the moral sense; and that physical science will give, as nothing else can give it.

Moreover, to revert to another point which we touched just now, man has a body as well as a mind, and with the vast majority there will be no *mens sana* unless there be a *corpus sanum*\* for it to inhabit. And what out-door training to give our youths, is, as we have already said, more than ever puzzling. This difficulty is felt, perhaps, less in Scotland than in England. The Scotch climate compels hardiness; the Scotch bodily strength makes it easy; and Scotland, with her mountain-tours in summer, and her frozen lochs in winter, her labyrinth of seashore, and, above all, that priceless boon which Providence has bestowed on her, in the contiguity of her great cities to the loveliest scenery, and hills where every breeze is health, affords facilities for healthy physical life unknown to the Englishman, who has no Arthur's Seat\* towering above his London, no Western Islands spotting the ocean firths beside his Manchester. Field sports, with the invaluable training which they give, if not

> The reason firm,

Yet still

> The temperate will,
> Endurance, foresight, strength, and skill,\*

have become impossible for the greater number; and athletic exercises are now, in England at least, so artificialized, so expensive, so mixed up with drinking, gambling, and other evils of which we need say nothing here, that one cannot wonder at any parents' shrinking from allowing their sons to meddle much with them. And yet the young man who has had no sub-stitute for such amusements, will cut but a sorry figure in Australia, Canada, or India, and if he stays at home, spend many a pound in doctors' bills, which could have been better employed elsewhere. 'Taking a wall',—as one would take a pill or a draught—seems likely soon to become the only form of outdoor existence possible for us of the British Isles. But a walk without an object, unless in the most lovely and novel of scenery, is a poor exercise, and as a recreation, utterly nil. We never knew two young lads go out for a 'constitutional', who did not, if they were commonplace youths, gossip the whole way about things better left unspoken; if they were clever ones, fall on arguing and brainsbeating on politics or meta-physics, from the moment they left the door, and return with their wits even more heated and tired than they were when they set out. We cannot help fancying that Milton made a mistake in a certain celebrated passage, and that it was not 'sitting on a hill apart', but tramping four miles out and four miles in along a turnpike road, that his hapless spirits discoursed

> Of fate, free-will, foreknowledge absolute,
> And found no end, in wandering mazes lost.\*

Seriously, if we wish rural walks to do our children any good, we must give them a love for rural sights, an object in every walk; we must teach them—and we can teach them—to find wonder in every insect, sublimity in every hedge-row, the records of past worlds in every pebble, and boundless fertility upon the barren shore; and so, by teaching them to make full use of that limited sphere in which they now are, make them faithful in a few things, that they may be fit hereafter to be rulers over much.

# EXPLANATORY NOTES

Compiled by Brian Alderson, and revised by Robert Douglas-Fairhurst

Readers approaching the unabridged version of *The Water-Babies* for the first time are often surprised by how densely packed it is with scientific and pseudo-scientific language, literary and historical allusions, and gleeful pirouettes of nonsense. They are not always reassured by Kingsley's observation that his hero was 'a little frightened at the long words . . . not understanding them the least; as, indeed, he was not meant to do, or you either' (p. 177). These Notes attempt to explain what can be explained, and give instances where Kingsley is being deliberately misleading or opaque.

## ABBREVIATIONS

CK     Charles Kingsley

*LM*     F. Kingsley (ed.), *Charles Kingsley: His Letters and Memories of His Life*, 2 vols. (1877; London: Macmillan, 1890)

*Misc.*     C. Kingsley, *Miscellanies; Reprinted Chiefly from 'Fraser's Magazine' and 'The North British Review'*, 2 vols. (London: J. W. Parker & Son, 1859)

*MM*     *Macmillan's Magazine* printing of the story (1862–3)

*ODNB*     *Oxford Dictionary of National Biography*

*OED*     *Oxford English Dictionary* (2nd edn.)

*WB*     *The Water-Babies*

Quotations from the Bible are taken from the Authorized Version.

3  *TO MY YOUNGEST SON*: this dedication was first published in the book edition of 1863; the opening of the story in *MM* was preceded only by 'L'Envoi' (see below).

*Come read me . . . can*: based on a traditional formula made popular by the song 'Allen-a-Dale' in canto III of Sir Walter Scott's poem *Rokeby*: 'Come, read me my riddle! come, hearken my tale!'

4  *L'ENVOI*: published in *MM* and in early copies of the first book edition, it was then 'suppressed lest it should be misunderstood and give needless offence' (*LM* ii. 187). It is not clear who might have been offended; possibly T. H. Huxley (see note to p. 38) and Bishop Wilberforce.

5  *I heard . . . made of man*: from 'Lines Written in Early Spring', first published in *Lyrical Ballads* (1798). Not in *MM*. The indenting of alternate lines is CK's invention.

*Tom . . . heard it before*: Tom was a popular boy's name in children's stories. The transformation of CK's hero into a creature less than 4 inches long may owe something to Tom Thumb, while more recent and realistic examples included *Tom Brown's Schooldays* (1857) and the sequel *Tom Brown at Oxford* (1861), both by CK's friend Thomas Hughes; CK had commented on a draft of the first story and reviewed the published version in the *Saturday Review*. Alternatively, this could be an allusion to William Blake's pair of poems in *Songs of Innocence and Experience* entitled 'The Chimney Sweeper', the first of which features a little sweep named Tom (see Introduction, p. xxiv), or possibly a private joke: Tom was the hero's name in CK's novel *Two Years Ago* (1857).

5 *in the North country*: the geography of *WB* is a composite one. Lewthwaite Crag may be seen as both Malham Cove and Ingleborough (see note to p. 24) and the river may be thought of as a Pennine river, flowing on through an industrial landscape but ending up at somewhere like Torquay or Clovelly. Several attempts have been made to locate it more definitely, the most sustained being that by Göte Klingberg in his *Besök i Brittiska Barnbokslandskap* (Stockholm: Sjöstrands Förlag, 1987), 98–103. For the 'great town' CK may have had in mind Leeds or Bradford, which he appears to have visited during his stay with W. E. Forster in 1858.

6 *velveteens*: trousers made of a cotton fabric simulating velvet. *OED* cites *WB* as the first usage in this sense, but notes also an earlier extension from the same period when Tom Brown mocks the under-keeper as 'velveteens' in *Tom Brown's Schooldays* (1857).

*ankle-jacks*: 'Jack-boots reaching above the ankle' (*OED*).

*drab*: dull-coloured; 'drab' is a form of undyed linen.

7 *frame-breaking riots*: a complicated anachronism. The frame-breaking riots occurred during the economic slump of 1811–12 and consisted of 'Luddite' attacks on wide-frame looms that were being used to undercut work done on traditional narrow-frame looms. Since *WB* is clearly set later than this date, CK has conflated the frame-breaking riots with the Chartist agitations against which Wellington (based in London rather than the North of England) had mobilized the army in 1848.

*a grand old man*: although *ODNB* claims that the character of 'the squire' was based on CK's friend Walter Morrison (1836–1921), the proof rests on little more than Morrison's ownership of Malham Tarn House. Sir John is more likely to have been a composite figure, owing much to CK's idealized version of such landowners as his patron Sir John Cope of Bramshill House.

8 *buirdly*: stout, stalwart (cf. 'burly').

*gradely*: graceful, bonny; a term still commonly used in Northern dialects, especially in Yorkshire.

*Government National School*: one of the schools designed to teach children to a rudimentary level under the nominal control of the National Society for Promoting the Education of the Poor in the Principles of the Established Church. CK's animus against this 'system' probably stemmed from its casual attitude towards both religious and educational matters, and from the low level of official expectations for the performance of teachers and children alike. Although CK often sniped at educational provision for the poor, he and his patron at Eversley were responsible for founding a national school in the village in 1853.

*piert*: obsolete or dialect form of 'pert' (*OED*).

9 *pit-bird*: reed-warbler.

*Soon they came up with*: the poor Irishwoman did not exist in *MM*, which continued with the paragraph 'At last, at the bottom of the hill . . .'. See Appendix I for the other textual changes CK made to accommodate this new theme.

*crimson madder*: the dye produced from the climbing plant *Rubia tinctorum*. Red flannel petticoats were characteristic dress for Galway peasant women, whom CK presumably encountered during his Irish fishing trip, but madder-dye production does not seem to have been a distinctive Galway industry.

10 *as you see here*: i.e. at Eversley.

11 *over into Vendale*: Göte Klingberg (*Besök i Brittiska Barnbokslandskap*) suggests that Vendale is Littondale, although that is north of Malham Cove. Klingberg also notes that Vendale figures as a place in the modern Dales stories of William Mayne, although in these examples Vendale is usually a mixture of Swaledale and Arkengarthdale.

*Martinmas*: 11 November, the date of the Feast of St Martin, and traditionally a day on which fairs were held.

14 *Clive's Indian wars*: Robert Clive (1725–74), also known as 'Clive of India', helped to secure India and its wealth for the British crown through a series of military campaigns.

*caves of Elephanta*: a network of sculpted caves on the island of Gharapuri to the east of Mumbai; sixteenth-century Portuguese settlers renamed the island Elephanta after the huge statue of an elephant's head located at the entrance.

*or under the earth*: the first of CK's pseudo-Rabelaisian catalogues, here poking mild fun at architectural descriptions as found in guidebooks. Despite the exaggerations CK may have been inspired by such houses as Malham Tarn House ('apparently late Georgian with an asymmetrically placed Italianate tower of c.1850') and Eshton Hall, lower down Airedale ('remarkably early . . . for a house in pure neo-Elizabethan style') (see N. Pevsner, *The Buildings of England: Yorkshire; the West Riding* (Harmondsworth: Penguin, 1959)). Both houses are still in existence: one is a Field Studies Centre, the other has been converted into apartments.

*Naboth's vineyard to critics, and architects*: Ahab, King of Samaria, coveted the vineyard of his subject Naboth, but Naboth refused to sell or exchange it: 'The Lord forbid it me, that I should give the inheritance of my fathers unto thee' (1 Kings 21: 3). Fortunately for Sir John the 'critics and architects' could not resort to *force majeure*, unlike Ahab, whose queen, Jezebel, arranged for Naboth to be stoned to death.

15 *ash-boy*: a younger version of the ash-man, 'a collector and remover of ashes' (*OED*).

*anastomosing*: cross-connecting between the main lines of a branching system. The term was used by Professor – later Sir – Richard Owen (1804–92) of veins, or connected bones, for example in his *On the Anatomy of Vertebrates* (1866). Owen was the country's leading authority on animal anatomy in CK's time and to him fell the task of analysing many of the newly discovered fossils and specimens of wild animals that so stimulated the debate on evolution. He was a difficult, self-opinionated man who earned the hatred of Darwinians for his obfuscation of scientific evidence. See also notes to p. 38.

16 *ewers and basons*: water-jugs and bowls ('bason' is a variant spelling of 'basin').

18 *at the headland*: the strip of land at the end of the furrows where the plough-horses are turned.

19 *stramash, charivari*: a 'stramash' (Scottish) is an uproar; a 'charivari' (French) is 'a confused, discordant medley of sounds' (*OED*).

*screaking*: screeching.

*gorilla*: at this time a novel discovery. Two skulls arrived in London in 1846, sent by the American missionary Thomas Savage, to be followed by a skeleton in 1851 and a full specimen preserved in alcohol in 1858. In 1861 a stuffed gorilla was the star attraction of the lectures delivered by Paul Du Chaillu (see note to p. 39), whose book *Explorations and Adventures in Equatorial Africa* featured a crouching gorilla embossed on the binding and another as a large frontispiece that could be unfolded to face the title page.

20 *hassock-grass*: clumps of coarse grass (cf. 'tussocks').

*lawyers*: long brambles (*OED*, citing *WB*).

*cock-robins covered him with leaves*: an allusion to the traditional ballad of *The Children in the Wood*, first published in 1595. The alternative title of 'The Babes in the Wood' became popular from the 1840s onwards, and the story was frequently dramatized as a pantomime.

21 *backed*: went in the opposite direction.

*over just such a moor*: 'Behind the acacia on the lawn you get the first glimpse of the fir-forests and moors of which five-sixths of my parish consist' (*LM* i. 75, dated 14 July 1842). Eversley was set on the edge of the sandy heaths, seen at their most characteristic in the heather woodlands around Bagshot.

22 *the twelfth of August*: 'the glorious twelfth' when the grouse-shooting season begins.

23 *poults*: grouse-chicks.

*whimberries*: a local term for bilberries or whortleberries (*OED*, citing *WB*).

*swallow-hole*: a vertical cavern, characteristic of limestone country, caused by the chemical action of rainwater on the soluble rock. In England the most famous examples are perhaps 'the Buttertubs' on the high pass between Wensleydale and Swaledale.

24 *a bit and a sup*: something to eat and drink.

*Behind him, far below*: the topographical description that follows is an epitome of the landscape in which *WB*'s opening chapters are set, but suggests the influence of Ingleborough rather than Malham Cove: 'Last night we went up Ingleborough, 2380, and saw the whole world to the west, the lake mountains, and the western sea beyond Lancaster and Morecambe Bay for miles' (*LM* ii. 58, July 1858).

26 *And is there . . . foe*: from *The Faerie Queene*, Book II, canto VIII, stanza i (modern spelling). Not printed in *MM*.

*the High Craven*: the wild fell-country that lies to the north of Malham, inspiring CK to an almost hypnotic litany of place names which, in his day, would have stood for grim and awesome solitude. Bolland Forest is the tract of open land north of Preston, now called the Forest of Bowland; Cross Fell is the highest point of the Pennines. Annan Water and Berwick Law stand at the western and eastern limits of the England–Scotland border.

27 *Mr George White*: gardener and general factotum at Eversley.

*baba*: an in-joke; this appears to have been how CK's son Grenville pronounced 'mama'. 'Mind and be a good boy and give Baba my love' (CK to Grenville, *LM* ii. 172, 1864).

28 *There has been a great black smudge*: a fanciful explanation for the real appearance of lichens that grow in damp streaks on the rock face.

29 *the frogs on the Great-A*: the Great-A is a triangular patch of land at Eversley, crossed by a footpath like the bar of a letter A. Below the bar the land was marshy and populated by frogs.

*dimity*: 'A stout cotton fabric woven with raised stripes or fancy figures; usually employed undyed for beds or bedroom hangings, and sometimes for garments' (*OED*).

*Chris-cross-row*: W. J. Frank Davies in his *Teaching Reading in Early England* (London: Pitman, 1973) suggests that early alphabets were written out in the shape of a cross with A at the top and Z at the bottom. More usually, 'crisscross-row' is taken to mean a linear alphabet preceded by a written or printed cross. Many examples of this usage as they appear in literary references are given by Andrew Tuer in his *History of the Horn-Book* (London, 1896), vol. i, ch. 5.

*old dame*: until the introduction of compulsory elementary education in 1870, many young children attended 'dame schools' run by women in their homes; a study conducted by the Statistical Society of London in 1838 concluded that nearly half the pupils were taught little more than spelling.

29 *I'm most clemmed with hunger and drought*: 'I'm almost starved with hunger and thirst'.

33 *Cousin Cramchild . . . Conversations*: probably a reference to the American Samuel Griswold Goodrich (1793–1860), who invented the sententious character 'Peter Parley' as a persona, imparting information on any number of subjects in books and magazines. *Tales of Peter Parley about America*, his first collection, was published in Boston in 1827 and was followed by many other works. In England the name was appropriated by several writers who published their own 'Peter Parley' books and also a long-running magazine and annual. Goodrich's own work was initially inspired by his abhorrence of traditional tales 'commonly put into the hands of youth, as if for the express purpose of reconciling them to vice and crime'.

*spirits . . . thumping on the table*: an allusion to the claims made by spiritualists that the dead contacted them during seances by 'rapping' on the table. The birth of the movement is usually dated to 31 March 1848, when the Fox sisters in New York State created a sensation by reporting that they had made contact with the spirit of a murdered peddler (although they later confessed that this was a hoax). Several spiritualist newspapers and periodicals were published in Boston, which according to E. W. Capron's *Modern Spiritualism* (Boston, 1855) rapidly became a centre for 'communications from the spirit-world' (p. 206).

*Aunt Agitate . . . Arguments on political economy*: cf. *Conversations on Political Economy; in which the Elements of that Science are Faithfully Explained*, by Jane Marcet (1769–1858). First published in 1816, the book was one of a series of 'conversations' by the same author, most of which were frequently reprinted. Her *Conversations on Chemistry* (1806) are said to have had a decisive influence on the 11-year-old Faraday. CK may also have had in his sights the nine-volume *Illustrations of Political Economy* (1832–4) written for the general reader by the atheistical Harriet Martineau (1802–76).

*C'est l'amour, l'amour, l'amour . . . à la ronde*: refrain from a French folk song, printed in *Chansons nationales et populaires de France* (Paris, 1850), ii. 180, also quoted by CK in ch. 11 of *Yeast*. A translation of the refrain is recited by the Duchess in ch. IX of *Alice's Adventures in Wonderland* – a passage which, like those on the Cheshire cat (see note to p. 58), did not appear in Dodgson's pre-*WB* manuscript of *Alice*. CK's grammatical error of 'la monde' for 'le monde' has been retained in most subsequent editions.

34 *no slot*: no animal footprint (usually of deer) for the hunter to follow.

*brow, bay, tray, and points*: the parts of a stag that a hunter might assess if he has the right to shoot it: the main, secondary, and tertiary antlers, together with its other qualities or features.

*between Haddon Wood and Countisbury Cliff*: presumably Heddon Wood on
the River Heddon, midway between Ilfracombe and Lynton; Countisbury
Cliff is at the headland east of Lynton.

*Mr Palk Collyns*: Charles Palk Collyns (1793–1864), surgeon at Dulverton,
and a noted Devonshire stag-hunter (misnamed 'Parker Collyns' in *MM*).
In 1862 he published *Notes on the Chase of the Wild Red Deer in the Counties
of Devon and Somerset*.

*stogged*: stuck or bogged.

*a heath-cropper*: one accustomed to getting a living from heathy (hence
boggy) land; cf. 'all the simple healthy comforts of a wild "heth-cropper's"
home. When he can, the good man of the house works at farm labour,
or cuts his own turf; and when work is scarce, he cuts copses and
makes heath-brooms, and does a little poaching' ('My Winter Garden', in
*Misc*. i. 161–2).

35 *first whip . . . second whip*: a 'whip' or 'whipper-in' is a 'huntsman's assist-
ant who keeps the hounds from straying by driving them back with the
whip into the main body of the pack' (*OED*).

36 *Malton*: a town north-west of York that featured four annual fairs and a
famous set of races on Longton Moor.

*noble old Beeswing herself*: a northern racehorse, foaled in 1833, and
described as 'the idol of her time'. She won the Ascot Gold Cup, the
Doncaster Gold Cup (four times), and the Newcastle Gold Cup (six
times). A race named after her was run at Newcastle from 1977 until 1999:
the Beeswing Stakes.

37 *the parotid region of his fauces*: another species of Rabelaisian trope: a
learned scientific definition, used with a mixture of mockery and display.
The phrase refers to gills formed below the ear connecting with the back
of the mouth.

*eft*: a young newt, with whose physical characteristics, especially their
slightly human 'hands', CK makes some play in the otter incident on
pp. 57–8.

38 *the coming of the Cocqcigrues*: i.e. an imaginary moment in the future that
could be either 'sometime' or 'never'. The source is Rabelais, *Gargantua*,
ch. XLIX: '[Pierochole's] kingdome should be restored to him at the coming of the Cocklicranes, which she calls Coquecigrues [*que son royaulme lui
seroit rendu a la venue des coquecigrues*]. What is become of him since we
cannot certainly tell, yet was I told that he is now a porter at Lyons . . .
enquiring at all strangers of the coming of the Cocklicranes, expecting
assuredly . . . that at their coming he shall be reestablished in his Kingdom.'
The first of five uses of the phrase in *WB*.

*Mr Garth*: Thomas Garth (1821–1907) from a wealthy family of sugar-
planters. He lived at Twyford, Berkshire, and was founder and first Master
of Foxhounds of the local hunt, which took his name in 1842. 'We had
a pretty thing on Friday with Garth's. The first run I've seen this year'
(CK to Thomas Hughes, *LM* ii. 55, June 1857).

38 *Illustrated News*: probably the *Illustrated London News*, the world's first illustrated weekly newspaper, founded in 1842; by 1863 it was selling more than 300,000 copies a week. CK used pages of it to paper his summer-house in Eversley.

*Professor Owen . . . Professor Huxley*: for Richard Owen see note to p. 15; Professor Huxley was Thomas Henry Huxley (1825–95), who in 1863 became both Hunterian professor at the Royal College of Surgeons and Fullerton professor at the Royal Institution. As a fervent Darwinian, he was strongly opposed to Owen's equivocations over evolutionary theory, but noted in a letter to H. Dyster in February 1860 that CK was 'a manly, right-minded person' and 'an excellent Darwinian to begin with'. Linley Sambourne's illustrations to the 1886 edition of *WB* included one of Owen and Huxley looking at a bottled water-baby.

*the shore of a boundless ocean*: 'to myself I seem to have been only a boy playing on the sea-shore, and diverting myself in now and then finding a smoother pebble or a prettier shell than ordinary, while the great ocean of truth lay all undiscovered before me'. Quoted in Sir David Brewster's *Memoirs of the Life, Writings and Discoveries of Sir Isaac Newton* (London: John Murray, 1855). CK returned to the idea when describing modern scientists in his essay 'The Study of Natural History': 'they stand upon the threshold of knowledge like (as Newton said of himself) children gathering a few pebbles, upon the shore of an illimitable sea' (*Scientific Lectures and Essays* (London: Macmillan, 1885), 303).

39 *Murchison . . . Grove*: a catalogue of some of the most famous names in science at this time: Murchison (1792–1871), a pioneer geologist and one of the founders of the British Association; Adam Sedgwick (1785–1873), Woodwardian professor of geology at Cambridge, who was for a considerable time a friend of Murchison's and worked with him studying early rock formations in Britain; Charles Darwin (1805–82), whose presence in *WB* is discussed in the Introduction, p. xiii; Michael Faraday (1791–1867), physicist and lecturer at the Royal Institution; William Robert Grove (1811–96), lawyer and physicist, who became a judge in 1871 and was knighted in 1872. For Professors Owen and Huxley see note to p. 38. A similar roll call of names occurs in the transcript of one of CK's lectures to the boys at Wellington College in June 1863 (*LM* ii. 167).

*M. Du Chaillu*: Paul Belloni Du Chaillu (1835–1903), explorer whose first expedition to Central Africa was recorded in his *Voyages*, translated into English in 1861 as *Explorations and Adventures in Equatorial Africa*. His tall tales of horrific gorilla attacks created such a sensation that *Punch* dedicated its 1861 Christmas Annual to the gorilla theme.

40 *Le Vaillant*: François Levaillant (1753–1824), explorer and ornithologist, who recorded his travels in such books as *Voyages dans l'intérieure de l'Afrique* (1790) and *Histoire naturelle des oiseaux d'Afrique* (1795–1808).

*king of the Cannibal Islands*: a favourite phrase with CK. It occurs on two occasions in *Yeast* (chs. VIII and XV), and once in *Alton Locke* (ch. X).

It was used as the title of a pantomime, first performed in 1845, and was also a popular comic song published in *Punch* in 1844 that was still being sold as a broadside ballad in the late 1850s.

*Pterodactyles*: lit. 'wing-fingers': the genus of prehistoric reptile which contrived to fly by developing extended webbing on its modified front legs. *OED* cites a first use of the term by Charles Lyell in his *Principles of Geology* (1830), following discoveries of fossilized remains.

*And has not . . . knows what is*: these two sentences were the subject of an erratum note printed on B1ᵛ of the first edition, in which CK pointed out that the statement that lizards had feathers was written 'before Professor Owen's Memoir of November 20, 1862, showing that the Archæopteryx is certainly a bird; and was unfortunately overlooked in correcting the proofs'. The *Memoir* in question was read to the Royal Society and established that the fossilized remains of a creature found in the Upper Oolite limestone at Solenhofen, Bavaria, were undoubtedly those of a bird, which was designated *Archaeopteryx macrurus*.

41 *green drake*: a species of mayfly, whose nymphs, like those of the alderfly and dragonfly, live on the river-bed before surfacing to hatch. CK expatiates on green drakes and alderflies as bait in his 'Chalk-stream Studies' of 1858.

*Proteus of the Adelsberg caverns*: 'At the caverns of Adelsberg in Carniola . . . in darkness from its birth until its death, lives that strange beast, the *Proteus* [*anguinus*], a sort of long newt which never comes to perfection— I suppose for want of the genial sunlight which makes all things grow' (*Madam How and Lady Why* (London: Bell & Daldy, 1870), 166). Adelsberg and its extensive cave system is now called Postojna, and is situated in western Slovenia.

*M. Quatrefages*: Jean Louis Armand de Quatrefages (1810–92) was a noted zoologist and ethnologist and was a foreign member of both the Royal Society and the Linnean Society. He published a number of papers on the annelids, which include the polychaete worm *syllis*, and on jellyfish; the source of CK's quotation is *The Rambles of a Naturalist on the Coasts of France, Spain, and Sicily*, trans. E. C. Otté (London: Longman, Brown, Green, Longmans & Roberts, 1857), i. 223, which has 'emerge from the egg' rather than 'come out of the egg'.

42 *goose-barnacles*: stalked barnacles which, in medieval times, were thought to turn into barnacle geese. By 'degradation' CK may be referring to their transition from free-swimming larvae to sessile crustaceans; the degradation of their 'cousins' may refer to the operations of the crustacean larva *Sacculina carcini*, which is parasitic upon crabs and consists of little more than a reproductive sac and a root system for intruding upon the body of the host. CK's interest in barnacles may have been inspired by his reading of Darwin, whose eight-year research into their various species underlay his work on evolution.

*the Great Exhibition*: the Great Exhibition, a vast array of manufactured goods, inventions, and machinery from all over the world, was the brainchild of the Prince Consort and was held in Hyde Park in 1851, housed in Joseph Paxton's 'Crystal Palace'. In 1854 this structure was moved to Sydenham in south London and continued to be used for public exhibitions.

42 *'We are fearfully and wonderfully made'*: 'I will praise thee; for I am fearfully and wonderfully made' (Psalm 139: 14).

43 *rapping on it*: see note to p. 33.

*caddis*: larva of the caddis fly or 'caperer'. CK gives a fuller fictional description on pp. 48–9 which stems from his observations as a fisherman. See his account in 'Chalk-stream Studies', in *Misc*. i.

*the Linnæan Society*: now spelt 'Linnean', the Society was founded in 1788 by James Edward Smith to promote botanical work.

44 *Botany Bay*: in New South Wales, Australia, the bay where James Cook anchored HMS *Endeavour* in 1770, and was later used to refer to the penal colony where British convicts were transported.

*not certificated*: part of the government's plan for expanding education widely and cheaply was to select bright pupils from national elementary schools and train them within the school, and later at training institutions, to become certificated teachers. At a pragmatic level the system worked, but CK deeply mistrusted the academic capacities of children 'forced' in this way. On the next page he mocks a pupil-teacher analysis of the word 'amphibious' which recalls (with more pronounced satirical overtones) Bitzer's mechanical definition of a horse in ch. 1 of Dickens's *Hard Times* (1854).

45 *as lively as a grig*: proverbial; a person who is full of joy and energy (a grig is a species of eel).

46 *He prayeth well . . . all*: from S. T. Coleridge's 'The Rime of the Ancyent Marinere', first published in *Lyrical Ballads* (1798). Not printed in *MM*. CK's error of 'men' for 'man' has been corrected, although his elision of the stanza break between lines 2 and 3 has been retained.

*Amphibious*: see note to p. 44 above.

47 *a wise man once*: William Wordsworth; the quotation is from 'Ode: Intimations of Immortality from Recollections of Early Childhood', first published in 1807.

48 *orthodox . . . on-all-accounts-to-be-received*: the first of several word lists compiled in imitation of Rabelais. Despite its nonsensical rigmarole it serves to emphasize the 'doctrine'—the central lesson—of CK's 'fairy tale'.

*sand-pipes*: not a recognized biological term. CK probably means tube worms, which, caddis-like, build themselves habitations out of sand.

49 *the Long Pond*: at Eversley. 'Many a time did he show his children, and other children too, the caddis-baits in the Long Pond in the glebe' (Rose Kingsley in her introduction to the Everyman edn. of *WB*, p. xii).

*spoon-bonnets*: ladies' hats, very popular in the early 1860s, with the brim rising concave above the forehead like a spoon. This gave no shade to the face, so a scarf-like attachment could be added, fittingly called an 'ugly'. Linley Sambourne illustrates a spoon-bonnet on p. 102 of the 1886 edn. and includes the date AD 1862 in the picture.

*one wonderful little fellow*: CK probably intended this to be a description of the tube-dwelling rotifer, which cements a protective sheath for itself and sweeps up food through currents created by its rotating cilia.

50 *howked*: hollowed out or excavated by digging.

51 *like the cats in Struwelpeter*: the German picture-book *Struwwelpeter*, written and illustrated by Heinrich Hoffmann, was first published in Frankfurt am Main in 1845 and was translated into English in 1848. It soon became famous throughout the world for its playful – but also startling – reworking of didactic themes. The cats appear in 'The Dreadful Story about Harriet and the Matches', where they 'scream'd for help, 'twas all in vain' after the disobedient girl accidentally burns herself to death.

*hover*: 'any overhanging stone or bank under which a fish can hide' (*OED*, citing this example).

*floushed*: 'Came with a heavy splash' (*OED*, citing this example).

53 *hare and hounds*: 'a cross-country race in which the runners follow a trail marked by torn-up paper' (*OED*).

*green caterpillars let themselves down*: cf. 'who knows not that [the angler's] best fish are generally taken under some tree from which the caterpillars (having determined on slow and deliberate suicide) are letting themselves down gently by a silken thread into the mouth of the spotted monarch, who has but to sail about and pick them up one by one' ('Chalk-stream Studies', in *Misc*. i. 202).

54 *neither Blondin nor Leotard*: circus performers. 'Blondin' was the stage name of Jean-François Gravelet (1824–97), celebrated for his high-wire acts, one of which had been performed at the Crystal Palace in 1861; Jules Léotard (1838–70) was the inventor of the flying trapeze and also first appeared in England in 1861, at the Alhambra. A mechanical toy was named after him, and his name is now preserved in the one-piece costume worn by dancers.

*duns and spinners*: duns are flies used in angling; spinner-flies are more commonly known as daddy-long-legs.

*as bold as nine tailors*: an adaptation of the satirical proverb about tailors, that it takes nine of them to make a man.

55 *nor Houdin, nor Robin, nor Frikell*: conjurors. Jean-Eugène Robert-Houdin (1805–71), from whom Houdini took his name; Henrik Joseph Donckel Robin (1811–74), a Dutch illusionist who performed at Windsor Castle in the 1850s and at the Egyptian Hall in London in 1861; Wiljalba Frikell (1816–1903), a sleight-of-hand performer who was famous for the simplicity of his sets and props.

56 *My wife shall dance . . . away*: from the second verse of the traditional English song 'Begone dull care'.

57 *Zoological Gardens*: now known as London Zoo, the Zoological Gardens were originally founded as a private collection for scientific study in 1828, and opened to the paying public in 1847.

*Cordery's Moor*: low-lying land to the west of Eversley, near the confluence of the Whitewater and Blackwater rivers.

58 *bogies*: goblins or other terrifying creatures.

*a fresh*: 'A rush of water, or increase of the stream in a river; a freshet flood' (*OED*).

*grinning like a Cheshire cat*: *OED* dates the phrase back to 1770 and explanations of its popular origin range from the appearance of a grinning cat on a Cheshire inn-sign to the moulding of a Cheshire cheese into a similar image. The Cheshire cat in *Alice's Adventures in Wonderland* (1865) may stem from the Revd Charles Dodgson's [Lewis Carroll's] reading of *WB*, since it was not present in his first draft of the story written for Alice Liddell in 1862–3.

60 *omnium-gatherums*: *OED* dates this term for 'a miscellaneous collection' back to 1530 and cites *WB* as an example of nineteenth-century usage.

61 *strids*: rock-walled gullies above a stream which can be jumped across; named after the strid in Bolton Woods in Wharfedale. 'Tell R[ose] I jumped over the Strid where young Romilly was drowned. Make her learn Wordsworth's ballad on it, "What is Good for a Bootless Bene"' (CK to his wife, *LM* ii. 80, July 1858).

*squatter up*: 'To make one's way among water with much splashing or flapping' (*OED*, citing *WB*).

*Dennis*: an Irish servant; cf. CK's jocular verses on a proposed fishing trip to Ireland (*LM* ii. 4): 'Blow Snowdon! give me Ireland for my pennies | Hurrah! for salmon, grilse, and Dennis, Dennis, Dennis!'

63 *Cythrawl Sassenach . . . Fan Quei*: the first is a mixture of Welsh and Gaelic meaning 'hostile English'; the Chinese phrase means 'foreign devils'.

*wise new fishing laws*: legislation passed *c*.1860 that banned roe-fishing and the use of the killing-pan.

*in the good time coming*: an echo of the Chartist song which features in *Alton Locke*.

*Arthur Clough . . . 'Bothie'*: lines from section v of Arthur Hugh Clough's long poem *The Bothie of Tober-na-Vuolich* (1848). 'So if you will keep your trumpet for "Ambarvalia", I will celebrate the birth of Clough's "Bothie" with penny whistle and banjo' (CK to J. Conington, *LM* i. 191, 30 December 1848).

*scald cream*: clotted cream.

*water-ouzel . . . stones*: a hazy echo of Tennyson's 'The mellow ouzel fluted in the elm' from 'The Gardener's Daughter' (1842).

64 *gilly*: a servant (from the Gaelic 'gille', lad).

*dear old Bewick*: Thomas Bewick (1753–1828), engraver on wood and metal, who brought to perfection the technique of 'white line engraving' on the end grain of boxwood, which enabled him to reproduce images of great delicacy. In CK's day he was widely famed for his compendia *A General History of Quadrupeds* (1790) and the two-volume *History of British Birds* (1793, 1804), which were illustrated with very accurate pictures of the animals described and also with beautifully wrought scenes set in Bewick's native Tynedale. CK refers affectionately to Bewick's work in several letters and essays.

66 *stake-nets*: fishing nets secured in a vertical position by means of stakes.

67 *as proud as Alcibiades*: an Athenian, born c.450 BC, who was a pupil of Pericles and a friend of Socrates. His turbulent career, marred by arrogance, is charted by Thucydides.

*hidalgo*: a Spanish gentleman or nobleman.

68 *Sweet is the lore . . . receives*: from 'The Tables Turned', the second part of 'Expostulation and Reply', first published in *Lyrical Ballads* (1798). Not printed in *MM*.

69 *muckle*: a heavy hammer used for killing fish.

71 *snob*: here referring to someone belonging to the ordinary or lower classes of society; cf. the battle between the squire's men and the gang of Cockney poachers who come down from London by rail in *Yeast*, ch. IX.

*millraces*: a mill race is 'the swift current of water that drives a mill-wheel' (*OED*), getting caught in which can be dangerous for swimmers.

72 *as some wise men tell us*: the philosopher Thales (b. c.624 BC) believed that water was the source of life, as dramatized in Part II of Goethe's *Faust*: 'Alles ist aus dem Wasser entsprungen!! | Alles wird durch das Wasser erhalten! | Ozean, gönn uns dein ewiges Walten.'

73 *sea-pies*: oystercatchers.

74 *a great lazy sunfish*: a fish native to the western Atlantic that occasionally wanders into British coastal waters.

*Chesapeake*: Chesapeake Bay, the largest estuary in America, covers 64,000 square miles of bays, marshes, and rivers, and contains over 300 species of fish, some of which migrate there during the year.

75 *threshers*: or 'thrashers': 'a sea-fox or fox-shark . . . so called from the very long upper division of the tail with which it lashes its enemy' (*OED*).

*collier brig*: a ship used for transporting coal.

*like a ribbon of pure silver*: probably a silver eel in its breeding livery, although they do not have 'very long teeth'.

*owl-rays*: a variety of ray (*OED*, citing this passage from *WB*).

*the forsaken Merman*: Matthew Arnold's ballad 'The Forsaken Merman' was first published in *The Strayed Reveller and Other Poems* (1849), and quickly became a favourite anthology piece.

77 *Victoria Cross*: introduced by Queen Victoria on 29 January 1856 to recognize acts of bravery in the Crimean War, and still the highest military decoration awarded to members of the armed forces in the Commonwealth (previously the British Empire) for valour 'in the face of the enemy'.

*old German bogy-painters*: e.g. Matthias Grünewald and Hans Baldung Grien. In a letter to the illustrator Charles Bennett in 1859, CK contrasts 'Greek health and accuracy' with German 'grotesqueness' as 'the only two root-schools in the world' and cites Dürer as his example of the latter (*LM* ii. 76–7).

*leap-frogs*: a home-made toy involving a string attached to the two ends of a goose's breastbone and wound tightly on a peg to form a spring. This could be secured with a piece of wax which would 'give' suddenly, causing the apparatus to leap in the air. Hans Christian Andersen celebrates the toy in his story 'Springfyrene' ('The Jumpers').

78 *the bench and the board of guardians*: thus administering justice as a magistrate, and determining admissions to and conditions in the Poor House as a guardian.

79 *mild applications of iodine . . . Parry's liquid horse-blister*: the presence of iodine in sea air was thought by many Victorians to be conducive to good health. (A more modern myth stresses 'ozone'.) Similarly the application of 'blisters' to the skin was often employed to promote healing by bringing humours to the surface through inflammation. The application of Parry's patent concoction to children would have had disastrous results; CK had himself been scarred in childhood by the application of some 'tartarised blistering stuff' when his left lung was discovered to be seriously congested.

*dead of bad smells*: alluding to the miasmatic theory of disease, which held that diseases such as cholera were caused by 'miasma' (pollution), a form of bad air that carried particles of decomposed matter; sanitation campaigner Edwin Chadwick summed up the theory by claiming that 'all smell is disease'. During the 1850s and 1860s it was gradually supplanted in scientific thinking by germ theory, but retained its hold on the popular imagination.

*Professor Ptthmllnsprts*: i.e. Put-them-all-in-spirits, a reference to the current enthusiasm for preserving specimens in alcohol. (Peter Raby's *Bright Paradise: Victorian Scientific Travellers* (London: Chatto & Windus, 1996) includes a photograph from London Zoo of a gorilla pickled in rum, p. 183.) CK's subsequent description of the Professor allows him to make a broad comic attack on various aspects of scientific and educational dogmatism.

80 *Curacao . . . know why*: the Caribbean island of Curaçao was occupied by the Dutch in 1634 and later became an important centre of the Atlantic slave trade; the Siege of Petropavlosk (Petropaulowski) in 1854 was a significant conflict of the Crimean War.

*Acclimatisation Society*: the Acclimatization Society of England was founded in 1860 by Frank Buckland, who was a naturalist and popular journalist. An earlier one had been set up in Paris by Isidore Geoffroy Sainte-Hilaire in 1854, with the view to introducing and acclimatizing new species, particularly in the colonies. Buckland's society, however, seemed to specialize in holding dinners to sample as many exotic animals as they could, following the example set by his father, Dean William Buckland. Frank Buckland had a standing order with the London Zoological Society for the bodies of all deceased animals which would then be served up at his dinners.

*sea-cockyolybirds*: see note to p. 161.

81 *"The Triumph of Galatea"*: presumably a copy of the fresco by Raphael, finished *c.*1514 for the Palazzo Farnese in Rome, although CK's description does not correspond in all details. His 'burning mountain' may be from a Pisan fresco, *The Triumph of Death*.

*John Locke . . . Plato*: the English philosopher John Locke (1632–1704), one of the founding fathers of the Enlightenment, whose pragmatic theories of psychology and education offended CK's Romantic inclinations. By contrast CK saw in Plato, whose *Dialogues* had influenced him since his student days, a precursor of Christian doctrines of the pre-eminence of Spirit. 'I confess myself a Platonist; and my aim is to draw men by showing them that the absolute "God the Father", whom no man hath seen is beyond all possible intellectual notions of ours' (*LM* i. 325).

*British Association . . . hippopotamus majors*: a satire on contemporary arguments over natural selection, which had been exacerbated by the discovery of the gorilla. Professor Richard Owen, who in 1858 became president of the British Association for the Advancement of Science (founded 1831), defended mankind from an implied simian ancestry by declaring a distinctive difference possessed by humans: a unique lobe which he termed the hippocampus minor. CK thought the idea ludicrous, and at the 1862 meeting of the British Association in Cambridge he circulated an imaginary speech by 'Lord Dundreary' (see note below) that confused 'hippocampus' and 'hippopotamus'.

*faith, hope, and charity*: 1 Corinthians 13.

82 *Lord Dundreary*: a foolish toff, the lead character in Tom Taylor's play *Our American Cousin* (1858). The make-up for the part included long sidewhiskers which then became fashionable as 'Dundrearies'. Tom Taylor was a third member of the fishing party to Wales in 1856.

*British Association at Melbourne*: the Association usually held its annual meetings in different provincial towns, as satirized in Dickens's *Mudfog Papers*, but did not venture beyond Britain.

*nymphs . . . or worse*: a globetrotting assortment of figures from myth and folklore, including 'nixes' (water sprites), 'wilis' (spirits of jilted maidens), 'kobolds' (spirits who are usually invisible but can materialize in the form of people, animals, or household objects), 'cluricaunes' (small creatures similar to leprechauns), 'follets' (Will-o'-the-wisps), 'lutins' (hobgoblins), 'afrits' (snake-bodied monsters), 'marids' (ocean-dwelling genies), 'peris' (winged, fairy-like creatures), and 'deevs' (demon fairies); for bogies see note to p. 58.

82 *bosh and wind*: stuff and nonsense.

*regular Sadducee . . . Pharisee*: two opposing groups within the Jewish faith, the first denying oral elements of the Mosaic Law, including the resurrection of the dead, the second often seen as too obviously advertising their adherence to every detail of the Law. Both groups figure in the cancelled 'Envoi' to *WB*.

83 *Holothurian . . . Synapta . . . Cephalopod*: spur-of-the-moment mumbo-jumbo by a scientist attempting to cover up his surprise and ignorance. Holothuria and Synaptidae are sea cucumbers; cephalopods are molluscs such as cuttlefish.

84 *wise old heathen*: Juvenal in his fourteenth Satire.

86 *A very terrible old fairy*: perhaps an indirect reference to Mother Carey, with some Kingsleyesque satire on prognostication.

*geryons*: in Greek mythology Geryon was a three-bodied, four-winged giant who lived on the island of Erytheia; one of the twelve labours of Heracles was to steal his red cattle.

87 *the beginning thereof—*: what follows is a nonsensical mixture of genuine and phoney scientific language.

88 *peth-winds*: convolvulus; given by *OED* as a variant of 'bethwine' and citing this passage in *WB*.

*Schedule D*: income tax was first introduced by William Pitt the Younger in 1798 to raise money for the French Revolutionary Wars; although abolished in 1802, Sir Robert Peel's reintroduction of the tax in 1842 saw the return of schedule D to cover 'annual profits or gains' from trade, commerce, and the professions on incomes over £150.

*Hippocrates*: the Greek physician (*c*.460–*c*.357 BC) who, because of his careful observations and records, has come to be regarded as the founder of scientific medical practice.

*Feuchtersleben*: Ernst, Freiherr von Feuchtersleben (1806–49), an Austrian doctor and poet whose ideas on the relationship between mental and physical health have been seen as anticipating modern psychiatry.

*Hellebore*: black hellebore is a purgative drug found in Greece and southern Europe. It must be used only in minute quantities because of its toxicity.

*Aretæus*: a Cappadocian physician (*fl.* second century AD). Like Galen (see note below) he was influenced by Hippocrates and took his practice to Rome. He was the first accurately to describe diabetes, to which he gave the name that is still in use.

*Celsus*: Aulus Cornelius Celsus (25 BC–AD 50), a Roman writer on medicine, who believed in letting nature take its own course. He became known as 'Cicero Medicorum' for the purity of his Latin style.

89 *Cœlius Aurelianus*: properly Caelius (*fl. c.* AD 150), a Roman physician who wrote a treatise on chronic diseases.

*Galen*: Claudius Galen (*c.* AD 130–201), a Greek physician whose writings on medicine were a major influence down to the Renaissance period.

*Borage*: a plant used for making cordials.

*Cauteries*: either heated metal instruments used for searing skin, or caustic drugs used for the same purpose.

*Gordonius*: Bernardus Gordonius (1258–1315), physician and medical writer, whose *De amore* is quoted in another work of fiction heavily influenced by Rabelais, Laurence Sterne's *Tristram Shandy* (1759–69).

*Bezoar stone*: a solid substance found in the stomach of some animals, chiefly ruminants, and thought to be an antidote to poison. It is mentioned for comic purposes by Rabelais.

*Diamargaritum*: powdered pearls used in the manufacture of medicines.

*Ambergris*: a secretion from the intestines of sperm whales formerly used in cookery and the manufacture of perfumes.

*Dormouse' fat*: historically used for medicinal purposes.

90 *Croquet*: the game (which features famously in *Alice's Adventures in Wonderland*) was introduced into England from Ireland in 1852, and by 1863 had become immensely popular.

*Aunt Sally*: recorded 1861 in *OED* as 'a game much in vogue at fairs'. A dummy woman's head was set up with a pipe in its mouth and contestants threw sticks to try to break the pipe.

*The Saturday Review*: one of the most influential weeklies of the Victorian period, published 1855–1938; the term 'muscular Christianity' was first applied to CK in its pages.

*outriders*: mounted escorts.

*Easthampstead Plain*: to the east of Eversley.

*Wellington College*: initiated in 1852 after the death of the Duke and with the eager sponsorship of the Prince Consort, it opened in 1859 under the headmastership of E. W. Benson, later Archbishop of Canterbury. CK's eldest son, Maurice, joined the school in its second term, and was a pupil there until 1866.

*black game*: heath-fowl (blackcocks) as opposed to grouse, etc. (red game).

*Suffumigations*: 'fumes or vapours generated by burning herbs, incense etc.' (*OED*, which gives an additional use for the term in incantations at ceremonies of sacrifice and witchcraft).

*Heerwiggius*: presumably Henningius Michael Herwig, whose tract on 'sympathetic medicine' (see also note on Weapon-salve, below) was translated into English in 1700 as *The Art of Curing Sympathetically or Magnetically Proved to be Most True . . . with a discourse concerning the cure of madness.*

90 *Dr Gray*: Asa Gray (1810–88), American botanist and Fisher professor of natural history at Harvard. He was a supporter of, and correspondent with, Charles Darwin.

*Metallic tractors*: invented by an American physician, Elisha Perkins (d. 1799), 'a pair of pointed rods of different metals . . . which were believed to relieve rheumatic and other pain' (*OED*).

*Holloway's Ointment*: a patent medicine manufactured by Thomas Holloway (1800–83) that was advertised as a cure for ailments including gout, rheumatism, ulcers, and sore breasts; in 1879 he used some of the profits to build Holloway College for the Higher Education of Women, now part of the University of London.

*Electro-biology*: 'A branch of biology dealing with electrical phenomena in living organisms' (*OED*), although CK's usage is probably related to its appearance in discussions of mesmerism (see note below) such as James Braid's *Magic, Witchcraft, Animal Magnetism, Hypnotism, and Electro-Biology* (1852).

*Valentine Greatrakes*: a Cromwellian soldier (1629–83) who claimed to cure scrofula and other disorders by laying-on of hands.

91 *Holloway's Pills*: see note on Holloway's Ointment, above. The pills included aloe, myrrh, and saffron, and the advertisements claimed that they could cure everything from 'loss of appetite' to 'dropsical swellings'.

*Morrison's Pills . . . Parr's Life Pills*: more examples of popular patent medicines. Both were mentioned by Friedrich Engels in *The Condition of the Working Class in England* (1844) as examples of the nation's apparent addiction to pills and potions: 'As our German peasants are cupped or bled at certain seasons, so do the English working-people now consume patent medicines to their own injury and the great profit of the manufacturer.'

*Mesmerism*: hypnotic powers, named after Franz Anton Mesmer (1734–1815), who launched a Europe-wide craze in the late eighteenth century. CK experimented with mesmerism as an undergraduate, and although he later expressed scepticism about its medical uses, in 1848 he was 'magnetized' by his old university friend Charles Blachford Mansfield while on holiday in Ilfracombe.

*Malleus Maleficarum . . . Wierus*: *Malleus* was the work of two Dominicans, Johann Sprenger, dean of Cologne University, and Heinrich Kraemer, professor of theology at Salzburg, published *c.*1486. It was used by both Roman Catholics and Protestants as a handbook for the extirpation of witchcraft, and remained in print for over 100 years. The other references here are to later writers who encouraged or, in the case of Wierus, protested against the cruelty of witch-hunting. The *Formicarius* was a five-volume work by Johann Nider, published at Douai in 1602; Martin Anton Delrio, SJ, published his *Disquisitionum magicarum libri sex* at Louvain in 1599; and the Belgian physician Johann Weyer sought to rationalize attitudes to witchcraft in several treatises published in the mid-sixteenth century.

*Hydropathy*: the water-cure, a fashionable form of medical treatment that was originated in 1825 by Vincenz Preissnitz at Gräfenberg in Germany, involving the external and internal application of water. Popular British centres included Malvern, where the visitors included Darwin, Dickens, Florence Nightingale, and Tennyson, who was said by Edward FitzGerald to have emerged 'half-cured, or half-destroyed' from one stay in 1848.

*Madame Rachel's Elixir of Youth*: a reference to the con-artist 'Madame Rachel' (Sarah Rachel Levison, d. 1880), whose beauty salon was based in New Bond Street, and who claimed to be many decades older than she appeared. Her pamphlet *Beautiful For Ever* was published in 1860, and her beauty products were also referred to in Mary Elizabeth Braddon's *Lady Audley's Secret*, published in the same year CK wrote *WB*.

*Poughkeepsie . . . Prophecies*: Andrew Jackson Davis (1826–1910), often referred to as the 'John the Baptist' of modern spiritualism, whose prophetic book *The Principles of Nature: Her Divine Revelations and a Voice to Mankind* (1847) was allegedly dictated while Davis was in a mesmeric trance.

*addle eggs*: unfertilized eggs.

*Pyropathy*: treatment by fire.

*Basil Valentine*: or Basilius Valentinus, the possibly spurious authorial name given to a sequence of alchemical works 'discovered' in Thuringia by Councillor Johann Thölde, who may have assembled them himself from earlier documents. Probably the most famous was the *Currus triumphalis antimonii*, containing a factual description of compounds of antimony (chiefly used in medicine as an emetic).

*Weapon-salve*: Sir Kenelm Digby (1603–65), courtier and diplomat, whose *Late Discourse . . . Touching the Cure of Wounds by the Powder of Sympathy* (1658) recommended that wounds should be treated by daubing a specially manufactured powder not on the injured part of the body, but on whatever had caused the injury. The *OED* traces the phrase 'hair of the dog', now commonly used to refer to a hangover cure, to Robert James's *A Treatise on Canine Madness* (London: printed for J. Newbery, 1760): 'The hair of the dog that gave the wound is advised as an application to the part injured' (p. 204).

*Ruggiero*: one of the heroes in Ariosto's Italian epic *Orlando furioso*, first fully published in 1532, and translated into English by Sir John Harington (1561–1612) in an edition published in 1591. CK here conflates (or confuses) this story with that of the English knight Astolfo, who borrowed Ruggiero's hippogriff and flew to the moon to recover Orlando's lost wits.

*hippogriff*: 'a fabulous creature, like a griffin, but with body and hind-quarters like those of a horse' (*OED*).

*'a man and a brother'*: 'Am I not a man and a brother?' was a phrase that had been incorporated into an anti-slavery medallion created by the potter

Josiah Wedgwood (1730–95), later adopted as a seal by the London Anti-Slavery Society. In May 1861 *Punch* had published a cartoon satirizing evolutionary theory that showed a gorilla asking 'Am I a Man and a Brother?' The phrase is also quoted on p. 128.

91 *Noodle . . . Foodle*: generic names for fools, as used in Henry Fielding's play *Tom Thumb* (1730), and more recently in Dickens's *Bleak House* (1852–3) alongside Boodle, Coodle, Doodle, Goodle, Hoodle, Koodle, Loodle, Moodle, Poodle, and Quoodle (ch. XII).

*black-fellows chipped flints at Abbeville*: during the 1840s Jacques Boucher de Crèvecœur de Perthes (1788–1868) made a series of discoveries of flint implements in the Somme Valley which carried the dating of man's existence back to the Pleistocene period. An extensive account was given by Charles Lyell in his *Antiquity of Man*, published in the same year as *WB*.

92 *Mr Weekes*: an elusive figure, possibly a friend of the Kingsley family, or William Henry Weekes (*fl.* 1835–46) of Sandwich, Kent, who published a number of papers on his experiments with voltaic currents and their relation to biology and meteorology.

*Macintoshes and Cording's boots*: the waterproofing of cloth by using rubber was patented by Charles Macintosh (or Mackintosh) in 1823. Cording's patent boots did not survive long enough to give the language an equivalent common noun.

*mesenteric . . . ventricles*: mock-medical nonsense; 'mesenteric' refers to the abdomen, and 'ventricles' to the heart, but 'apophthegms' are pithy sayings.

94 *Ode to Duty*: Wordsworth's 'Ode to Duty' was first published in 1807. Not printed in *MM*.

*Vick . . . Lioness*: dogs at Eversley.

*withes*: flexible pieces of willow used for weaving and basket-making.

95 *'I can't get out'*: alluding to the caged starling in Laurence Sterne's *A Sentimental Journey* (1768) which laments 'I can't get out,—I can't get out'.

96 *Polonius*: a character in Shakespeare's *Hamlet* (1603), father of Ophelia.

*girn*: 'To show the teeth in rage, pain, disappointment etc' (*OED*, citing this passage from *WB*).

97 *It was something of a bull, that*: i.e. a contradictory piece of behaviour. Such contradictions, often funny or unintended, had come to be especially associated with the Irish; a study written by Maria Edgeworth in collaboration with her father was published in 1802 as *An Essay on Irish Bulls*.

*'What . . . in the morning?'*: a traditional sea shanty.

*cut my capers*: to dance or frolic, from the Italian *capriola*.

*the Mewstone*: a rock near Wembury to the south of Plymouth Sound.

98 *sand . . . in the tobacco*: the adulteration of common foodstuffs was a matter of increasing concern. A. H. Hassall wrote a series of outraged pieces in

*The Lancet* (1851–4) which were later turned into a book; the matter was also discussed at a special conference in Birmingham in 1854, which led to articles such as 'The Poisoners of the Present Century' (*Punch*, 9 December 1854) and informed Tennyson's *Maud* (1855), in which the speaker complains that 'chalk and alum and plaster are sold to the poor for bread'. In *London Labour and the London Poor* (London: Griffin, Bohn, and Company, 1861–2) Henry Mayhew reports that 'I was assured, by a leading grocer, that he could not mention twenty shops in the city, of which he could say: "you can go in and buy a pound of ground coffee there, and it will not be adulterated"' (i. 184).

*black diver*: a seabird.

101 *St Brandan's fairy isle*: the earliest extant version of the *Navigatio Sancti Brendani* is an eleventh-century MS in Latin. St Brandan (or Brendan) is said to have lived in the sixth century and his seven-year voyage was undertaken in search of an earthly paradise somewhere in the Atlantic Ocean. His legend is part of a much larger body of Celtic lore – including the story that formed the subject of Tennyson's 1880 ballad 'The Voyage of Maeldune' – that plays on the theme of voyaging among mysterious islands.

*potheen*: illegally distilled Irish whiskey.

*pater o'pee*: a form of jig.

*old Dunmore*: Dunmore Head, the westernmost point of Ireland, overlooking the group of islands and rocks known as the Blasquets (or Blaskets). This area of Kerry is steeped in Brandaniana, and Dunmore is not far from Clogher, where the saint is said to have died.

*that I had wings as a dove*: Psalm 55: 6.

*hooker*: 'A one-masted fishing smack on the Irish coast' (*OED*).

102 *locks and friths*: i.e. lochs and firths.

*Atlantis*: described in Plato's unfinished dialogue *Critias*.

103 *Fourier*: François-Marie-Charles Fourier (1772–1837), a French social philosopher whose ideas for communal groups of producers anticipated some of the anti-capitalist ideas of Karl Marx.

*Nereids*: in Greek mythology the fifty Nereids were the daughters of Nereus, a sea-god, and the nymph Doris. Amphitrite was one of these, called queen because of her union with Poseidon, lord of the sea. Zoologists adopted the term *Nereidae* for the ragworm family within the larger class of marine bristle worms; other families are the *Eunicidae*, the *Polynoe*, and the *Phyllodocidae* (or paddle-worms).

*Scythes . . . Needles*: another Rabelaisian list. A *Yataghan* is 'a sword of Mohammedan countries, having a handle without a guard, and often a double-curved blade'; a *Cneese* is 'a Malay dagger with the blade in wavy form'; a *Tuck* is a kind of rapier; and a *Gisarine* (more usually Gisarme) is a battleaxe 'having a long blade in line with the shaft, sharpened on both sides, and ending in a point' (*OED*).

104 *overlaid*: suffocated through having someone lie on top of them.

105 *most immaculate, potentate*: in 1859 Napoleon III made a secret deal with Cavour, prime minister of Piedmont, for France to assist in expelling Austria from the Italian peninsula, in exchange for Piedmont relinquishing Savoy and the Nice region to French control.

108 *calomel*: mercurous chloride, a white, tasteless powder, widely used in the past as a purgative and antiseptic, but liable to result in mercury poisoning. CK claimed that the heavy doses he had been given for 'biliousness' as a child inhibited the development of his jaw, creating the stammer that afflicted him in adult life.

*jalap*: a purgative made from bindweed (*Ipomea jalapa*) that could be given in sugar or jam to disguise the taste.

109 *Pope Gregory . . . chair*: alluding to the popular belief that Pope Gregory I (*c.*540–604) was responsible for introducing a form of plainsong to church services (hence 'Gregorian chant'); he is the one of the patron saints of musicians and singers.

110 *butties*: middlemen in collieries who undertook to meet a production target and had few scruples about how it was done. 'Nailers' ran nail-making shops and were allegedly similarly ruthless with their apprentices.

111 *bathing-women*: supervisors of sea-bathing who often stood in the sea to dunk their customers.

*the naughty boys in Struwelpeter*: see note to p. 51. Hoffmann's 'Story of the Inky Boys' tells of the retribution visited upon three children who mock a 'woolly-headed black-a-moor'. 'Der grosse Nikolas' who effects this appears in English editions as Agrippa, so presumably CK knew the German version.

114 *Thou little child . . . life*: from section VIII of Wordsworth's 'Ode: Intimations of Immortality from Recollections of Early Childhood'.

115 *the people in America; and . . . in the Bible*: 'But Jeshurun [i.e. Israel] waxed fat, and kicked' (Deuteronomy 32: 15). *WB* was written during the American Civil War (1861–5).

116 *howk him, hump him*: kick him, beat him black and blue.

*like Ishmael's*: see Genesis 16: 11–12.

117 *Kings of Naples*: a reference primarily to King Ferdinand II, whose repressive reign lasted from 1830 to 1859. Gladstone was in Naples in 1851 and, in a letter to Lord Aberdeen, referred to Ferdinand's government as 'the negation of God'.

*Solomon*: 'Train up a child in the way he should go: and when he is old, he will not depart from it' (Proverbs 22: 6).

118 *a sea-egg*: sea urchin.

*people's souls . . . snail makes its shell*: cf. letter from CK to Professor Rolleston (12 October 1862): 'I am glad to see that you incline to my belief . . . that the soul of each living being down to the lowest, secretes the body thereof, as a snail secretes its shell, and that the body is nothing more than the expression in terms of matter, of the stage of development to which the being has arrived' (*LM* ii. 133); the same idea is repeated in an 1863 letter to Revd F. D. Maurice (*LM* ii. 156).

119 *like the Test out of Overton Pool*: source of the River Test, one of the great trout streams, south-west of Eversley.

121 *holy child ... worship idols*: possibly Agapetus, who 'loved Jesus so much ... that he refused to worship idols', and was tortured by being hung up by his feet while boiling water was poured over him, before finally being beheaded (see *The Children's Treasury* (1868), 15–16); there are many other candidates.

123 *the new philosophy*: a double strike, first at the mid-nineteenth-century interest in spiritualism and seances (see note to p. 33); and secondly at the scientific materialism which attributed all thought processes, etc., to physical causes.

124 *twinkling of an eye*: 1 Corinthians 15: 52.

*photographs*: once the collodion process was freed from patent restrictions in 1855, photography quickly became a national hobby. In his *Lewis Carroll: Photographer* (London: M. Parrish, 1949) Helmut Gernsheim suggests that portraits of CK often found a place in Victorian photograph albums.

*The History of ... the Doasyoulikes*: CK had earlier used the concept of evolution (but going forwards and not backwards) in the dream sequence of ch. 36 of *Alton Locke*.

*Jews'-harp*: a simple metal instrument, struck while being held in the mouth, the pitch varying with the size of the mouth cavity made by the player.

125 *Peter Simple*: a novel by Frederick Marryat (1792–1848), first published in 1834. See ch. 28: ' "It's my opinion, Peter, that the gentleman has eaten no small quantity of *flap-doodle* in his life-time." "What's that O'Brien?" ... "Why, Peter ... it's the stuff they *feed fools on*".'

*tufa*: porous stone.

128 *M. Du Chaillu*: see note to p. 39.

*'Am I not a man and a brother?'*: see note to p. 91.

130 *And Nature ... universe*: stanzas 2–4 of Longfellow's 'The Fiftieth Birthday of Agassiz. May 28, 1857', from *Birds of Passage*, 'Flight the First' (published in *The Courtship of Miles Standish and Other Poems*, 1858), with some minor changes of punctuation introduced by CK. Not printed in *MM*.

131 *quarter*: 'The upper part of a ship's side aft of the beam' (*OED*).

*quarter-gallery*: 'A kind of balcony with windows projecting from the quarter or quarters of a large sailing vessel' (*OED*).

132 *Her voice was so soft and low*: cf. *King Lear*, v. ii: 'Her voice was ever soft, | Gentle and low, an excellent thing in woman'.

132 *Allalonestone . . . Gairfowl*: Alfred Newton in his *Dictionary of Birds* (London: A. & C. Black, 1893–6) devotes some five pages to the Gare-fowl (also known as the Great Auk), an apparently flightless bird that was hunted to extinction across the North Atlantic, and praises 'the happy exercise of poetic fancy with which Charles Kingsley was enabled to introduce the chief facts of the Gare-fowl's extinction . . . into his charming *Water-Babies*'. From the extended description given on p. 133, the Allalonestone is presumably St Kilda.

133 *Two little birds . . . fal-lal-la-lady*: Iona and Peter Opie, in their *Oxford Dictionary of Nursery Rhymes* (Oxford: Oxford University Press, 1951), trace the first printing to *Mother Goose's Melody* (*c*.1795), and cite CK's variant version. CK may have known it from an oral source, or from the version printed among the 'Songs' in the widely disseminated editions of nursery rhymes edited by J. O. Halliwell from 1842 onwards.

134 *marrocks*: or 'marrots'; a local name for guillemots, razor-bills, and puffins (*OED*, citing *WB*).

*dovekies*: 'black guillemots' (*OED*).

135 *Gairfowlskerry*: Geirfuglaskér, which disappeared under the sea after an eruption in 1830, was a habitat for the Great Auk, as was the rock known as Eldey. According to Newton (see note to p. 132), the Gairfowl's account is indeed 'true'.

*deceased sister's husband*: an Act of 1835 had made it illegal for a man to marry the sister of his deceased wife. Nevertheless concern about the subject continued, especially among Liberals, and the year after *WB* the Liberal MP for Marylebone introduced a Bill to make such marriages lawful. CK clearly approved of this attempt, unlike his contemporary Matthew Arnold, who made ironic play with the idea in *Friendship's Garland* (1871).

137 *dear old Hakluyt*: Richard Hakluyt (1552?–1616), whose *Principall Navigations, Voiages, and Discoveries of the English Nation* was first published in 1589 and in a much enlarged form in three volumes 1598–1600. It was one of CK's favourite books, and a significant source of inspiration while he was writing *Westward Ho!*.

*Tennyson*: two lines from 'Morte d'Arthur', first published in *Poems* (1842). CK misquotes the first line (an error he repeats in *LM* ii. 222), which should read 'The old order changeth, yielding place to new'.

138 *stump-orators*: a term, originating in the USA, for politicians making speeches in public places (as from the stump of a tree). Martin Gardner in his *Annotated Alice* (1960) notes that CK's use of 'caucus' may have influenced Lewis Carroll's invention of the Caucus-Race in ch. III of *Alice's Adventures in Wonderland*. 'But', he reasonably adds, 'the two scenes have little in common.'

*hokany-baro*: 'giant teller-of-lies'.

139 *bent-ropes*: ropes made from woven fabric or reeds.

140  *Jan Mayen's land*: an island north-east of Iceland, midway between there and Spitsbergen; also known as Hudson's Tutches.

141  *molly-mocks*: a form of 'mallemuck': the fulmar; also abbreviated as 'molly'.

*lubbers*: sailors' slang for clumsy or unseamanlike individuals.

142  *plucked*: plucky, courageous.

*horse-whales*: walruses.

*Hendrick Hudson*: actually Henry Hudson (*c*.1570–1611): CK may have taken the Dutch spelling from a reference to Hudson's service with the Dutch East India Company.

143  *white gate that never was opened yet*: the Northwest Passage, a trade route it was hoped would act as a short cut between the North Atlantic and North Pacific, but had so far stubbornly resisted discovery. The explorer Sir John Franklin died in 1847 after his ships *Terror* and *Erebus* were frozen into the Arctic pack ice, although the fate of the remaining members of his expedition (including rumours of cannibalism) continued to be the subject of heated debate.

*sea-moths*: small marine animals with large wing-like dorsal fins; dried specimens were often brought back as curios by sailors travelling to the waters of East Asia and the South Pacific.

144  *Mount Erebus*: the Antarctic volcano discovered by James Clark Ross (1800–62) in 1841. He named it after one of the ships in his expedition rather than the cavern of Greek mythology that leads to Hades.

145  *salpæ*: 'gelatinous, transparent marine animals, generally found in the form of a chain' (*The Zoologist*, 2 (1867), 844).

*whalebone net . . . from which bourne no traveller returns*: an echo of *Hamlet*, III. i, joined with a reference to the fringed plates in the upper jaws of the baleen whales. These take the place of teeth and allow the feeding whale to filter plankton from the seawater.

146  *a grand answer*: the implication is that nature takes its own way within divinely ordained limits.

148  *Prometheus . . . Epimetheus*: 'Forethought' and 'Afterthought'. The legend of Pandora was probably invented by Hesiod in his *Works and Days*; CK's use of it for his own purpose here unusually denigrates Prometheus (creator of man, and bringer of fire) in favour of his less adventurous brother. A curious 'Proem' is given to Epimetheus and Prometheus at the start of CK's verse drama *The Saint's Tragedy* (1848).

*Ptinum . . . Laciniarum*: a mixture of genuine and invented pharmacological terms: *acaris* is a mite which burrows under the skin; *tinea* is a fungal infection of the skin.

*ills which flesh is heir to*: cf. *Hamlet*, III. i: 'the thousand natural shocks | That flesh is heir to'.

149  *lucifers*: matches which worked when struck against a rough surface.

150 *President Lincoln's policy*: an allusion to the diplomatic wrangles involving
Britain during the American Civil War (1861–5), particularly over the
Union's naval blockade of the South, which had a devastating effect on the
Lancashire cotton industry. CK supported the Confederacy, and consid-
ered Lincoln to be a 'poor cute honest fellow' unsuited to high office.

*Old Mother Shipton . . . Old Nixon*: a miscellany of fortune tellers, mages,
etc. drawn from history and popular legend.

*senior wrangler*: the student who achieves the highest first-class degree in
Cambridge University's mathematical tripos.

152 *Come to me . . . dead*: the first and the last pairs of stanzas from 'Children'
in Longfellow's *Birds of Passage*, 'Flight the First' (1858), with some minor
changes of punctuation introduced by CK. Not printed in *MM*.

154 *madreporiform tubercle*: a perforated swelling.

155 *Baron Munchausen*: more properly, Karl Friedrich Hieronymous, Freiherr
von Münchhausen (1720–97), a German nobleman whose tall tales of his
travels were collected by Rudolf Erich Raspe (1737–93) and published in
1785 as *Baron Munchausen's Narrative of his Marvellous Travels and
Campaigns in Russia*.

*Ballisodare*: or Ballysadare; a river in Sligo which in its course from Lough
Arrow to the sea drops down over a series of rock ledges, one of which is
10 feet deep.

*Everton toffee*: a superior toffee sold by the confectioners Barker & Dobson,
who began a retail business in Liverpool in 1834.

*Dr Letheby and Dr Hassall*: Henry Letheby (1816–76) was an analytical
chemist, much concerned with food safety, who served as medical officer
of health for the City of London. In 1850 *The Lancet* set up an Analytical
and Sanitary Commission headed by himself and A. Hill Hassall (1817–
94). The latter was an authority on adulteration, pioneering the use of
the microscope, and publishing *Food and its Adulteration* in 1855. Their
work eventually led to the first Food and Drugs Act of 1860. See also note
to p. 98.

*the names of the books*: a satirical hit at the long, but very popular, *contes
larmoyants* that came to Britain from the United States: *The Lamplighter*
was by Maria Susanna Cummins (1827–66); *Queechy*, *The Wide, Wide
World*, and *The Hills of the Shatemuc* by 'Elizabeth Wetherell' (Susan
Bogert Warner, 1819–85). *The Children's Twaddeday* may be a satirical
version of 'The Children's Holidays', a series of Sunday school books
published in New York by Appleton in 1858.

156 *spirit-rapping*: see note to p. 33.

*good old Lord Yarborough*: Charles Anderson Worsley Anderson Pelham,
second Earl of Yarborough (1809–62), may have been known to the
Kingsley family when CK's father was rector at Barnack, near Stamford.
He was a captain in the Lincolnshire yeomanry, Lord Lieutenant of
Lincolnshire, and, from 1846, Master of the Brocklesby Foxhounds. He is

remembered now for his willingness to lay odds of 1,000 to 1 against a bridge hand being dealt that was void of all cards above a nine.

*Polupragmosyne*: meddlesomeness.

*Bramshill Bushes*: this topographic feature, with its 'Rogues' Harbour', has now disappeared from local memory. Clumps of trees in the parish were often called 'bushes', and this may have been a thicket used by poachers and ne'er-do-wells.

157 *'Parliament of Man . . . World'*: 1. 128 of Tennyson's 'Locksley Hall', first published in 1842. To be 'on the wrong side of the house' would presumably be to oppose the millennial dream: 'There the common sense of most shall hold a fretful realm in awe, | And the kindly earth shall slumber, lapt in universal law.' Parts of the subsequent string of examples suggest that CK is reworking contraries found in the popular tradition of 'The World Turned Upside Down'.

*the Trafalgar Fountains*: the first fountains to be built in Trafalgar Square, in 1845, were a fine example of a Great British Cock-up, and were the subject of much mockery in *Punch*. The flow – from pumps and cisterns in an engine house in Orange Street – was variable, the ceremonial opening began with gurglings and spouts of muddy water, and wells sunk for the water supply were found to have drained water from other pumps in the neighbourhood.

*Victrix causa diis placuit, sed victa puellis*: 'the cause that conquered was pleasing to the gods, but the conquered were pleasing to the girls'. A parody of Lucan's 'Victrix causa diis placuit, sed victa Catoni' (*Pharsalia*, i. 118).

158 *gastrocnemius muscle*: a large muscle running down the back of the calf of the leg.

*Gotham*: the town of popular tradition inhabited by foolish people. References to it and to 'the wise men of Gotham' date back at least to the fifteenth century, and by 1863 Gotham stories often appeared in nursery literature.

*expanding their liturgy*: i.e. introducing elaborations to the ritual of a kind which CK would deem Romish and unnecessary.

*Golden Asses*: Lucius Apuleius (b. *c.* AD 120) was the son of a Roman provincial magistrate, who in *c.* AD 155 wrote his classic *Transformations of Lucius*, which Augustine referred to in *The City of God* as *The Golden Ass* (*Asimus auereus*). The main plot features a hero who is transformed into an ass through a failed attempt at magic; his subsequent adventures produce a series of fanciful and titillating stories that include 'Cupid and Psyche'.

*mokes*: donkeys.

159 *fugleman*: leader.

*cockered up*: coddled. The giant may be CK's attempt at a self-portrait, like Lewis Carroll's White Knight in *Alice's Adventures in Wonderland*, although Darwin (whose autobiography dwells on his enthusiasm for catching beetles) has also been suggested as a model.

159 *Canada balsam*: 'A transparent gum for mounting microscopic objects' (*OED*).

160 *Dominie Sampson*: in Walter Scott's *Guy Mannering* (1815).

161 *a malignant and a turbaned Turk*: *Othello*, v. ii.

*Mr Joseph Ady*: a fraudster (1770–1852) who obtained money through the post by offering to tell people 'something to their advantage'.

*one of the sons of Epimetheus*: see note to p. 148. This character, who is an invention of CK's, not only 'thinks after' but 'travels after'. His presence, perhaps as a satirical comment on Baconian science, parallels that of Professor Ptthmllnsprts in Ch. IV.

*cockyolybirds*: a nursery, or pet, expression for 'dear little bird' (*OED*, citing *WB*). Compare 'sea-cockyolybirds' on p. 80, presumably used here to refer to marine creatures.

162 *Oniscus . . . Podurellæ . . . M. le Roi des Papillons*: nonsensical use of scientific language (*Oniscus* is a species of woodlouse, and *Podurellae* are fleas), with a made-up name that means 'King of the Butterflies'.

*sow by the right ear*: heart of the issue (proverbial).

*Jack shall have Gill . . . all go well*: from *A Midsummer Night's Dream*, III. ii, slightly misquoted by CK.

*the Isle of Laputa*: in Part III of *Gulliver's Travels*, Swift's satire on those given to formalized abstraction: 'Imagination, fancy, and invention, they are wholly strangers to . . . the whole compass of their thoughts and mind being shut up within [mathematics and the science of music].'

163 *distance between . . . Camelopardalis*: constellations of stars.

*Mutius Scævola*: hero who saved Rome from the Etruscan king Lars Porsena in *c.*509 BC.

*Graidiocolosyrtus Tabenniticus*: a piece of pseudo-intellectual invention; 'Tabenniticus' refers to the author (possibly a monk from the monastery at Tabenna in Egypt), and 'Graidiocolosyrtus' translates roughly as 'a noisy rabble of old hags'. CK had printed 'an unpublished fragment' of the work in *Hypatia* (1853).

164 *tide-waiters*: 'Customs officers awaiting the arrival of ships' (*OED*).

*cornetcies*: commissioned officers in troops of cavalry who carried the colours.

*nimble-comequick*: an invented word the *OED* glosses as 'of rapid growth'.

165 *Roger Ascham*: classical scholar (1515–68), tutor to Edward VI and the future Elizabeth I, and author of the first great treatise on education in English, *The Scholemaster*, published posthumously in 1570. Ascham's fundamental belief that 'Love is fitter than Fear, Gentleness better than Beating' strongly appealed to CK.

*dance . . . gooseberry bush*: according to A. B. Gomme's *The Traditional Games of England, Scotland, and Ireland* (1898), this is a local variation on the game in which children link hands and dance in a circle singing 'Here we go round the mulberry bush, | The mulberry bush, the mulberry bush, | Here we go round the mulberry bush, | On a cold and frosty morning', changing the words and performing suitable actions for each alternate verse.

166 *like the Scribes and Pharisees of old*: 'The Scribes and Pharisees sit on Moses' seat; all things therefore whatsoever they bid you, these do and observe: but do not ye after their works; for they say and do not. Yea, they bind heavy burdens and grievous to be borne and lay them on men's shoulders' (Matthew 23: 2–4). Cf. CK's cancelled 'L'Envoi' with its critique of the legalism of the Sadducees and Pharisees.

*Aldershott*: the army training camp, quite close to Eversley, was established at the end of the Crimean War. Soldiers from the camp and officers from Sandhurst would come to the parish to hear CK preach.

*no more was John Bunyan*: lengthy evidence of Bunyan's lacklustre poetic gifts can be found in his didactic *A Book for Boys and Girls; or, Country Rhimes for Children* (1686), frequently reprinted under the title *Divine Emblems*. In his preface to *The Pilgrim's Progress*, illustrated by Charles Bennett (1860), CK discusses more warmly Bunyan's poetic visualization of human character.

167 *fettle*: to 'do for', to beat (*OED*, citing *WB*).

*Powwow man . . . with his thunderbox*: presumably a witch doctor with a box of tricks. In the theatre, a 'thunderbox' was a container filled with cannonballs that could be rolled around to create rumbling sound effects; the word can also refer to a kind of portable toilet, although the *OED* does not record any citations earlier than 1939.

*served her Majesty at Portland*: given the Powwow man's eccentric behaviour, this reference is presumably to a convict incarcerated in the prison on the Isle of Portland whose inmates worked in the stone quarries. Her Majesty was also served by naval contingents who made regular use of the fortified roadstead at Portland.

*'Here we are again!'*: the catchphrase of Joseph Grimaldi (1778–1838), the most famous nineteenth-century clown, whose *Memoirs* were edited by Dickens in 1838.

*corrobory*: the native dance of Australian aborigines.

*turnip-ghosts . . . sallabalas*: toys and games; 'turnip-ghosts': hollowed-out turnips carved into faces and illuminated from the inside by candles (cf. Halloween pumpkin heads); 'magic-lanthorns': lanterns that projected ghostly images; 'bogies': goblins; 'spring-heeled Jacks': bogeymen (based on the nineteenth-century legend of a serial killer with a seemingly supernatural ability to leap over walls); 'sallabalas': not described elsewhere in the period, they may be CK's invention or a private joke.

168 *palanquin*: 'A covered conveyance, usually for one person, consisting of a large box carried on two horizontal poles' (*OED*).

*as Sinbad carried the old man of the sea*: on his fifth voyage Sinbad met an evil spirit who forced him to carry him everywhere on his shoulders. See Nights 83–4 in Galland's version of *The Arabian Nights' Entertainments*, first published in twelve volumes between 1704 and 1717.

169 *Crystal Palace*: see note to p. 42.

*a certain new lunatic asylum*: probably the asylum at Colney Hatch, Barnet. When it was completed in 1850, it was described as the largest asylum in England and the most modern in Europe. (See Richard Hunter and Ida Macalpine, *Psychiatry for the Poor* (London: Dawsons, 1974).)

*naviculæ*: small spindle-shaped cells of algae.

171 *Lemnius, Cardan, Van Helmont*: a random selection of Renaissance scholars: Simon Lemnius (*c.*1505–50), a German humanist, pupil of Melancthon at Wittenberg and an opponent of Luther; Girolamo Cardano (1501–76), an Italian polymath, notable especially as mathematician, physician, and astrologer, whose biography by Henry Morley (1854) is recommended by CK in his lecture on Paracelsus (*Historical Lectures* (1880), 362); Jean Baptiste van Helmont (1579–1644), a Flemish doctor and chemist who invented the term 'gas' and was the first to use melting and boiling points as standards for measuring temperature.

*Punch*: alluding to the resilient hero of traditional Punch and Judy shows, who has a habit of comically popping up whenever he seems to have been defeated.

*atomy*: mite.

172 *everybody must help themselves*: a summary of Samuel Smiles's argument in his popular recent book *Self-Help* (1859).

175 *ticket-of-leave*: 'Since 1840 the usual colloquial name for an "order of licence" giving a convict his liberty under certain restrictions before his sentence has expired' (*OED*).

179 *blazing light*: an allusion to Christ's transfiguration on the mount (Matthew 17: 1–9, Mark 9: 2–8, Luke 9: 28–36).

*dog-days*: the Romans believed that the sun in conjunction with Sirius (the Dog Star) during high summer led to the increased temperature, a period termed *caniculares dies*.

180 *thirty-seven or thirty-nine things*: an allusion to the Thirty-Nine Articles of faith whose acceptance was obligatory upon Anglican clergy.

*vivariums*: aquariums.

181 *haddened doun*: held down.

*good Bishop Butler*: Joseph Butler (1692–1752), bishop of Durham, whose *Analogy of Religion, Natural and Revealed, to the Constitution and Course of Nature* (1736) was one of CK's favourite theological works. The reference is to Butler's argument for redemption through an awareness of the presence of God in the believer's conscience.

## APPENDIX II

190 *philosopher of old Greece*: probably Aristotle (384–322 BC), who was invited by Philip II of Macedon to become tutor to his son Alexander the Great in 343 BC; during his time in Macedon he also taught two other future kings, Ptolemy and Cassander.

*works . . . this Article*: 'The Wonders of the Shore' was published as a review of Revd D. Landsborough's *A Popular History of British Zoophytes or Coralines* (1852) and *A Popular History of British Sea-weeds* (1851), Philip Gosse's *A Naturalist's Rambles on the Devonshire Coast* (1852) and *The Aquarium* (1854), William H. Harvey's *The Sea-side Book* (1849), and Ann Pratt's *Things of the Sea Coast* (1850).

*Mr Gosse's presages*: *A Naturalist's Rambles on the Devonshire Coast* (London: John Van Voorst, 1853) concluded with Gosse expressing his 'confident expectation' that 'an elegant vase stocked with algae and sea-anemones' would shortly be manufactured 'for the Parlour or Conservatory' (p. 441).

*Bewick's 'British Birds'*: see note to p. 64.

191 *White's 'History of Selbourne'*: Gilbert White's *The Natural History and Antiquities of Selborne* (1789) recorded the natural history of the area around his vicarage in the Hampshire village of Selborne.

*Don Saltero*: a coffee shop in Chelsea, founded in 1695 by James Salter, which became famous for its display of curiosities; an advertisement from 1728 promised 'Monsters of all sorts here are seen, | Strange things in Nature, as they grew so, | Some relics of the Sheba Queen, | And fragments of the famed Bob Crusoe'.

*Ferrante Imperato*: a Naples apothecary (1525?–1615?) who published an influential work of natural history in 1599, illustrated with an engraving showing his own cabinet of curiosities, a collection that included shells and sea creatures as well as fossils, minerals, and gems.

*'bigarrures . . . humain'*: 'motley of the human spirit'.

*Linné*: Carolus Linnaeus (1707–78), also known as Carl von Linné, a Swedish botanist and zoologist who established the first generally accepted system for the classification and naming of living organisms. The Linnean Society (see note to p. 43) was named after him.

*vis plastrix*: cf. *vis plastica*, a shaping force.

*Ray*: John Ray (formerly Wray) (1627–1705), naturalist and theologian, whose works included a natural history of fish (1686) illustrated by 187 plates.

192 *Seba and Aldrovandus; to Pomet*: Albertus Seba (1665–1736), Dutch apothecary and collector, whose *Thesaurus* of animal specimens (1734) included 446 engravings; Ulisse Aldrovandi (1522–1605), Italian naturalist described by Linnaeus as the father of natural history, whose botanical garden in Bologna was one of the first in Europe; Pierre Pomet (1658–99),

French pharmacist whose illustrated *Histoire générale des drogues* was published in 1694, and was translated into English as *A Compleat History of Druggs* in 1712.

*'homo diluvii testis'*: in his book *Lithographia Helvetica* (1726) Johann Jakob Scheuchzer described a fossil as *Homo diluvii testis* (evidence of a diluvian human), believing it to be the remains of a child who had drowned in the biblical flood. In 1831 the fossil was revealed to be that of a salamander and renamed *Salamandra scheuchzeri*.

*"Deus quidam deceptor"*: 'God who is sometimes a deceiver', a phrase CK would later use when writing to Philip Gosse about his study *Omphalos* (1857).

*Buckland . . . Sedgwick, Lyell . . . Jameson*: major figures in the development of geology: William Buckland (1784–1856); Sedgwick: see note to p. 39; Sir Charles Lyell (1797–1875), author of *Principles of Geology* (1830–2), whose last major publication *Antiquity of Man* was published in the same year as *WB*; Robert Jameson (1774–1854).

*Fairholme . . . Granville Penn*: George Fairholme (1789–1846), whose *General View of the Geology of Scripture* (1833) and *The Mosaic Deluge* (1837) argued that geologists should not depart from the Bible when interpreting their findings; Granville Penn (1761–1844), whose study *A Comparative Estimate of the Mineral and Mosaical Geologies* (1822) concluded that 'The science of Geology . . . not only conducts the intelligence . . . to the discernment of the God of Nature, but advances it further, to a distinct recognition of that God of Nature in the God of Scripture'.

193 *Hugh Miller*: geologist and Evangelical journalist (1802–56), whose books *Footprints of the Creator* (1849) and *The Testimony of the Rocks* (1857) argued that the appearance of complex animals early in the fossil record refuted theories that proposed a simple evolutionary progression from primitive to advanced organisms.

*monsters . . . Crystal Palace*: a series of life-size models depicting various dinosaurs and extinct mammals (with varying degrees of accuracy), designed by the sculptor Benjamin Waterhouse Hawkins, was unveiled in the grounds of the relocated Crystal Palace in 1854.

*scientia scientiarum*: science of sciences.

*zoophytology*: the natural history of zoophytes (animals that resemble plants, such as sea anemones).

*those who have eyes . . . understand*: Deuteronomy 29: 4.

*Mr Ellis*: John Ellis (*c.*1710–76), a zoologist whose longest and most influential works were *Natural History of the Corallines* (1755) and the posthumously published *Natural History of Zoophytes* (1786).

*Dr G. Johnston's British Zoophytes*: George Johnston, *A History of the British Zoophytes* (Edinburgh: W. H. Lizars, 1838).

*Dr Landsborough's book . . . subject*: see note to p. 190.

194 *Marsigli or Bonnet . . . Pallas*: Count Luigi Ferdinando Marsigli (1658–1730), Italian naturalist, widely considered to be the founding father of modern oceanography; Charles Bonnet (1720–93), Swiss naturalist and philosopher; Peter Simon Pallas (1741–1811), German zoologist and botanist.

*Dr Parsons*: James Parsons (1705–70), physician and Fellow of the Royal Society, who claimed that the 'jelly-like animals' observed in coral had nothing to do with its growth.

*Baker*: Henry Baker (1698–1774), a naturalist who received a gold medal from the Royal Society in 1744 for his work on the crystallization of saline particles.

*Leith*: the nearest port to Edinburgh.

*polypidoms*: organisms with a supporting structure to which individual polyps are attached.

*Musselburgh*: a settlement in East Lothian on the Scottish coast.

*congeners*: members of the same kind or class.

195 *'dead man's hand'*: a zoophyte which takes the form of fleshy fingers.

*madrepore or brainstone*: madrepore is a coral with a hard, perforated structure; brainstone is a form of coral thought to resemble the human brain in appearance.

*'walk by faith . . . sight'*: 2 Corinthians 5: 7.

*Oh . . . their nation*: from *The Faerie Queene*, Book IV canto XII.

*'Oh . . . for ever!'*: a canticle from the Book of Common Prayer.

196 *mangosteen*: a tropical fruit.

*Colonel George Montagu*: (1750-1829), one of the first naturalists to exploit the microscope to describe small species, and a key figure in the history of British ornithology.

*Mr E. Forbes*: the natural historian Edward Forbes (1815–54); the quotation is taken from his study *A History of British Starfishes* (London: J. van Voorst, 1841), 46.

197 *Lord Bacon*: Francis Bacon (1561–1626), author and polymath, who wrote about the investigation of nature as part of a larger project of extending 'the power and dominion of the human race itself over the universe' (*Novum Organum*).

199 *sciolism*: superficial knowledge.

200 *mens sana . . . corpus sanum*: a healthy mind in a healthy body.

*Arthur's Seat*: the tallest hill in Edinburgh, rising to a height of 822 feet, and popularly associated with the legend of King Arthur.

*The reason firm . . . skill*: from Wordsworth's 'She was a Phantom of Delight', ll. 25–6.

201 *Of fate . . . lost*: a slightly misquoted version of Milton's *Paradise Lost*, ii. 560–1.

American Literature

British and Irish Literature

Children's Literature

Classics and Ancient Literature

Colonial Literature

Eastern Literature

European Literature

Gothic Literature

History

Medieval Literature

Oxford English Drama

Philosophy

Poetry

Politics

Religion

The Oxford Shakespeare

---

A complete list of Oxford World's Classics, including Authors in Context, Oxford English Drama, and the Oxford Shakespeare, is available in the UK from the Marketing Services Department, Oxford University Press, Great Clarendon Street, Oxford OX2 6DP, or visit the website at www.oup.com/uk/worldsclassics.

In the USA, visit www.oup.com/us/owc for a complete title list.

Oxford World's Classics are available from all good bookshops. In case of difficulty, customers in the UK should contact Oxford University Press Bookshop, 116 High Street, Oxford OX1 4BR.